Prai

THE FLAME AN

“Rossetti offers an inventive tale of magic [illegible] ture that deftly combines an otherworldly setting with characters you care about. *The Flame and the Shadow* sparkles with excitement!” —Shana Abé, *New York Times* bestselling author

“Rossetti creates such lovably flawed characters in Cenda and Gray that it is hard not to laugh (and cry) . . . *The Flame and the Shadow* is exceedingly hot! Explicitly hot! Beware to keep a glass of ice water or a cool shower handy so that you can maintain your own cool while the sparks fly . . . the perfect blend of science fiction and erotic fantasy romance. I can’t wait to read about the water, air, and earth witches, as well as the mystery fifth element belonging to this pentagramic group.” —*Romance Reader at Heart* (Top Pick)

“Should appeal to fans of Storm Constantine and Laurell K. Hamilton.” —*Library Journal*

“A wonderful new erotic romance novel that goes way out there and brings the reader in. A wonderful fantasy approach to the genre, with many new concepts and ideas that I’ve never read about. A stunning print debut.” —*Night Owl Romance*

“An erotic, evocative fantasy . . . If this thriller is any indication, Denise Rossetti is a welcomed newcomer to the fantasy genre.” —*Midwest Book Review*

“Simultaneously heartbreaking and heartwarming. With people who inspire through their own growth a compelling plot, and passion as incendiary as the fire witch’s power, Denise Rossetti offers readers a novel that is hard to put down until the last page.” —*Wild on Books*

“Denise Rossetti has taken the fantasy genre by storm with her print debut. *The Flame and the Shadow* bursts with action, mystery, and passion.” —*Romance Junkies*

continued . . .

"I was so captivated . . . I couldn't put it down. *The Flame and the Shadow* is darkly intense, warmly romantic, and blazingly erotic." —*Publishers Weekly*'s WW Ladies Book Club Blurbs

"A dark erotic tale that is satisfying on many levels. Rossetti's first installment of the Four-Sided Pentacle series is exciting and full of passion and intrigue. I will be anxiously awaiting the second book." —*ParaNormal Romance*

"The connection between Cenda and Gray explodes with excitement in this wonderful read." —*The Romance Studio*

"Denise Rossetti creates an erotic, mystical, futuristic world full of excitement and intrigue, promising even more adventure in the next book in this thrilling series. This is a great read!" —*Fresh Fiction*

"The erotica is in high supply and the sexual tension is repeatedly built up and released only to be built again. If you enjoy reading about sensual sex, and like the sex to be flaming hot and steamy, this erotic romance in an unearthly universe will seductively draw you in." —*SFRevu*

"Readers will delight in the author's rich imagination as they are caught up between the dilemmas of the main characters, the fight for power between the magic-wielding Pures and Technomages, and a thorough fall into love."
—*Love Romances & More*

"Ms. Rossetti has developed an intriguing fantasy world that begs for further stories." —*Eye on Romance*

THE FLAME AND THE SHADOW

DENISE ROSSETTI

BERKLEY SENSATION, NEW YORK

THE BERKLEY PUBLISHING GROUP
Published by the Penguin Group
Penguin Group (USA) Inc.
375 Hudson Street, New York, New York 10014, USA
Penguin Group (Canada), 90 Eglinton Avenue East, Suite 700, Toronto, Ontario M4P 2Y3, Canada
(a division of Pearson Penguin Canada Inc.)
Penguin Books Ltd., 80 Strand, London WC2R 0RL, England
Penguin Group Ireland, 25 St. Stephen's Green, Dublin 2, Ireland (a division of Penguin Books Ltd.)
Penguin Group (Australia), 250 Camberwell Road, Camberwell, Victoria 3124, Australia
(a division of Pearson Australia Group Pty. Ltd.)
Penguin Books India Pvt. Ltd., 11 Community Centre, Panchsheel Park, New Delhi—110 017, India
Penguin Group (NZ), 67 Apollo Drive, Rosedale, North Shore 0632, New Zealand
(a division of Pearson New Zealand Ltd.)
Penguin Books (South Africa) (Pty.) Ltd., 24 Sturdee Avenue, Rosebank, Johannesburg 2196, South Africa

Penguin Books Ltd., Registered Offices: 80 Strand, London WC2R 0RL, England

THE FLAME AND THE SHADOW

A Berkley Sensation Book / published by arrangement with the author

PRINTING HISTORY
Ace trade edition / November 2008
Berkley Sensation mass-market edition / October 2009

Excerpt provided courtesy of Denise Rossetti
Cover art by Jim Griffin
Cover design by Judith Lagerman
Interior text design by Laura K. Corless

ISBN: 978-0-425-23135-7

BERKLEY® SENSATION
Berkley Sensation Books are published by The Berkley Publishing Group,
a division of Penguin Group (USA) Inc.,
375 Hudson Street, New York, New York 10014.
BERKLEY® SENSATION and the "B" design are trademarks of Penguin Group (USA) Inc.

PRINTED IN THE UNITED STATES OF AMERICA

10 9 8 7 6 5 4 3 2 1

For Mike, who never worried and always believed

1

The flames had been singing to her, so loudly Cenda could almost catch the words. She tugged at the heavy fabric of her gown. Five-it, the small chamber was stifling! But Krysanthe had lit the fire with her own hands and closed the windows tight to keep out the night air. Outside, below the sill, lay the vegetable garden of the Wizards' Enclave, the plants pushing slowly through the soil in the chilly dusk of early spring. She couldn't stand having the healer cluck over her like an irritated hen. There'd been enough of that since—

Without taking her gaze from the flames, she shifted in the big, shabby armchair, tucking her long, narrow feet under her, unlacing the front of her gown. She could let the fire die so the room cooled, but she didn't want to.

No, no, keep the fire. Cenda ripped the gown off over her head. Absently, she tossed it aside. Beneath, her lanky body was clad in nothing more than a shift, worn thin and soft with frequent washings. Ah, that was better.

Resting an elbow on the broad arm of the chair, she propped her chin in her palm and returned to the contemplation of the cheery blaze. Yellow and orange ribbons leaped and writhed, dancing for her, crackling, hissing. Was that Elke's high thread of a baby voice, singing a nonsense song? The one about the fishie in the lake. *Are you lost, little fishie, are you lost? Where's your mama, little fishie, where's your mama?*

They'd both liked that one, though not even a mother's love could persuade Cenda her daughter had had anything but a tin ear.

Are you lost, little one? Where'd you go without your mama?

Cenda blinked, the tears sizzling on her cheeks. A log shifted and sparks leaped. She seemed to see Elke's sturdy little body running away from her, down that long, shimmering tunnel, the curls bobbing, Booboo the furrybear toy clutched tight in one chubby hand.

Faithful Booboo. She didn't need to turn her head even a fraction to locate him, because he sat on her pillow, keeping her company through the interminable nights.

In fact . . . Cenda uncurled her legs, wincing at her stiffness. How long had she been sitting before the fire? Shadows had pooled in the corners of the room. She rose and took two steps to the bed, almost upsetting the unlit lantern on the small side table in the process. Absently, she steadied it with one hand as she smoothed a palm over Booboo's well-chewed ears. "Look, sweetie," she whispered, picking him up and hugging him to her chest. She sank back into the sagging embrace of the chair. "There she almost is, my darling. Do you think I'm mad?"

Booboo refused to be drawn, so Cenda set him on her lap and leaned back, losing herself in the flames again. Yes, there was the curve of Elke's cheek, the twist of a curl, fat little hands, fingers spread like a starryfish. In a strange way, the pain was welcome, the piercing agony of regret better than the odd numbness that had afflicted her for months, so that life went on around her, separated by a gray veil behind which people moved and spoke and existed. And touched her not at all.

A bright eye winked from the other side of a burning log. Cenda watched with complete attention, holding her breath. If she concentrated, she might see Elke's face. A flame flickered like a tail, like an animal darting into the undergrowth. Cenda blinked. A tiny lizard lay on the log, its body sculpted of moving flame, minuscule claws gripping the charred wood.

"Oh," she breathed, no more than the smallest exhalation.

The little creature tilted its head to one side, watching her carefully. Its eyes were the same shade of blue as the heart of flame.

Great Lady, what a sweet dream!

The seconds tiptoed past. From deep in the Enclave, Cenda heard the Moonsrise chant, the strange five-beat rhythm familiar, haunting. Her fellow wizards, the Pures, would be filing out into the twilight to raise the Dancers, to pay homage.

She hummed along under her breath. She could hold a tune, but only just. Choir Master used to insist she mime the most complex passages, but the flame beast didn't seem to mind her vocal deficiencies. Its head bobbed, and it crept closer along the burning log. "Pretty thing," crooned Cenda, abandoning the chant. "Sweet, pretty thing."

A second lizard crawled from between two glowing coals, and Cenda's smile widened, her fingers buried in Booboo's fur. She was undoubtedly mad, but what did it matter? Singing softly, completely off-key, she gazed dreamily at her strange audience, her long body relaxed in the chair, one foot tapping time.

Now she had three, sitting on the tiles of the fireplace, each a jewel of flame no longer than her middle finger. Steadily, they advanced until one reached the threadbare rug. At the first touch of a tiny claw, the rug began to smolder, and Cenda laughed, the rusty sound so loud in the quiet room it startled her. "Watch the furnishings, little one."

The fire lizard quivered, but held its ground. Then it made a dash for Cenda's bare toes. She yelped and jerked her foot away, but she couldn't move fast enough. A leap, a scramble, and the little creature was sitting on her foot, hanging on with its talons, tail extended for balance.

Cenda froze. It didn't burn. Sweet Lady, it didn't burn!

That was— That was— She swallowed.

Pinpricks dug into her flesh, but the fire lizard's body felt hot and smooth, like sun-warmed stone. Its little sides heaved, and she could swear she felt its heartbeat flutter against the top of her foot. "Sshh," she soothed. "Sshh. I won't hurt you, I promise."

Very slowly, she leaned down and extended her hand, the way she would to one of the Enclave's cats. An excruciating pause and the creature stepped onto her longest finger, as delicately as a maiden lady. It paced across her palm, advancing until it reached her thundering pulse. There it lowered its head, nosed her skin. Apparently satisfied, it curled up in her palm and appeared to fall asleep.

"Goodness," said Cenda, lowering her hand gingerly to her lap, next to Booboo. "Goodness." How Elke would have loved them!

Sharp as a blade in the guts, it all came crashing back. *My darling, oh, my darling. My baby.* A vise made of bitter regret closed around her chest. She couldn't catch her breath.

Something tickled up the back of her calf. "Hey!"

The second lizard skittered over her knee and made a dash across her thigh, leaving a pitter-patter of scorched tracks on her shift. The third followed, right behind. Together, they made a leap for her forearm and curled around it, an improbable pair of exquisite bracelets.

Completely bemused, Cenda watched their heads lift, the sapphire eyes glowing as they stared deep into her soul.

At her back, the latch clicked. A brisk voice said,

"Five-it, Cenda, what do you think you're doing? It's freezing and you're sitting in your— *Aaaargh!*"

Grayson of Concordia, known in a hundred dives on a hundred worlds as the Duke of Ombra, lay naked in the velvet dark, long fingers wrapped around his aching erection. Temptation besieged him.

It was never as good as when Shad did it.

He'd held out against Shad's cool touch for almost a year this time, since long before he'd arrived on the small, crowded world of Sybaris.

Which was why he'd closed the rickety shutters and drawn the dusty curtains right across. No shadow could exist in darkness this total—*Shad* couldn't exist.

He wouldn't have to look at him, a man-shaped slice of midnight stretching over the floor and up the wall of the cheap inn room. He wouldn't have to feel the shadow Magick smear his soul, remember the horror in his mother's eyes that sunny winter's day on the way home from Devotions, the first time she'd seen his shadow move.

All by itself.

The flick of her fingers in a warding gesture, her choked whisper. "*Abomination!*"

But his body didn't care. It was never as good as when Shad did it.

Infinitely preferable to take care of his own needs. He slid his fingers up and down, dragging the satiny skin over the blood-engorged hardness beneath, his balls drawing up in anticipation.

Noises filtered up from the street below. Stumbling footsteps, a wandering, reedy tenor, clearly affected by alcohol. A woman spoke sharply; the singer grunted as if in pain or shock; a door banged. Gods, what a place!

Likely she'd been right, his mother.

Looking back, he'd done so many murky things to stay alive—starting with the price he'd paid to stow away at fourteen. His mouth twisted. His coltish, rawboned beauty had proved a useful commodity, but Judger God, it had hurt! And it had soiled his soul, all the way to the bedrock of his masculinity. Perhaps it was fortunate he hadn't got his full growth 'til later, or he would have killed the first mate. He didn't know anymore.

And now— He gripped the threadbare covers. His breath came a little faster. The inn was perfect for his purposes—for all that it was so shabby—only a short walk from the Wizards' Enclave. *She* would be there now. Sleeping, unaware. His commission on the pleasure planet had begun.

Gray's lip curled. Pleasure planet! He knew he was fastidious, but he'd never seen such a slattern of a world. Whores for every taste, every purpose. All sexes, all colors, all ages. A tawdry smorgasbord of misery and sleaze.

The Technomage Primus of Sybaris had a commission for him, and she wasn't renowned for her patience. A kidnap. The target was reputed to be a fire witch, though he'd never heard of such a thing. *Ah shit, why did it have to be a woman?* But conscience was a luxury he couldn't afford, not if he wanted his dream, his life whole and clean.

A double game, a game of dodge and deceit and shadow. Ah, but he walked a razor's edge of risk!

The tension had destroyed his erection. One problem solved. Gods, he needed air! With a sigh, he rolled toward the window, reaching out to pull the curtains and push the shutters wide. A few hours ago, he'd grabbed an ale jug and climbed up six flights of narrow stairs to the flat roof of the building so he could watch the dusk draw down over Sybaris. Ironically, the lights scattered below shone like glittering baubles, jewels in the velvet dark. But he knew what lay concealed beneath the kindly cloak of night—an endless stretch of teeming, festering cities, gambling hells, brothels, and taverns. The single dark patch on the far horizon was Remnant One, fifty square miles of the last native feather forest. Remnant Two, renowned for the exquisite beauty of the Rainbow Lakes, wasn't visible.

A Technomage flitter hummed past, skimming a couple

of hundred feet above the slums, a sleek winged shape across the face of the moon. The first of the Dancers, the five famous moons of Sybaris, had risen already, high and silver over the planet's blowsy shoulder, ribbons of light streaming into the narrow room and over Gray's lean, bare torso. He sensed movement behind him. Ignored it. Which moon was that? Arabesque?

A cool fingertip touched the back of his thigh, almost shyly.

Gray reared up, so quickly the bed frame creaked in protest.

His shadow lay behind him, half on the bed, half on the floor. As he watched, it coalesced, gaining density until it sat up, next to his hip. Shit, not now! Why was it Shad was at his strongest when Gray felt unclean? When he felt *wrong*?

"No! I don't want—"

The eyeless, featureless head turned toward him, a black silhouette against the wall. His straight blade of a nose, the lock of hair that fell over his brow, the stubborn jut of his chin. *Yes, you do.* Not even a whisper in his mind, more like a thought, suddenly apparent, seeming to spring from nowhere, the way thoughts did.

Gray came up on his elbows and glared down the length of his body, knowing what he'd see. No more than a blink, and he'd swelled again, his shaft so high and full and fat, it strafed his navel, barely quivering. A shadowy hand reached for it, the fingers closing over him with absolute certainty.

Gray grunted with shock and horror and pleasure. Shad's grip was cool, smooth, hard.

Perfect.

Fuck, it was always perfect! How could it not be, when Shad was the other part of himself? The worst part, the darkest part, the soiled underbelly of his soul he tried so desperately not to expose.

Gray grabbed for his shadow's wrist, even as a slick palm cradled his scrotum and a knowing thumb rasped over the sweet spot under the head of his cock. The seed boiled, pressing hard against tender skin. "Stop," he groaned. "Stop!"

We need. Shad pumped, exquisitely deft, milking and squeezing exactly the way Gray liked. *Both of us.* His shaft slipped through the black fist, appearing and reappearing, the ruddiness of lust washed pale by the moonlight.

Gray arched and shook, helpless, fingers gripping the bedclothes. Ah fuck, it was fine! Fuck, fuck, fuck! His brain gone foggy and slow, he thought, *Once, just this once, then never again. I promise, I'll be good. I'll—*

A confident fingertip slipped between the cheeks of his ass, and the thought shattered, lost in a maelstrom of physical sensation. With a choked cry, the Duke of Ombra spurted all over his stomach, the orgasm so brutal, so gorgeous, only his head and heels touched the mattress.

Ah, Judger God. Tears stood in his eyes.

Abomination.

Gray fell back panting on the pillows, one arm thrown over his eyes. A whisper of movement and a soft cloth swiped across his belly, cleaning him as if he were an infant. *Get the fuck away from me.*

Why?

Because— Shit! Gray snatched the cloth and waved Shad away.

His shadow retreated a few steps. *You'll miss me.*

Gray snarled. *Like hell I will.*

Squeezing his eyes shut, he thought of old Deiter standing in the precise center of his tower room in Nakarion City on Concordia, the chalk lines glowing an eerie green on the polished floor.

"I can cure you of your shadow, Grayson, my friend," the wizard had murmured in his cracked old-man's voice, shrewd eyes gleaming with gentle malice. "But it will cost." And he'd named a price that made Gray's blood congeal. His very soul to save his soul. A bargain with the devil.

His mind gone quiet and clear, the way it used to do in battle, he'd stepped forward, scuffing the lines on the floor, chest to chest with the old wizard. He'd wrapped his fingers in Deiter's tripartite beard and hauled him up until they were nose to nose. "Deiter," he'd said, almost tenderly, "if you're lying to me, I will kill you." A little shake. "Do you understand?"

"Yes." The old man's breath smelled of wine. "But you're not a killer."

Gray bared his teeth. "Not by inclination, no. But I've done almost everything in my time. I was a mercenary before I was a musician. Play me false, and I won't hesitate."

Releasing his grip, a finger at a time, he stepped back, leaving the wizard standing. He threaded his way through the cluttered room—the rows of jars containing strange floating objects, the bundles of dried herbs, the skeleton on a stand, the grimoires shackled to the dusty desk. It reminded him of a stage set for a rustic pantomime—Wizard's Lair. Wondering where Deiter did the real work, he turned at the door for a last glare. "Remember, old man. Don't cross me."

"Don't be foolish." Deiter straightened his robes with an irritated rustle and flapped a hand. "Begone."

And they *had* gone, he and the Duchess, his antique lap harp, all the way to Sybaris, holiday destination for the crass and gullible, happy playground for the criminally inclined.

To play the double game. Dodge and deceit and shadow.

2

The flame lizards disappeared in a shower of sparks. The fire flared.

Cenda twisted to look over her shoulder. Krysanthe the healer stood at the door, her plump, pretty face slack-jawed with astonishment. "They've gone," said Cenda, feeling gray again. She turned back to stare moodily into the dying fire. "But you saw them, too, didn't you? So I haven't lost my mind."

No answer.

Cenda closed her eyes and leaned her skull against the high back of the chair. The old feeling of dislocation returned full force, making her head swim.

She heard the scrape of a stool as Krysanthe settled next to her. "I never thought—" said the healer. She cleared her throat and started over. "I suspected—oh, yes—for the last two months. In fact . . . But I hardly dared hope."

"Get to the point, Krys," said Cenda wearily. All the wonder of the fire creatures had leaked out of her. Six months ago, she wouldn't have been so curt, but six months ago, she'd sat in this very chair with Elke in her lap, heavy and warm, the curly head resting sleepily on her shoulder. Elke, the child of her autumn years, the child she'd never thought to have, never—

"Salamanders," said the healer, with something that sounded very like glee. "That's what they are. I started my research into fire Magick the night you melted all the candles in the dining hall. Remember?"

Ah, yes. Cenda bit her lip, feeling the flush stain her cheeks. She pleated the fabric of her shift with fretful fingers. Her first meal in public since . . . since they'd been so ill, she and Elke. An ordeal in itself, the cautious, assessing glances, the scarcely there pats on the arm, the murmurs of sympathy. A well-meaning gauntlet to be run.

She'd found the silence of the blessing a relief, a small space she could use to put herself back together. Each of the Pures, witch or wizard, standing with head bowed, holding a small candle to symbolize the presence of the Lord and Lady. On the last phrase of the invocation, the custom was to focus your will on the candle, light it, and set it at your left hand. A lighting spell, not easy to master for all that it looked so simple, but the first of the Magicks required for entry to the First Circle.

Cenda had failed her First Circle practicals twice before she made it through, though she'd had no problem with the theory. And that night she wasn't . . . herself. Shakily, she'd gathered her will and focused fiercely on her candle, determined not to look stupid.

But somehow, the Lady only knew how, she managed to overdo it. Every candle in the hall, more than fifty of them, flared, shooting flame to the high ceiling before slumping into puddles of melted wax.

Absolute silence.

The fishy eye of Purist Matthaeus, who was presiding at High Table that evening, turned unerringly toward her. "Cenda," he said delicately, "perhaps—?" He waved an elegant, be-ringed hand in the direction of the tall, carved double doors.

"Yes, Purist." Head bowed, she'd fled. It was only when she reached her room and uncramped her fingers that she realized her metal fork had flowed and melted in her grip until it formed a right angle.

Now Krysanthe said, "It caused a lot of talk, you know. That much power, used indiscriminately. We tried to hose it down, Matthaeus and I, but . . ." She rubbed her nose. "Rumors get about."

Cenda shrugged. "I made a mistake; that's all. I make a lot of mistakes. You know that."

"No, no!" The healer sprang to her feet and began to pace, her choppy stride betraying her excitement. "It all adds up, don't you see?" Her hair had begun to come loose from its braid in soft wisps of salt-and-pepper. Seizing the cold lantern, she thrust it toward Cenda. "Light this for me, dear, will you? I'm too excited to concentrate."

"Mm." Her gaze still fixed on her friend, Cenda flicked a finger in the general direction.

The lantern blazed up in the healer's face. "Lord's balls!" She dropped it with a tinkle of broken glass. "Uh, sorry." Crouching, she grabbed Cenda's water jug and upended it. The flames died. When she looked up, her face was bright with triumph. "See?" she said. "I told you. Fire Magick."

Cenda gaped. Then she shook her head. "Don't be ridiculous," she said. "Not me."

Not Cenda the clumsy, Cenda whose gifts of Magick were so small, she'd barely qualified for the First Circle. So awkward that the visiting wizard who'd fathered Elke had quickly grown impatient, though he'd found her inexperience a charming novelty in the beginning.

Krysanthe stroked Booboo's head with a gentle finger. Unobtrusively, Cenda moved him aside. The healer said, "I think you're the first true fire witch on Sybaris. Matthaeus agrees." Her dark eyes, usually so soft and calm, grew flat and purposeful. "If you don't learn to master the powers, you'll be a danger, Cenda. To yourself and everyone around you."

Rising, Krysanthe lit the fat candles on the mantel with a wave of her hand.

Bemused, Cenda stared at her friend. "Ah, Krys . . ."

"Don't you see? It's the only answer! Great Lady, you must be the last person in the world to know, you poor love. You don't feel the cold anymore, do you? Hadn't you noticed?"

Cenda started to shake her head, then stopped. Krysanthe was still wearing a heavy all-weather cloak, while Cenda sat in her shift, perfectly comfortable.

"And your hair . . ."

"What about it?"

The healer reached under her cloak and rummaged through the jingling chatelaine she wore at her waist. She came up with a small round mirror on a short handle. Unclipping it, she thrust it into Cenda's slack fingers. "Look."

She couldn't remember the last time she'd brushed her hair properly. Once, it had been her only vanity, a thick, lustrous black, waving down to the middle of her back. No gray, though at forty-one, there should have been.

Tilting the mirror, she peered. No, just the same, though a little wilder than usual. New frown marks graven between her brows, her lips thin and tight. Wait! What was that?

Helpfully, Krysanthe grabbed a candle and held it close. Cenda grunted with surprise.

A few threads of red shone at her temples. True red, blazing red.

"Then there's this." With cold deliberation, the other woman brushed the length of Cenda's forearm with the candle flame.

Cenda yelped and jerked aside, but Krysanthe clamped a ruthless hand over her wrist and did it again. Lady, it felt like the fire lizard! Warm, yes, but almost pleasant, ticklish even. Nothing like the searing pain of a burn.

Together, they stared down at her unmarked flesh.

"You could walk through a forest fire and emerge unscathed." The healer let out a long breath. "And then there were the salamanders. How many? Two, was it?"

"Three." Her brain seemed to have turned to soup. "But why? How?"

"Something happened the night your fever broke, didn't it?" Krysanthe took Cenda's hands in a strong grip. "Tell me, sweetie."

"Elke died," said Cenda flatly. "And so did I."

Elke had been whiny, fretful, whereas normally she was a cheerful little body, bright and sweet as a new moon, always into mischief. Cenda had sighed and cuddled her close, rocked her and told her stories. "The winter ague," said Krysanthe's apprentice, Tai Yang. "Be sure to make her drink."

And she had, though she could feel the first effects of the ague herself, nibbling at her bones and joints, sapping her strength. Then Elke had begun pushing the cup aside and screwing up her eyes against the light. When Cenda stroked the hair off the child's forehead, the skin was dry and hot.

Tai Yang had been busy, but he'd come straightaway when she sent for him. His almond eyes fierce with concentration behind his spectacles, he'd examined both of them. Then he'd drawn a deep breath. "I need Purist Krysanthe's opinion," he'd said. "Nothing to worry about."

But she heard his footsteps receding rapidly down the passage. *Running.* Tai Yang, who was such a scholar, so self-contained. Terror swam like a monstrous, twisted fish in Cenda's belly; her head thumped as though a demon used it for an anvil. Though every muscle screamed in protest, she'd gathered Elke's little body into hers. It felt hot and brittle, like a dried leaf, and the child whimpered at her mother's touch.

The fever took them both like some great ravening beast, roaring with delight and fury as it ate them up, burned them alive. Cenda was only peripherally aware of Krysanthe barking orders, of people rushing about with cold cloths and infusions and ice packs. With every fiber of her being, she yearned to touch the little body lying in the next bed, to offer her breast. Somehow, she was convinced that if she could only hold Elke close and let her suck, the way she used to, all would be well, the fire beast vanquished.

"Mama's here," she murmured foolishly, though the words got tangled in the agony in her throat. "Don't cry, sweetheart. You're safe. Mama's here."

But she'd been wrong. Ah, Great Lady, so very, very wrong!

By the time Elke's convulsions began, Cenda was deeply unconscious, though she fought bitterly against the swelling tide of it, every step of the way.

It could have been a moment later, or a century, but the darkness fell away, leaving her floating, disembodied, voiceless, looking down at her own lanky limbs on the bed, the cluster of figures working frantically over Elke's small body. In one corner of the infirmary, just under the heavy beam that supported the ceiling, an oval of light shimmered into being, cool and golden. It expanded, grew into an aperture that opened onto a long tunnel, stretching far away into infinite space. And somehow, Cenda was not surprised to see Elke trotting away from her toward the distant glow, Boohoo bumping along behind, dangling from one fat little fist.

"Sweetheart!" she'd called. "Wait for me. Wait for Mama!"

Elke had glanced over her shoulder and chuckled, a rich baby chuckle, one that showed her bright new teeth, but she didn't stop. "Mama!" she'd caroled. "Mama!" Her sturdy little legs twinkled along, with that toddler gait like a tipsy sailor's.

And beyond her, Cenda had seen it.

A huge wall of flame, flickering and shifting. Behind, dimly seen figures. A queenly woman with five moons circling above her head, a broad-shouldered man wearing a horned headdress.

The woman crouched, holding out her hands through the flame curtain, her smile so tender, so loving, Cenda's eyes filled with tears of joy.

Yes, yes! Exerting her will, she hurried after her daughter, skimming down the tunnel like a twig carried by a summer stream. Laughing, Elke stepped through the flame as if it wasn't there and was gathered into the Lady's embrace.

But when She rose, She looked directly at Cenda and shook Her head, the moons dancing in the swirl of Her hair, Elke tucked into the crook of Her arm. *Not yet,* She said, Her voice like a silk-and-silver bell in Cenda's mind. *Not yet, my dear.*

"Yes!" insisted Cenda. "Oh, my baby, my baby!"

And she hurled herself into the wall of fire.

Agony licked over her skin, crisped her bones. It took her lungs in giant, greedy fists and wrung them dry, sank taloned fingers into her heart and guts. Her skin sizzled and she threw her head back, screaming without sound.

Through the torment, she thought she heard the Lord's voice, deep with wonder and respect. "Ah, no love like that of a mother."

"Give. Me. Back. My. Baby," gritted Cenda, writhing.

"Quickly, my Lord," said the Lady. "If we are to do this, let it be done quickly!"

Cenda was wrenched away, to tumble down, down, down, until she jolted into the cage of rib and muscle and tendon that was the body on the bed, arching in a paroxysm of pain and grief, her bones cracking, tears streaming down her face, her nose running.

And she'd turned her head to see no more than a child-shaped husk on the other bed.

Empty.

Krysanthe's cheeks were wet. "Oh, my dear," she said, her voice shaking. "My dear."

Awkwardly, Cenda patted her shoulder.

"She gave you the gift of fire for your courage," breathed the healer. "The Lady Herself. Oh, Cenda."

"No," said Cenda grimly. "She paid me for the life of my child."

Krysanthe reared back, fingers spread in the sign of the Five. "Don't— I'm sure that's not—"

Cenda shrugged and turned away to stare into the embers. She supposed she should get up, but all she could do was hunch her soul over the place inside that felt so flayed, so bloody, she couldn't bear to touch it.

"You need to rejoin the human race," said Krysanthe firmly. "Get out a bit. And Purist Matthaeus insists on taking you for private classes. Think of it as a prescription."

"I'll get over it—is that what you mean?"

The healer flinched, very slightly, but she persisted. "There's a new troupe down at The Treasure. From off-world, too. Here." She pulled a crumpled sheet of paper from a pocket and smoothed it over the arm of the chair.

Cenda flicked a glance at it. "Unearthly Opera and the Duke of Ombra. Who are they?"

"You haven't heard of them? Unearthly Opera do everything from pantomime to oratorio. They're pretty good, and this time Erik the Golden's with them. He's supposed to be incredible. Women swoon." She chuckled. "As for the Duke of Ombra . . ." Her eyes glazed over. "He's . . . Well, I saw him last time they were here. He's a fine singer, and not in the ordinary way, either."

A smile tugged at Cenda's stiff lips. "Five it, Krys, you fancied him!"

The older woman flushed. Then her shoulders relaxed and she grinned. "There's a good deal to be said for a man that dark, that dangerous. Gets the blood pumping."

Not for the first time, Cenda wondered about the dynamics of the relationship between Purist Krysanthe and her handsome protégé, Tai Yang. Her friend could be surprisingly earthy in her appetites.

"A man like the Duke would do you good," said Krysanthe.

Abruptly, Cenda wanted to slap her. Instead, she stared fiercely into the flames that roared suddenly in the fireplace. "Some rough, sweaty sex, and I'll get over it—is that what you think?"

"I want you to live, Cenda. Laugh, love. Be all that you can be."

Cenda picked at a loose thread on the arm of the chair. "Time heals—isn't that what they say?" She cast an angry, sidelong glance at her friend. "I should have another baby. I'll be all better then."

"No." Krysanthe reached forward and took both Cenda's hands in hers. "Sweetheart, you're only the third fire witch in the history of the known worlds. Tai Yang and I spent the whole of last month searching the Purist records. Great Lady, he even got us access to the Technomages' Library! The other two . . ." Her cool grip on Cenda's fingers tightened. "Neither had children, though they were both married. At least to begin with."

Cenda's heart began a slow, slamming beat. "So?"

"Your hands are so hot." The healer's gaze slid away from hers. "Your body temperature . . ."

"Don't stop there. What about it?"

At that, Krysanthe's dark eyes rose to meet hers. She looked grossly uncomfortable. "I think it's too high for a man's seed to survive inside you," she said, all in one breath. "No children."

"Is that all?" When she was sixteen, she'd sliced the pad of one finger with a ritual blade. One of many, many accidents. This was how it had felt—the bright, icy burn of the knife, the numbness of shock, the welling crimson. And last of all, the hurt. Vaguely, Cenda wondered when the pain would choose to strike. She shrugged. "Elke was my miracle. I'm too old for another."

A wave of weariness swept over her, and for a moment, her friend's intent face swam in her vision. "Krys, I need to be alone," she said. "Now."

"All right." The healer rose. "Matthaeus expects you in his rooms first thing tomorrow."

Cenda's stomach rumbled, so loudly she clamped a hand over it, startled.

Krysanthe grinned. "You need fuel to feed the fire. I'll

send an apprentice with a tray." Her hand drifted over Cenda's hair in the lightest of caresses. "Lady love you, sweetheart."

The door shut softly behind her.

A moment later, it swung open again. "Eat up, you hear? Tomorrow night we're going to The Treasure. And no arguments." This time, the latch clicked.

Cenda sat, staring into the fire, carefully thinking of nothing at all, until a shy tap announced a boy with her supper. With a murmur of thanks, she seized the tray, whipped off the cover, and dug in.

Five minutes later, she drained the last of the ale and licked the crumbs from her fingers. Lady, that was better! She couldn't remember the last time she'd felt hungry, but even after the meal she'd just bolted, her stomach still felt so empty it was clamped hard against her spine. Rising, she scrabbled through the drawers in the rickety dresser, coming up with a small bag of waynuts and some dried fern fruit.

As she crammed them into her mouth, she glanced down at her long body, noticing the hip bones thrusting like blades against the fabric of her shift. Still chewing, she drew the garment off over her head and tossed it onto the chair. Standing naked before the fire, she ran her palms over small, unremarkable breasts, the corrugations of her rib cage, down to the hollow of her belly.

Lady, she was nothing but a bag of bones!

The warmth of the fire kissed her bare shins, and she shivered with pleasure. Fire witch. *Fire witch.*

Nonsense. It had to be nonsense. Not her, not silly Cenda.

Frowning with concentration, she stared into the glowing coals. *Where did you go, whatever you are? Salamanders?*

Nothing. She sagged. Ah, well.

A log at the back caught, the flame flaring in a long tongue of blue orange.

Cenda set her jaw and concentrated fiercely. *Come. Come to me, little ones!*

When the first of the tiny lizards scrambled out of the coals, tears sprang to her eyes. She fell to her knees on the rug before the fire, holding out her hands. The salamander tensed and leaped. Then it skittered up her inner arm, over a biceps, and across the meager slope of her left breast, where it clung, directly over her beating heart.

At the prickling touch of the tiny claws, a great rush of sensual feeling swept down Cenda's spine to pool between her thighs. Her skin rippled with gooseflesh, her nipples furling into tight, rosy buds.

Utterly astonished, she gasped aloud. "Great Lady!"

Tears trembled on her lashes. So long, it had been so long since her body had been real—*there*. And now physical hungers overwhelmed her. Her mouth watered for the taste of something savory. Her skin ached for the brush of hard fingers. Hot chills fluttered in her belly, heating her sex so that it wept, too, spilling down her thigh.

Needing an anchor, she grabbed Booboo and clutched him to her chest. The salamander clambered over her collarbone and up the side of her neck, finally draping itself across the top of her ear.

Cenda huffed out a laugh. Then she snatched up her shift and blew her nose on it. "Five-it, I'm still alive," she murmured. "Who'd have thought it?"

Her breath coming shallow and fast, she found an old summer gown and struggled into it. The fire lizard was not at all discomfited. It clung easily enough, and she imagined she heard it purr.

There was no doubt the body was an amazing machine, even her body. But there wasn't much she could do about the skin hunger, not given who she was, not given the way she looked. Still, she could fill her stomach. She knew her way to the kitchen, and Cook had been a friend of hers before—

Cenda braced a hand against the wall and pulled in a deep breath. The playbill Krysanthe had brought fluttered from the arm of the chair, caught an updraft, and sailed over to the fireplace. Immediately, a salamander darted from behind a log and pounced on it, worrying at the edges like a playful kitten. The paper caught and crackled.

As Cenda walked down the passage toward the kitchen, she could still see it in her mind's eye—the bold, slashing script, and the last words to curl and blacken and die.

And featuring . . . the Duke of Ombra!

3

Gray finished tuning the Duchess and tucked her under his arm. In his usual graceful fashion, he threaded his way through the scantily clad dancers milling about in the practice rooms of The Treasure, so accustomed to the careless display of bosom and leg that he barely noticed. Reaching the wings, he slid open a peephole. Where the hell was she, this supposed fire witch? The Technomage Primus had guaranteed she'd be there.

Thus far, the Technomage had proved formidably efficient. And she had a long arm. Tonight, he'd opened his instrument case to discover a small, square sheet of some flexible substance, taped to the Duchess. A portrait and accompanying text, the briefest of dossiers.

Quickly, he'd absorbed the single paragraph of information about the fire witch and stared at the picture, imprinting it on his mind. So her child had died? No wonder she looked so gaunt, so sad. Her lips had a thin, bitter line, and the shadows beneath her eyes flowered like bruises, emphasizing the delicacy of her bone structure. But a glory of dark hair spilled down her back, almost to her hips, and the line of her thigh showed long and strong beneath the tattered gown. It looked as if her image had been captured while she was digging among serried rows of plants. A vegetable garden? Her slim fingers were clenched on the handle of a hoe, and dirt smeared her cheek.

Cenda.

He'd lifted it to peer more closely, intrigued by her eyes. They looked light. What color—?

Without warning, the document had dissolved in a puff of noxious gas. Filthy, stinking thing. As he scanned the eager faces of the crowd, he ran the palm of his right hand down the seam of his slim-fitting black trews.

Concentrate, concentrate. Drawing a calming breath, he ran a caressing fingertip over the small chips of contrasting wood inlaid on the pillar of the harp. His lips quirked in a wry grin. The only female he'd ever loved.

The smile disappeared. Save for Mother and little Gracie.

"I thought I'd do 'The Death of the Firebreath's Bride,' " rumbled Erik from behind him. "Harp accompaniment only. Something different, you know?"

"Fine." The neatly written note clipped to the dossier had said she'd be accompanied. Two women paused in the foyer area just inside the swinging doors, one short, the other tall, her shoulders slumped. Gray's eyes narrowed. The tall one had a lot of dark hair, tied back.

Erik's big hand closed over his biceps. "Gray? That all right?"

"Good idea." Gray spun around and clapped Erik on one massive shoulder. "There won't be a dry eye in the house." Erik Thorensen had the most beautiful baritone he'd ever heard. Together with blond good looks and sunny charm, it was enough to have the singer beating women off in droves.

Onstage with Erik the Golden, he might as well be invisible. He could sit at the back, hidden in the shadows where he belonged, and study his fire witch while he played. He still hadn't really decided how to go about it. The kidnap.

A knife-edge of dark excitement twisted in his belly. The game had begun.

Gods, it was going to be chancy! His preferred option had always been seduction, because he couldn't bear the thought of raising his hand to a woman. Sentimental fool that he was. Though he'd never had a problem with a pursuit, not once he'd set his mind on a woman he wanted, but this time . . .

His guts clenched. Ah, shit, she must still be grieving! The death of a child was a sad, evil thing. He remembered the three tiny graves behind the barn, his mother rocking herself, keening softly.

Ah, the poor woman. He pulled in a rasping breath. Her sorrow didn't matter; he couldn't *let* it matter. Not when the price was his very soul.

Krysanthe piloted Cenda into The Treasure, a firm hand on the small of her back. As the swinging doors snicked shut behind them, Cenda blinked and stumbled. She would have fallen if not for her friend's support. The impact of so much energy packed into such a confined space hit her like a clenched fist. Five-it, she hadn't realized how long she'd spent alone, locked up with her pain.

The day she'd just passed in the chilly company of Purist Matthaeus, sweating and straining to perform even the tiniest piece of fire Magick, hadn't been much of an improvement. In the end, he'd put the tips of his fingers together and leaned over his massive desk. "Cenda," he'd said, "fire Magick is not a gift you can spurn. And despite what you may think, that is what it is—a gift of the gods, freely given."

When she'd turned her head away, he'd snapped, "Don't be more of a fool than you can help."

Stung, she'd tried again. As many times as it took until she managed it at last, just before dusk.

Could she—? Concealing her hand in the folds of her tunic, she stared down at her palm, gathering up the heat that danced under her skin, the hot lick of impotent fury that singed her soul. Gathered and *pushed.*

The tiniest flicker of flame skittered over her skin. *Yes!* Triumph blooming within her, she closed her fist over it, her heart thundering. It wasn't much, but it was more than anyone else could do, even the so very pure Purist Matthaeus. But it made her weary bones ache. And she was still hungry—ravenous.

Surreptitiously, she took a step sideways, leaning against the wall while she got her bearings. After the cool of the evening outside, the interior of The Treasure was hot and fusty, the splintery smell of flesh-warmed wood mixing with ale and sweat.

Krysanthe flagged down a harried serving girl who led them to a booth. When she pulled aside the privacy curtain to usher them inside, the healer smiled. "Excellent view. Well-done, my dear." She pressed a coin into the girl's hand.

Sets of padded wooden benches were set aside for the offworld tourists, the economic lifeblood of Sybaris, coming in by the flitterload from the spaceports. The less fortunate stood shoulder to shoulder at the back, a kaleidoscope of jarring, cheerful color.

When the girl returned with spiced wine and a tray of vegetable pasties, Cenda brightened. As the orchestra struck up, she sat back to watch the dancers, one hand creeping up to pat her hair, where a single salamander nestled like a fancy golden comb. She hadn't wanted to take the little creature out with her at all, but Purist Matthaeus had set the task as a test of her control. One glance at the cool arch of his brow and her protest had died unborn.

Don't you dare move, she thought at it now, concentrating fiercely. But all she felt were the warm spot against her scalp and a tiny purr of contentment.

As she worked her way methodically through the meal, the acts followed in cheerful succession. There were tumblers, dancers and singers, a man who told jokes, a short pantomime. Cenda relaxed, stretching her legs under the table, leaning against the back of the padded bench. When Krysanthe gasped and dug strong fingers into her arm, she was almost asleep, far away with Elke, reading a story, the little body heavy and relaxed on her lap, curved into her breast.

"That's him!" hissed the healer. "About time!"

What a lovely dream. Blinking away the tears, Cenda pried her eyes open as the first notes floated out. Startled, she sat up with such a flurry that she knocked her wine cup with her elbow. It fell, rolling back and forth across the table, the last sip trickling out of it to form a small puddle.

Two performers occupied the small stage. Foursquare in the light stood a huge, blond bear of a man, singing. Though that was a pale description. An exquisite river of melody flowed out of his mouth, falling into a pool of absolute silence. Every face was rapt, turned toward the stage like flowers seeking the sun. A serving wench poured ale 'til it overflowed the tankard and slopped on the bar. Cenda shot a glance sideways. Krysanthe's mouth hung slightly open; her eyes were round.

The singer's accompanist sat on a stool in the farthest corner. Because he wore a black shirt and trews, he merged with the shadows as if he were part of them, scarcely there, his face a pale blur marked by dark brows. But the light washed over elegant, long-fingered hands, the lap harp he played gleaming with the rich patina of old wood and pearl inlay.

Dark and dangerous, as Krys had promised. Cenda dragged a breath in and didn't let it out.

He'd rolled up his sleeves, and she focused on the strong wrists, the muscles flexing in his forearms, the delicate precision of his movements. The extraordinary feelings that had washed over her in front of the fireplace returned in full force. Abruptly, her skin felt too tight for her body, as though she were netted in fire.

Long fingers moved in a leisurely fashion, picking out the lilting melody that wove above and beneath and around

Erik's magnificent baritone. The song took flight, the notes almost visible as crystal motes, they were so beautiful. No, not crystal, thought Cenda suddenly—long, smooth ribbons of flame, twisting in the air.

What a flight of fancy! Too much fire Magick had fried her brain. Her lips curved without real amusement.

Erik drew out the final, throbbing note. Love and loss and regret.

An instant's silence, as if the world held its breath. Then a storm of applause, shouts, stamping feet. Under cover of the noise, Krysanthe leaned over to whisper in her ear, "Great Lady, he's something, isn't he?"

Cenda could only nod. She licked dry lips. "Wish it wasn't so dark. I can't see."

"What? Actually, I meant the singer." Krysanthe's dreamy sigh sounded like a girl's. "Erik."

At the rear of the stage, Gray reached for the wine jug under his stool and drained the last of it in a single reckless swallow. The weight of the fire witch's gaze pressed against his body like caressing fingers, and he couldn't suppress the delighted spurt of vanity. But gods, she'd ignored Erik the Golden as if he weren't there. *Erik!*

Woman has taste, murmured Shad in his mind.

Gray's lips twitched. *Yeah, she sure*—Annoyed with himself, he cut off the thought with the ease of long practice.

She hadn't worn a gown. Instead, endless legs stretched under the table, sheathed in soft, hide leggings. The square neck of her overtunic exposed the ridged, complex architecture of her collar bones, but though she was definitely too thin, the garment draped sweetly enough over small, high breasts, the curve of her ribs. Put a bit of weight on her, and she'd still be slender, but queenly with it. Muscles slid under pale, smooth skin as she fiddled with the end of a dark braid as thick as his wrist. He couldn't recall the last time he'd slept with a woman, truly *slept*, with her head resting on his shoulder and her hair drifting across his naked chest. Such peace.

The fire witch swept a small, pink tongue over her lips. As she tilted her head to speak with the woman beside her, the gold comb thrust into the dark waves of her hair glittered as if it had a life of its own. Alcohol and anticipation roared a challenge in Gray's blood, the edginess making his heart pound. His cock gave a single, hungry twitch. Gods, this wasn't going to be any hardship, after all!

Nice, whispered Shad. A pause the length of a heartbeat. *So sad.*

Gray's train of thought came to a shuddering halt. *I know,* he thought savagely. *Now shut up and let me get on with it.*

Erik had bowed himself off. Gray's turn. Rising, he stepped forward, into the light. His fingers flashed, the Duchess sang the opening chord, and they were away.

Cenda couldn't decide whether heart, guts, or loins took the brunt of it, or all three. But she couldn't look away, not even when the aching regret reached ruthless fingers deep inside her and tugged at the roots of her soul. It was an ancient melody, a strange choice for a man. The Duke sang a mother's lament for the son gone to battle, achingly, desperately beautiful, threaded through with hope and fear, and futile, empty yearning.

She didn't know what kind of voice she'd expected, something hard-edged and silvery, to go with the aristocratic regularity of his features. But though his tenor was true and strong, it was husky rather than smooth, ripe with feeling.

Ah, Great Lady . . . How was it that he made it seem he sang for her alone? Hot tears slipped down her cheeks. *Come back, oh, come ye back . . .*

After the last of the applause died away, he spoke, dropping the words into a pool of silence. "Something different, now." The tone was dark and coolly sweet, deeper than his singing voice. "Sing the chorus with me." A quirk of one flyaway brow and he'd launched into "The Milkmaid's Jugs." The crowd roared with delight, belting out the vulgar chorus with relish. Cenda used the time to dry her eyes and regain her composure.

When the lights came up for interval, the serving girl appeared at her elbow, a covered dish in her hands. "Mistress." She bobbed a curtsey and placed it on the table. "The Duke of Ombra's compliments. And he's sorry he made you cry."

Five-it! The blush scorched her cheeks, the salamander shifting uneasily in her hair. First she'd bolted her food, then she'd sniveled like a child. And all in plain view.

"Well, well, the Duke no less. Go on," said Krysanthe, nudging Cenda's shoulder. "Eat. It smells wonderful. Anyway, I told you, you need fuel for the fire."

Cenda picked up the fork, then laid it down. She shook her head. "Can't."

A strong hand covered hers, fork and all. "Yes, you can," said a dark voice, perfectly pitched for her ears alone.

Cenda's breath caught and her gaze flew up to meet his.

The Duke smiled, though his eyes remained steady and serious. "May I join you?" He removed his hand, leaving Cenda's to lie abandoned on the table, limp and awkward. The harp was slung over one shoulder, and he had a stoppered wine jug tucked under his arm.

"Of course!" said Krysanthe, leaping to her feet. "Please. I'm just . . . ah . . . off to see a friend." She patted Cenda's shoulder. "Be good, now."

"Krys!" hissed Cenda, making a furious grab for her friend's skirt.

"Have fun." With a final twinkle, the healer drew the privacy curtain behind her, cocooning Cenda with the Duke in what was now an alarmingly intimate space.

She'd thought his eyes must be as dark as his hair, but this close, they were a clear, limpid gray. Long-lidded eyes, full of secrets, shielded with extravagant lashes, surely the gift of some besotted goddess. His brows were strongly marked, with an upward slant at the corners. They gave him a sardonic air that went well with his lithe, self-contained grace.

"Mistress, may I sit?" he asked patiently, obviously not for the first time.

At her nod, he slid onto the bench beside her, bringing with him a wave of body heat, the clean, earthy scent of healthy male. His shadow wavered behind him, dark as slate. All the hair rose on the back of Cenda's neck. She gripped her hands together in her lap. That way she wouldn't be tempted to reach out and touch.

The Duke didn't seem at all discomposed by the silence. Calmly, he studied her face, cataloging her features one by one. It should have been insolent, the action of a man confident of conquest, but he looked almost . . . concerned. On the other hand, the expression in his eyes wasn't the least brotherly. Under the table, Cenda pressed her thighs together to still the sudden liquid ache.

She frowned. What was a man like this doing here? With her?

Finally, when she was sure he must be able to hear her heart knocking against her ribs, he asked, "Did you enjoy the music?"

Cenda bit her lip. Five-it, she was practically in her dotage! Surely she could speak to an attractive man as if she had all her wits. She smiled with all the self-possession she could muster. "Oh, yes. I've never heard anything like it."

"I hadn't, either, not 'til I joined the company. He's unique."

"No, not Erik." The words slipped out. "I meant you."

"You flatter me." Absently, he set the harp beside him, picked up her fallen wine cup, and righted it. But his remarkable eyes had gone silver with pleasure.

Cenda fought not to grin. It wasn't as if she'd had a string of lovers—rather, the reverse—but she knew what men liked to talk about. Barton, Elke's father, had spent hours informing her of his brilliance. Relaxing against the high bench at her back, she gave the Duke an opening. "It must be exciting, traveling with an opera company," she said.

"This is an individual deep-dish pie. The specialty of the house." Casually, he picked up the fork and wrapped her lax fingers around it. "Eat it for me and I'll tell you." Lifting her hand, he guided it to the plate and speared a fat noodle.

"You need it," he said, so gently she couldn't take offense.

As the pie disappeared, bit by bit, the Duke told stories in his sweet, husky voice. If she stopped eating, he stopped talking. His observations were fascinating, spiced with a wry, wicked wit. Sometimes the things he said made her chuckle. Once, she even blushed. He was enthralling, and she'd never met anyone like him.

With some surprise, she regarded the empty dish. "You should have been a storyteller," she said. "Or a magician."

"Oh, I have." As he uncorked the wine jug, his shadow flickered. His lips went tight. "I've done a great many things."

Refilling the cup, he swallowed, his gaze burning into hers over the rim. Finally, he said, "My name is Grayson. Those who care for me call me Gray."

Deliberately, he turned the cup and lifted it toward her lips. "Will you drink with me, sweetheart?"

The seconds stretched, the chatter of the crowd suddenly as distant as surf on a faraway shore. All she need do was lean forward a scant inch to touch her lips to the place where his had been. Within her, Magick moved, uncoiling in her pelvis, her breasts. Like fire Magick, but darker, hotter, *wetter*. Female Magick.

Cenda teetered on the brink.

The Duke—no, *Gray*—cradled her cheek in his other hand. "I'd wondered about your eyes," he said in a deep murmur that thrilled along her nerves. "They're gold."

"Light brown," she whispered back.

"Gold like an old coin." He drew callused fingertips down her cheek, across the cushion of her lower lip. "And your skin's perfect. Like honey and cream."

Dark and dangerous, full of secrets. But oh, so beautiful, so practiced. And he was a traveling player; he'd be gone in a few short weeks. Why not? She had nothing left to lose.

Lord and Lady, give me strength.

Cenda laid her fingers over his on the cup and lowered her head. The spiced wine slipped over her tongue, filling her mouth, rich and heady and warm, replacing the very blood in her veins. Her whole body flushed with heat.

When she would have taken a second gulp, he removed the cup. "Slowly," he said. "Very. Very. Slowly."

There was no mistaking that intent, predatory expression, the smoky heat of his gaze. Great Lady, he was going to kiss her! Disconcerted, she moved her head the wrong way and their noses bumped. The Duke murmured a curse, and the hand on her cheek slid under her hair to clasp her nape. A hard thigh pressed all along hers under the table.

Barton had always been at her to open her mouth, but it was so . . . so . . . wet. Kissing him was a sloppy discomfort to be endured. She'd actually preferred the sex, but even that—

Gray nibbled her lower lip, licked the spot, and all thoughts of Barton dried up and blew away. Gray's mouth was smooth and soft and firm all at once, and sweet with wine. Wicked bursts of fire licked up her spine, tingled in her breasts, her belly. When she gasped, he slipped his tongue into her mouth, but true to his word, he did it all slowly—so slowly, she found she was desperate for more. If she could have freed her lips, she would have begged—faster, stronger, *deeper*—but all she could do was hang on, her head spinning.

Gods, she'd had no idea!

Floundering after her composure, Cenda clutched at his shoulders, but he wound her braid around his wrist and tugged her into his lap so that she sprawled against him, her breasts mashed against his hard chest. Crooning deep in his throat, he ran his palm the length of her spine, molded the curve of one buttock. Something like a bar of molten metal pressed insistently against her hip.

He wanted her—he really did—this extraordinary man! *Her*—clumsy, skinny, used-up Cenda. With a sort of grim astonishment, she surveyed her own confusion. Then she let it sweep her up and carry her away. Every particle of common sense she'd ever possessed slithered off. Somewhere dark and fiery and pulsing.

She'd lost herself sufficiently to nip gently at his bottom lip, to thread her fingers through the cool silk of his hair, when something sharp and hot prickled against her scalp, tiny claws gripping hard. *Lord's balls!* How could she have forgotten the salamander, the fire Magick? She was on fire with lust, almost literally. Only the gods knew how dangerous she really was. Had she scorched him, hurt him?

Fumbling a hand free, she pushed against the solid wall of his chest, mumbling a protest into his mouth. For a moment, he held her fast, his tongue still cajoling, caressing. But in the end, he pulled back, kissing the tip of her nose, her eyelids, one after the other. Then he let her go. Slowly.

Panting, they stared at each other. The Duke's shadow loomed over the booth, looking almost predatory. He flicked a glance at it, then back at her. "Gods, who knew?" he murmured. His cheekbones were flushed with hectic color and his chest rose and fell as if he'd been running, but he didn't seem to be in any pain. A bead of sweat coursed down his neck to pool in the soft pit at the base of his throat, and she had the insane desire to burrow there, to nuzzle and lick.

Who, indeed?

On the other side of the curtain, the serving girl shuffled her feet and cleared her throat. "Five-minute warning, Gray," she said loudly.

Cenda put a shaking hand to her lips. They still tingled. "Duke, I—"

He clamped his hand over her wrist. "Call me by name. Say, 'I'll wait right here 'til you've finished, Gray.'" His eyes had gone so smoky they were almost black.

Rising, he pulled her to her feet, hard up against him. She couldn't stop the instinctive flinch. Five-it, she was so tall, they were almost eye to eye.

Immediately, he frowned and his arm tightened around her waist, forcing her to stand straight. "Never think it,

Cenda. You're perfect. See?" He pressed a hard, swift kiss to her quivering lips.

"Three minutes, Gray!" called the girl.

"Promise me," he insisted. "Promise!"

4

In her cool, airy office high above the teeming tourist traps of Sybaris, the newly appointed Technomage Primus leaned back in her plaswood chair, her brain buzzing with stimulation. As was her usual practice, she'd been doing four things at once: scanning the data on her current experiment, annotating correspondence in her bold, angular hand, double-checking the spaceport budget, and thinking about the fire witch.

She took a moment to sigh and rub her aching neck, but her lips curved with satisfaction. Her judgment had proved sound—again. Which went to show that reason was all very well, but a Scientist's intuition must never be discounted. Especially hers.

Hiring an offworld adventurer had been a stroke of genius. Sharanita had handled all the arrangements personally, and her loyalty to the Primus was ironclad. Given that her position as Primus was far from secure, the Secundus and his allies still scheming against her, the whole situation was perfect. Nothing like having an extra card up your sleeve, top-secret data, exclusively yours.

As if her thought had called the woman, a discreet cough came from the threshold. Suppressing the surge of irritation, the Primus turned her head. "Nita, how many times have I told you to use the deskvid?"

Sharanita hovered, not an easy feat for such a tall, raw-boned woman. She topped her employer by a foot. Bobbing her head, she said in her slow, deep voice, the slum accent still marked, "Hate t' things, Primus. Sorry."

"Well, get used to it," snapped the Technomage.

"Yah, Primus." Sharanita flushed, her body blocky and awkward in one of the vulgar flowered smocks she favored. She dropped her eyes to the sheet of paper in her hand. "T' Quartus is here, ten minutes early." A pause. "Have ye eaten?"

Not for the first time, the Primus congratulated herself on her choice of Prime Assistant. Her colleagues had been appalled at the thought of inserting an ignorant Sybarite peasant into the white-coated hush of the Technomage Tower. "She'll never understand us, our work," one had muttered. "Never!"

Always subtle in his opposition, the Secundus had said, in his usual dry manner, "The ethical quibbles will be inevitable, my dear Primus. Annoying at best, dangerous at worst. Not to mention the sheer stupidity."

He couldn't have been more wrong. Sharanita had no social graces or academic ability, but she'd been schooled by a local moneylender, and numbers held no terrors for her. Nor did hours and hours of mind-numbing detail. Within a week, awe shone in her eyes whenever she glanced at the Primus. Another week of cultivation, the occasional word of praise, and the awe had become devotion.

Now, the Primus noted the hurt in the other woman's broad face. She summoned up a tired smile. "You're right." She waved a careless hand. "Get me something, would you please, Nita? Just a snack. You know what I like."

Sharanita glowed. "Yah, Primus, of course. An' t' Quartus can wait?"

The Primus shot her Assistant a conspiratorial glance full of weary humor. "That's right. Until the appointed time."

It took so little to be a leader, just a moderate degree of appreciation, judiciously applied. The Primus had had Sharanita extensively investigated. A childless widow, there wouldn't be more than a ripple in her home slum if she disappeared. Such a necessity would be damnably inconvenient, but it was good to know, nonetheless.

"Oh, an' Primus?"

"Mm?"

"T' Duke made contact las' night."

The Primus straightened, her blood bubbling. "Excellent," she said. "When do you estimate he'll deliver the witch?" She couldn't wait to get the subject into the lab and start testing. The ability to produce flame, to *throw* fire. She had to admit, as a Scientist, she was skeptical about Magick on general principles, but there was no denying the existence of hard evidence. A pity Magick research was regarded as somehow reprehensible, a shoddy, second-class field of study.

"He's slippery." Sharanita shrugged. "Our operative couldn' get him t' say."

If it should be true . . . there'd be nothing she couldn't do, couldn't achieve, with such an energy source. Especially if it was reproducible.

"Never take no for an answer, Nita." Crisply, the Primus reiterated her original orders. Then she steepled her fingers under her chin, considering ways and means. The logistics of the delivery were going to be a challenge, because the fire witch was hers and hers alone. The slightest hint of this research and every member of the Ten would be avid.

With her fingertips, she caressed the numeral one embroidered on the collar of her white coat, feeling the slight roughness where she'd unpicked the five with her own hands. She'd made a private ceremony of it, alone in her luxurious apartment in the Tower of Residence. A meteoric rise that was the culmination of decades of determined effort. The alliances, the bribes, the results she'd fudged, the papers she'd written, one carefully arranged accident. Regrettable, but the Technomage who'd been her superior had left her no options, not when he'd demanded sexual favors she was unwilling to provide.

When in doubt, think outside the box. "Nita," she said slowly, "we need a more efficient intermediary. Who do you know who'd collect the woman from the Duke, no questions asked?"

"I guess . . ." Her Assistant dried up. Then she shook her head.

The Primus smiled her encouragement. "Go ahead, dear," she said. "Speak freely. We're just considering possibilities."

Sharanita raised unhappy brown eyes. "Where I live, it's t' Fixer," she said in a husky whisper. "But he's a bad man, Primus. Wicked."

"Ah." The Primus drummed her fingers on the desk. "I rather think the Fixer has met his match. Contact him, Nita." She bared her teeth. "And send the Quartus in. I look forward to her explanation of the discrepancies in the West Sector spaceport budget."

Gray strode toward the Wizards' Enclave in a filthy temper. He must be losing his touch. He could have sworn he'd had Cenda in the palm of his hand the previous night. His body had certainly been convinced of it. Irritably, he recalled the awkward, eager press of her tongue, the long, lithe body and small breasts crushed against his chest. His fingers curled in memory, the silk of that long braid soft in his palm.

Tonight, the tourists had been more than usually enthralled. Erik had taken ten curtain calls. *Ten!* Gods, he'd thought the show would never end.

Looming over the slums, a cluster of Technomage Towers pierced the night sky, four thick, glowing needles of light. Gray turned his back on them with a muttered curse. The greasy food stalls with their garish colored lanterns jostled for frontage in laneways worn down by centuries of passing feet, while thieves and whores were dark shapes glimpsed in darkened doorways.

Gods, it wouldn't take much to light the mean streets of Sybaris with the occasional glowglobe, but no, the Technomages kept their Science and their money clasped to their white-coated chests. Their invention of the slingshot sails that catapulted starships through the Discontinuity Tunnels between worlds had been a source of unimaginable riches. Even the most minor factotum in the Tower was wealthy beyond a Sybarite's dream of avarice, while the Technomage Primus wielded powers a god might envy. Bastards, all of them.

Without withdrawing his attention from the street behind him, Gray glanced up at the natural glory of the Dancers. Arabesque and Pointe were highest in the night sky, Pirouette just rising. Tap and Tango, the smaller twins, circled each other with endless, glowing grace. The colors made an extraordinary blend—the silver of stately Arabesque bleaching Pointe to a pale rose gold, while Tap and Tango were subtly different shades of orange, like two fat manda fruits hanging in the sky. Pirouette, the largest of the moons, shone blue, its face still stained with the dusk of evening.

Five moons made for complex, multi-edged shadows. Set in a twenty-foot hedge of fragrant Lady's lace, the tall, wrought-iron gates of the Enclave cast mad, curlicued patterns over the rutted dirt of the road. *P-p-pretty,* said Shad, his presence fragmenting.

Gray snorted with grim amusement. *You're stuttering.*

His shadow made the mental equivalent of a rude noise.

Deliberately, Gray stepped into the complete darkness at the foot of the hedge, and the weight of Shad's presence lifted. Breathing more easily, he watched a small carriage pull up, drawn by a team of dogs, the largest working animals the Technomages would permit on Sybaris. Three flitters buzzed overhead in neat formation, and Gray growled a curse. *Dogs*, for the gods' sake!

A couple paid, climbed out of the dogcart, and spoke with the gatekeeper. They disappeared into the Enclave, to be followed a few moments later by a rowdy group of apprentices, boys and girls both.

Gray strolled in their wake. After all, he had nothing to hide, not yet. "I'm here to see Cenda," he told the old woman in the gatekeeper's cubby. Rheumy eyes surveyed him with remarkable keenness. Gray looked down his nose, resisting the urge to check the fit of his trews.

"If she wishes," said the old woman at last.

"Where . . . ?" He gestured at the crazy hodgepodge of buildings, their dark bulk outlined against the night sky. For all the world, it looked as if the Enclave had been dropped on Sybaris, a single piece at a time, from the Dancers. Light shone from windows of every conceivable shape, an erratic illumination for narrow paths that corkscrewed in all directions. But thank the gods, it was quieter here, the unnerving hum of drinking and gambling and all the attendant collateral damage muted by the thickness of the hedge.

"Follow Titfer." The old woman snapped her fingers, and a huge tabby cat sauntered out of the bushes to rub against her legs. "He'll show you."

Completely disregarding Gray, the animal strolled down the nearest path, tail waving behind him like a furry flag.

"Go, go." The old woman flapped her hands in a shooing motion, but Gray hadn't moved more than a few yards when she called after him, "Don't trip over your shadow." She cackled when he missed a step.

Gray flexed his fingers, testing the reassuring weight of the dagger in its forearm sheath. Feeling more like a fool with every moment, he drew a breath and strode after the cat. They progressed in a series of infuriating fits and starts, his feline guide pausing at intervals to sniff at clumps of grass or to stare idly at the moons, but eventually they stopped outside a building so small it barely qualified as a cottage. The cat planted his backside on the step, curled his tail around neat feet, and said, *"Perroww!"* in a decided sort of way.

"This the one?" Gods, he must be mad, talking to a cat!

You talk to me, said a sly, smoky voice in his head.

Gray ignored it.

Titfer regarded him with an inscrutable green gold gaze. *"Prrrrt!"*

With wry humor, Gray glanced over his shoulder, recognizing the back wall of the gatekeeper's cubby. The bloody animal had led him through the Enclave in what was virtually a complete circle. "Think you're clever, don't you?"

Titfer didn't reply, but he looked smug.

Gray sighed, conscious of such tremendous reluctance he was hard put not to turn away and forget the whole fucking thing. There'd been desolation swimming deep in her gold brown gaze, self-hatred even. Though he doubted she named it that. Not many would. It wasn't an easy matter to stare your soul in the eye and know yourself for what you were . . . to see all the ugly smears that were the real you, the utter selfishness of the human animal, its greed, violence, and inherent cruelty.

But if he moved two steps, directly under that light, that part of himself would rise up and stand before him, a being of impenetrable darkness, speaking in his mind.

Oh, gods, to be free of Shad! Free before he lost his grip on sanity entirely.

Memory rose up in a suffocating wave, Deiter's voice cutting through, sharp and ironic. *I can cure you of your shadow, Grayson, my friend.*

But Judger God, the price!

"Bring me the fire witch," Deiter had said.

Gray curled his lip. "Alive or dead?"

The old wizard frowned. "Alive," he'd said. "If she can't function, our bargain is void." Then he'd grinned, not a comfortable sight. "The word off the starships says the

Technomage Primus of Sybaris is also, ah, interested." He wagged a gnarled finger. "A small matter of a double-cross, dear Grayson, and there'll be a nice profit on the side."

He could always use money, no question of it, but Judger, he hated what he was going to do to her.

Not . . . all . . . of it. Shad's voice, the thinnest of whispers in the faint shadows cast by the Dancers.

I know I'm a bastard, all right? Now shut the fuck up. But the blood pounding in his temples sang a song of dark anticipation, and the tension in his guts worked its way down to tighten the skin over his balls. Gods, he'd never expected the untutored touch of her mouth to affect him so. She hadn't really known what she was doing—that much was clear—but the strange innocence of her, the fresh taste, the warm, slender limbs clinging, pressing . . . For some godsbedamned reason, he found it unbearably erotic.

"Is that you, Krys?" Quick steps from inside. "I thought—" The door swung open just as he raised his fist to knock, and there she was, the fire witch, salvation and damnation combined in a single dowdy, extraordinary package. They both froze. "Oh," she said. "Duke. It's you."

"Yes." As he dropped his hand, the shaft of light from inside streamed across the step, throwing his shadow into sharp relief behind him. *And me,* murmured Shad.

Gray blinked. Cenda had a towel wrapped around her head, strands of wet, dark hair plastered to her neck, her forehead. Beneath the bulk of the makeshift turban, her face appeared small and pointed, as fey as a fairy's in an old book. "You washed your hair," he said stupidly.

"Yes." Her throat moved as she swallowed, drawing his attention downward. The fire witch wore a thin shift, a dust-colored shawl thrown over her shoulders. With the light behind her, he could make out the long curves of her slender body. The shawl covered her breasts, but he thought he caught a glimpse of the dark crescent of a nipple.

With a supreme effort of will, he wrenched his gaze back to her gold brown eyes. "You promised." It came out more aggrieved than stern, so he said it again, frowning. "You promised. You said you'd wait."

"I know. I—" Her tongue crept out to moisten her lips, and in the back of his mind, Shad growled softly. Fingers clenched on the door frame, she held his stare. "I lost my nerve." She squared her shoulders. "I'm sorry."

"Merroww!" The cat rose and butted his head against her shins.

As she turned her attention to the animal, he saw Cenda bite her lip. "Why thank you, Titfer," she said. When she bent to stroke the cat's head, the towel came undone and fell off. The great, damp mass of her hair slid down over her shoulder and brushed Titfer's back. With an indignant hiss, he stalked past her and into the cottage.

Gray laughed. "No one does offended like a cat." Smoothly, he scooped up the towel and handed it over. "What sort of name is Titfer?"

Her lips curved in an almost smile. "Tit for tat. Cat. See?"

Arching a brow, Gray looked over her shoulder at the feline stretched out in a lordly fashion before the fire. "Seems a bit beneath his dignity."

"Oh, it's not his True Name." Cenda stepped back. "I guess you'd better come in," she said, but she didn't sound any too pleased.

Nettled, Gray moved past her, ensuring that their shoulders brushed as he did so. With grim satisfaction, he heard the breath catch in her throat. "So what is it, his True Name?"

"Oh, I couldn't tell you that." Her eyes opened very wide and some of the high color faded from her cheeks. "Knowing a creature's True Name gives you power over it. Anyway," she finished prosaically, "it's really hard to pronounce."

The cottage was essentially a single room, dominated by a huge, shabby old armchair angled toward the fire. A drawn curtain revealed a bed tucked into an alcove. Another concealed what he assumed to be cooking or bathing facilities. Everything was worn, well used, but the general effect was cozy, welcoming.

Cenda tossed the towel onto the bed and adjusted the lamp. Shad flared into solid, dark existence behind him. Gray gritted his teeth. *Keep out of this, you hear?*

Shad said nothing, but his silence was ominous.

"Please, sit down." Cenda made a jerky gesture at the chair. "Can I get you something?" She used both hands to shove the hair out of her face. It was beginning to dry, twisting into long, crazy curls.

You, naked in my lap, he thought. *Let's get it done. Finished.*

Gray didn't speak, only looked at her, allowing the hunger and impatience to slip the leash for an instant. She reddened. "Something hot, I mean."

He quirked a brow, and her lips tightened. "Uh, something hot to drink."

Shad stirred. *Stop it.*

"Thank you, I'd like that." He dug into his belt pouch, extracted a small paper bag. "Here. I thought you might enjoy this."

"Oh!" Her eyes sparkled, a rich amber. She lifted the bag to her nose, sniffing with delight. "Sweet Lady, what a gorgeous smell! What is it?"

Gray lowered himself into the chair and stretched his legs toward the fire. "It's called chocolat." He smiled, enjoying her lack of artifice, the honesty of her pleasure. Would she be this sensual in bed, this innocent? "I brought it with me from Concordia. For a special occasion."

She stilled, her fingers clutching the bag. "Is this"—she cleared her throat—"a special occasion?"

As if her husky voice had tripped a switch inside him, blood pooled in his groin, spilling into his cock. He didn't have the luxury of time to waste. Deliberately, he slid a palm up over her forearm, kneaded her biceps. Gods, her skin was warm! "Oh, I think so, don't you?" He tugged, very gently, and she came stumbling into the side of the chair. Gray ran his hand up the back of her neck, into the damp thickness of her hair, pulling her down toward him.

"You remember?" he murmured, scant inches from her lips. "About slowly?"

"Yes," she croaked, dropping the bag and closing the distance to his mouth in an awkward lunge. In the fireplace, a log caught in a shower of sparks and her lips collided with his.

When he'd kissed Cenda in The Treasure, he'd had to lure her in, seduce her with his mouth, so the heat had ambushed him in the most disconcerting way. Need had flashed through his blood like a forest fire, expanding his cock against the fabric of his trews. This time, he'd been confident he'd be prepared, in control, but Judger God, her kiss was going to kill him!

The unabashed greed of her hot, sleek tongue, combined with the uncertainty of her clutching fingers on his shoulder made his head reel. Shad was growling, a continuous ground bass that vibrated at the base of his skull. Gray caught himself a split second before the hand in Cenda's hair closed into a fist, before he hauled her right over the arm of the chair and into his lap.

He didn't doubt she'd come willingly, but then Shad would shred his self-discipline, and he'd end up terrifying the life out of her. As if giving her to old Deiter wouldn't be a terrifying experience! Shit, shit, *shit*! Through the tangle of lust and conscience, he focused on two things. One, this was a battle for his soul, his sanity. He couldn't lose, no matter the cost. He *couldn't*. Two, Cenda might have had a child, but she was so inexperienced, it was almost painful. An innocent in every possible way.

He opened his eyes to see a shadowy hand stroking her hair. *Don't touch,* he growled at Shad. *And shut up that noise.*

Why? Can't concentrate?

Tilting his head back, Gray opened to her, letting her take the lead, find a rhythm that pleased her. Pleased him.

Ah, she was a quick study, his fire witch! Gray gentled his grip on her hair, holding himself still with an effort of will while an agile little tongue flicked over his, twining and flirting with a kind of desperate joy.

He registered the instant she recalled who she was, what she was doing. When she would have pulled away, he tightened his hold. "No," he growled. "Again. Kiss me again."

Instead, she whispered, "When do you leave?" But she tempered the question with a kitten lick to his bottom lip that made his cock twitch.

"A week, ten days if the crowds are good." *And you'll be with me, sweetheart; conscious or not, it makes no matter.* "Time enough for us to play, Cenda."

She surprised him. Her brow still knitted, she straightened, maintaining her grip on his shoulder. She looked him dead in the eye. "Why?"

"What do you mean, why?"

"Why me?" Her face shuttered and she shrugged. "You're not only a duke, but the Lady gave you the gift of music. And you have to know you're beautiful." Her cheekbones flew flags of color. "You could have any woman—any man, for that matter. Why me?"

Shad flexed, dark against the wall. A derisive snort. *Beautiful?*

Fuck off. If it wasn't for you, I wouldn't be doing this.

Really?

"Don't be ridiculous." He hooked an arm around her waist, but she resisted.

"Duke, look at me."

"I told you. That's a stage name. My real name is Gray." He managed a grin, though his lips felt stiff. "And I'm looking."

"What do you see?"

"What do—?" Gray stared, his brain racing. The abyss yawned before his feet. She was too intelligent to fool, too wary to accept flattery. The truth, then. "You really want to know?"

She nodded.

"Come here, then." Taking both her hands in a firm grip, he drew her to stand between his knees. He rested his head against the high back of the chair and studied her tense face. Threaded through the crackle of the fire, he could hear the steady rumble of Titfer's baritone purr. At last, he said slowly, "I see a woman who hasn't realized her potential."

Her fingers moved convulsively in his. She bit her lip, and her lashes swept down, concealing her eyes.

"You're too clever not to see it, and it makes you angry, I think." He shrugged. "Understandable."

Lifting their clasped hands, he rubbed his cheek against her knuckles. "And I only just realized I've never seen you smile, not really."

At that, her golden gaze flashed up. "No," she agreed. "I haven't felt much like smiling lately."

Now they were getting to it. Gently, gently. He lowered the timbre of his voice, using it as an instrument of persuasion, the way he did when he was singing. "What happened, Cenda?"

But she shook her head, a wild jumble of curls falling forward across her cheek. From behind their protection, she whispered, "Later. Later I'll—Maybe." She rallied. "You still haven't said why me." Shooting him a narrow glance, she said dryly, "I don't imagine I'm your usual type."

5

Cenda watched amusement flash across the Duke's face. His elegant lips quirked and those clear gray eyes gleamed. "No," he said, "you're not."

He looked so relaxed in her shabby chair while she stood caged between his knees, acutely conscious of his muscular warmth, the possessive firmness of his hands clasping hers. She'd been stupid, launching herself at his mouth like that, but his touch, the texture of his skin, were so startling, so addictive, she'd been lost, unable to wait another moment. If truth be told, she'd been lost from the first time she'd seen him, wreathed in shadows, making his music.

Her body still wept for him, a heated trickle slipping down her thigh, the tips of her breasts stiff and aching.

Five-it, no fool like an old fool!

The bracing heat of the fire licked up her spine, giving her strength. What was it Purist Matthaeus had said? "Remember that Magick is a matter of the will, Cenda." He'd studied her over his steepled fingers. "Therefore, it is linked inextricably with your emotional state. That you are using rage and grief as triggers for the flame is understandable in the, ah, circumstances, but it will not do in the long term." He fixed her with a dispassionate gaze. "Discipline is what lies at the heart of true Magick, young lady. Cultivate it."

Discipline be damned! He was laughing at her, this beautiful man, and Great Lady, how it hurt!

She tried to wrench her hands away, but he shook his head, holding her fast. Impelled by inner pain, Cenda drew a preparatory breath. She doubted she could muster even enough power to scorch his fingers, but by the seven circles of hell, she was going to try!

The Duke spoke. "You have no idea, do you?" he said in that dark, sweet tenor.

"Idea?" Everything inside her went still. She wet her lips. "Of what?"

"Of how much I want you. That I'd want you even if—" His eyes went deliciously smoky and the slanted brows drew together. "I honestly don't know why. Oh, you're pretty enough, or you would be if you ate properly. But that's not it. Gods, I can't—"

Abruptly, he pulled her hand down and slammed it down over his groin. "Feel that?" Beneath the black fabric of his trews, the solid, uncompromising length of his cock throbbed against her palm.

Cenda gasped with shock and arousal, and her fingers clenched. The shawl began to slip from her shoulders.

The Duke's flesh leaped under her touch. From the corner of her eye, she saw his shadow jerk hard against the wall. He grunted a word that sounded like a curse, something about judgment or judging. His other hand shot out, spearing into her hair, tugging her down to sprawl against his body, breast to breast and thigh to thigh. The shawl slithered over her hips to pool on the floor, but she didn't notice.

When he took her mouth in a deep, possessive kiss, she realized with a tiny thrill of fear that he'd been holding back. This was nothing like their previous kisses, and nothing could have prepared her for it. It wasn't slow. Or sweet.

There was an edge of desperation to it, an iron-hard focus. The sensation of his thrusting tongue was so intoxicating, so masterful, Cenda could do nothing but cling, her eyes squeezed shut, her heart thundering. Long fingers dug mercilessly into the curve of her buttock, pressing her hips into his, the wedge of his erection insistent against her pubic mound. Breathy moans bubbling in her throat, Cenda shifted her thighs to accommodate him. The ridge of his cock split her sex lips perfectly, setting nerves jangling in the most exquisitely agonizing way. Fire streaked from her pelvis up her spine, wrapped around her ribs, fingered her nipples with a sly burn.

Great Lady! Cenda's eyes flew open. The Duke's extravagant lashes lay against his cheek as his mouth worked its dark Magick on hers. Her horrified gaze fixed on her left hand, gripping the back of the chair in a white-knuckled clench. Where her fingers dug in, the upholstery was beginning to scorch.

Before she could jerk away, something blessedly cool enveloped the nape of her neck, and the fiery tingle in her fingertips receded. A long shudder ran through the hard body beneath her. The Duke ripped his lips from hers with a growl of "No, don't—" He broke off, panting, his eyes gone so dark they seemed drowned in shadow.

Then his gaze sharpened and he cradled her cheek in one hand, as if he had every right to hold her steady for his scrutiny. "Are you all right?"

"Yes. Are you?" It must have been her imagination, that fleeting sensation.

"Me?" He arched a cool brow. "Why shouldn't I be?" Stroking his knuckles along her jaw, he frowned.

Gods, now she'd insulted his masculinity.

"Let me go." Her voice hardly shook at all. Cause for pride. "There's something I have to tell you."

The Duke lifted his hands, but when she would have levered herself off him and out of the chair, he shook his head and drew her back. "Nuh-uh. I like you on my lap." So she snagged the shawl, curled up her long legs, and settled into the crook of his shoulder, surprised that she fit so well. Barton had complained she was too lanky, too heavy. Cuddling had been beneath his dignity. A little twist of pleasure unfurled inside her and she let one hand rest over Gray's heart, featherlight.

Not willing to spoil it just yet, Cenda turned her head to watch the fire, letting her pulse slow to something approaching normal. He didn't speak, but his fingertips skated over her thigh, drawing random patterns on the thin fabric of her shift. His cock throbbed against her hip. She could feel it, like the beat of a salamander's heart against the inside of her wrist. Beneath her, his lean, muscular body was tense, but he held her lightly.

Barton would have had her flat on her back by now. He'd never been able to wait, but the Duke—*Gray*—didn't seem to be in any particular hurry, though his heart thudded hard and fast against her palm, the peak of a nipple brushing the heel of her hand through the fine linen of his black shirt.

Cenda watched the salamanders frisking in the flames, smiling a little. Gray had given her more physical pleasure in their few moments together than Barton had in a period of months, the pompous idiot. The only gift the wizard had given her was Elke. She closed her eyes on the shaft of pain, and Gray said, "What is it?"

"Nothing," she said automatically.

"You had something to tell me?"

Cenda sighed inwardly, reminiscent tremors running through the folds of her sex, the skin of her breasts still swollen and tight. Her belly fluttered. Gods, she wanted more—more mind-numbing pleasure, more abandonment of the senses, more oblivion. Just . . . *more*. For a second, she toyed with the idea of saying nothing, but there was no way she knew to hide it, what she was.

She let her head drop back against the firm muscle of his upper arm, holding his gaze. "You know I'm a witch." She made it a statement.

He regarded her steadily, his slate gray eyes wary, opaque. "Of course."

"I've never been very good at Magick." It was surprisingly easy to admit. "But a few months ago, I was very sick and the fever—" She stalled.

"And?"

"Apparently I'm a fire witch now." She bit her lip. "But I'm not very good at that, either." Her time with him had been something she'd always remember, a glimpse of a whole new world: earthy, sweaty, and sweet. So very, very good.

"Go on." He concentrated on winding a long curl around his fingers.

"Gray." Cenda touched his cheek, willing him to understand, not to laugh. "I don't have much control. I could hurt you."

"Hurt me?" One corner of his beautiful mouth tucked up.

She dragged in a breath. "Any powerful emotion is a trigger. If I—I could burn you."

He stiffened. "Nonsense."

Her nerve snapped. "Look, look here!" She pointed to the singed upholstery, the five scorch marks that fitted her fingers perfectly. "See what kissing you did to me?"

His eyes went silver, the way they had in The Treasure. "That good, huh?" His shadow flickered behind him, shifting.

"Will you listen to me?" Cenda struck his shoulder with her fist. "I'm dangerous!"

Gray grasped both her hands in his. "Do you want to cause me pain?"

"No, of course not!"

"Well, then." Releasing her, he leaned back. "You won't."

Cenda stared, aghast. But deep inside, her empty flesh contracted with greed, as if he were already embedded high and hard within her, instead of pressing into her hip, firm and insistent. "You should go," she managed. "Right now."

"I can't." He blinked once, slowly, the inky lashes sweeping down, as if he were listening to an inner voice. In the lamplight, his shadow loomed behind him, a man-shaped cloak made of impenetrable, velvety darkness. "For you, sweetheart, I'll risk the blisters."

"But—"

Gray nipped the side of her neck, then soothed the spot with his tongue. Into her hair, he murmured, "Don't incinerate my balls just yet, sweet Cenda. Wait 'til tomorrow."

Cenda jerked her head aside. "I'm not joking!"

"Neither am I." He favored her with a lazy smile. "Show me this fire Magick then."

He didn't believe her! Why, the arrogant, beautiful—He didn't believe she could do it.

Cenda wrenched herself out of Gray's lap with little dignity and less grace, disregarding his pained grunt. Her breast heaving, she stood on the rug before the fire, filling her senses with the crackling song of the flames, the sweet smell of burning feather wood and the more acrid undernote of pseudocoal. Colors danced behind her eyelids, orange and white and blue. Ah, what a blue, the blue of salamander eyes. Falling to her knees beside the snoozing cat, she thrust a hand into the blaze, only half hearing Gray's startled oath from behind her. The shawl tumbled from her shoulders to the rug.

Come. Come to me now.

Nothing.

Magick is a matter of the will, Cenda.

But what of courtesy? Of honor?

Disciplining her breathing the way Purist Matthaeus had taught her, Cenda shaped her thought until it seared like the flames. *Come, my bright darlings. Please. You are so lovely. Come show yourselves. For me.*

The salamander crawled slowly out from behind a log, its head tilted to watch her. Only one, but bigger than ever before, almost six inches from nose to tail.

Cenda smiled, joy and triumph burning hot in her veins. "Come, sweetheart," she whispered. "Come." The creature advanced, more stately than its smaller brethren, until it reached the tiled edge of the fireplace.

She knew the instant Gray recognized its existence as separate from the fire. A single, abrupt movement and everything behind her went still. "Judger God!"

Titfer opened his eyes and yawned, only to find himself nose to nose with a lizard made of flame. With a hiss, he shot across the room and up a curtain, his tail a brush behind him.

Cenda let the creature climb from her fingers to her wrist and up onto her shoulder before she turned. She'd apologize to the cat later.

Gray stood a good three feet away, balanced on the balls of his feet. In his left hand, he held a long dagger in an expert grip. "What the fuck *is* that?"

"A salamander. Isn't it beautiful?" Gently, Cenda ran a finger down the creature's spine, and it arched into the caress like an affectionate cat, its body smooth and warm to her touch. "Purist Matthaeus says it's a fire elemental."

Gray shook his head. "And I thought I'd seen everything." Absently, he lifted his free hand to the creature and it stretched forward as if to sniff his fingers. "Shit!" He snatched his hand back. "It burns!"

"Told you so," murmured Cenda, unable to resist.

"Your shift's on fire."

"Five-it, I keep forgetting!" Cenda urged the salamander down to coil about her bare wrist, while she clamped her other hand over the shoulder of her shift and snuffed the flames.

"You keep forgetting?" repeated Gray, fascinated.

"Yes, and I'm running out of clothes."

At that, he chuckled outright and Cenda froze, arrested by the amusement in his expression. The lines of strain had disappeared from around his eyes and mouth, and he looked years younger. It hadn't occurred to her to wonder how old he was. She sighed. Yet another complication.

The Duke sheathed his dagger in a forearm harness, shaking his head as he did so. "Cenda," he said, and she thought what she heard in his voice might be truth, "you're the most amazing woman I've ever met." The humor fled. "You're not as defenseless as you look, are you?"

Nonplussed, Cenda stared. As she watched, Gray's face hardened, taking on an intent, predatory expression, totally *male*. Feathery wings of delight and apprehension fluttered under the skin of her belly, brushing her clitoris with a gossamer touch. It throbbed.

"Put your little friend back where he belongs and let's see how hot I can make you."

Cenda wavered on her feet, and Gray grasped her free hand, steadying her. The salamander slithered down her other arm and disappeared into the fireplace in a shower of sparks.

"Come here, little one," murmured the Duke.

She had to smother a snort. Little one? Long, skinny Cenda? *Little one* was what you called a child, a beloved child. An endearment intended to comfort and reassure.

Ah, five-it, she'd forgotten. *Forgotten!* Guilt and bitterness dug talons into the soft breast of her soul, and she bled afresh. Lady, you'd think the scar would have scabbed over by now!

But he was pulling her close, his hands sliding firmly around to the small of her back, one palm rubbing soothing circles over her spine, the other gripping her bottom in a proprietorial kind of way. And when she laid her head on his shoulder, she did feel a small measure of comfort, a sense of protection. Which was undoubtedly an illusion, but nonetheless . . .

It had been so long. Cenda sighed and let herself snuggle.

"What else can you do?" said a dark voice in her ear.

"Not much." Cenda held out a clenched fist, exerted her will. When she opened her fingers, a tiny rill of flame skittered over her palm and winked out almost immediately. She sighed. "Purist Matthaeus is not impressed."

"You'll get better with practice."

"Perhaps I should run away." Cenda forced a smile. "Join the Unearthly Opera like you."

She'd said it lightly, but the lean body against hers tensed. "No," Gray murmured, brushing her hair aside so he could feather his lips over her neck. "If you know what's good for you, you'll stay far, far away from me." He lapped at the soft skin behind her ear and then blew on the spot. The tingle streaked straight to her already swollen nipples. Cenda shivered with delight. "But Judger God, I hope you won't."

Don't worry. I've nothing left to lose.

Had she spoken aloud? Apparently not, because he gazed down at her in silence, his slashing brows drawn together in concentration. Gently, he placed his hands around her throat, those long musician's fingers encompassing her easily. His thumbs brushed rhythmically along the line of her jaw. "I don't want you to have any illusions, Cenda. You know what I want."

The temptation to laugh was shockingly strong. *You're safe, Duke. A woman can't fall in love without a heart. And mine is ashes.*

She stared deep into that clear gaze. A week or so, and he'd be gone. "The same as what I want." His hands slid up and tunneled into her hair, shaping her skull in his palms. A wave of delicious gooseflesh tightened her scalp, and she shivered with the strange heat of the sensation. *Kiss me. Just kiss me before I die. Leave me with the memory of glory.*

Slowly, his mouth curved. Though the banked heat in his eyes didn't change, his soot black lashes swept down, his limbs tensing, and she had the oddest thought. He looked like he readied himself for some act of reckless bravado. A man about to launch himself into battle, or to utter the words that would change his life forever. She had the sense of existence teetering on the brink, of the lines of the future and the past forming and re-forming in an incomprehensible pattern, a dance as complex as that of the five moons.

"Gray, I . . . I need this." Cenda clamped her hands

over the strong wrists, and he murmured something in his throat. She couldn't catch the words.

He backed her into the wall, pinning her with his hips, and the strange fancy blew away in a whirlwind of sensation. She gasped as fire shot straight up her spine.

"You couldn't need it as much as I do, sweetheart, believe me."

As the Duke lowered his dark head to hers, his shadow bent behind him, its posture a dark echo of his.

6

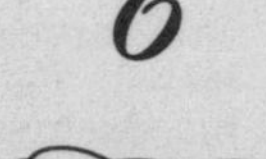

Gray could feel the sharp angles of her shoulders under his palms, sense the fragility of her slender frame, sandwiched between the solid muscle of his body and the unforgiving wall. But it made no difference. Dark tides surged inside him, ebbing and flowing as he and Shad battled for supremacy.

Fire witch, indeed. Gods, her mouth was so sweet, so *hot*! Her tongue fluttered against his in a feminine panic, but experience told him arousal was sweeping over her, drowning the uncertainty in a woman's wet heat. Gray exerted his will and gentled the kiss, but he couldn't resist the tantalizing press of her breasts against him, a nipple as hard as the marbles he and Shad had played with when he was a boy. A lifetime ago, together . . .

Keeping one hand anchored in the heavy mass of her hair, he cradled a small, firm curve with the other and rasped the crest with his thumb 'til it stood proud under the threadbare fabric of her shift.

Cenda panted into his mouth, her pelvis moving against

his in an instinctive rhythm. Shad roared, *Inside, inside! Now. Need inside now!*

Gray shuddered under the wave of driving lust. *Wait, wait. Nooo!* A guttural moan. *Hard, hurting. Fuck her, fuck her.*

The fire witch whimpered, and his head spun. When her hot, slim hands moved over his chest and slid up behind his neck, he lost his grip on sanity for a moment. Shad surged over him and rolled him under. His eyes slammed shut and the world became an interior one of the senses, a blur of instinctively driving hips, his rampant cock jutting obscenely into the sleek, strong curves fitted against the hard planes of his body.

Cenda flinched and jerked back, but it took Gray long moments to comprehend, to hear her gasping his name. The shock was like a punch to the gut. He pulled back, staring, his blood chilling. He'd pulled one long, slender leg up over his hip. Strong musician's fingers dug into the satiny flesh of one buttock under the shift. Judger God, one more second and he'd have her splayed wide and be ramming inside her without any kind of preliminary.

Shad snarled his frustration.

Shut the fuck up! Gray growled back. *Shit, you nearly made me—*

"Gray, my hair! Sorry, but you're—" Cenda reached up to where he gripped a fistful of her hair.

His chest heaving, Gray stared into her golden eyes, almost hating her. "Sorry," he said curtly, withdrawing his hand and stepping back.

What the fuck was wrong with him? He'd spent all the years of his adult life locked in battle with Shad. The gods knew how many women he'd had, but never—*never!*—had his shadow come so close to breaking through his iron control. He prided himself on his skillful lovemaking, loved and enjoyed women for their own sake, for their amazing strength and beguiling fragility. Judger, he'd been brought up in a society that revered and protected its females! Now Shad had pushed him to the point where their combined lusts had caused a woman distress, pain. Fuck, they'd frightened her!

He stared into Cenda's pale, set face, spots of color burning on her cheekbones.

In fact—guilt twisted its dark claws inside him—it was her artless, unpracticed mouth, the slightly awkward way she held him, the unashamed delight she took in his touch, that inflamed him almost beyond bearing. The thought of pleasuring her, watching shock flare in her eyes along with the helpless rapture. And gods, teaching her to pleasure him—!

And after he'd fucked her senseless, *used* her, he was going to hand her over to old Deiter in exchange for the rotten piece of garbage he called his soul.

Judger God, beyond redemption! His gut turned over. There was little enough left in him of the devout simplicity of his home world, but this—! His mother's calm, gentle face rose before him, bewilderment and grief mixed in her expression. "Oh, my son, what hast thou become?" He imagined her lips trembling as she spoke. She'd use the edge of her veil to blot her eyes, the way she'd done the last time he'd seen her. The very last time.

He'd turned and strode toward the door before he even knew he was going to do it, dragging his shadow behind him. No more tonight, he couldn't take it, not another bloody second.

A bestial grunt. *Fuck, no! Want, want!* Shad putting a shoulder to his will, shoving hard.

"Gray, wait."

He glared back over his shoulder, the bile of self-disgust rising in his throat. Cenda's long body was hunched in a defensive posture against the wall, the creamy skin of her cheeks stained an ugly red. She moved her hands in an abrupt gesture, then stilled, her spine stiffening. Her chin went up. "Aren't you going to . . ." She stumbled, then rallied. ". . . say good-bye?"

"Cenda, I . . ." What was he supposed to say now? What could he say? Fuck, she had guts. More than he did.

"I'm sorry," he said. "I didn't mean to hurt you." He could feel the heat rising to his cheeks. "I'm shamed."

The fire witch looked at him oddly. "You didn't, not really. It's just"—her lips curved in what could have been the beginnings of a smile—"my hair dries so fast these days, it tangles straightaway if I don't brush it. You pulled on a knot."

"So it wasn't . . . ? I didn't . . . ?" The Duke of Ombra wasn't accustomed to feeling like a fool.

Suits you.

Shad was going to drive him mad, no doubt of it. Always pouncing when he was weakest, knowing him better than he knew himself, the black underbelly of his soul. *This is your fault. Abomination.*

Her cheeks a fiery crimson, Cenda shook her head.

Gray counted five breaths while her golden brown eyes tangled with his. Whichever way he turned, he was caught. He felt Shad gloating. Godsdammit, if he left now, Cenda would do the typical female thing and assume she was ugly or undesirable or some other stupidity—he just knew it. In comparison with the ultimate betrayal he was planning, abandoning her now would be a pinprick, but he couldn't do it.

He moved back to the chair and sat. "Find me a hairbrush and come here." He indicated the rug before the fire.

But she shook her head. "No need. I can brush my own hair."

"There's every need." Somehow, Shad's growl emerged together with his. "Just do it, Cenda."

She pressed her lips together, hectic spots of color still on her cheeks, but she took a sturdy wooden brush from the top of a dresser and handed it to him, sinking to the floor between his feet.

"Eat your chocolat and sit still."

Cenda craned back over her shoulder, fixing him with a gaze brimful of female skepticism.

"I used to do this for my mother." Her lips brushing his brow at bedtime, after Last Devotions. Shad's recollection and his, an effect like double vision.

Cenda relaxed with a sigh, leaning back between his knees, and Gray began. Her black hair was thick and unruly, and he took his time, sliding the warm weight of each silky lock between his fingers so it didn't tug her scalp, working the brush carefully until her hair shone, going on to the next curl. The fire crackled, and Cenda stared into the heart of it, the bag of chocolat in her lap. When Gray followed her gaze, he thought he glimpsed the salamanders frolicking, but he couldn't be sure. He didn't speak, because he couldn't think of anything to say. His lips quirked in a wry smile. The Duke of Ombra sitting like a block, all his polished elegance come to nothing. Struck dumb by an untutored fire witch.

And his memories.

His mother had been called Modesty, named for a virtue, as was the custom of the people of Judger's Gift. And truly, the name had suited her; her soft voice, the long curve of her eyelids lowered over clear gray eyes exactly like the ones that looked back at him from the mirror. Gods, how they'd loved her, he and Shad. Looking back now, from the perspective of manhood, he thought she'd been merely pretty, plain even, her face illuminated by her simple faith and by her love for the husband her parents had selected for her with such care.

Judger's Gift was an agricultural world, but the fertility it gave in such wild abundance in the form of crops and animals had its cost in the wombs of its women. Full-term pregnancies were precious; few children survived infancy, especially females, and childbirth was fraught with more than the usual dangers.

The men of Gift treasured their womenfolk, none more so than Justice, Gray's father. Gray had never doubted Father loved him. Even now, when Justice must surely be dead, worn-out with grief and heavy labor on the farm, he knew it still. But Modesty and Grace had been the sun, moon, and stars of Father's existence, the central point around which all else revolved.

Involuntarily, his lips curved. Ah, little Gracie! With her quick, high voice and incessant questions, her skinny brown legs twinkling as she tagged along behind him, the big brother she adored. He'd been gruff with her, offhand, but he'd never been able to hide how much he loved her. And in the end, she'd cost him—

A long, black curl clung to his fingers, and he feathered the end of it across his palm. Mother's hair had been brown, liberally streaked with gray. In the evenings, after supper was over and Thanks had been given, she'd remove the veil all adult women of Gift wore in public, and Father would brush out her hair 'til it lay in a soft cloud down to her hips. Sometimes, Gray was allowed to help. Mother would hum under her breath: cradle songs, hymns. Whatever music he had in his soul had been hers to bestow.

Cenda's hair lay in a gleaming shawl over her back, but he had to go on touching it, as if the connection sealed them in a bubble of quiet, a glowing silence in which he was able to remember without pain. *Pretty,* whispered Shad, but not even that disturbed him. He started again at her temples, drawing the brush through in a strong, steady rhythm that made her purr, noting absently the hint of auburn, a deep, deep red that shone in the firelight like spiced wine. When she turned her head, he could make out the fan of her lashes lying against a clean-cut cheekbone. She'd closed her eyes with pleasure, the way Mother used to do.

Mother hadn't known that Shad loved her. She hadn't known about him at all. No one did.

Everyone had a shadow. Gray had understood that, right from the time he could toddle. He'd become aware of Shad as a presence only gradually, as he developed his own sense of self, so that it seemed there'd never been a time they weren't inextricably tangled, happily linked. He was such a solitary, self-sufficient little boy, his shadow trailing behind him, that no one paid him any particular attention. After his chores were done, he'd loved to roam the gentle, wooded hills behind the farm, going about a child's business of coming home grubby, tired, and happy.

Ah, they'd been so happy, he and Shad! Reserved by nature, Gray had never felt the need to confide in anyone, not even Mother, and by the time they were old enough to realize they were *different*, concealment had become instinctive, automatic. It was another couple of years before it dawned on Gray and Shad that they were *wrong*.

Anyway, what did he need friends for when he had the best friend in all the world? Someone who shared his adventures, liked what he liked, endured all the boyhood scrapes and bruises right along with him?

He smiled a little, lost in the rhythm of the brushstrokes, remembering the time he'd stubbed his toe, the bright blood welling from under the flap of detached skin. He'd hopped on one foot, Shad hopping beside him. "Ow, ow, ow!" And then, greatly daring, "Fuck!" The youngest farmhand had muttered it when the milkbeast kicked over the bucket. Shad had chimed in, an echo in his mind, less than a heartbeat behind. *F-fuck!*

They discovered early on that Shad was hopeless at any kind of ball game, the ball slipping out of his dark, elongated hands. Gray used to jeer and Shad would pounce, holding him down and digging those skinny fingers into his ribs until he shrieked with laughter and begged for mercy.

He'd never been able to hurt Shad physically. The only way he could cause his shadow pain was with the rapier of his thoughts. He hadn't known that—not until that terrible day, the one that changed his life.

The fire witch popped a chocolat in her mouth and murmured with pleasure, her head lolling back against his knee. Gray laid the brush aside and took a generous handful of hair. He divided it into three locks and began to braid, his fingers still deft, even after all these years. Mother had always said he could plait better than she could. He was her good boy.

At Devotions, Gray and Shad were very nearly perfectly behaved: Gray washed and brushed, the stiff collar of his best suit digging into the skin of his neck; Shad barely there in the diffuse light inside the small, whitewashed building. It always took Gray the first twenty minutes to quell his fidgets, and sometimes Father had to give him a quick frown, tempered by a light touch on the shoulder. Mother would smile a gentle reproof. Allowing his thoughts to wander or singing little songs in his head, Gray would listen with half an ear to the low, rather nasal voice of the pastor. He liked the smells: wood polish and flowers and starched clothing.

". . . rid thyselves of the shadow of sin!" The pastor thumped the worship table with his fist, and Gray sat up straight on the wooden bench, his eyes opening wide. Shad wasn't sinful! But the man went on, using words Gray didn't quite understand, though his stomach clenched at the sound of them, with their dark, doom-laden emphasis, rolling out over the heads of the congregation.

Evil. Abomination. Works of the Devil. Weighed on the Judger's Scales.

Again and again, the pastor spoke of the *shadow* of sin, the *shadow* of death, the *shadow* of evil. Each phrase settled like a drop of icy water in the pit of Gray's belly. That couldn't be right. His shadow was his friend. He *loved* Shad!

Much later that afternoon, he sat in the grass with his back against the barn, Shad stretched out beside him. Without really seeing them, he stared at the three tiny graves in the small fenced cemetery, the babes that had been lost between him and Gracie.

Stupid pastor, he'd grumbled to Shad. *Thou art a good shadow!*

Shad patted Gray's ankle. *Thy shadow.*

"Son!" Mother's voice calling. "Come in now. Aunt Charity and Cousin Temperance art here!"

Gray made a face. Temperance was bossy. And whiny. Aunt Charity had a forward-thrusting bosom like a plowshare and an eye like a gimlet.

Rapid footsteps. Temperance's shiny boots, buttoned right to her plump little calves. "Hulloo? Cousin, where art thou? Wilt thou play tea parties?"

Hastily, Gray scrambled to his feet. Where to hide?

Here. Shad pointed to the solid block of shadow on the other side of the barn.

She'll see.

Hide thee. Trust me. Please?

And because he *did* trust Shad, he'd stepped into the

shadow. The sensation was not unlike being immersed in cool, heavy water, slick and flowing over his skin, a translucent veil across his face. All the fine hair on Gray's body stood up. "Shad!" he gasped in panic, clawing at his eyes.

Sshh. 'Tis fine.

And so he'd disciplined himself to stand quietly and watch Temperance search the barn, the outbuildings, the yards. Several times, she looked right through him, her lower lip quivering, and he'd almost laughed. At last, she flounced back to the house.

That was how Gray had learned that while Shad was always part of him, he could choose to be part of shadow. They didn't do it often. At first, it had been a novelty, a handy trick, but as time went on, Gray found the merging made him increasingly uncomfortable. It was disorienting, seeing the world through the smear of the shadow veil, being present and yet unseen, overhearing half-understood adult conversations. It made him feel greasy.

And now, the very thought of it made him physically ill. *Never again.*

"I'm sorry. Would you like one before they melt?"

Cenda held up the bag of chocolat, turning her head with care because Gray still held one thick braid, though his fingers had ceased moving sometime ago.

He forced a smile. "No, they're for you." He didn't have a tie to finish the plait, and he didn't want to ask for one and have her get up. The warm, confiding weight of her shoulder pressed against his leg felt oddly comforting, the urgency of his lust cooled by the memories. Lifting his hands away, he watched the heavy silk of her hair begin to unravel. Was that the ghost of Shad's sigh?

The fire witch licked her fingers like a child. She huffed with pleasure. "I've never— They're gorgeous, but they melt awfully fast."

Gray had to chuckle. "Do you think that might have something to do with the salamanders?"

She had three of them now, their glowing sapphire eyes fixed on her face. Two small ones curled around her forearms, the largest perched just above her knee. She'd hiked the shift out of the way, undoubtedly to save it from scorching. The fire lizard was draped over a curve of smooth white skin. It blinked slowly.

"Mm." Cenda rested her cheek on Gray's knee and closed her eyes. "Must be."

From his vantage point above her, he could see her small breasts rising and falling beneath the thin fabric, no more than two scant handfuls. Her nipples looked surprisingly broad and dark. Her skin was so fair, he would have expected a rosy pink.

Sweet, came the shadow of a whisper.

Yes, he agreed, his mouth watering. *Like chocolat.*

Firelight played across her cheek, illuminating every curve and hollow, the finest of lines crinkling the corners of those gold-coin eyes. Gray had the fancy he could read the grief written in the droop of her lips, the translucency of her skin, stretched tight across the bone. She was four years older than he, according to the Technomage's dossier. Not that it mattered.

In fact, it wouldn't have mattered if she'd been thirty years older, he told himself brutally. He'd still have to seduce her.

But you want to. Real bad.

Gray cast an irritated glance at the dark, flickering bulk extending up the wall. Arguing was futile, especially when Shad had the right of it. His shadow's head moved sharply, as if he'd nodded.

The cat had returned to the warmth of the fire, his chin pillowed on Cenda's ankle, an unwinking green gold gaze on her fingers as they stroked the salamander perched on her leg. The little creature arched into the touch in obvious pleasure.

Judger, it was extraordinary! Gray had never seen anything like it, hadn't imagined such a thing as a fire elemental might exist. To be sure, the vagabond life he'd led had shown him very quickly how narrow and circumscribed his existence on Gift had been. Away from the cultural backwater that had been his home, he'd grown accustomed to the casual display of Magick, though it had taken him quite some time. There were Pure Enclaves like this one on almost every world. But Magick was a delicate power, subtle in its effects, chancy and difficult, even for a powerful wizard like Deiter—whereas Technomagery was predictable, a blunt instrument that *worked.*

This sad, slender woman had an uncertain, fledgling command of one of the most awesome powers in the universe. An *element.* What might she become? A tool? A weapon? Gray shivered, remembering the way she'd thrust her hand into the flames without a moment's hesitation.

Grimly, he thought of the greed that had thickened the voice of the Technomage's go-between under the concealing hood. No wonder the Primus wanted Cenda. As badly as Deiter did? Or more, perhaps?

Not for the first time, Gray wondered about the other Pures. Her tutor—what had she called him? Purist Matthaeus?—already knew. Which meant others did, too.

Fuck, the only thing keeping her alive was the fact that no one believed a fire witch could be real! He'd be lucky to get them offworld in one piece once word spread through the underworld of Sybaris.

We can do it, murmured Shad.

Yes, they would do it. Giving in to temptation, Gray leaned forward to smooth a fingertip over her eyebrow, the creases at the corner of her eyelid. Without opening her eyes, Cenda reached up and touched his hand with sticky fingertips. Something in Gray's chest tightened painfully, but he ignored it, the same way he ignored Shad.

He was out of time.

On with the seduction, the debauching of the innocent.

7

The warmth of the fire, the comfort of his hands moving in her hair, the scent of his skin. It was all so good, so perfect, he'd almost lulled her to sleep. But five-it, the Duke was a strange man! Not so long ago, he'd kissed her with a ferocity and sensual skill that made her head reel. Then he'd pushed her away, glaring as if he loathed her. And the next moment, he had her seated before the fire, brushing her hair like a man worshipping at an altar.

Lord's balls, she couldn't keep up!

If it hadn't been for the chocolat, Cenda might have made an excuse, asked him to leave. But the dark, silky flavor had exploded on her tongue, demanding her complete attention. It filled her mouth and nose with a child-like, wriggling delight that was better than any sex she'd ever had.

How Elke would have loved it! And what a mess she would have made! But Elke would never taste chocolat, never learn her first spell, never fall in love, never . . .

A questing fingertip feathered over her eyebrow and slid

down her cheek. Breathing heavily, Cenda shoved the pain away, walled it off. She touched Gray's hand, feeling his long fingers close hard over hers.

We don't have long. Make it stop. Make me forget.

As if he'd read her mind, Gray murmured, "Put your pets back in the fire, Cenda." Clumsily, Cenda leaned forward, shooing the salamanders past Titfer's offended nose. After that, she didn't know what to do, how to get from her crouch on the floor into his arms.

Gray rose, so lithe and graceful. Smiling gravely, he offered her his hand. But when she grasped it, she underestimated his lean strength, so that she overcompensated, stumbling into his chest, knocking him back into the wall. He grunted.

Then he laughed. "Come here, sweetheart." Spreading his legs, he pulled her between them, sealing their torsos together from neck to hip.

Cenda swallowed. She'd never felt anything remotely like it before, a hard wall of muscle, all warm planes and uncompromising masculine solidity. Barton had been soft and plump, cushiony. The rigid bulk of Gray's erection pressed insistently into her belly. Her fingers curled hard in the fabric of his shirt, almost as if they wanted to hold him off, while the rest of her waited for his kiss, shaking with anticipation.

Instead, he bent his head, sampling the skin under her ear. Lady, he was *licking* again, nibbling all down the side of her neck, crooning in his throat! Cenda's fingers flexed, gripping the shirt with the strength of desperation, while her stomach fluttered as though it were the skin of her belly he tasted.

Under her clutch, a button popped off the Duke's shirt. The tiny clatter as it bounced off his boot and onto the floor fell on her ear like a brief mocking laugh. Cenda froze. Ah, shit! She was going to ruin the most exciting sensual experience of her life, and the Lady knew, she'd never have another opportunity. How was it he made every rational thought in her head fly out the window? A clumsy fire witch was a recipe for disaster. And when the said fire witch was barely in control of herself or her power . . . Stupid, stupid, stupid!

Straightening her elbows, she levered herself away, and Gray lifted his head, his eyes dark as smoke.

"Duke, stop. I can't— This isn't going to work."

"Why not?" he asked calmly, slipping a finger under the neckline of the shift, tracing her collarbone.

Cenda shivered, goose bumps parading down her spine, tightening the skin over her breasts. She pressed her thighs together. "I told you . . ." Dropping her head, she took a step backward in the circle of his arms. "You'd better go," she said stonily, addressing the loose threads where the button had been.

"Look at me." His hand on her jaw was gentle but firm.

Reluctantly, she raised her eyes to his.

"You're thinking so hard I can hear you," he said. He brushed his lips over hers. "All you have to do is feel."

"But what if I—"

He laid the pad of his forefinger on the center of her lower lip. "Sshh. If it hurts—either of us—I'll stop." A smile flickered across his elegant mouth. "I'm not one who enjoys pain." His voice dropped to a husky murmur, dark with sensual promise. "Trust me, Cenda."

But his lips had an ironic twist, thoughts scudding behind those magnificent eyes like storm clouds passing.

"But—"

"You can trust me with your pleasure, sweetheart. Judger God, I can swear to that, if nothing else."

Cenda searched Gray's face, her heart thudding. There was nothing to be seen on his regular features but clear, masculine purpose spiced with a kind of guarded affection. His shirt had fallen open to reveal a wedge of firm, smooth skin, a shade lighter than his neck, and his chest rose and fell with the force of his breath. Five-it, he was a handsome man! Krys had been more right than she knew.

Cenda pulled in a huge breath. *Nothing left to lose.* "All right," she said. And waited.

For a moment longer, he stared, those slanted brows drawn together. Then his shoulders relaxed. He smiled with genuine pleasure and what looked oddly like relief.

The smile changed his whole face, as if a lantern had been lit inside him, illuminating his eyes, giving them an extraordinary clarity. Cenda had seen a mountain stream like that just once, years ago in Remnant Two, flowing clean and limpid over a granite bed, but she'd never forgotten its crystal beauty.

"Do you have a scarf?" he said. "A dark color, preferably."

"What?"

"A scarf," he repeated. "Or a stocking."

Cenda closed her sagging jaw. "Yes, but why?"

One corner of his mouth kicked up. "You need a blindfold."

When all she could produce was a gurgle, the smile broadened. "To stop that busy brain of yours." He drew her firmly against him, his palms traveling down her spine in a leisurely caress. "I want you mindless with pleasure, Cenda—screaming, crying, begging-me-to-fuck-you pleasure."

Cenda jerked with the impact of the word. *Fuck.* No one spoke to her so crudely, so directly. No one!

Gray held her firmly, circling his hips into hers, the hard length of his cock rubbing over her mons, making the nerves there flutter deliciously with shock. "That's what it's called, sweetheart. Fucking." It sounded so raw in his dark, sweet voice, so wanton. He licked the corner of her mouth, sucked on her lower lip. One hand cradled her breast through the shift, the nipple thrusting shamelessly into his palm. "Fucking's sweaty, messy . . . wet. There's nothing better, nothing in this life. Ah, Cenda"—he transferred his attentions to her throat, stringing soft nibbles over her thundering pulse—"you're going to be so good at it. Scarf?"

"Dresser." Cenda fought for breath. "Second drawer."

Gray slid an arm around her waist and swung away from the wall. Holding her sealed against his side, he took two steps and yanked the drawer open one-handed. Her silky winter scarf, light and warm. Last time she'd worn it, she'd tickled Elke's nose with the fringe, making her giggle.

"Cenda."

She looked up, wondering if the pain showed on her face.

"Feel, sweetheart. Just feel." Dark fabric, scented with the dried dillyflower blossom she used to keep her meager cold-weather wardrobe fresh and sweet, masked her eyes. Deft fingers tied it firmly, but not too tight.

Cenda patted it with her fingertips. "But I want to see." She'd imagined the perfection of that lean, toned body beneath the clothes, and the thought of the long line of his thigh, the taut, muscular rise of his buttock, made her mouth water.

Warm breath ghosted over her cheek. "Later. You can take it off later. Stand still now."

Rustling noises, the sense of his body turning away for a moment. "Here. Touch me." Grasping her hands, Gray slapped her palms on a warm, hard, breathing surface.

Cenda gasped, her fingers flexing. Oh, oh, he felt amazing, the hair-dusted skin of his chest covering layers of hard-packed muscle, all intriguing planes and long, sweeping curves. She was so absorbed by the luscious, masculine solidity of him that it took her a couple of seconds to realize he'd asked her a question. "Hmm?" Helplessly drawn, she leaned closer, brushing her nose over his skin. Only a smattering of hair on his chest, then. And it would have to be black, as black as the raven lock that fell over his eye when he was intent on something.

"Do you take mothermeknot, Cenda?" His hand rubbed the nape of her neck, under the cloud of her hair. "Quickly. Yes or no?

"What? Oh yes." She'd always quite liked the sweetness of mothermeknot tea. It was not only an effective contraceptive, but calming for the nerves. Krysanthe the healer had prescribed it for that reason, even though she'd said the fire Magick would make Cenda barren.

Barren. Oh, Lady. Elke . . .

"Good." Gray unlaced the front of her shift, the backs of his knuckles brushing what little cleavage she had. "Stop thinking."

Slowly, he drew the two halves of the garment aside, baring her breasts.

Silence, save for the crackling of the fire and the drumbeat of her pulse in her ears.

Cenda's nipples felt so tight and swollen, they were almost painful. And every sensation was intensified by the loss of sight. The licking warmth of the fire all along her side, the heat of Gray's body before her, the way his breath hitched for a moment and then his long exhalation.

Squaring her shoulders, Cenda forced herself to stand straight, her heart banging against her ribs. The stretch marks were on her belly, not her breasts, but she'd long since left the perkiness of youth behind. Before panic could swamp her completely, he said, "Sweet," in a whisper so husky and low, it sounded as though an echo followed a heartbeat behind. *Sweet.*

A hot mouth closed over her nipple. Cenda cried out, clutching his shoulders, panting with shock. Wet, warm, firm. Gray's lips tugged rhythmically, while his tongue lashed the sensitive flesh and his free hand cradled her other breast. Brutal tingles flashed down her spine, sizzled across her belly, plumped the lips of her sex. Droplets of silky moisture slipped down the inside of her thigh. Five-it, she hadn't thought it was possible to be so wet, to feel such an intensity of desire!

As if he'd caught the thought, Gray murmured against her nipple, "Are you wet for me, sweetheart?" He slid a hand up her inner thigh, under the shift, and automatically, she opened her legs, spread for him.

Never, *never*, had she felt like this!

"Aaah." Gray petted her thatch of dark, springy hair, drifted a slow, inquiring fingertip the length of her slit, starting with the quivering apex, dabbling into the clutching little mouth of her sex. All the way to . . .

She jumped. "Gray!"

"Sshh." He pulled her even closer, the pressure of his body all along hers giving her the only solid point of reference in a reeling universe. But he didn't stop, grasping her calf and hitching it over his hip so he had complete access. He dipped a finger into her sheath, no farther than the first knuckle. Gently, he rotated it, pressing against the walls of the tight little opening, making all the nerves there flutter with delight. Cenda found she was breathing with the rhythm of the caress. It felt so good, so hot, so *naughty.*

Gray grasped her firmly about the waist and took a step forward, tipping her onto the bed. He raked the shift off and down, and she lifted her hips to help him. When she sensed him step away, she sat up, wrapping her arms around her rib cage, hiding her breasts, feeling like a long, skinny lump of dough, acutely conscious of the small pouch of her belly, the jut of her hip bones. But this vulnerability was part and parcel of what she'd asked for. She couldn't have what she wanted so badly without it. Slowly, she released the death grip she had on herself and stiffened her spine, straining her ears.

A thump as one boot hit the floor. Then the other.

A tingling pause, then a light touch at the base of her throat, hesitating there for a split second, skimming down between her breasts, over her quivering solar plexus. "Ah, Cenda." The merest husky thread of sound. It must be the back of his knuckles, drifting over her stomach, making the nerves under the skin vibrate like flutterbyes tossed in a windstorm.

Hot sensation bloomed in the center of her chest, unfurling like the petals of some exotic flower from a fire forest. It could have been relief or lust or even pride. She wasn't sure.

Gray's hands grabbed hers and placed them on the waistband of his trews. "Help me." She'd never heard that tone from him before, so tight and edgy that his musical voice sounded flat and curt.

"Yes. Gods, yes." Gasping for breath, she dug her fingers

into the fabric and pulled down, pressing her forehead into his flat belly for leverage. She could smell him, the musky scent of aroused male, feel the heat radiating from the blood surging beneath the skin.

Heat. Ah, gods, beautiful heat.

Not just hers—his, too.

Cenda turned her head and took a cautious lick over warm, breathing muscle. Gray jerked and swore, but his fingers tightened in her hair, so she giggled and did it again. This time she led with her nose, bumping over the intriguing indentations of his stomach, finding his navel and nuzzling into it. Unable to resist, she slid her hands under the loosened trews, around to the small of his back, shaping the curves of his ass with her palms, digging eager fingers into taut, resilient muscle. Five-it, she'd had no idea a man could feel so wonderful, so hot and hard and . . . beautiful.

Something warm, blunt, and velvety nudged her throat, and Cenda froze.

With a curse, Gray grabbed the trews and ripped them the rest of the way. "Touch me, love," he grated. "Touch me before I bloody die."

Cenda ran her palms up his braced thighs, the muscles as hard as stone, but trembling beneath her touch. Spreading her fingers, she brushed her thumbs along the delectable crease between groin and thigh. The breath sawed in and out of her lungs, rasping in her throat. It was amazing, what Grayson, Duke of Ombra, had done, what he'd given her.

Here she sat, naked, helpless, deprived of sight. Yet she'd never felt more powerful, more free. The blindfold was a gift, something she hadn't known she needed. Because it concealed her eyes, it set her free—free in the strangest way. And because it gave him control, it meant she didn't have to worry about her long, awkward limbs or fret over her tenuous grip on the fire Magick. Nothing was required of her, so she could relax and give it all. A sliver of unease worked its way through the fog of desire. How was it Gray was so insightful, so clever? He must be enormously experienced, far more than she.

Nonetheless, he was a man, wasn't he? And Barton had taught her something of what men liked. Tentatively, she drew her hands together, her fingers curling over a column of living, pulsating heat. Immediately, Gray pushed forward into her grasp, as if he couldn't help himself. "Harder," he snarled. *"More."*

Cenda gripped, running her thumb over his cock head, the dome of it dense and spongy, smooth as satin and slick with desire. She dropped her other palm between his legs and cradled his testicles, so hot and round and tight.

Gray grunted, a deep, primitive sound, and his hand came down to spear into her hair. He said, very low, "You should see yourself, Cenda. Judger God, you should see. So beautiful." A pause for breath. "So pale and smooth. With your sweet chocolat nipples and your hot fingers wrapped around my cock. Squeeze, little witch. Squeeze."

Beautiful? Cenda felt her lips curve. She flexed her fingers, and Gray's cock leaped in her hand. Later, she couldn't be sure how long she held him there, trapped by the rhythm of her massage, but the memory of the life force throbbing hard against her palm—that, she knew, would never leave her. The power of it stole her breath.

His whole body shuddering, Gray's hands closed hard over her shoulders. The shock of that masterful touch rang all the way from the base of her spine to the top of her skull. "Stop," he growled. "I can't—" Breaking off, he pressed her back across the bed, and she went willingly, her thighs falling open beneath him. He leaned into her, a welcome weight, his mouth open against her throat, his cock nestling into the notch of her weeping sex.

Cenda's hips arched up of their own accord. "Now," she whispered. "Do it now."

His lips curved against her skin. "I said you'd beg. What do you want, sweetheart? This?"

Something smooth and hard and fiery hot slicked through the petals of her labia, nudging her clit at the top of the stroke, setting off a spangle of fireworks. Flames licked up Cenda's spine, the sensation so vivid a ribbon of fire seemed to lace up her back, twisting and twining through each vertebra, slipping through bony channels and hollows. "Yes," she moaned, beyond caring how she sounded. "Yes!"

Gray froze, hissing in a sharp breath. "Don't," he snapped. "No, leave—"

He exhaled, a long, shuddering breath, and sank the first inch into her tight opening. Lost in the fire, Cenda barely registered the fleeting touch on her breast, the cool fingers cradling her burning flesh, stroking the skin over her galloping heart.

All the muscles in her neck went loose, and her head rolled on the edge of the mattress. He stretched her so wonderfully, the walls of her sheath tingling with delight and panic mixed. Raising one leg, she clamped it over his hip, and Gray braced his forearms on the mattress near her head, the heat of his skin searing her ears and cheeks, while cool hands sifted through her hair, keeping the inferno from exploding and taking the top of her skull off. Five-it, he was wonderful, perfect—hot and cold at once—exactly what she needed!

Inch by inch, he worked his way inside her, peppering kisses over her cheeks, her chin, nipping her jaw, mumbling nonsense all the while. "No," he muttered, punctuating each gliding thrust with the word. "No." He pulled out, the friction so sumptuous that Cenda's eyes rolled behind the blindfold.

Hooking her ankles together in the small of Gray's back, Cenda raised her pelvis and he slid home, hilting with a choked curse. "No, I don't need—"

What in the world—? Great Lady, she had to see! Gasping, Cenda clawed at the blindfold.

Gray hung over her, his eyes almost black with concentration, a lock of hair flopping over his forehead. Feverish spots of color flared on his cheekbones. The wonderful width of his sweat-slicked shoulders more than encompassed her, his chest a wall of muscle compressing her breasts. He smiled crookedly, but his gaze flicked up and away, to where his shadow hung on the wall behind her head. Then he dipped his head and kissed the tip of her nose. "All right?"

Cenda released her death grip on his hard biceps to brush the hair back out of his eyes. "Yes, but—" Gray switched to shorter, harder strokes, and all the air punched out of her lungs. "Gods, I'm so hot." She writhed, a crowd of punishing tingles gathering behind her clit, tormenting her almost beyond endurance. "Five-it, Gray, am I burning you?"

His chuckle was breathless, though no humor showed in his face. A drop of sweat coursed down the side of his neck, and he grunted when she reared up to lick it off. "Don't worry about it." His shadow fell over her shoulder and upper arm, cooling the fire in her blood enough so she could see straight. At once, Gray frowned and his jaw went tight. "Come for me, Cenda. I need you to come."

Without warning, he set up a hard, slamming rhythm. It was brutal. Beyond gorgeous. Flinging her head back, Cenda gave herself to it, body and soul, her cries rising above the violent creaking of the bed.

Gray slipped a hand between their sweaty, straining bodies. "Now. *Now!*" He pressed, and Cenda's quivering flesh convulsed. For endless, shuddering moments, she hung, writhing and whimpering, in a world of soft, dark, mind-numbing fire.

From very far away, she heard Gray grunt as if he'd been gut-punched. "Judger! Fuck, oh *fuck*!" The words disappeared, overtaken by a groan so deep it sounded as though the heart were being ripped from his chest. A dark echo of the sound faded slowly in the small room.

Silence.

8

Either the one-legged beggar was out late, or he started work early. The cool, unfeeling light of dawn fought with the smoke pall that hung over the mean streets. It dwelled on a red-veined nose, lingered on the clumsy darns in the workingman's shirt straining over a paunchy gut. The beggar propped himself on a rough stick, hand cupped suggestively. "Alms, by yer kindness."

Judger knew what showed in Gray's face, but when he turned to glare, the beggar recoiled, paling. He waited 'til Gray was almost at the end of the alley before he shouted, "Fook ye, ye cold bugger!" A door banged decisively.

Cold? What a joke! Gray lengthened his stride, growling under his breath, but the action rubbed the crotch of his trews over his tender genitals and he slowed to a halt, so furious he could hardly see straight. Attenuated and wavering on the smoke-stained stone wall of the gambling hell beside him, Shad said nothing, but his very presence in Gray's mind was creamy with satisfaction.

Gray clenched his fists. *Say it, damn you.*

No need.

And that was true enough. If he hadn't long since given up believing in gods of any kind, he would have assumed he'd been Judged, Sentenced, and Punished. Competing fragments of thought jostled in his head, clamoring for attention. One of the best fucks of his life—if not the very best, which was crazy enough in itself—and Shad had ruined it.

Saved it, came the inevitable whisper in his head.

Gray turned in to the long, crooked alley that led to the back entrance of his inn. Experience had taught him never to make a habit of using the same approach twice. The sour smell of stale beer assaulted his nose. When he stretched to step over the slimy gutter, he flinched.

Fuck, it had been good at the beginning! Perfect. Cenda had been shy—but so delightfully eager the blood had deserted his brain with a speed that made him dizzy. Even now, the mental vision of the torrent of dark hair tumbling over her bare shoulders, her pale, slender body, the long, warm fingers gripping his girth as she pumped him . . . And Judger, the trust she'd given him! Helpless behind the blindfold, open to anything he desired. All pink and wet and vulnerable, his to pleasure, to ravage, to fuck, to suck, to— He stopped, breathing hard. His cock stirred, the stupid thing, still game for more.

All ball-hardeningly good. Until he got inside her and her arousal had really begun to build. From the first, she'd been magnificently blood-hot, her wet, satiny tissues clasping him from crown to root, as he slid back and forth, his passion ramping up to levels he'd never experienced before. The sensation had been exquisite, keeping him poised on the delicious cusp between pleasure and pain, his heart hammering with apprehension and desire.

And then . . . He pressed back against the wall to allow a small dray loaded with ale barrels to pass, the lead dog lifting a lip in a canine snarl as the team trotted by. The balance had tipped, the heat becoming decidedly threatening. It had been all he could do not to pull out.

Judger God, Shad had leaned down and *touched* her! Shad, who had touched no one *ever* save Gray—and Gracie, just that once. He'd laid a cool, dense palm over her sweet little breast, caressing her dark nipple until it jutted. The fire had banked, enough that Gray's pleasure returned in a thrusting rush. But instinctively, he'd tangled his will with Shad's. "No," he'd rasped. "No." *Get off. Leave her. Mine!*

Shad had simply growled in reply, an inchoate negative. He sank his shadowy hands into the splendor of Cenda's hair, wrist-deep, and she arched into that touch, trembling, crying out in her pleasure. But then she'd ripped off the blindfold, Shad had withdrawn, and sweat had popped from every pore of Gray's body.

"Five-it, Gray, am I burning you?" And she'd licked his neck, a searing brand that nearly sent him through the ceiling.

"Don't worry about it," he'd managed, and then Shad had shifted, his darkness falling across her upper body, and Gray could breathe again. By some miracle, he was still hard, a measure, he thought now, of how desperately he'd wanted her. After that, he'd been ruthless, he knew, shoving her over the peak before she was properly ready, but he'd had no choice. Ah, she'd responded magnificently, the lusty little darling!

He leaned against the wall, not caring about the filth staining the back of his shirt, his breath coming short. Against his will, Gray's lips twitched. He'd found her expression of surprise, her wide, shocked eyes, downright cute. The Judger knew what the father of her child had done to her in bed. If anything. And she hadn't even been a fire witch then, if what she'd said was true. The man might have been a wizard, but he was a fool.

Forget the salamanders, the fire. What would she be like once she truly understood the power of her female Magick? He'd hardly dared to think. Yet he couldn't wait to find out, to teach her. Even if it killed him.

Because when her climax had triggered his, it set off a

conflagration of the senses such as he'd never known, never imagined. The burn had started deep inside his pelvis, spread to his ass, and ignited a fireball that shot straight up his spine. It flashed from his balls to surge into his cock in a seething, boiling flood. Looking back, he was pretty certain he'd screamed. He might even have passed out for a second, because when he came to, the fire witch was sobbing into his shoulder, her tears scalding on his skin.

But Judger God, it had been worth it! Even now, he could feel the residual effects, the tremor in the muscle of his thigh, the quiver at the base of his spine.

Me, need me, whispered Shad.

The backyard of the inn looked blowsy and tired in the foggy halflight, like a slattern after a busy night. Gray curled his lip. *No, I won't let you soil it. There'll be a way. There must be.* The ragged child rummaging in the woodpile took one startled look at his face and darted into the tumbledown dogshed. A chorus of snarls and yips ensued.

Soil it? A mental snort. *Remember Deiter,* said Shad, the words enunciated with more precision than usual.

Gray stopped dead. Then he swore for three minutes straight, in every language he knew, without repeating himself. The child's face hovered like a pale ghost in the gloom of the dogshed.

What would life be like without Shad? He could scarcely imagine. Blessed silence in his own mind. Calm, peace.

A huge, exaggerated yawn. *Boring. Boooring.* And then more quietly: *Lonely.*

Gray ran a furious hand through his hair, then he stomped up the stairs to his room, conscious of the weight of the urchin's thoughtful gaze.

"Where ye wan' 'em?" It was the child. Gray couldn't make out the sex, but the skinny arms were full of lanterns, all battered and well used.

Gray frowned, rescuing the biggest one, which was dangling precariously from a small, filthy finger. "Put them on the floor. I'll do the rest." When he'd demanded another half dozen lanterns, he'd expected the innkeeper to bring them personally, not send a scullery rat.

With a grunt, the child squatted and set them down, oblivious to the rattles and clanks. Gray made an arbitrary decision, wrinkling his nose at the odor wafting off its ragged person. Male.

Flat, dark eyes looked up at him, black as pitch under an unkempt fringe. "Skeered of t' dark?"

Shad snickered, and Gray stared coldly down his nose, fighting to keep his face straight. Must be a male, because he sure had balls.

Oh so casually, the child laid a hand on the latch, though Gray noticed the grimy fingers trembled. So why didn't he run?

The mystery was solved when he tilted his head, took a short step forward, and held out his other hand, cupped like the beggar's.

"What?" said Gray, deliberately obtuse.

The cautious look changed to an all-out glare. "Carried 'em up frum t' basement. There'm roaches." He scratched the back of his neck and glanced up from under his lashes. "An' rats."

Cynical amusement curved Gray's lips. The lad was what? Eight? A perfect little Sybarite citizen already. "Here." He dug an oct-cred out of his belt pouch and tossed it. The boy snatched the small coin out of the air. Excellent reflexes.

Gray studied the small figure, cataloging the seamed lines on the pointed face that spoke of semistarvation, the world of weariness in the snapping black eyes, wary as a feral dog's. But behind the studied belligerence were a survivor's cunning and an iron will; that much was clear already. Hmm. And no one noticed a child, especially a beggar child.

"Want to earn more?" he asked.

The lad's stare grew sharp with interest, but he fumbled

behind him for the handle of the door. "Ain't no bum-boy," he muttered, clearly torn.

Gray's guts lurched with remembered dread. Moving slowly and keeping his hands in plain view, he took a step away, widening the distance between them. "That's not what I want." The boy relaxed infinitesimally. "I need eyes and ears. Can you watch someone for me? Get others to help if you need to, but no adults."

"Mebbe." The lad released his clutch on the door frame. "How much?"

Midway through the bargaining, Gray revised his original estimate of the child's age. He had to be around ten, but so undernourished he could have passed for several years younger. The smallest finger on one hand crooked away from the others, bent and stiff. Grimly, Gray wondered how it had happened.

"What's your name?" he asked.

"Slop."

"That's not a name."

The boy shrugged. "It's me job. T' piss pots 'n' pails."

Gray raised a brow. "Your real name?"

A long pause. "Don' matter."

"Do you have a family? Somewhere to sleep?"

Every meager muscle went rigid. "What's it t' ye!"

"Never mind." Gray cleared his throat. "Do you know a witch called Cenda?"

Slop stared. "Yerss," he said slowly. "T' fire witch. So you're t' one."

Gray tensed. "The one what?"

"Word's out. T' Fixer'll pay good creds fer t' fire witch. Ye got 'er then?" He looked around the cramped room as if he expected Gray to produce Cenda out of thin air.

Gods, already! "Who?"

Slop's dark eyes narrowed. "T' Fixer," he repeated, louder this time.

Gray thought some of the color had left his cheeks, though it was hard to tell beneath the grime. Some local crime lord, undoubtedly. He fished out another oct-cred. "Tell me about this Fixer."

The boy's bony shoulders moved in a shrug. "Whatever ye wan', he fixes it, see? T' grog, t' crazy powders. Ye wan' a death? All quiet like. Ask t' Fixer." He stared at his dirty toenails. "Or screamin', if you wan'. Ye wan' a doxy? Or—" His lips twisted and he fell silent.

Ah, well, a phenomenon he'd encountered before. Every town had a hard man, a boss. Still, it always paid to be cautious. "How many men does he have?"

For the first time, Slop smiled, a flash of still-white teeth. It wasn't a pleasant expression. "T' Fixer owns everyone in t' Sector. Dunno know how many. Thousands?"

Gray grunted, absorbing it. *Shit.* "Including you?"

"Yah."

"But you're still taking my money?"

"Yah." The boy looked him straight in the eye. "I'll do me best, but if it comes t' it . . ." Another shrug. "Ye're frum offworld. I ain't." He concentrated on picking at the scab on one bony elbow.

"All right. I'm crooked enough to understand that kind of honor. Every man for himself." Gray held out his hand.

Slop whisked himself half out the door. He lifted his lip in a truculent sneer, reminding Gray of the dray dog. "Nah," he said, but his voice shook.

"Where I come from, men shake hands to seal a deal."

"Mebbe." The boy took a step back into the room. "Not here."

Poor little bastard. Nonetheless . . . Gray stiffened his spine. He knew where matters stood. Slop's loyalty was a commodity for sale. The child had made that clear enough.

"We'll skip it, then." Gray sat on the side of the bed. "Do you know what Cenda looks like?"

Slop nodded. "Seen her once wit' t' kid."

Gray couldn't resist. "You saw the child?"

"Yah." The boy cocked his head to one side. "But she'm dead. T' winter ague."

"I know." Judger, this was stupid! "What did she look like, the baby?"

Slop shrugged, puzzled, but obliging. "A bebby. Black hair." A sigh whispered out of him. "Fat."

Gray could see her in his mind's eye, a chubby little thing with her mother's dark curls. No wonder Slop was envious. Well fed, well loved.

"What was her name?"

"Ellen, mebbe? El . . ." The boy's frown cleared. "Elke."

Elke. How his mother would have loved her!

And this was *fucking* stupid! Regrets were useless. With an effort, Gray pulled his thoughts out of the morass.

He counted out half the creds they'd agreed on. "She's safe enough until midday . . ." After the crying jag, she'd made it impossible for Gray to stay, though that would have been ideal from his point of view. But no, she'd said there was barely time for a visit to the bathhouse before her class with Purist Matthaeus. Left with no alternative, Gray had gritted his teeth and smiled, but he flung the sheet aside with studied deliberation and watched the fire witch dress with unwinking attention, enjoying the sidelong glances she couldn't resist, dwelling on the smooth, feminine lines of her body. She had a superlative ass, creamy and round and biteable. Even now, his mouth watered.

"After that, I want you to watch the front gate of the Enclave. I'll take the back."

Slop laughed aloud.

"What?"

"T' Pures use Magick, special wardin' spells on t' Enclave, all round. T' gate's only way in. True."

Gray thought about it. He had preparations to make. And he had to sleep sometime, because he had a performance tonight—two performances, if he counted the one he'd have to give for Cenda after he'd finished at The Treasure. His balls drew up tight, his thoughts a tangle of lust and ironclad purpose. Judger, there had to be a way, because he wasn't letting her go; he *couldn't* let her go. Not if he wanted his soul and his sanity.

Unobtrusively, a dark hand gave the back of his neck a soothing rub. *You know the way.*

Shut up. Gray pinched the bridge of his nose. He hadn't even tasted her yet, listened to the chokes and whimpers as he licked a leisurely way around all her most secret places, pink and musky and sweet. He'd be willing to bet she'd never experienced it.

And after he'd gained her trust, made her his . . .

He pulled in a breath. Every man for himself—wasn't that what he'd told the boy? Him or her. And Deiter was a better option than the Technomage; of that he had no doubt. The lesser of two evils.

Noble, aren't you?

I said shut the fuck up.

He loathed it when Shad was right.

"All right," he said curtly. "I'll give you a message for the fire witch. Stay with her after that, but don't let her see you watching. You'll need a runner. Got someone?"

Slop nodded.

"If anything happens, you send the runner here to me and you follow Cenda. Understand?"

"Yah."

"Come here."

The boy shook his head.

"Come here if you want the money."

With the greatest reluctance, Slop took a pace forward, then another. Gods, he reeked!

"Hold out your hand."

A grubby paw was extended. It trembled.

Gray slapped the money into it and gripped the boy's wrist, staring deep into the wary black eyes. "Keeping her safe is everything. Got that?"

"Yah."

Gray opened his fingers, but Slop stood, rubbing his wrist. His eyes gleamed with speculation. "Ye're sweet on 'er." It wasn't a question.

"No." Gray turned away, retrieving his pack from where it hung on a hook on the wall. "This is business."

He extracted paper and pencil and scribbled an invitation to supper. With a flash of wry humor, he added a brief postscript. *Deep-dish pie.*

"Mmm." The boy didn't sound convinced.

Gray folded a chit for tonight's performance of the Unearthly Opera inside the note. "Put it directly in her hands."

"Yah." The latch rattled.

"Wait!"

Halfway out the door, Slop paused to look back over his shoulder.

"Here." Gray tossed the small packet across the room.

The boy raised it to his nose and sniffed. He froze.

"It's Concordian chocolat." Gray smiled, enjoying the reaction. "There's only two pieces left, but it's good."

A gasp and a flurry and Slop disappeared. His bare feet were pattering down the stairs before the door swung to.

Sobering, Gray turned to stare at the lanterns. One in each corner of the room and two near the bed, and he could have a little peace.

Killjoy, muttered Shad.

Fuck you.

Gray sat at the bar of The Treasure, nursing a drink. Brooding. The tourist benches were full again. Erik would be pleased. He'd dozed for a couple of hours, but his sleep had been restless, his mother's thin, sweet voice singing in his dreams. Godsdammit, he hadn't thought about the "Lullaby for Stormy Eyes" for years, but now he couldn't shake the lilting melody—or the memory of Mother bent over Gracie's bed, stroking her hair.

Something small plopped into his ale, and he glanced up. The pale blur of Slop's face peered down out of the rafters, and a hand gestured toward the back of the building. Casually, Gray rose and set his tankard aside. The Judger knew what sort of object the lad had used, but he wasn't going to risk it.

Without haste, he made his way through the crowd, acknowledging the good-natured quips, smiling, accepting friendly slaps on the shoulder with the best grace he could muster. Backstage, all was the usual purposeful chaos, the smells of the fresh paint on the flats almost smothering the odors from The Treasure's kitchen. Without pausing, Gray headed for the stage door and the slim figure sitting bolt upright on a stool in the corner, her hands folded tightly together in her lap, a salamander shining in her hair.

9

Gray's note had been short and specific. *Come to the stage door. Jonas will let you in. Wait there for me.* And this time, Cenda had done as he asked. But she hadn't been bored, no, not at all. Eyes wide, she'd drunk it in, everything larger than life—the stout, bustling man who brandished scripts and scores, the stagehands who swarmed up and down the sturdy wooden ladders or wrestled with sets, the musicians tuning their instruments in a corner. But it was the half-naked dancers who fascinated her. She supposed she'd led a sheltered life, but they were so *bold*, so lithe and young and unashamed, their inviting bodies barely covered with strategic feathers and filmy skirts as they flirted with the stagehands. A few were using the time to limber up, bending sideways or raising a high-heeled dance shoe against the wall to stretch a toned thigh. She could almost hate them.

"Gray!" exclaimed a curvy blonde, with an unmistakable note of pleasure.

And there he was, clad in his customary black, the harp slung over one shoulder, coming toward her with his characteristic self-contained grace. Dark and dangerous. Without warning, the vision sprang to the forefront of her mind, as if it had been painted on the inside of her eyelids. Gray lounging back against her pillows, nude and indolent, a smattering of hair drawing attention to the breadth of his chest, arrowing down to his navel, finishing in the dark curls between his thighs. His cock nestled there, still half-hard, implicit with all the power of a male of the species.

Cenda gasped, a reminiscent wave of heat surging out of the modest neckline of her best blue gown. The salamander in her hair moved abruptly, the pinpricks of its tiny claws needling her scalp. How she wished she'd had the nerve to explore all those intriguing dips and hollows! Perhaps tonight.

Her heart hammered.

"Hullo, Sydarise," she heard him say, a smile warming the habitual coolness of his voice. He bestowed an absent-minded peck on the blonde's cheek, but he didn't pause. They'd been lovers; that much was obvious. Likely they still were. Cenda fixed her gaze on her hands, watching the tiny tongues of flame licking at her clasped fingers, willing them to subside.

Because it didn't matter. Her decision had been made last night. The Unearthly Opera would leave soon, and Gray with it, but while he was here . . . Her breath hitched. His hands and mouth, his body, his *cock*— He'd given her such pleasure she'd been certain she would die in the firestorm, but that had been followed by an even greater gift. She'd slept a scant hour or so in his arms, but she hadn't dreamed. *Great Lady, there'd been no dreams!* Just blessed oblivion, her body humming, replete.

"Cenda."

She looked up, striving for dignity, ignoring the scarlet staining her cheeks.

Gray smiled down at her, so confident, so *complete*. "You got my message." His gaze flicked up to the salamander in her hair, and one slanted brow quirked.

Cenda took the hand he offered and rose, uneasily

conscious of the dancers' curious glances. "A beggar boy brought it."

"Good." Gray slipped an arm around her waist. Right there, in front of everybody. "I'm not on until after the break. Let's have supper."

Cenda didn't mention she'd taken her evening meal an hour ago in the Enclave's dining hall. Well, she'd been *hungry*. As she was again. All that—she hauled in a breath—*f-fucking* took it out of a woman. She cast a sidelong glance at his calm face, scarcely able to credit she'd seen it distorted by the agony of pleasure. Because of her. "You promised me deep-dish pie."

"So I did." He drew her to a halt at the foot of a narrow ladder behind the last set of flats. "You afraid of heights, little witch?" Grinning, keeping a wary eye on the salamander, he tweaked one of the curls that had escaped her thick braid.

Cenda frowned, puzzled. "Not especially."

"Good." Completely brazen, he patted her bottom, then administered a crisp smack. "Up you go, then."

"Up?" Cenda tilted her head, staring into the maze of catwalks, lights, ropes, and pulleys in the shadows of the canvas roof.

"You get an amazing view. Of everything." His eyes gleamed. "Go on, I'll be right behind you. I won't let you fall, trust me."

He nuzzled his nose into her neck. "Mm. Wait." Without haste, he cupped her shoulders, bent his head, and kissed her. Slow, sweet, and remorselessly tender. Five-it, exactly like that first kiss.

Gratefully, Cenda sank into it, slipping her hands into his hair, feeling the solid, stubborn shape of his skull beneath her fingertips. How quickly she'd come to crave his touch, his skill. There might be other lovers after he'd gone—Lady, she hoped so!—but she knew already they'd never set her alight like Grayson, Duke of Ombra.

When he released her, it took her a moment to regain her focus. His eyes had gone the silver that meant she'd done something to tickle his vanity. Five-it, he had an almost feline self-assurance. Like a great cat, Gray knew exactly who and what he was. How she wished she could say the same!

His thumb caressed her cheek. "Climb, sweetheart," he murmured.

Blindly, Cenda gathered her skirts and set a foot on the first rung, Gray only one step behind her, his chest a blanketing wall of muscle at her back. The ladder trembled a little with their combined weight, but she was too keyed up to be concerned. It ended in a small platform surrounded on three sides by a wooden wall, waist-high. The catwalk stretched away into the gloom. Peering, Cenda could just make out a similar platform at the other end, two stagehands busy with some complicated pulley system involving sandbags.

"Make yourself comfortable." Gray indicated a fat, shabby cushion on the floor. He picked up a wicker basket and moved it aside. "The curtain goes up in a few minutes."

Bemused, Cenda sank down against the wall. Her feet dangled in midair and she wiggled them like a child. "We won't be in the way?" Far below, members of the Unearthly Opera scurried about, strangely foreshortened.

Gray shook his head, kneeling to open the basket. "They're flying the sets in from the other side tonight." With quick, efficient movements, he spread out a small cloth and set out two covered dishes, two cups, and a small jug of wine. Cutlery and napkins followed.

Cenda laughed aloud. "A picnic! Oh, Gray!" She and Elke had gone on a picnic once. Only as far as the herb garden she cultivated for Krysanthe, but nonetheless . . . It had been a considerable expedition for little legs. She smiled even as tears burned behind her eyes.

Gray handed her a cup of wine. In the pervasive gloom, he had no shadow. Instead, the shadows lived in his eyes, making them smoke dark again. He smiled gravely and raised his cup. "Here's to deep-dish pies and feeding the fire."

"Yes." Suddenly short of breath, Cenda buried her nose in her cup.

"Damn!" Gray had lifted a lid, his face dark with displeasure. "These are cold!"

"Never mind. I'm hungry."

"You're always hungry," he said absently, still frowning.

"Krysanthe says it's the fire."

"Makes sense." He looked up, his gaze suddenly intent. "How did your Magick lesson go, Cenda?"

She'd shown real improvement this morning. Purist Matthaeus had been pleased. "You're an instinctive practitioner, Cenda," he'd said. "You do better when you stop thinking." She'd blushed so hard she thought she might self-combust.

Now she wet her lips. "Give it here," she said. "The Magick might as well be useful for something." Leaning forward, she picked up a dish, cradling it in both hands, conscious of Gray's fascinated gaze. "Don't watch," she said. "I can't concentrate with an audience."

"All right, I'll look at something else." Gray chuckled. "But I want my supper hot." He shifted his attention, sliding a hand up under her skirt, stroking from her ankle to her knee. "I want you hot."

Five it, how was she supposed to [illegible]? Cenda swallowed the whimper, clutching the dish between her burning palms. Gods, his touch felt good. Her skin broke out in goose bumps, and steam began to rise from the pie dish, together with savory smells.

"Excellent." Calmly, Gray used a napkin to take it from her. "Here, do the other one."

This time, all she had to do was lay her fingers against the curve of the bowl. The salamander pressed its belly against her scalp, emitting a tiny rumble.

"Eat up, little witch. You're going to need your strength."

Cenda's loins clenched as if a great, gentle fist had taken hold of her and squeezed.

Below them, the curtain rattled open to a storm of applause.

Acutely aware of the warmth of Cenda's shoulder touching his, Gray watched the dancers' heads and shoulders forming and re-forming in complex patterns. Erik the Golden belted out popular love songs, the crowd swaying to the beat like a field of multicolored flowers in the wind. Gods, the man was good! Relaxing, he rubbed his cheek against the thick silk of her hair, relishing Shad's absence, the light directly under the roof of The Treasure too diffuse for him to exist. He was so preoccupied, he didn't notice the catwalk bounce at first, despite the fact he was expecting it. Hell, Shad would have known the moment the boy set foot on the first rung.

When he turned his head, Slop's dirty face appeared in his field of vision. Gray raised an inquiring brow, and the lad clambered onto the platform. He produced a grubby parcel from down the front of his ragged trews and handed it over. Gray winced, but he nodded his thanks.

Cenda craned around his shoulder. "Hullo," she said next to his ear, the greeting directed at the boy. "Was it good?"

The lad ducked his head, a strangely shy gesture. His mouth moved, forming words over the sound of the music. "Yah." He paused. "Mistress."

Erik finished his bracket and bowed himself off, the center of a moving knot of dancers. Gray watched them vie to escort the big man into the wings. He'd never seen anything like it. Erik attracted women as if he'd bespelled them.

Over the rising rumble of the audience's conversation, Gray asked, "Was what good?"

"I sent him to the kitchen," said Cenda. "Cook's a friend of mine." She bent a stern gaze on the boy. "Show me your hands."

Muttering obscenities under his breath, Slop extended his hands. Gray bit back a laugh. A tide line circled each skinny wrist, and below it, the skin was several shades paler. Even his fingernails were clean and clipped.

"What happened to you?" he said.

"She'm did." Slop cast Cenda a resentful look. "Sed I had t' fookin' wash up."

"Watch your mouth!" snapped Gray, but the boy only looked puzzled.

"You can't eat with dirty hands," said Cenda reasonably. "You'll get sick."

Slop glanced at her sidelong, an expression that said he'd humor any lunatic with access to food and the inclination to share it.

"I have a gift for you." Gray put the parcel in her lap, his pulse quickening. "Something I thought you might find useful."

Cenda's mouth fell open and she flushed with pleasure. Poor little witch, she'd never been spoiled. The faded blue gown she wore hung on her. He narrowed his eyes, thinking. She'd look good in jewel tones, to play up the fire in her soul and showcase those amazing eyes.

Smiling a little, he watched her rip open the parcel and remove the black leather gauntlets. Her puzzled gaze rose to meet his. "Gray, I don't need—"

"It's to save your clothes. Put one on, and I'll show you."

The gloves weren't new—they were even a little battered—but they were meant for winter, supple and thick, covering the arm as far as the elbow. It had taken him a precious couple of hours to find what he wanted in a backstreet bazaar, and he'd had to pay through the nose to have them properly cleaned. A worthwhile investment, he'd thought.

"Oh! Oh, I see!" Hastily, Cenda pulled on a glove. Then she coaxed the salamander out of her hair and onto her finger.

"Fookin' 'ell!" Slop shuffled backward so rapidly Gray grabbed his bony knee to keep him on the platform.

"Oh, Gray!" Her eyes shone pure gold with happiness, and abruptly he felt like shit.

"It's nothing," he said curtly. "I have to go. I'm on soon."

The gold clouded and she turned her head away, blinking. Fuck. *Do what you have to; just do it.* "Cenda." Gently, he touched her shoulder. "Promise me you'll stay here. I need—" He broke off, with absolutely no idea of what he'd been going to say.

"You, too." He caught the boy's sullen gaze. "You are not to move from this spot, understand?"

"Yah." Slop's gaze skittered over the bright body of the salamander and he swallowed.

"But, Gray—" she said.

He leaned forward to rub his cheek against Cenda's. "We have so little time, sweetheart," he murmured into her hair. "Let's not waste it."

"No," she agreed. "No."

One last swift kiss, pressed firmly to her sweet lips, and Gray swung onto the ladder. A couple of deep breaths in the wings, and Erik was introducing him. Once onstage, the Duchess sang a couple of the strangest discords before he could discipline his fingers to work properly, but after a few moments, the benefit of rehearsal cut in, and the harp blended with Erik's sumptuous voice, the way they always came together, a harmony profoundly satisfying. Judger, it felt good!

But when it came to his solo bracket, he was preternaturally aware of the attention from above and behind, as if her gaze were a weight pressed against his skin. He stiffened his spine, wanting to show her what he could do, impress her. And how juvenile was that? He didn't need anyone's approval, much less that of a half-trained witch. In the end, he did well, or certainly no worse than usual, the music coming as he willed it. When the crowd stamped and clapped, ringing the rafters, Gray felt defiance bloom in his soul. Why not? Why the fuck not? He'd do it as an encore, and then it would be exorcised. Gone.

"One more." He smiled out over the footlights in his serious, easy way. "This is an old song, centuries old. Some of you may know it." Bending his head over the Duchess, the first notes of the "Lullaby for Stormy Eyes" rang out, crystal clear, the minor key tugging at the heartstrings.

Storm clouds gather, love,
In your eyes, in your pretty eyes.

Gray's fingers moved in the final glissando, then stilled, Mother's face so clear in his memory, he was almost surprised to raise his head and not see her before him. He blinked.

Utter silence, as if the world held its breath.

Two heartbeats. Three. Then a patter of applause, building rapidly to a crescendo of stamping, whistling, and clapping.

As they passed in the wings, Erik thumped him on the shoulder, making him miss a step. "Gods, Gray, where did that come from? You had them in the palm of your hand."

"No idea," said Gray briskly. A small, ragged figure darted behind one of the pantomime flats. *What the hell?* He headed for the spot, his heart hammering.

"*What?*" he hissed, gazing studiously toward the orchestra pit.

The whisper came from behind him. "T' Fixer's here."

Gray's head whipped around. "Where?"

"Back near t' bar. He'll be lookin' fer ye."

Gray slid one of the peepholes open and set his eye to it. The Fixer's men weren't difficult to spot. They looked big and tough, with that understated air of menace that meant they knew there was nothing left for them to prove. And the way they stood, each close in the others' space, showed they were accustomed to acting as a unit.

And Judger, what *was* the mountain of fur and muscle crouched at their feet? A dog?

"Cenda?" Gray asked the air.

"She'm still oop there."

"Don't let her down. Even if you have to sit on her. I'll deal with the Fixer."

A sharply indrawn breath. Then the patter of bare feet receding. The ladder creaked.

Gray slipped from the wings, took the route through the kitchen and around to a side servery door. As he followed a buxom serving wench, sliding into the narrow, dimly lit gap between two booths, Shad shivered into being at his side. *Careful, careful.*

Gray didn't bother to reply. A single step and he merged with the crowd, offering the Fixer's men his back.

Just in time. He exhaled, slow and even, watching from the corner of his eye. The shortest of the Fixer's men was scanning the booths, a systematic sweep that passed right over Gray without pause, traveled up to the stage, and worked its way down the other side of The Treasure.

It was extraordinary, the way the tide of eager drinkers broke and flowed around them. At all times, a few feet of wooden floor were visible in a wide circle, a little no-man's-land of caution. On the other hand, it was no wonder, given the monstrous dog.

On many worlds, including Concordia, they had big, beautiful riding animals called horses, plant eaters with long, strong legs, powerful hindquarters, and huge dark eyes. Gray had loved them from the first, becoming a more than competent rider. Now he wondered if a species cross was possible, because this dog was the size of a small horse.

Even across the width of The Treasure, he could see the way it turned its massive head, watching people pass with a predator's intensity. It wore a heavy leather collar at least three inches wide, studded with dark spikes and attached to a heavy chain. The chain was wrapped twice around the big fist of a man who had "thug" written all over him, from the scar bisecting his eyebrow to the dome of his shaved head. Every now and then, he planted his feet and hauled back on the chain, muscles swelling in his beefy forearms, and the dog would turn its head to stare at him.

Which meant . . .

The one in the middle had to be the Fixer. No more than middle height, soft and paunchy. Neat, but not flashy, in a workingman's shirt and trews. Gray narrowed his eyes. The man wore a ring on his left hand, the stone fracturing the light as he gestured, saying something to the dog handler. A novarine, flung from the heart of an exploding star, all that escaping light trapped in a black so dark it was every color and none. Worth more than The Treasure and everyone in it. Gods, likely worth more than the whole Sector!

Gray waited 'til a dozen tipsy offworlders reeled by, heading back to the bar. Must be a package tour, fresh off the flitter from the spaceport. Smoothly, he stepped up behind the group, sticking close. When they parted around the Fixer and his men, Gray was left standing quietly, like a purposeful piece of driftwood left high and dry by the receding tide.

"Grayson, Duke of Ombra." Gray flexed on the balls of his feet, glad he'd left the Duchess with Erik. The weight of the blades in his forearm sheaths was reassuring. For once, Shad's wavering presence, created by the lanterns hanging in the bar, was welcome.

You ready?

Always.

Gray looked from one face to another, raising an insolent brow. "Which of you is the Fixer?"

10

Four pairs of eyes regarded Gray in silence, the dog's such a pale blue they were almost white. They were steady, calculating, and hot with banked rage. A growl rumbled in its chest and it lifted a lip, exposing long, white fangs. Judger God! The fine hair on Gray's neck stood up.

"That'd be me." The man in the middle cocked his head to one side, and though his gaze was a warm, genial brown, it reminded Gray of the dog's. "Shut up, Tiny." He sank his fingers into the brindle ruff around the animal's huge shoulders. It flinched and quivered, its head dropping.

"So," said the Fixer, "ye're a duke?"

Gray shrugged, waiting.

For a moment's ticking silence, the Fixer studied Gray's face, then he grunted and leaned back against the bar. "Ye got 'er?"

"Got who?"

The Fixer's smile didn't alter, but the dog snarled, very softly. "Don' fook wit' me, son. T' fire witch."

"Why ask me?"

Another thoughtful silence. The Fixer clicked his fingers in the dog handler's face, the cabochon stone in his ring swallowing the light. With a hard glare at Gray, the big man extracted a folded slip from an inner pocket. The Fixer jerked his head, and the man held it up between two fingers, grinning. A tooth was missing from the side of his jaw.

Gray flicked a glance at the dog. One crushing bite from those pile-driver jaws and he'd lose a hand. Deliberately, he relaxed his stance. "What's that?"

"From t' Technomage Primus. Instructions, like."

Gray's pulse quickened. He narrowed his gaze, staring into the dog handler's small, dark eyes. *It lays a fang on me and you're dead.* Casually, he let a knife drop into his left hand, held out his right.

The dog handler turned his head aside and spat. Then he jerked hard on the dog's chain, simultaneously slapping the message into Gray's palm. The animal snarled and lunged, and the big man set his feet, swearing, the chain humming taut.

Gray couldn't prevent the instinctive flinch, the rapid step backward. Cursing inwardly, he unfolded the sheet, keeping his fingers steady with an effort of will. *Screamin', if you wan'*. Slop's thin voice rang in his head.

Scary bastard, whispered Shad.

You got that right.

A small sheet of some thin, flexible substance, exactly like the one he'd discovered in his instrument case. He rubbed it between his fingers, disliking the cool, greasy feel. Presumably, this one wasn't set to disintegrate. The upright, impersonal clerk's script was short and to the point. *The Fixer acts for me. Deliver the witch to him in good condition.* No signature.

Gray raised his eyes. "And the fee?"

"Yah." The Fixer scooped a handful of waynuts out of the bowl on the bar and crammed them into his mouth. "Gimme t' woman first," he said, chewing. He swallowed, wiped his fingers on his trews, and backhanded the third man hard across the face. In the sudden silence, a female voice in the crowd made a startled noise. "Salted, not boiled, ye stupid git," the Fixer said calmly. He looked at a point past Gray's shoulder and his brows drew together. "What ye starin' at, woman?" Heels beat a rapidly receding tattoo on the wooden floor.

The third man said nothing, just wiped the blood off his lip with the back of his hand, the red smear absurdly cheerful against his chalk white cheek.

The house lights flickered. "I have to go," said Gray.

"Yah." The Fixer's affable gaze met his. "T' Primus ain't a patient body, son." He dropped a hand to scratch the dog behind one torn ear. It froze, shivering. "Me, neither." The Fixer ran his thumb over a scab in the fur, picking at it. "Two days. No more."

Gray nodded. "I'll send word." He stepped back, fading into the crowd. The last thing he heard was the Fixer saying gently to the third man, "Ye missed 'im, laddie. Not pleased, not pleased at all."

Judger!

Back up on the catwalk platform, it wasn't difficult to persuade Cenda to spend the night with him. Gray simply made it clear he assumed she would, and no contradiction was forthcoming. In fact, her cheeks went a delightful pink, and even under the loose bodice of the gown, he could see her nipples bead up tight.

If he hadn't been so worried, he would have been charmed.

It took a real effort to smile, to meet Slop's cynical, knowing gaze as the boy lounged in the corner, skimming a finger around the inside of a pie dish. Gray watched the pantomime dragons cavorting below, his brain whirring with conjecture, creating and discarding plans, one after another.

He wasn't fool enough to think the Fixer had come to The Treasure with just two men and a dog, not when the Technomage was offering a fat fee. A careful survey revealed another three men studying faces in the crowd, their eyes hard and wary. Slop nudged Gray's shoulder and jerked a chin in the direction of a heavily painted whore working the bar tables and an old woman selling dubious sweets from a tray. Gray frowned. Thousands, the boy had said the Fixer owned. *Thousands.*

Shit.

Sydarise and the other girls high-kicked across the stage, scantily clad as nymphs, distracting not only the dragons but every man in the audience. Gray slipped an arm around Cenda's shoulder, and she relaxed into his side, stroking the salamander that clung to her leather gauntlet. He could probably trust the dancers. And Erik, for sure. The members of the Unearthly Opera were a small, tight-knit, theatrical family. It wasn't that they couldn't be suborned, but achieving it would take the Fixer precious time.

The staff of The Treasure, however, were a different matter entirely. As was the boy.

Cenda the fire witch was a marked woman. The moment she climbed down from the catwalk, she was as good as dead. He was out of options.

The dragons and nymphs bowed themselves off to thunderous applause and the curtains rattled closed. Gray watched the stagehands swarm out of the wings to begin striking the sets. He had to bind her to him, and quickly. Fear and pleasure. Pleasure and fear. Both so powerful, but he had no doubt as to which he preferred. Pity he couldn't have one without the other.

With an inward sigh, he took both her hands in his. "Cenda." The contrast was marked, the warm, bare skin of her left hand and the cool brush of the leather covering her right. "Have you heard of a man called the Fixer?"

"Of course." Her brow furrowed. "All Sybarites have. Why?"

"He's here," said Gray slowly, hating this more than he'd thought possible. "And he's looking for you."

Her eyes went wide. "Five-it, whatever for?"

"For your Magick."

Cenda stared a second longer, then her lips twisted and

she pressed his fingers. "That's just silly." She glanced down at their clasped hands. "Everyone knows I'm not much good."

Gray took her face between both palms, refusing to let her look away. Below, the musicians packed up their instruments and filed out. "It's your potential they're after," he said grimly. He forestalled her before she could speak. "Think of it, Cenda. The ability to *throw* flame, to trigger firestorms, explosions. The possibilities are endless."

"No," she whispered. "No." She tried to shake her head, but his grip was too strong. "I can't. I *couldn't*." She lifted her gloveless hand and wrapped her fingers around his wrist.

"Yes, you could." He stared deep into horrified gold brown eyes, willing her to understand. "You're getting better at it, aren't you? *Aren't you?*"

She swallowed. "Purist Matthaeus said—"

"What would happen if you were angry, Cenda? Really angry?"

She squeezed her eyes shut, her brow creasing. "I don't know."

"Yes, you do." He pulled in a preparatory breath. "What if I told you your baby died because of me?"

Her eyes went molten, incandescent.

"Shit!" Gray jerked his wrist away as flames burst from her fingertips. The pie dish slipped out of the boy's grasp and landed with a tinny clang. He snatched it back before it could tumble off the edge of the platform.

"*What do you know about Elke?*" hissed the fire witch, her eyes blazing.

Judger, he'd never seen anything like it! As if the flash fire of her anger had ignited an inferno in her eyes. "Nothing, Cenda, I swear it. The boy told me about her. That's all."

Slop nodded as he turned the pie dish round and round in his hands. "Yah," he agreed, his voice thin with shock.

Gray gritted his teeth. "It was a bastard of a thing to say. I'm sorry, sweetheart." He reached out to stroke her burning cheek, and she jerked her head away. "But I had to show you."

"I didn't ask for this," she said, low and fierce. The gloved hand flashed out and gripped his forearm so hard he knew he'd have bruises on the morrow. Not that he didn't deserve them.

"I don't *want* it!" Her body vibrated with tension, tears spilling from her golden eyes. Gray would not have been surprised to see the water steam on her cheeks. "My baby." She wrapped both arms around her middle and bent double, rocking herself. "They took my baby and gave me *this*!" She flung out her naked hand, wreathed in flame, ribbons of it trailing up her wrist, singeing the cuff of her gown.

From behind, Slop hissed, *"Fookin' 'ell."*

Cenda raised her eyes, and now they were swimming with misery. "Take it away," she whispered, and Gray knew she was no longer speaking to him. "Take it away and give my Elke back. I miss her." Her voice dropped to a keening murmur, the last three words repeated over and over, a litany of utter desolation.

Her long body folded in on itself as if all the strength had leaked from her bones. She curled into a surprisingly small bundle on the floor, her head buried in her arms. The salamander crept up over her shoulder until it could nose her cheek.

"Cenda." Gray touched her arm, his guts a cold, spiky tangle. "I'm so sorry. For everything." He was intensely grateful Shad couldn't exist in the gloom, couldn't agree with him. "Do you believe me now, about the Fixer?"

"Doesn't matter." She sniffed and wiped her face with her sleeve, the salamander sidestepping neatly. "Nothing matters."

The catwalk shook as pulleys creaked. On the other side of the curtain, the noise level ebbed and flowed as patrons rushed the bar and gamblers set up their tables. The Treasure would be in business until the wee hours.

Gray hardened his heart. "You *want* to be a weapon? Because you will be, Cenda. You will be."

Her muffled voice floated back to him, low and thready. "I'd rather die." A pause, and she hunched further into herself. "Perhaps it would be better."

Better, *better* . . . Why, the little fool! Something dark and angry wrapped iron bands around Gray's chest. He swooped, gripping Cenda's shoulders, hauling her up until they were nose to nose. The salamander dived into her hair. "And what about me?" he hissed. "What happens to me if you die? Had you thought of that, fire witch?"

Cenda stared into his face, her gaze dull and flat. "You?" Her lips twisted in a travesty of a smile. "Why, Gray, you'll go on, just as you've always done." She lifted her fingertips to his cheek, a warm, fleeting touch. "Handsome, clever, confident." Her hand dropped to her side. "Complete."

The laugh rose in Gray's throat, ugly and jeering, but he managed to choke it down. "No." He shook his head. "Not complete. I haven't finished with you, Cenda," he said, knowing she'd see the truth of it in his eyes, knowing it *was* the truth—savage, ironic, and a godsbedamned bitch, but truth nonetheless.

He stroked both thumbs over her temples. "There's so much I have to show you." Feathering his lips over hers, he murmured, "Please let me."

She closed her eyes, turning her cheek into his palm. His heart leaped, and he slipped an arm around her waist, rocking her gently against him. "Going back to the Enclave right now would be stupid, with the Fixer waiting. Stay with me for a little, sweetheart."

At that, she placed both hands on his chest and pushed. Reluctantly, Gray loosened his hold. "Gray, you must have it wrong somehow." She frowned. "The Fixer wouldn't want *me*."

"You think?" He glanced at the boy, sitting cross-legged in the corner, dark eyes flicking from one face to the other. "Tell her."

"Yah." Slop gave a prolonged sniff and dragged his sleeve across his nose. "Word's out, Mistress. T' Fixer wants ye. Sez he's got a buyer."

"A *buyer*?" Cenda choked.

"Yah. Or he'd use ye hisself."

"He's here, Cenda," said Gray. "Come down, and we'll show you."

In the end, he had to nudge her onto the ladder. She descended stiffly, like an old woman. Gray guided her toward a peephole. "Look for three men and a bloody huge dog. At the bar, see?"

She nodded, her breath coming in shallow gusts.

"The Fixer's the one in the middle."

A stool scraped and Slop scrambled up beside them. "That's Tiny wit' 'em." A small hand crept out and clutched Cenda's skirts, the stiff finger jutting out at an angle. "He'm a killer, Tiny. Fookin' crazy."

"Show her the others, Slop," ordered Gray, and the boy pointed them out, one by one. By the time he finished, Cenda was shaking as if she had the winter ague. Gray stepped up behind her and wrapped his arms around her rib cage, just under those sweet little tits. He rubbed his cheek against her hair, fixing the salamander with a warning glare. It glared right back, as if it could see all the way to the black depths of his soul.

"Come with me?"

"All right," she said, her voice a thread.

"You want me to *what*?" said Sydarise the dancer, her carefully plucked brows arching.

Cenda tried not to stare as the girl propped her fists on trim hips. Five-it, her cleavage went all the way to her navel. How in the Lady's name did she keep the thing on?

"Disguise her," repeated Gray. "I need to smuggle her out of here and back to the inn."

"But—"

Cenda stirred, slipping her gloved hand into Gray's. "It's my . . . um . . . husband," she offered.

Sydarise chuckled. "Gray," she said, "not again."

Gray shrugged and smiled, though he didn't look

amused. "Can you do it, Syd? For me?" He dug in his belt pouch. "I've got a few creds for your trouble."

Sydarise waved the money aside. "For old times' sake," she said with a twinkle, and Cenda sank her teeth into her lower lip. Surreptitiously, she curled the fingers of her free hand into her palm, and the flames winked out. The girl asked, "What did you have in mind?"

"I thought a dancer. Then she could leave with the troupe."

Sydarise laughed outright. "Just like a man, go for the maximum amount of skin. Let's see then." She took Cenda's arm and turned her in a circle, her gaze assessing, but not unkindly. "Hmm, you've got the height for it, dearie, and the legs, but can you move like a dancer?"

"No," said Cenda, her heart sinking. For a split second, she'd imagined herself in the skimpy wisp of nothing, relishing Gray's startled expression, the smoky shadows of desire darkening his eyes. Great Lady, how stupid! "I'm not young enough to pass. They— He'd know."

Sydarise shot her a shrewd glance. "Knocks you about, does he? Not to worry—we'll fool him, the bastard. Wait here, Gray. Should be about ten minutes." She bustled Cenda into the back of the building, to a poky room that smelled of makeup, perfume, and sweat. "Strip," she demanded.

It was more like twenty minutes later in the end, but when Cenda strode past Gray carrying a box on her shoulder, he looked straight through her. He frowned at Sydarise, who'd given her a few minutes' start. "It's taking long enough. Everything all right?"

The dancer giggled. "I'd say so." She jerked her head to where Cenda was lowering the box to the floor.

Gray's slanted brows flew up in surprise, and though it was difficult to move her jaw, Cenda smiled with genuine amusement. Great Lady, how long had it been since she'd smiled? Or laughed outright? It felt like forever.

She clomped across the stage toward him in the heavy work boots. When she'd looked into the cloudy mirror in the little dressing room, her jaw had dropped. The lanky stagehand staring back at her looked nothing like Cenda the fire witch. Loose overalls and a rough shirt hid her feminine shape, meager as it was, and Sydarise had bundled her hair up under a cloth cap. The line of her jaw remained too fine for a man, but the dancer had shoved some unpleasant-tasting wadding in her mouth and glued a wispy beard to her chin, a young buck's first effort. The leather gauntlets still covered her hands, the salamander clinging unobtrusively to the inside of one wrist.

"The boys will be carrying the dragons out any minute," said Sydarise. "She can help."

One corner of Gray's mouth tucked up. "Syd, you never cease to amaze me."

The dancer blushed. "Oh, I don't know," she murmured, but she rose on tiptoe to return the kiss he dropped on her lips.

Deliberately, Cenda removed her gaze and made a discovery. "Where's the boy?"

Gray broke off his low-voiced conversation with Sydarise to glance over his shoulder. "I sent him away."

"Gray, no! How could you?"

His face hardened and he shrugged. "He's a street rat, Cenda. We can't trust him. He as good as told me that himself."

"But—"

"You're too soft." Gray came to loom over her, all flinty and grim. "I'm not."

Cenda stared into his eyes, gone slate dark with purpose. No, he wasn't soft, the Duke of Ombra. And yet . . . he'd entranced the rough crowd with nothing more than a tenor like spiced wine and the power of his personality. And when he'd sung the "Lullaby for Stormy Eyes," his face intent, his attention turned inward . . .

She inhaled, bracing herself against the prickle of returning tears. The ache that had roughened the smooth edges of his voice was that of a grief still raw. Words trembled on her lips. *Who died, Gray? Who was it you loved and lost?*

11

The dogs penned in the shed set up a furious cacophony of barking. Crouched behind the woodpile in the yard of the inn, well out of the moonslight, Cenda shoved a shaking fist against her mouth. A door creaked and a slice of yellow illuminated an untidy stack of empty barrels. "Fookin' beasts!" roared a gravelly voice. "Belt oop!"

Cenda shrank back, cupping the salamander in both gloved hands, masking its glow. A slam, and the blessing of darkness returned. She bent double, breathing in great, choppy gusts. Her tongue felt like a plank of wood, the wadding in her cheeks absorbing all the moisture in her mouth.

She'd had no idea of how frightened she'd be. Not when she'd already passed through the veil of fire to face the Lady Herself and survived the experience, not when she'd lost the most precious life in the world. But the physical body had a logic of its own, and the thought of her flesh savaged, bitten, torn, had every limb trembling with the desire to flee.

Great Lady. Oh, Great Lady . . .

At the stage door of The Treasure, Gray had issued a stream of curt orders, making Cenda repeat them back to him until he was satisfied. She was to cuddle up with Sydarise as if they were a courting couple and stick close to the men who carried the snarling dragon masks. Once at the inn, she was to walk in with them, enter the stairwell, and fade away, out the back door and into the yard. "Find a dark corner and wait there for me. I won't be more than a few minutes behind you, I promise. Got it?"

She'd wanted to clutch his arm, blurt out her protests, but big Erik had ambled over and given Gray a genial buffet on the shoulder. "Man out there asking questions about you, my friend." He'd grinned, eyes bright with interest. "Tough-looking character. Got the biggest fuckin' dog I've ever seen. You owe money?"

The sour burn of bile rose in Cenda's throat. Gray said lightly, "Not this time." His eyes moved from Cenda to the dancer and back, as clear as a shouted order. Deliberately, he turned away, falling into conversation with Erik and a couple of horn players.

And so she'd done as she was told, because she didn't know what else to do. Things like this didn't happen to Cenda—not Cenda the supremely ordinary, the awkward, the well-intentioned. A sense of unreality made her head swim, her spine crawling with tension as if eyes followed her from the darkened doorways. Crossing a street crowded with tipsy, happy tourists, Sydarise had giggled loudly. "Ooh, you naughty devil!" Boldly, the dancer reached across and groped Cenda's crotch. Cenda managed to swallow the all-too-feminine squeal, but it was a close-run thing. The pockmarked man lingering at the noodle cart on the corner favored Sydarise with a gap-toothed leer. His gaze passed straight over Cenda.

"Come on." The whisper came from the patch of inky darkness directly behind her. A pale hand beckoned.

Gray!

Cenda launched herself at him with the strength of

desperation, burrowing her face into his shoulder, inhaling great gulps of that essential Gray smell, spicy herbal soap mixed with the warmth of his skin and something else, something indefinable, almost like home.

His arms closed hard about her. "Sshh," he whispered into her hair. "I've got you. Nearly there."

Peeling her off, he flung a long, dark cloak around her shoulders, removing the stagehand's cap, adjusting the hood to cover her head. Finally, he did up the front fastenings for her, batting her hands aside when she tried to help. "Come." Taking her hand, he glanced up at the Dancers shining like a fistful of multicolored coins flung across a baize table, frowning as if he measured the mettle of a foe. Then he slid into the fivefold shadows like a swimmer breasting a soft sea, drawing Cenda stumbling along behind him.

She lost track of the twists and turns. They jinked in and out of so many buildings, her head spun—two gambling hells, a whorehouse, three storehouses and a bazaar, another inn. Each time, they entered by one door and left by another. Her pulse skittered, her heart blundering about against her ribs. Gray drifted down the crooked alleys like a smoke wraith, so light on his feet she knew he must be a beautiful dancer. Pity she'd never learned.

"Bend your head." Obediently, she ducked, and Gray pulled her through a low, dark opening. Straightening up, she had the sense of an echoing, cavernous space above her head.

"Where—?" she whispered, pushing back the hood.

"An abandoned palazzo." He guided her down a passage and through another door, closing it behind them.

Cenda focused on the pale oval of his face. "I don't understand. What happened to staying at the inn?"

"I can't see a damned thing. Make us a light, sweetheart."

"A light? How?"

She felt rather than saw him shrug. "You're the fire witch."

An instinctive practitioner, Purist Matthaeus had said. Cenda tugged off her gloves. The salamander scampered down her forearm and leaped onto her palm, its small body shining gold even in the gloom. *Shine more, little one,* Cenda pleaded. *Show me we're good for something.*

Abruptly, a flare more than a foot high exploded on her palm. Gray swore, swaying backward. Cenda glared at it, frowning. *Too much, just . . .* She made a mental adjustment, molding, compressing . . . The flame became a fireball about four inches in diameter, the salamander curled happily inside it. Ah . . .

Pretty. Cenda pulled the wadding out of her mouth and smiled for the first time in hours.

"Good," said Gray briskly, as if she'd done nothing out of the ordinary. Her heart warmed with a small pleasure, as if the fireball had migrated to her chest and settled beneath her breastbone. "I paid for candles. Ah, here we are."

Still smiling, Cenda reached out and touched a fingertip to each wick in turn. The flicker of candlelight smeared its buttery fingers over Gray, his shadow springing into being behind him, his gaze steady on hers, his handsome face unreadable. A battered pack sat at his feet; an instrument case was slung over his shoulder. Beyond the charmed circle of light, the room stretched, vast and dusty, the ceiling lost in swirling gloom. Over Gray's shoulder, she could see an enormous sagging bed, a four-poster festooned with rotting drapes. She fought back the desire to sneeze. Next to the bed stood a rough wooden box, like an old packing crate. On it was a battered water jug with a chipped handle, and he set the candles beside it. Four of them. At the other end of the chamber was an elegant mantelpiece, framing an empty fireplace big enough for a child to stand upright inside.

Cenda lifted the fireball high. A procession of tall windows, all boarded up, peeling wallpaper, trails of mold slithering over graceful plaster molding, age-spotted mirrors. What in the world—?

Her face must have betrayed her confusion, because

Gray said, "It was the ballroom once; now it's a squat. We weren't followed—I made sure of it. The Fixer won't find you here." He shrugged. "For a day at least. Maybe two."

"Two days!" Cenda dragged in a deep breath. "I have to get back to the Enclave. They'll be frantic."

His face hardened. "You can't trust them, Cenda. Not with so much at stake."

"Not trust—" The fireball flared with the sudden spurt of anger and hurt. "The Pures are my family, Gray. There's not enough money in the world."

He stepped forward, grasping her shoulders. "You think money's the only temptation?" He gave her a quick shake for emphasis. "You represent power without limit, you little fool. More than enough to challenge the Technomages for control of this world. What would your precious Enclave, any Enclave, give for that?"

"Nonsense, that's just . . . nonsense." Cenda set her jaw. "You don't trust anyone, do you, Gray?"

He gave a dark chuckle. "Not even my own shadow, sweetheart." But he stroked her cheek with the back of his knuckles.

"That's it, isn't it?" Cenda swatted the caress aside. "That's why we're not at the inn. You don't trust the boy."

Gray let his hand drop. "Right about now, young Slop will be showing the Fixer's men to my room. In fact, I'm depending on it." He stepped away to lift the pack onto the wooden box and rummage inside it.

The shakes began without warning, starting as a tremor in Cenda's hands, spreading to her spine, her legs, until she feared she might collapse where she stood. Everything she knew about her world was inside out, upside down—*wrong.* She had the curious sensation that the floor shifted beneath her feet, as fluid as the colored sands on the shores of the Rainbow Lakes. Moving cautiously, she reached out and wrapped her fingers around one of the bedposts. Thus anchored, she hefted the fireball, shining in her other hand. "What should I do with this?" Amazing. Her voice came out sounding almost normal, though she couldn't be completely certain.

Five-it, she knew she was naive, just a simple witch from a backwater Enclave, but how stupid did the Duke of Ombra think she was?

He glanced over his shoulder, those deft fingers busy unwrapping a lumpy bundle in a folded cloth. "Put it out. We don't need it now."

But she didn't want to. Cenda released the bedpost and navigated her way to the fireplace, crouching to deposit the fireball there. It looked so small, as lost in the big space as she was with Gray. But the salamander glowed happily enough, pleasure radiating from its little body, the heat a tangible presence against her cheek.

She couldn't put it off any longer. Cenda rose and turned, her back to the fireplace. Under the cloak, she folded her arms together to still the trembling, to shore up her courage with her anger. "Why are you doing this?"

He froze for a second, his shadow hanging on the wall, then he was moving smoothly, straightening, spinning to face her. She still couldn't read his expression, his eyes opaque in the soft light. "What do you mean?"

"Why are you helping me? Is it for the money?"

A slanted brow arched. "No." He took a leisurely step toward her.

"Because I can't compete with the Fixer. Or his buyer." She had to stop and catch her breath before she could continue. "I can't pay you, not even for this." She waved a hand at their surroundings.

Another two paces. Five-it, he was graceful, almost feline in his movements. She hadn't realized a man could move so beautifully. "Cash is always useful." He smiled, very faintly. "But I have enough to get by. So no, not this time."

"The power, then? My—" She choked. "My so-called potential."

Gray stood so close she could see the faint rise and fall of his chest beneath black linen, watch the pulse ticking in the soft hollow of his throat. "Power of that kind doesn't interest me."

Cenda searched his face, seeing nothing but guarded calm. Her heart sank. Such complete composure, such total control. Truth or falsehood, she'd never know—not until it was too late. "Then, Great Lady, *why*? Why take such a risk?"

He bent his dark head, fingers working the fastenings of her cloak. "Is it so hard to believe I'd do it for you?"

"Yes," she said baldly, spoiling the effect by swaying closer. Only half an inch, but she hadn't meant to do it at all, the comfort of his touch like a drug.

He drew the cloak away and tossed it onto the bed. "Cenda," he said in his cool, dark voice, "you'd be wise not to trust me." He fanned the fingers of one hand over her cheek, his thumb caressing the underside of her chin, inches from her vulnerable throat. "Whatever honor I had I lost years ago. But know this." Something flat as stone gleamed in his eyes. "I will not give you to the Fixer. I swear it."

She should leave it at that—she knew she should—but some dark impulse spurred her on. "That's no answer. *Why?*"

"I wouldn't give my worst enemy to that bastard." He grinned suddenly, fierce and wild, an unsettling glimpse of a man she didn't know. "Or perhaps I would. But you—" His voice dropped to a practiced, seductive purr. "You underestimate yourself, little witch." His head dipped toward hers.

Cenda braced her palms on his chest, the prickle of furious tears burning behind her eyes. The words jerked out of her. "You think I'm stupid?" Her chest ached.

Gray stilled. "No."

She ripped herself out of his arms. "Then don't treat me like a fool!"

He spread his hands, a picture of reason. "I'm not."

Cenda drew herself up to her full height, which meant she had to look up only an inch or so to meet his interested gaze. "I know what I am, all right? There's no need to pretend."

Gray raised an inviting brow. "Go on."

Five-it, she was making a mess of this! "I can't imagine the lure of—of—" Her tongue got tangled in her mouth.

"Fucking you," he said helpfully.

"Yes. The lure of f-fucking me is enough for any man to risk his life, let alone you."

"You think I don't want you?"

"Oh, I'm sure you could manage." She couldn't prevent the bitter twist of her lips. "We've already established I'm pathetically eager, and you're a man, after all."

Gray's curse was all the warning she got. His shadow swooped past her, racing along the wall as Gray's strong arm slid around her waist and lifted her off her feet. The room spun as he swung her up in his arms, thrusting his face into hers, his eyes blazing. "You don't know a fucking thing!" He dropped her in the middle of the bed. It creaked and a little cloud of dust arose, tickling her nose. Following her down, he straddled her body, pinning her in place. "Not about me or what I want. And gods, you don't know a bloody thing about yourself."

Cenda gaped. "But—"

"Shut up!" Slowly, he sat back on his heels. For what seemed like the longest time, he just studied her, lying sprawled beneath him, his elegant lips pressed together, the dark, slashing brows giving his handsome face an almost demonic cast. When Cenda opened her mouth, he shook his head, and she subsided, her heart beating its way up into her throat.

"Your eyes are so wide," he said at last, the harsh note easing from his voice. "So pretty. Relax, Cenda. All you have to do is listen." His lips thinned. "You're not beautiful. There. Does hearing it make you feel better, more justified?" One of corner of his mouth tilted up. "And I can't say the beard's an improvement."

"Oh!" Cenda's fingers flew to her chin.

"Don't worry. Syd gave me a salve. We'll get it off later." His eyes narrowed. "Are you listening?"

When she nodded, he said, "Good. Because I won't

be repeating myself." A tinge of pink suffused his cheekbones. "It's a simple thing to praise a woman's looks, especially if you want to bed her. I could tell you how much I love your hair." He rubbed a strand of it between his fingers. "How just the thought of it wrapped around my cock makes me hard." He shot her a sharp glance. "Did you say something?"

Cenda shook her head, swallowing. Low in her belly, something unfurled, warm and quivering.

"You're definitely too thin. No question. You need feeding, spoiling. But Sydarise would kill for legs like yours. Any dancer would. Perfect." Slowly, Gray placed his palms on her knees, his sure touch gliding up her thighs to her hip bones, thumbs brushing into the notch between thigh and hip through the coarse overalls. His breathing quickened. So did Cenda's. "They go on forever, all the way to this gorgeous ass." His hands slipped beneath her, and automatically she raised her hips so he could cup her buttocks, his fingers flexing.

"But I've had more beautiful women."

Cenda licked her lips. "Yes," she croaked. "I know."

"No, you don't." Calmly, Gray withdrew his hands and unfastened the overalls, ignoring her gasp, the way she grabbed at his fingers. "Looking back, I'm not sure I liked more than a couple of them." He shrugged, folding the bib front down to her waist. "That's hardly to my credit, but beauty has a way of leaving a man alone in the bed."

Not last night, she thought. *You're the beauty, but I wasn't alone last night.*

"Cenda—" His smile came out crooked. "We both know this isn't love eternal." The flush faded suddenly, leaving him pale, dark stubble showing clearly on his cheek. Those extravagant lashes swept down, concealing his eyes. "Sweetheart, one day you're going to hate me, but until then—" Lightly, he ran his index finger down her nose, sending her cross-eyed. "I *like* you, all right? I like being with you and I purely *love* fucking you."

"I didn't—I mean, was it—?" She broke off. Gods, she was a fool!

He paused infinitesimally, his nimble fingers busy with the top button of her shirt.

When would she learn to keep her mouth shut?

"You were amazing, Cenda. I've never—" He broke off to slip the button. "And no, you didn't hurt me."

There must have been a draft in the room, enough to make the candles flicker, because his shadow jerked violently against the wall. She hadn't caused him pain. Cenda's relief was so great, she squeezed her eyes shut for a moment. Oh, thanks be to the Lady.

Never? Never what?

Cool air whispered across her torso and she reared up on her elbows. *"Gray!"*

He raised a brow. "Cenda?"

"What are you—?" Well, that was patently obvious. She grabbed at the open shirt, hauled in a breath, and tried for some degree of composure, sophistication.

His eyes glittered silver with amusement. And anticipation. "You insulted me, sweetheart. You implied I'd fuck anything female provided it held still long enough."

Cenda held the edges of the shirt closed with a white-knuckled grip. She wouldn't apologize. She *wouldn't*.

"I've got a point to prove, so we're going to play a game, you and I."

"A game?" Her brain spun. "The Fixer's out there with his dog and you want to play games? Are you mad?"

"No." Unperturbed, Gray leaned forward and kissed her, soft and slow, his lips lingering on hers. It was only as he drew back that he whisked his tongue over her lower lip. Her mouth tingled.

"Danger's a powerful aphrodisiac, sweetheart. But I'm sure you know that. We've got food, a bed, and a safe place for tonight and tomorrow. You need spoiling, Cenda, and I'm going to spoil you every way I know." His eyes darkened. "I may never get another opportunity. And it's what you want." He smoothed a leisurely forefinger over one eyebrow, brushed her hair back off her forehead. "Isn't it?"

She wasn't going to lie—either to Gray or to herself. "Yes," she said. "But I'm not exactly in the mood. Sorry."

He didn't smile or attempt reassurance, though she'd expected he would. Instead, he raised a brow. "I said once you could trust me with your pleasure. Do you, Cenda?"

She searched his face, but there were no answers there. "Tomorrow I go back to the Enclave," she said slowly. "But for tonight . . ."

His sudden smile was dazzling, like a shaft of sunlight spearing though a rain cloud. "Well, then." He grew serious, intent. "You're going to drive us both crazy and I'm going to hold out until the candles burn down." Gray lifted his chin, staring across the room at his shadow on the wall, but now she couldn't interpret the expression on his face. It looked almost like challenge, but she couldn't imagine why that might be so. Five-it, he was strange! Enigmatic, fascinating—and dangerous in every possible way.

His gaze returned to Cenda, and tremors broke out across her chest. Beneath the shirt, the skin over her breasts contracted, her nipples drawing up painfully tight.

"There are only two provisos . . ." His lips curved in what was probably meant to be a devilish smile, but it reminded her more of Elke, hell-bent on some toddler mischief.

She relaxed a little. "And they are?"

"You do what you're told and you do it naked."

12

Her face was an absolute study. Gray very nearly laughed aloud, the combination of huge, shocked eyes and wispy tufts on the chin almost too much for him.

Innocent, whispered Glad, and Gray's amusement evaporated.

Yes, he thought. *A virgin in every way that matters. Poor little fire witch.*

Ah, she's perfect.

"I promised to feed you. Are you hungry?" he said, and watched her scramble to refocus, regain her balance.

"Yes." She made a face. "I'm always hungry."

"Come on, then." Gray shifted back to give her room to sit up, but he kept his grip on the open collar of the shirt. As soon as she moved forward, it would slide off her shoulders. He knew the moment she realized and everything in him stilled, waiting for her to decide.

Because this was all the time he had, this one night. His heart leaped. If he could make it good enough, addictive enough, she might even come with him to Concordia of her own free will. Gods, the perfect solution! And as a bonus, he'd be able to keep the truth from her until the last possible moment.

Those amber eyes flew to his, searching for something. The gods knew what. Reassurance?

When her pretty mouth thinned, he thought for a horrible moment he'd lost. "You brave enough to play, sweetheart?" he murmured, the merest breath of sound.

Cenda didn't reply, but she shoved herself off the mattress in an awkward rush. Gray let the shirt slip away and braced a hand on the small of her back. With his support, the movement became a smooth, graceful arch until she sat bolt upright, his hand resting against the warm knobs of her spine, her sweet little breasts trembling with her quickened breath.

His fingers drifting across satiny skin, he released her slowly. "You're going to kill me, you know," he said conversationally.

She swallowed, her fingers knotted together in her lap. "I am?"

"Touch me. Feel what you do." When she hesitated, Gray seized one hand and pressed it against his groin. Delightful, stimulating warmth. His cock kicked against her palm, filling.

Her mouth rounded in a perfect pink O, and the tip of her tongue peeped out. Unbidden, a vision seared his mind. Cenda on her knees, sweetly submissive, his cock jammed down her glorious throat, the hot velvet of her tongue rasping over the ultrasensitive spot under the head, his fingers buried in that glorious hair, Shad's dark figure enveloping her from behind, long fingers tweaking her distended nipples so her moans of pleasure vibrated around the thickness in her mouth, Shad moving, bending his dark head to feather kisses down her neck, while Gray shook with—

Shad, stop it!

You like this better? Gray, yelping with pain, wrenching the fire witch off him by her hair, crouching to cradle his scorched privates. Her face, at first aghast, then horrified, then appalled. The guilty tears streaking her cheeks, the pity in her eyes—

He had to step away from her touch before he could catch his breath. *I don't have to fuck her to seduce her, make her come.*

But you want to; you want her under you. Close and wet. Shad shoved the visceral memory of it at him, thickening his cock, pulling the skin over his scrotum tight and hard.

And to that, there was no answer, save self-discipline.

"I like to look at you," Gray said. "Don't move." He picked up the package of bread and soft cheese he'd placed on the top of the wooden crate and drew his knife. "Undo your hair and fluff it out. Do you like cheese?"

Wordless, she nodded, her cheeks scarlet.

He found the wine jug and levered the cork out with the tip of the knife. "What about wine?"

Cenda's fingers trembled on the binding of her plait. "Just a little."

Gray poured. He'd brought only the one cup, and that was fine. His eyes on hers, he sipped, swallowed. When he moved closer, she reached out, but he shook his head. "No." One hand on her cheek to keep her steady, he held the cup to her lips. He hadn't thought her eyes could get wider, but they did.

Crumb by crumb, sip by sip, he fed her bread, cheese, and wine, taking scrupulous care, falling into a kind of rhythm, until the fire witch was opening her mouth for each morsel like a trusting child, her lips and tongue swiping against his fingers, soft and wet and warm.

Neither of them spoke, the huge, empty space of the old ballroom quiet save for their breathing and the occasional rattle or shout from the street, thin and faraway. Shad was mercifully silent, but Gray had a sense of him, in a kind of limbo, waiting and yet somehow content.

When the plate was empty, Gray brushed the last of the crumbs from Cenda's chin. "Better?"

"Yes." A pause. Her gaze flicked across the front of his trews. "Thank you." It came out high and breathy.

Excellent.

He smiled, taking Syd's salve from his pack. "I said you'd kill me." Without changing his inflection, he said, "Your tits are playing peek-a-boo with your hair."

Immediately, her hands flew up in a shielding motion, but when her gaze collided with his, she let them drop. Her chin firmed and she straightened her shoulders. Gray sifted a silky lock of hair through his fingers. "Good girl."

Cenda shot him a glare, then apparently thought better of it and stared down at her restless fingers, pleating the strap of the overalls lying in her lap.

Trying so hard, said Shad. *Brave.*

Yes, she is, the little darling.

Aloud, he said, "Tilt your chin, sweetheart." The salve smelled green and minty, with an earthy undertone. When he smeared it on, the false beard lifted away from her skin. Carefully, he wiped the whole mess off with the square of soft cloth Sydarise had thoughtfully included, making sure to clean every trace of the cream from his fingers.

"Have I told you how much I love your pretty tits?" Gray didn't wait for a response. Gently, he brushed the curtains of her hair aside, exposing her small breasts, each no more than a rounded handful for a man with long fingers.

But the fire witch surprised him. "Chocolat," she whispered. "You said my nipples were like chocolat."

"You remember that?" They were drawn up so tight and stiff, they must be hypersensitive by now, aching. At least, he hoped so, because the candlelight fondled the pale, tender undercurves of flesh in a way that tested his willpower. Only fair that Cenda suffered, too. "They make my mouth water. When a woman's suckled just right, she makes the most beautiful noises, like music." He drifted his knuckles over the outer swell of her left breast, and she gasped. "Will you sing for me, Cenda?"

"I can't—"

Gray shifted his attention to her areola, circling the furled, velvety flesh with a fingertip.

"Oh, Great Lady—*oh!*" She swayed into his touch.

Satisfaction moved through him in a warm tide. Perfect!

Shad growled, a reverberating rumble of frustration. *Go on. Suck.*

Not yet.

Hauling in a fortifying breath, Gray sank to his knees and untied the laces of one clumsy boot. "Cup your breasts," he ordered. "Both hands."

"What?"

The boot fell to the floor, and he peeled off the rough, thick sock beneath. Gods, even her feet were slender, fine-boned with a high arch. He grasped her heel firmly. "Cenda," he said warningly.

She did it, though the flush over her neck and cheeks intensified.

Gray ran both thumbs over the sole of her foot, pressing lightly. "How's that?"

"Good." She swallowed.

"Excellent." He showed his teeth. "Match me, now. Stroke for stroke."

She didn't move, except to squeeze her eyes shut.

Gray removed the second boot and sock, cradled her foot against his chest, and waited her out. Eventually, her lashes lifted, her eyes glowing amber with shock and desire. Ah, yes, and wonder. "Sweetheart." He stroked up to her ankle. "Have you never played a game like this?"

Cenda shook her head. No.

He smiled. "There's no greater pleasure than arousal denied again and again." He pressed his thumbs into the ball of her foot and rotated them. Her eyelids fluttered and a sigh whispered out of her throat. "All inflicted, all endured, in the full knowledge that you can't bear the torment another moment. When you'll say anything, do anything, to end it and reach fulfillment. Beg, plead." He paused. "Scream."

Her lips parted. "Or you will."

The chuckle bubbled out of him, dark and wicked, and though he hadn't meant to laugh aloud, Gray was delighted to watch the sound skitter over her skin, tiny shivers following in its wake. Judger, she was so responsive! He hadn't had this much fun with a woman in—He couldn't remember how long it had been.

Yes, fun, whispered Shad, for once in complete accord.

"You never know—I might beg. See if you can make me." He set his thumbs at her heel and stroked all the way to her toes, pushing harder into the instep this time. "Pleasure your breasts, Cenda. I'm sure you know how. And look at me while you do it."

Hesitantly, she rasped her thumbs over the taut, dark crests. When she gasped and her lashes swept down, Gray said sharply, "Eyes on me." Without giving her any further time to think, he began a firm massage, feeling the tiny bones and tendons under his strong musician's fingers, the waves of comfort and pleasure rolling through her.

She lowered her gaze to his hands and he let her, because she really was matching him now, her thumbs flicking over her stiff nipples every time his fingers flexed on her foot. "Arch your back," he murmured, and she did, the small swell of her belly rising and falling with her rapid breath, her ribs making a prominent pattern under smooth, pale skin. Gray made a mental note to feed her the honeyed fern-fruit cakes he'd brought, every crumb. Later.

He pulled at her toes, one by one, and she moaned, very softly.

So did Shad. *C'mon, c'mon.*

Gray switched to her left foot, propping the right against his belly. Immediately, her toes flexed against his shirt as she braced herself, her heel almost brushing the head of his rigid, aching cock. He glanced at the candles, pacing himself, hearing Shad's rumble of disgust in the back of his mind. *Too bad,* he snarled in reply, running his hands up a slim calf, feeling her muscles tighten, then relax.

But it was more powerful than he'd expected, watching his fire witch quiver with the effort of processing such wildly different sensations. She'd stopped thinking about the Fixer, about dogs and thugs and violent death, about what to do tomorrow. Her world had narrowed to this moment, to him. It surprised him, the sheer joy he took in the giving of this gift. The strong, relentless stimulation on her nipples would be warring with the soothing rub on her feet, while the heady novelty of being half-naked, exposed to his intent, admiring regard, had clearly affected her deeply.

Wet. Shad slipped the word in like a sly rapier thrust, under his guard. *Smell it. Hot, wet cunt.*

It was like being gut-punched. Inadvertently, Gray inhaled. Deep. All the way to the balls.

Judger!

He surged to his feet, reaching for Cenda's shoulders. He bore her backward, onto the cloak spread over the sagging mattress. Ignoring the little shriek of surprise that stirred his hair, he clamped his mouth over one dark, furled nipple, rolling it between his tongue and his hard palate, tugging with relish. A frozen instant and her back arched, her hips driving up into his. She fumbled a hand out from between their bodies and buried it knuckle-deep in his hair, holding him to her.

Somewhere on the very periphery of his consciousness was a reason he should slow down, stop, but he ignored it, Shad's presence a continuous background roar of approval, urging him on. Gods, delicious—sweet as Concordian chocolat, with the same smooth, dark feel in the mouth. Exquisitely sensitive. Gray dropped his free hand to her other breast, interlacing his fingers with hers, so that they cupped the warm, tender weight together.

Cenda raised a leg and wrapped it around his thigh, her pelvis tilting up to cradle the solid ridge of his erection against her pubic mound. Automatically, Gray shoved forward with his hips and she whimpered, throwing her head back. The fabric of his trews rasped over the broad head of his cock, the brutal caress making it jerk in the confines of his pants.

Gray lifted his head, Cenda's nipple slipping from between his lips, shiny with his saliva and ruched up as tight as a fern bud just born. On the wall, Shad loomed over the bed, his edges clearly defined in the steady light of the candles.

Slender fingers whispered over his jaw. They shook. A husky voice said, "What happened to the game?"

Cenda lay quietly beneath him, staring into his face, her pupils so huge, all that remained of the iris was a golden rim. Though her lips trembled, they curved in a teasing smile. The warmth of her body pressed all along his, her palm resting on the nape of his neck, her fingers stroking his hair, though he had no doubt she was completely unaware of the caress.

The fire witch. Hot and sweet and brave.

Gray felt a grin stretch his lips, reckless and wild. Fuck it, but he wanted her! And the darkest irony of all was that he desired Cenda more than anything since they'd left Judger's Gift so many years ago, he and Shad. Ah, fuck it! "Sweetheart," he said. "You just took the game to a whole new level."

In a single smooth movement, he pushed himself off her, gripping the waistband of the overalls and peeling them down her legs with a flourish. He tossed the ugly garment over his shoulder and licked his lips. "Spread for me, fire witch."

Cenda struggled to her elbows, fighting the dip in the bed. Cloaked in her hair, she looked like a slender, fey goddess, her golden eyes sparkling with nerves, excitement, and passion—and the first dangerous intimations of a woman's age-old power. "Gray?" Her throat moved as she swallowed.

"What?" he said, lost in the line of an endless leg, the hard, fine bones of the ankle, so vulnerable, the swooping curve of her calf, the creamy smoothness of her thigh. Last night, she'd wrapped those legs around his waist, pulling him deep inside her, totally abandoned in her passion. His gaze tangled in the precious notch where thigh tucked into hip, the rise of her belly, and the dip of her navel. There were fine silvery streaks there, marks that showed her body had fulfilled the function for which Judger God had designed it. Irresistibly drawn, he leaned forward. First, he was going to kiss every one of those marks, until Cenda wore them like the badges of love and courage they were. And then . . .

Yes, hissed Shad. *Oh, yes.*

Pearls of moisture clung to the thatch of dark curls between her thighs, lassoing Gray's complete attention, making his mouth water. Luxuriously, he inhaled, pulling the primitive, musky smell of aroused female deep into his lungs. Without shifting his gaze, he reached for the foot he hadn't finished massaging. Unlike the rest of her, the outer lips of her sex were plump, a fleshy purse for the pink folds peeping from within. So good. It was going to be so good to hear her scream under his mouth, to have her thrash and beg, to send her over, again and again until she was limp, to—

Do it.

Yes.

But when he gripped her ankle so he could splay her wide, Cenda resisted with surprising strength. "Gray." And then more loudly. *"Gray!"*

Gods, Shad had him so far under, he could hardly
Fuck, always when he was weakest. With some difficulty, Gray focused on her face. He shook his head to clear it. "What?"

"You're still"—color rose in a wave from her breasts, up over her throat to her cheek—"dressed."

"So?" He ran his palm up her calf, stroked the hollow behind her knee.

"I want . . ." Her lips tightened, then she said, all in one breath, "Take your clothes off."

Judger, he'd felt more alive, more *present*, here with her in this one night than for all the days and nights of the previous year. The blood tumbling through his veins in a singing rush, Gray held out a hand. "Come here and do it for me."

Cenda shoved the hair out of her eyes. Then she grasped

his wrist and let him haul her out of the embrace of the mattress and into a sitting position on the edge of the bed, her knees pressed primly together. With trembling fingers, she undid one shirt cuff for him, then the other, while Gray watched the light spark deep red gleams off her bent head, as though she'd dipped her hair in garnet wine.

When she shifted her attention to the first button on his shirtfront, glancing up into his face as she did so, her soul shone out of her eyes, bright with the return of hope. Gods, it was impossible to quell the demon of hope; it sprang up in the human heart like a determined weed through cracked masonry. There was no armor of the soul proof against it, not even layers of scar tissue. Even he . . . Hope was a deceiving bitch, holding out the sly, beguiling promise of sanctuary, of comfort. A future.

Because Cenda had no future, save as a tool for Deiter's use. Gray stepped back so abruptly, she lurched forward with a choked cry, clutching at his waist.

One of the candles sputtered out, subsiding in a puddle of wax. Shad grumbled a protest as his outline wavered.

His sanity or his honor. Not much of a choice.

He bent, cupping the back of her skull, the silk of her hair whispering over his palm. "Remember what I said, sweetheart," he said harshly. "It's only a few fucks, not love eternal."

All the color drained from her face, and suddenly, she was just a tall, skinny woman, hunched naked on a ramshackle bed in a slum.

Cenda whipped her hands away from his body and dug them into the bed at her sides, her knuckles shining white, the breath sawing in her lungs. When her chin came up, she was glaring, though her eyes were sheened with tears. "You flatter yourself, Duke," she said, her lips barely moving.

Fool! hissed Shad, and Gray had to agree. The fireball in the fireplace flared and Shad thickened, becoming dense and solid. Under Cenda's fingers, tendrils of smoke curled up from the mattress.

Gray ripped the shirt off over his head and pulled off his

boots. "I told you you'd learn to hate me." Carefully, he set his forearm blade and harness on the top of the crate. When he put his hands to the lacings of his trews, Cenda froze, but she bit her lip, watching. With an effort, he gentled his voice. "But you still want it. As much as I do, sweetheart." Slowly, he pushed the pants off his hips, stepped out of them. "Bank the fire, Cenda, and let me in."

13

It was beyond Cenda to tear her gaze away. As she stared, fascinated, Gray thickened, his cock rearing high and rosy over his flat belly. A wave of embarrassment surged up over her throat and cheeks until even her scalp felt hot. It almost obliterated the confusing mix of fury and hurt and desire. Almost.

"The fire, Cenda," he reminded her.

Last night, she'd felt that silken length pulse in her grasp. She couldn't doubt he'd taken pleasure in her touch, but she'd had no idea of what he would look like aroused. *Great Lady.* Her previous experience had led her to view the male genitalia as inherently ridiculous, so . . . *dangly.* She'd always averted her eyes. Five-it, she'd never thought of a man's organ as imposing, let alone beautiful. But his was, the shaft engorged with life and power, the broad head flushed a tender rose pink. Her mouth watered.

Cenda slammed her eyes shut so she could concentrate on reducing the heat in her fingertips. Gradually, the frantic beat of her heart slowed, and the fireball subsided. The outer reaches of the vast room sank back into the dark, and another candle hissed and died.

"That's better. Kiss me." Gray hauled her to her feet and plastered their bodies together from neck to knee. The impact of so much skin on skin was deliciously shocking, her whole body tingling with it. She'd been right—there was very little hair on his chest, and what there was of it was a dusting of silky black, arrowing down to the dark curls between his thighs. He was delightfully solid, so very different, hard where she was soft. They fit together like the pieces of a puzzle, a spell cast with perfect precision, her breasts crushed against his chest, his cock pressing insistently into her stomach, one muscled arm wrapped around her waist, the other hand cradling her jaw. The horrible empty feeling in her stomach eased a fraction.

And then he kissed her.

He sank into the kiss as if the world were normal, safe, sane, as if there were nothing else he'd rather be doing, as if her mouth were a treat to be savored, seduced, nibbled. Ah, gods, her head was spinning; she couldn't accommodate so many wildly differing emotions simultaneously. The demands of her body rose, clamoring, and Cenda sank gratefully into the soft red heat, running her fingers into his hair and letting her head fall back. All the tension in her neck and upper back unraveled. She drifted in the remorseless tenderness of it, her tongue dancing shyly against his, growing bold enough to flirt and suck. Gray grunted, slipping a hand under her thigh to lift it over his hip. The kiss deepened, reaching a whole new dimension: darker, wetter, more intense. Cenda began to feel light-headed, the liquid ache between her thighs becoming unbearable. The room swung, then steadied.

When she opened her eyes, she was looking at the mold-spotted curlicues on the ceiling. Gray nipped along her jaw, kissed his way over her eyebrow, her nose, her eyelids. "All right now?" he murmured into her neck, delivering a nibble to her earlobe that made something low in her belly clench, as if a line of fire connected the two points. How odd. How wonderful.

He didn't wait for a reply, transferring his attentions to her collarbones, the points of her shoulders. No part of her body was left unaffected by his touch. Her ribs, the insides of her elbows, her wrists, the palms of her hands. The undersides of her breasts. Her—*Great Lady!*—nipples. He suckled gently but oh so firmly, so that the taut flesh ached with a pleasure so acute it was almost pain. Surely she'd never been so sensitive before? It must be the result of nursing Elke. For a surreal instant, she felt the pull of a hungry baby mouth, and then Gray was releasing her breast, moving down to brush his nose over her belly, murmuring, "I said you'd sing, little witch."

All thoughts of Elke evaporated. Cenda reared up and tried to clutch his hair. "What are you *doing*?"

He drifted a fingertip around her navel, shifted down to lick over her hip bone. "What do you think?" He blew on the wet skin and she gasped, the nerves there flickering with silver lightning, as though the Duke of Ombra had set skeins of Magick whipping about inside her with his clever mouth.

"No!" Gods, she was so wet, the poor man would drown. Or pull back in disgust. "Gray, you mustn't."

But he was lying between her thighs, his shoulders preventing her from closing her legs. He turned his head to nip the inside of her thigh, a series of tiny stinging bites, followed by a leisurely lick. When he looked into her eyes over the length of her body, he was smiling, his eyes dark as water on a moonless night. "Cenda," he said, his voice cool and sweet, the voice of seduction, "believe me, I've been dreaming of how you'll taste." He planted a soft sucking kiss on her clitoris, right where the pressure was worst.

She bucked, all the air rushing out of her lungs in a breathy scream. He'd been dreaming? Of *tasting* her? *There?*

Gray slid an arm under her hips and tilted her up.

"You're so pretty." His touch was featherlight but thorough, traveling from her clit to her anus and back again. "All pink and puffy and delicate. So female." This time, the caress was more of a stroke, firmer. Her nerves twisted in a little spasm of joy and anticipation.

"You've never had this, have you, Cenda?" But he didn't appear to require an answer, because he angled his head to take an unhurried lick, to nibble and suck on her quivering folds.

Cenda threw an arm across her eyes and collapsed into the mattress, every muscle in her body dissolving with pleasure, while a dark ache like a striding line of rain clouds gathered in her pelvis. Gray purred, a totally masculine sound of satisfaction, and stepped up the luxurious torture. Slipping a forefinger deep into her sheath, he crooked it, massaging a pleasure point inside her she hadn't known existed.

All remaining thoughts stuttered to a halt, a helpless litany of *Gods, oh gods, oh gods* . . . Gray was crooning something in his throat, the Lady knew what, his mouth vibrating against her quivering flesh, his tongue dancing, while he braced his forearms across her thighs to keep her from writhing right off the bed.

Another candle went out, and he froze for an instant. Cenda had the sense of something moving at the outer edges of the reduced circle of light, something huge and amorphous. Then Gray wrapped his lips over her clitoris and began to suck, softly, relentlessly, while that diabolical fingertip stroked, exerting exquisite pressure against sensitive tissues.

She was aware she was making the most undignified noises, but she couldn't seem to care. Her blood was bubbling, the coiling tension fiery and vicious, and he was pushing her closer and closer to a peak both terrifying and rapturous. Cenda thrashed, strands of her hair catching in her open, gasping mouth. With her last particle of sense, she gripped her fingers together, so she couldn't ignite the mattress.

Gray jerked away, muttering, "Shit!" A sharp inhalation, and he returned with a swoop, his lips closing hard on the throbbing knot of nerves, compressing it unbearably.

Cenda's body bowed right off the bed. Something deep inside her *gave*, and she tumbled off the edge into a dark firestorm of release. She screamed, the fireball flared, Gray reared back with another curse, and the last candle flickered out.

Over her own harsh panting, she heard Gray say, "Judger, Cenda, that was close."

She couldn't seem to get her thoughts together. Stupidly, she stared, trying to make out his expression, but the only source of illumination left in the room was the slowly dwindling fireball. "Did I—? I didn't—?"

She sensed him shake his head. "No." The bed dipped with the weight of his body. "I'm fine." The salamander's eyes glowed like twin sapphires from the fireplace, the darkness so absolute as to be impenetrable, but she could smell Gray's skin, the intoxicating scent stamped on her senses, never to be forgotten.

His voice floated out of the night, husky with satisfaction. "That should've taken the edge off." Slowly, he lowered his body over hers, settling into the cradle of her thighs. The velvety head of his cock nudged the entrance to her body. "Ready for me, sweetheart?"

Savoring the sensation, Cenda ran a palm over the firm swell of his biceps, up to his shoulder. His skin was warm, already a little sweaty, hard-packed with muscle and bone. She rubbed her cheek against his arm, knowing she was lost. "Oh, yes." She felt so boneless, so sated, he'd slide right into her as if he were greased. But five-it, she hoped he wouldn't be disappointed. There was no way known to the gods she'd reach another cataclysm like the one he'd just given her with his mouth.

"Mmm." He bent his head and kissed the side of her jaw, licked her lower lip. Then he said the oddest thing. "Just you and me now, sweetheart." Even his tone was peculiar. If it hadn't been so unlikely, she would have said he sounded smug, but the major impression was flinty, as if he was absolutely determined on a particular course of action.

In the concealing dark, she could grasp her thighs and pull her legs back, offering everything, exposing everything, without feeling like a wanton or a fool. His exhalation of pleasure whispered over her cheek as he worked the head inside her, the mouth of her sex opening greedily, sucking him in.

"Good?" she whispered, tilting up a little farther.

"Gods, yes!" A pause, while he fed her another inch. "So tight." He sounded as though he spoke through clenched teeth. "Still so hot."

"Gray?"

He rocked into her body, sliding deliciously back and forth, setting off tingles and sparks. "What?"

"Go ahead. Do whatever . . . whatever you want."

"Sweetheart, I intend to." His breath washed warm and moist over her collarbone, his cool hair brushing her neck. Another sumptuous slide, all the way to the hilt this time, his balls colliding softly with her perineum. "Fuck, that's good."

"Because I don't think I can do that again."

"Mmm. Do what?"

"C-climax like that. Not again."

Gray froze for a moment, buried so deep inside her, she could swear he nudged her heart. "You will if I want you to," he said.

Cenda gave a breathless chuckle. "Arrogant."

"No, a fact." He swiveled his hips, catching her at a different angle, and she heard him murmur with satisfaction when she gasped.

Regrouping, she said, "Don't be silly. It's not a contest, you know. Barton never—"

"Who?"

"Elke . . . Elke's father . . ." The words were sucked out of her mouth into a vortex of regret and guilt. She hadn't thought of Elke, of her precious baby, for the Lady knew how long. Gods, how could she have abandoned her darling, her sweet—

Suddenly, she was freezing, her skin clammy and chill where it pressed against Gray's warm body.

"Cenda!" he said sharply. "Cenda, come back!"

Her legs slid off his flanks, flopping down to the mattress. "It's all right." Deliberately, she smiled in the dark, so the misery wouldn't show in her voice. "Please." The smile congealed into a polite rictus, despite her best efforts. "Don't stop. Enjoy yourself."

"Fuck, you're allowed to go on living." Long fingers slid up her throat, cradled her jaw. His tone gentled. "Come on, Cenda, don't leave me all alone here."

She stroked a hand down over his shoulder blade, feeling a series of ridges under her fingertips. Strange. "I'm . . . not."

Gray made a noise of disgust and fury, deep in his throat. "No," he gritted. "You. Will. Not."

He reared back, still wedged hard and high inside her, seized an ankle, and hauled her left leg up over his shoulder. Cenda thrashed on the bed. "Five-it, Gray, what—*Nngh!*" He lifted the other leg, leaning hard into her, braced on strong forearms. Because of his size and the acute angle, it was an extraordinary sensation, on the borderline between pleasure and pain. Every thought flew out of Cenda's head as he began to thrust, long, ramming strokes, strafing unmercifully over that spot inside her, the one he'd teased with his fingers. He hit her clitoris full on every time he hilted, their bodies slapping together in a hard, jolting rhythm.

Gods, the high, tight friction was building, building to a pleasure point so fiery it was agonizing. "Come," he panted, thundering into her. "Damn you, woman, fucking come!"

She couldn't breathe. She was numb, every nerve dead with an overload of sensation.

Lady, no! Cenda struggled, striving for the rapture just out of reach. She was going to die, explode in a conflagration of wet, searing heat. Vaguely conscious of the hungry roar of flames from the fireplace behind her, she stared up into Gray's face, contorted with pain or ecstasy—she couldn't tell which. Blood welled over his lower lip, trickled down his chin.

"Now! Please, love, I can't—" Tears stood in his eyes.

Something huge and dark bent over Gray, wrapping long arms around his chest. Teetering on the cusp of culmination, trapped in her physical response, Cenda choked. Gray tried to throw it off, roaring, *"No!"* but his hips snapped forward one last, brutal time. He froze, jammed all the way to her throat, groaning long and deep in his chest.

The inferno swarmed over her, licking her body with tongues of flame, sizzling up and down her spine. Cenda screamed into the hard palm he clamped over her mouth. Squeezing her eyes shut, she gave herself up to the pyre and was consumed.

"Judger God. Shit, shit, *shit.*" Someone was swearing, a litany under his breath. "Oh, fuck! Get off, you bastard! I'm all right." A pause. *"Will you fucking get off?"*

Cenda's eyes flew open, her body still humming. Gray knelt on the bed, struggling with a creature of impenetrable darkness, his hands around its throat. She scrambled upright, a cry of rage bursting from her. "Leave him alone!" Though what help she thought she could provide was debatable. Distract it—she had to distract it. Perhaps she could throw a fireball? Her brain reeled. Lady, why hadn't she paid attention in demonology lectures?

But Gray glared at her. "Shut up!" he hissed. "Do you want to bring the whole world in here?"

Cenda's mouth fell open. Slowly, the demon released Gray and stepped back, so she could see it had no features, only a silhouette that was oddly familiar. Its head tilted to one side, watching her with unnerving concentration. She fumbled out a hand and clutched the first part of Gray she could reach, which was his bare knee. "What is it?" she whispered, trying not to startle the creature. "I've never seen a demon like that." Warding spells tumbled through her head, but the only one she could remember in its entirety was for keeping chew worm out of the vegetable patch.

Gray barked out a bitter laugh, a world of weariness in it. "Demon?" He glanced at the creature, then away, as if he couldn't bear the sight of it. "Near enough." He was so pale even his lips were white, his satanic brows the only slash of color in his face, his eyes like pits. "It can't exist without light. Put out the fire."

Cenda turned her head to stare at the blaze filling the huge fireplace, the salamander, now a foot long, dancing happily in the flames. The demon twisted to follow her gaze, but it made no move toward her. "Did I do that?" she whispered, awed.

Gray wiped the blood from his mouth, then stared at his fingers. "Yes," he said. "When you came."

"Gods." She couldn't help it—her gaze dropped immediately to his groin. His cock lay flaccid against his thigh, gleaming with their combined fluids. Still pretty. Unmarked.

"Not even singed."

"But how—?"

The demon took a step forward, closer to the bed. "That will do," snarled Gray. "Go." He pointed to the far corner of the room. "Over there."

"It does as you command?" Cenda extended her Magickal senses, searching for the stink of evil, the rotting-flesh smell of necromancy. Nothing. It felt . . . human, as complex and difficult as the man beside her.

But the dark creature walked steadily forward, its posture just like Gray's, lean and fluid and graceful. "As you see." Gray's laugh was closer to a jeer. "Shad, for the last fucking time—"

"It has a name?"

Gray ignored her, his stare locked with the creature's, combative reflections of each other, light and dark, life and shadow. Cenda had the sense of an unheard conversation passing over her head. Under her hand, Gray's body drew as taut as a strung bow. He lunged, interposing his own body between her and the demon.

Not at all discomposed, it sauntered up to the bed and bowed low, all lithe grace and dark charm. Peering around Gray's shoulder, Cenda laughed. "Why, Gray, he does that just like you."

Gray flinched.

So quickly she had no time to react, the demon reached a long arm past Gray, pried her hand from its death clutch on his biceps, and kissed her knuckles, a real kiss from cool, soft lips. Cenda gasped, delightful frissons traveling up her arm, soothing, tempering the heat in her blood. The roar of the fire muted to a hiss as the blaze moderated.

And she knew.

"You!" She gasped. "It was you! That's why I could—Why I didn't burn him!"

The demon glanced at Gray. Then he nodded.

Cenda pushed past Gray's unresponsive body, holding out both her hands. "Thank you," she said. "Oh, thank you. Shad? Is that your name?"

Another crisp nod, and the demon sank to his knees beside the bed, grasping her hands in his strong, dark fingers. Slowly, he bowed his head, as if honoring a queen, and drew Cenda's palms to his cheeks. Smiling, she flexed her fingers. His skin was smooth and strangely slick, not like living flesh, save for the hard bone of a strong jaw under her palms, her thumbs brushing a straight blade of a nose.

Beside her, Gray made a choking noise of sheer fury. One hand flashed out, gripping Shad's shoulder, sending him sprawling. "Get your filthy hands off her!" He sprang to his feet, fists clenched, so unlike the self-contained man she thought she knew that Cenda could only stare.

"Gray," she said gently, touching the bunched muscles in his shoulder. "He's not doing any harm. He *helped* us, don't you see?"

"You said"—Gray hauled in a breath—"a demon."

"I'm a real witch, even if I'm not very good." Cenda shrugged. "I've met quite a few demons. Mostly, they're low-level entities. Stupid. Easy enough to control."

Shad was shaking his head, and she fought the desire to laugh. "It's all right, Shad," she said. "I'm not calling you stupid."

But Shad kept shaking. Cenda frowned. "Then . . . you're not a demon?"

Shad shook again. *No*. He looked straight at Gray.

Cenda turned. "I think he wants you to do the introductions."

She'd never seen a man faint before. Cenda leaped forward and grabbed Gray by the upper arms. He staggered, then steadied, so milk pale he glowed like fine porcelain, his face almost translucent in the flickering light. "I . . . *can't*."

Abruptly, a flood of color ran up under his cheek. His lips twisted in a feral snarl as he glared at Shad. A Concordian tygre could have done no better. "Fuck, I hate you! If it wasn't for you—" Breaking off, he spun on his heel and rammed his fist into the wall, all his compact strength behind the blow. Chips of plaster drifted down, eddying around his beautiful bare shoulders like shoddy snowflakes.

14

For the first time, Cenda got an unobstructed look at his back. The smooth flesh was crisscrossed with raised welts, from waist to shoulder. They were pale and old, barely there. Mercifully, she had little experience of such violence, but the conclusion was inescapable. Sometime, many years ago, Gray had been flogged—savagely. Great Lady, enough was enough!

"No!" Cenda grabbed his forearm. "Not your hand!"

Gray spun around, slumping against the wall, his bloodied knuckles cradled against his bare belly. He squeezed his eyes shut. "Cenda, I—"

Shad walked straight past her and leaned against the wall next to Gray. He lifted one fist and pressed it to his stomach, turned his head, and gazed at her, just as Gray was doing.

Cenda looked from the pale face to the dark one. The lock that fell over his brow, the stubborn shape of his skull, the set of the square shoulders, that nose. "Lord's balls," she whispered. "He's you!"

Gray's lips parted, but nothing came out. After an eon, he inclined his head.

So did Shad.

The silence became glutinous.

Finally, Cenda faltered. "I don't . . . I don't understand. What Magick is this?"

"No Magick." Gray moistened his lips with the tip of his tongue. "Just wrong. Abomination."

Shad reached out and put a shy hand on Gray's shoulder. Gray batted it aside with a curse.

Cenda took a step forward. "Gray," she said very softly, "I think he loves you. How can this be abomination?"

Gray pushed away from the wall to scoop his shirt off the floor. He shrugged into it, not speaking.

"Gray?" prompted Cenda. Shad's cool fingers slid into hers and gripped hard. She pressed them reassuringly.

"He's . . ." Gray fixed his gaze on the salamander dancing in the fireplace, his face like flint. "The worst of me, the black heart of my soul." He rubbed his forehead. "Made manifest."

"I don't understand."

"I don't give a shit." Gray shrugged. "That's the way it is." He cast her a look of pure dislike. "You should be running for your life, little witch, not holding Shad's fucking filthy hand."

"He *helped* us."

One flyaway brow arched, and Cenda's palm tingled with the urge to hit him. "Oh, yes, he's all heart." Gray shifted restlessly, and her attention got tangled in the hem of the shirt, brushing the taut curve where ass met thigh. He had the most beautiful legs she'd ever seen on a man, lean and powerful, roped with long, graceful muscle.

Shad took a lock of her hair between two fingers and tugged, very gently. Cenda turned to stare up into the featureless face. "You can't speak, can you?" she said.

Gray snorted. "Never bloody shuts up. Always yammering in my head. It's—" He broke off and rubbed his forehead. "Drives me fucking crazy."

Without lifting his gaze from hers, Shad made a rude

gesture in Gray's direction, one long, dark finger jabbing the air. Cenda chuckled. She was sure Shad had smiled, though there was no way of telling. Struck by a sudden thought, she asked, "Can you sing?"

She'd managed to surprise them both. They exchanged a long, unreadable glance across the width of the room.

Eventually, Gray said, "No, no, he doesn't sing . . . But sometimes, I hear . . ." He frowned at the instrument case on the floor near the box-table. "Something like an echo, a dissonance that isn't." He bared his teeth. "In a minor key."

Shad's shoulders slumped.

Cenda gritted her teeth. "How can you be so cruel?" she demanded. "Poor thing. He's done nothing wrong."

"Nothing—?" Gray's handsome features twisted into an ugly sneer. "Fuck, Cenda, you know nothing about me and even less about Shad. It's none of your fucking business how I treat my own shadow."

Cenda blinked back the tears of hurt. "Your what?"

But Gray turned his head away, his jaw bunching.

His *shadow*? Cenda looked from one to the other, her mouth falling open. Now Shad appeared to be wearing the same shirt as Gray, the fall of it making his silhouette appear blocky and square-set. Of course.

"Shadow Magick," she whispered. "I didn't know it existed, but that's what you are, Gray. A sorcerer of shadows."

He laughed, a jarring sound. "Witch, you see Magick everywhere." Abruptly, he strode back to stand before her, gazing from her face to Shad's, his own features tense and purposeful. "Listen to me well, Cenda, because I'm warning you." He bit out the words, each one clipped and hard. "Don't delude yourself with romantic notions. Shad is my *curse*, the shadow on my soul." His hand shot out and gripped her jaw, forcing her to meet his turbulent, smoke-dark gaze full on. "And I would do anything—*anything*—to be rid of him."

Shad's fingers closed over Gray's wrist and drew it away, releasing her.

"Would you—?" Cenda licked her lips. "Would you kill the innocent, Gray? Do murder?"

A hot wave of color ran up under his cheek, then receded abruptly. He swayed a little on his feet. "Judger God," he said huskily, "I'd think about it." He jerked his arm out of Shad's grip.

Cenda's knees went out from under her and she sank to the bed. Spots danced at the edges of her vision and her stomach growled. With a whimper of embarrassment, she clapped her hands over it. Immediately, Shad's touch feathered over the back of her neck, and Gray's warm fingers stroked her shoulder.

As if in answer to a question, Gray's voice said, "Of course I remember. I'll get them." Then to her: "Put your head down for a minute, Cenda."

Shad pressed her down without missing a beat of that soothing rub on the back of her neck. Something clinked close by.

"Here." Gray raised her up and pressed a wine cup to her lips, but all it held was water. She gulped gratefully, her shaking fingers clutching the smooth pottery. "We forgot to feed the fire, little witch. You've expended a lot of energy tonight." His voice hardened. "Shad, get off her."

A pause, and Shad's fingers slid silently away.

"You have, too," she murmured.

"Yes, me, too." The bed dipped as he climbed up behind her. "Lean back and open your mouth."

Honeyed fern fruit on her tongue, chewy biscuit dough. Five-it, she was starved! Greedily, Cenda chewed and swallowed. Gray drew her into the circle of his arm and she sighed, relaxing into his shoulder and letting her lids droop. Lady, she was tired, but somehow, she couldn't bear to let him feed her again. The time for games was past.

With a huge effort, she lifted a hand. "I can do it."

Gray said nothing, but he put two fat, sticky cakes in her palm.

Between hasty mouthfuls, a languid procession of yawns worked their way out of her. "Sorry," she mumbled, but she couldn't take her eyes from Shad, lounging against the wall. Amazing.

Gray's cheek moved against her hair. "It's been quite a day. Go to sleep."

"Mm." Cenda stretched, and another problem became embarrassingly evident. "Gray, I need— Where's—?"

But he just said, "Good idea." Uncoiling, he rose and pulled her to her feet. "Come on, then, but you'll have to make your own light, I'm afraid. We're fresh out of candles." His voice was very dry. "Wait, hold still a minute."

It wasn't until the cloak dropped over her shoulders that Cenda realized she was still naked and she'd forgotten all about it. Great Lady, the man had her completely hypnotized!

Gray drew the hood up over her head. As he fastened his trews, he said, "There's a communal privy and what passes for a bathhouse on the next floor. It stinks, but they have to make do, the squatters." He retrieved their boots and handed hers over. "Hold your breath and for the gods' sake, if we pass anyone, don't speak. Don't even look up. And cup the fireball in your hand so it looks like a candle."

Shad drifted closer, wavering against the wall.

Cenda smiled. "You coming, too, Shad?"

"He's got no choice on that," said Gray. "And neither have I. Unless you'd rather piss in the dark."

Her cheeks warm, Cenda bit her lip and shook her head.

The privy was as noisome as Gray remembered. The fire witch had coped quite well, despite her instinctive recoil when the stench first hit them. He estimated it was a few hours after midnight, the ruined palazzo quiet enough, though it wasn't empty. They didn't encounter another living soul, coming or going, although there were creaks and rustling aplenty, the crawling sensation of beady-eyed attention from the gloom. He hoped to the gods it was just the scuttleroaches. He'd certainly never seen such big ones, swarming on the edges of the small circle of light, longer than his longest finger. Cenda's fireball struck bluish brown gleams off their hard, flat carapaces.

She'd insisted on dividing the fireball in half, though it took her several minutes of puzzled concentration to work out how to do it. "Five-it, Gray!" she'd hissed. "They're huge, the horrible things. If I leave you out here alone in the dark, there won't be anything left but your boots." Shad had thought it all vastly humorous. Of course.

But strangely enough, Gray had found the little sphere of light a comfort. He avoided the knowing, basilisk gaze of the tiny salamander inside it.

Shit, he was still shaking—somewhere deep inside, in a place he couldn't reach. Gingerly, he leaned back against the wall, and humiliation surged over him in a cold, greasy wave.

Gray squeezed his eyes shut, breathing through the nausea, the way he centered himself for a demanding performance. Why hadn't he offered her a blade so she could flay him, peel the skin away like a ripe manda fruit? Judger, it would hurt less. This was like waking from a nightmare, a dream of standing naked before a jeering, pointing crowd, only to feel their hot breath foul on your skin, your ears deafened with the catcalls.

Trust, murmured Shad. *Trust her.*

Will you fucking leave me be!

He didn't realize he'd spoken aloud, shouted, until the words reverberated in his skull, echoing up and down the dark passageway.

Cenda's head appeared around the door. "Gray? You all right?"

No.

"Of course." He straightened. "Finished?"

Back in the ballroom, he whipped the cloak away before Cenda could protest and spread it across the bed. "Don't argue," he said curtly. "It's better than the mattress cover. Go on."

Muttering darkly, she bent to snag the stagehand's coarse

shirt from the floor, showing him her pale, round ass, a glimpse of the sweet cleft between her thighs. Gray and Shad growled as one, their thoughts meshing perfectly. *Mine.*

Gods, yes.

The fire witch shrugged it on and did up every single button, her lips tight, though there was no way she could conceal the glorious length of those endless legs.

The question trembled on the tip of his tongue. Abruptly, he felt as though he were six again, gazing in horror at the broken bowl on the floor, the splatter across the rug. "Art thou mad with me, Mother?"

She'd ruffled his hair. "No, son, but thy carelessness means no biscuits for Father's supper." Looking back, he knew he would have preferred a whipping, but that was not the way of the Judger's people.

Shad gave him a hard mental nudge, and he opened his stupid mouth, as desperate for reassurance as that little boy, so long ago. "You're not revolted?"

Cenda sighed as she stretched her long limbs on the bed. "By what? Your Magick?" She pushed the hair out of her eyes as he stood watching her, his pulse thundering in his ears. "Fascinated would be closer. I've never seen anything like it. But Gray, Magick is what it is." She shrugged and the shirt slid a tantalizing inch up her thigh. "Why should I be revolted?"

"He . . . touched you."

The corners of her mouth tilted up. "It didn't hurt. And it helped, remember?"

"But—"

"Tomorrow, I'm going straight to Purist Matthaeus. He'll know what to do about the Fixer." She yawned delicately, like a cat, covering her mouth with slender fingers. "Lady, I'm tired." She curled into a ball, a hand beneath her cheek. "Let it go, Gray," she murmured. The fireball began to dim. Shad faded to a murky outline.

Well, hell, it hadn't worked. "Godsdammit, Cenda—" A wave of depression swept over him. For a minute there, as she'd writhed and whimpered, her long limbs wrapping him up, pulling him deep into her body, he'd thought . . .

Shit, he'd keep trying, though, because otherwise she'd be coming with him the hard way. And he was finding it more and more difficult even to think of it, let alone make the necessary plans.

She'd slipped into sleep, her hair tumbling over her shoulders in a profusion of dark, silky curls spiced with those wine red streaks, the tiny creases at the corners of her eyes smoothing out. It was astonishingly easy to imagine her at twenty, young and full of coltish promise.

Gray stripped and slid down beside her, settling her head on his shoulder. Cenda jerked. Then she let out a long, rasping breath and relaxed, snuggling, throwing one leg over his. The fireball winked out and the dusty dark fell like a blanket. Shad's presence disappeared. The perfection of the fire witch in his arms served only to emphasize his shadow's absence. Judger God, he told himself, peace at last!

Humming under his breath, Gray sank his fingers into her hair, drawing a swathe of it over his naked chest. The whispering weight was scarcely there, but his skin tightened at the sleek brush of sensation, and he hissed.

Her sleepy voice floated out of the dark. "What did he do, Gray? What did he do that you hate him so much?"

For a crazy moment, he was unbearably tempted, but cold, hard reason came to his rescue. She wouldn't understand; he'd be exposing his shame, his dirty secret, for nothing. Besides, the words would refuse to form in his mouth; his throat would close up and choke him. He *couldn't.*

He drifted his fingertips over her upper arm, feeling the warm, smooth flesh. "Sshh," he said. "Go to sleep." Resolutely, he shut his eyes. Surely there was no greater peace than a woman in your arms, trusting and sated, her hair spilling over your chest. Keeping loneliness at bay.

He'd been fourteen, rawboned and serious. Such a good lad, everyone said, so responsible, so studious. But they knew better, Gray and Shad. They knew Gray had stolen a kiss from Hope, the prettiest girl for miles around. They knew he dreamed of her budding breasts, bare and soft in his palms, while he rubbed himself furtively under the sheets.

But none of that was particularly unusual. Because he had Shad, Gray didn't need close friends, but he belonged to a loose circle of boys, all of whom were preoccupied with the forbidden and mysterious pleasures of the flesh. One day, Justice, his father, would speak with Hope's parents and everything would be arranged. His life mapped out ahead.

On that sunny winter's day, Gray and Shad had spent Devotions watching Hope in the pew two over, her eyes downcast, her bright hair veiled, as was proper.

Dost thou like her? he'd whispered silently to Shad.

Aye. 'Specially her bum.

Shad! That's . . . that's . . .

Truth?

Gray had smiled, his irrepressible cock twitching in his pants. *Truth,* he agreed, fixing his gaze safely on his boots.

And afterward, they'd strolled home together, the two families, the adults conversing about matters of feed and livestock, Gray and Hope walking side by side, not speaking. He'd been in a kind of exalted state, acutely, painfully aware of the sway of her hips, the smell of her skin.

The afternoon sun was at their backs, long shadows preceding them down the rutted lane, Shad's among them. The angelbark trees swayed in a brisk breeze, their trunks pale and beautiful, their branches creaking. After the storm of the previous day, the air smelled fresh and crisp, and was a little chill. When Hope smiled at him, Gray was grateful for his hip-length jacket, and not only because it kept him warm. Little Gracie had lagged behind, her cheeks rosy with the cold, hopping and skipping, playing some game only she understood.

"C'mon, Gracie," he'd called. "Keep up! We're nearly home."

Even now, he could see the mischief spark in her eyes.

Part of his punishment, this pinpoint recollection. "Race thee, slow coach. Race thee to the gate!" And she'd darted ahead.

He never knew what made him glance up. Some perverse blessing of the gods? A sound?

The ancient angelbark shading the gate swayed, the heavy branch seeming to peel away from the trunk and fall in slow motion. The air turned to glue, clinging to Gray's limbs, miring him in terror. *Gracie!* he screamed without sound.

But he wasn't close enough to reach her. No one was. Except . . .

Shad! he yelled, suddenly released. "Shad!"

A dark, elongated body barreled into Gracie, long arms wrapping around her skinny little waist, pushing her out of the way, so she sprawled headlong, the branch thudding to the ground just behind her.

An instant's silence. Then Gracie sat up in Shad's arms, took one look, and screamed like a high-pitched whistle, again and again. Gray stood stunned, his heart hammering, while the adults swept past him, shouting and exclaiming together.

Hope's mother shrieked, "A demon! Judger save us, a demon!"

15

Shad leaped to his feet and backed away, hands raised, but Father hefted his walking stick and beat at him, while Mother grabbed Gracie and held her close. But of course, hitting Shad had no effect except [illegible] him. At Gray's elbow, Hope began to pray aloud, her voice breathy with fear.

Still, he might have got away with it if it hadn't been for Shad. Gray stared into the cavernous gloom of the ballroom, blinking. Then he shifted, curling around the fire witch in his arms. She barely stirred, her body a warm presence all against his, that superlative ass pressed to his groin. Gray buried his nose in her hair and closed his eyes.

He and Shad had been everything to each other, so when Shad ran to him for comfort, he shouldn't have been surprised, but he was. Automatically, he slid an arm around Shad's waist, hugging him into his side.

Kneeling in the dirt, Mother had stared from Gray to Shad and back again, Gracie's head pressed to her bosom. Her face as pale as paper, she'd made the sign of the Scales. *"Abomination!"* she whispered. "Oh, my son. My son!"

"No! Mother, 'tis not like—" But when he'd looked into the faces ringed around him, he couldn't continue.

Father's jaw set like granite. "Get the pastor," he said to Hope's father. "And take thine womenfolk home."

"Judger help thee, Justice," said the other man, his voice cracking as he backed away. "'Tis an evil thing to have a child possessed. We'll pray."

Hope tucked herself into her mother's arm, shot Gray one horrified, reproachful look, and stumbled away, tears streaking her cheeks.

Father's big hand gripped Gray's shoulder. "Get rid of it," he grated.

"I can't!"

"Send it back to the hell thee got it from, boy."

"But I *can't*! He's my shadow!" Gray tried to free himself, but Shad clung, shaking.

"Darling?" Mother struggled to her feet, Gracie still huddled against her skirts. "For me? For thy mother? Send the abomination away."

"Mother . . ." To his horror, Gray felt his lips tremble, his eyes fill. "Shad saved Gracie's life. Doesn't that mean anything?"

"I'd rather she died than have her saved by thy dark arts," said Father, in a voice like winter iron.

Mother flinched, tears dripping slowly off her chin, her veil askew. "This is all an awful dream," she whispered. "I'll wake in a minute."

"Modesty," said Father, "pray, pray as thou hast never prayed before. We're fighting for the boy's soul here."

Gray rounded on Shad. "Go!" he hissed. "Leave me!"

Leave? Slowly, Shad relaxed his grip, stepped aside.

"Yes, leave! I don't want thee!"

Oh.

Shad drifted away down the path, until he stretched before Gray like the other afternoon shadows, the real ones, the normal ones. *Far enough?*

"No. Go right away. Disappear forever!"

Can't. The wealth of misery in the word made Gray's stomach cramp.

He swallowed. "There, see?" he pointed out. "Thou hast a shadow, too."

"Yes," said Father, "but only thine is listening to every word we say."

The short walk from the gate to the house was accomplished in a silence so wretched, it was still graven on Gray's soul. Father made him go ahead, Shad keeping pace. From behind, he heard his mother's quick breath, her muttered prayers. At one point, Gracie said, "I think Gray's clever. How—?"

"Hold thy tongue," said Father curtly.

Gracie gasped, a soft, startled "Oh!" Father never spoke harshly to her, never raised his voice.

Gray's stomach heaved.

Sorry, so sorry, whispered Shad, in a voice thick with tears.

"To thy room," said Father, crowding him up the stairs.

Gray turned, his hand on the latch. "Father, I'm sorry. Please—"

Father only shook his head and shoved him inside, but Gray saw the tears standing in his eyes.

Numbly, he sank to the narrow bed as the key turned in the lock. How could everything have changed, so quickly? His whole life turned upside down and inside out by a single instant. Gutted.

All because Shad . . . When his shadow slumped down beside him and dropped his head to Gray's shoulder, he shoved him away.

He'd thought nothing could be worse, but he was so wrong. So very wrong.

Half an hour later, he heard the rumble of masculine voices, heavy footsteps on the stairs. Ushering the pastor into the room, Father set down the armful of lanterns he carried. Bemused, Gray stared. Every lamp on the farm had to be there, even the old one they kept in the barn.

Shad clasped his hands over his head, cowering back against the wall, and the pastor hissed, making the sign of the Scales over the front of his stiff black jacket. "Judger have mercy!" Falling to his knees, he began to pray. By the time Father got every lantern lit, he was on the third repetition of the Sinner's Entreaty, and the small whitewashed room was unbearably bright.

Shad winked out and Gray breathed more freely.

The pastor rose. "Dost thou repudiate the abomination, boy?" he asked, gently enough.

Gray blinked. "Uh . . ."

"Dost thou repudiate the abomination?"

"Of course," said Gray. "I would if I could."

The pastor's jaw bunched. He turned to Father. "Justice," he said, "dost thou love thy boy enough for what must be done?"

Father said nothing, but he nodded, his throat moving as he swallowed. Gray's stomach clenched.

"Dost thou repudiate the abomination?" The pastor repeated it.

"Oh. Oh, yes," said Gray.

But the pastor only sighed. "Do it, Justice," he said. And Father snuffed out the lights, one by one, until only a single lantern burned.

Shad sprang up, seated on the bed next to Gray, his posture a slightly out-of-kilter echo.

Shit! Stop it, stop it! Go away!

Can't. So sorry, so . . .

"Father, please. He can't help it. *Please!*"

His mouth a grim line, Father lit all the lanterns again. Shad disappeared, his last whisper fading to an eerie moan. *Sorry, sorry . . .*

"There's something hideous deep in thine heart, boy," said the pastor. "Foul and wicked, a creature of the dark, spawned in sin." He put a hand on Father's rigid shoulder. "But Judger give us strength. We shall root it out of thee. For thy soul's sake."

Cenda snuffled in her sleep, her breath hot on Gray's

neck. He knew she'd seen the scars on his back, the marks of the flogging. He'd seen her eyes widen. Thank the gods she hadn't asked. What would he have said?

That they'd tried at first to be merciful, but the purge hadn't worked? Even with his bowels empty and burning, his guts cramping, Shad reappeared every time they got down to a single source of light. Starving didn't work, either. By the fourth day with nothing but water, Gray was off his head, babbling. He said whatever they wanted to hear, repeated the prayers, sang the hymns in a voice cracked with terror and an adolescent's uncertain command of pitch.

But each time, Shad betrayed him. Every single, godsbedamned time. The evil bastard couldn't even keep still long enough to be a convincing shadow, an *ordinary* one. Judger, surely Shad must realize no one had ever looked at him with such concentrated attention before. Who noticed a child's shadow? But now, for the first time in their lives, Shad was the focus of all eyes, and he'd freeze or twitch or tremble and give it all away. Gray cursed. He pleaded, begged, demanded, cajoled, even bargained. None of it made any difference, save that Shad now swung between frantic, suffocating concern and raw frustration, an overwhelming, confusing presence in Gray's head. One moment, he'd be crooning, pressing his cool, dark palm over Gray's aching belly; the next he'd snarl, *Fool, art a fool. Run, run!*

But there was nowhere to go. The door was locked. Even though the window was open, it was twenty feet from the ground. And why should he, anyway? He'd done nothing wrong. It was Shad who was the problem.

Always bloody Shad. *Fucking* Shad.

On the fifth night, he heard his mother's voice, raised in a sobbing wail. "No, Justice, no! Judger God, I beg thee." It dropped to hopeless, breathy gasps. "Not my baby, my baby . . ."

Father growled something in reply, the stairs creaked with his weight, and Gray's guts turned over. When the door opened and Father stood there, the belt gripped in his white-knuckled fist, Gray very nearly fainted.

The children of Judger's Gift were cosseted, loved. Discipline was by love and example. Father had never so much as cuffed Gray around the ear. When the first blow landed, Gray's yelp got lost in the loud cracking sound of leather on flesh. Judger, it *hurt*! He hadn't known anything could hurt so much.

After that, the memory was gone in a merciful blur. The passage of years had taken the worst of it from him. He no longer even remembered the precise number of blows. Gray stared into the darkness, thinking, his fingers drifting in a slow circle on the fire witch's smooth arm, her warm body a sleek, limp weight all along his side. Comforting.

No, not the worst. Some images would never leave him.

Looking down to see Shad, lying sprawled, skinny arms wrapped around Gray's knees, his dark head bent, shaking with sobs. The pain escalating, until his back was on fire, every nerve screaming. The moment when it finally ceased and he turned his head to see Father leaning against the wall, dry retching, his lip bloody where he'd bitten it, the tears streaming down his face and into his beard. "Judger God, son." He swayed where he stood. "The evil, root it out, I beg thee. Or the Judger's Scales condemn thy soul to everlasting torment."

Gray had nodded, unable to speak. Yes, yes. Anything.

But Father's gaze had traveled to Shad, crouched like a dog on the floor at Gray's feet. "I love thee, son," he whispered, and stepped forward, the belt swinging.

Gray cried out, and Shad surged to his feet and stood, his arms spread, shielding Gray's back with his dark body. The ultimate betrayal.

Father froze. He swallowed, his eyes stretched wide. "Pray," he rasped, making the sign of the Scales. "My son, if thou art in there somewhere, pray for thine immortal soul. I'm going for the pastor." He reeled out, slamming and locking the door behind him.

Gray sagged, subsiding into a huddle on the blood-splattered rug, so light-headed with starvation and pain, he must have passed out for a moment. Strong fingers tugged at his arm. *Get up! Run, run! Pastor will kill thee!*

Yes, he would, thought Gray, his brain foggy and slow. And the agony would be over. Good.

But Shad wouldn't let him rest. He pulled Gray to his feet and pushed him toward the open window. *C'mon. Out.*

Because the light was behind Gray, Shad's silhouette slid out past him, stretching down the wall and out across the yard. "No," Gray said aloud.

Shad painted the vision of Father's agonized face on the inside of Gray's eyelids, refusing to let him blink, look away. He added the sounds of Mother's despair.

Gray looked over his shoulder at the cozy world of his childhood, the books, his music, the bed with the patchwork quilt Mother had made, his rock collection. Everything collided inside him, guilt and fear and grief swirling and crashing, all of it overlaid with the excruciating pain of the bloody welts on his back. He had to grab his skull with both hands to stop it from exploding.

Condemned. Judger God, weighed on the great Scales and condemned. *Filth. Iniquity,* so soiled with the shadow of evil, his own mother couldn't bear to look at him. While Father—

Gray choked. He'd lost their love, thrown it away for the sake of an abomination, for Shad. *I'll never forgive thee. Never, as long as I live.*

Shad flinched, but he said nothing, reaching up from the yard with one impossibly elongated arm to hook behind Gray's neck and pull him out of the window. The veil of shadow closed over him, drowning him in the cool, slippery dark. He had the sensation of tumbling, as if he slid down a greased tunnel, Shad steadying him at the bottom. He thrashed, hitting out with a futile fist, but there was nothing tangible for him to strike.

Only Shad, pulling him to his feet in the yard, insisting, *Run, run!*

Clawing at his eyes to clear his vision of the taint of the shadow veil, Gray stumbled toward the barn. The house loomed, the dark bulk of it very quiet, lamplight streaming cheerfully from his window. *Shut up!* he snarled at Shad, lurching across the back pasture at a staggering run, heading for the road to Town.

It took him three days to reach the settlement, hiding by day and traveling by night. By the time he got there, he was delirious, the wounds on his back puffy with infection, his guts rebelling against the raw tubers he'd plucked from the fields. But for the first time, he saw the Technomages' starships, lifting from the horizon in a beautiful, soaring rush, defying gravity, and his jaw dropped.

Run, insisted Shad. *Far and fast.*

It was Shad who got them to the spaceport, darting and dodging through the alleys, hauling Gray into the shadow veil whenever anyone passed, despite his furious, feeble protests. The faithful of Judger's Gift tolerated offworlders for the vital goods they brought—the medicines, the seeds, the clever machines—but that didn't mean they approved of the ungodly. This close to midnight, only a couple of portside taverns were open, doing a desultory business. Shad gave them a wide berth, heading instead for the loading dock and the blunt-nosed starship squatting there. He hustled Gray onto a pallet of goods, wedging him into the narrow space between two crates, pulling a tarpaulin over his head. Completely beyond caring, Gray had closed his eyes and given himself to the dark.

Cenda's warm hand rested over his heart, her fingers loose in sleep. Moving slowly, Gray slid his palm over the back of it, linking their fingers. He'd spent only three months on the *DJ1952* before he'd jumped ship in Concordia, but the memory still had the power to turn his guts into a heaving, oily void. He disciplined his breathing, using the singer's exercises Erik had taught him.

Where was Scullyjon now? He'd be an old man. Was he still cheerfully molesting his cabin boys? The moment Gray had finished his first mercenary contract, he'd taken his severance pay and his bonus, and gone hunting, a grown man with murder in his heart. But there'd been no trace of the *DeeJay* and its first mate. No end to the sickness, the pain.

Gray shifted Cenda's hand down to his belly, the warmth of her flesh seeping into his skin, soothing the hollow places.

More than twenty years now, but he could still see Scullyjon's surprised, unshaven face staring down at him in the fitful light of the glowglobes in the ship's hold. Traveling from his heels to his skull, he felt the distinctive thrum of the sail winch engaging in the bowels of the ship, followed by the jerk as the first of the gossamer-thin slingshot sails was deployed.

"Well, now, what have we here?" The heavy face creased in a sly grin. "Who are you, lad?"

"I'm . . ." He wet his lips. Judger, he was hollow, a nothing, as dark and empty as his shadow. Gray, inside and out, with no more substance than ashes. "Call me Gray," he said. "I'll work for my passage, I swear."

Scullyjon hauled him out from between the crates and looked him up and down. The grin grew. "Aye, that you will." And he'd taken Gray to a small, stuffy cabin near the engine room, lit by a single dull glowglobe. He fed him, doctored his back, and let him sleep for three days straight.

Then he raped him.

16

Gray had been so innocent, he'd had no idea one man could do that to another, let alone how. After the first few seconds of utter shock and disbelief, the pain flared, and he thrashed, screaming, hitting out blindly. Scullyjon had only chuckled, breathless with pleasure, squeezed Gray's throat so hard he saw black spots, and thrust harder.

His face smeared with tears and snot, Gray stared at the shadow on the wall next to the bunk. Shad was shuddering to the harsh rhythm, too, his head thrown back, partly in agony, partly because the mate had a good grip in Gray's hair. *If it hadn't been for thee. Oh, gods, thy fault, all thy fault.*

But after Scullyjon had finished with him, that first time, it had been Shad whose hand he clutched as he curled into a fetal ball. He'd shuddered so hard, sobbed so desperately, that if it hadn't been for the grip of those dark fingers, he might have shaken himself to pieces.

Give me thy pain, whispered his shadow. *Let me help. Give the darkness, the shame, to me.*

And it seemed only right, because without Shad . . .

So he got through the first dreadful week by fleeing somewhere else, a place inside that was small and dark and huddled, far away from his abused body, his ravaged soul, his soiled shadow. But as his body became accustomed to the harsh use, the agony in his soul grew worse, not better. How had it come to this? He knew he'd been a good son, no better and no worse than any of his friends. How was it he'd been Judged so harshly on the Great Scales?

There was only one answer, one thing that made him different.

Abomination.

Even at the time, he'd been aware he was going mad. It had taken about a month. With every rape, every indignity, the pressure in his mind grew and grew. Mother and Father had begged him to put the abomination away. The Judger was merciful; if he could do it now, separate his immortal soul from the stain of his shadow, he might yet be forgiven. His old life was waiting, like a beautiful dream just over the horizon. Mother, Father, little Gracie. Even Hope . . .

But Shad wouldn't go, the shit. He fought back, begging, pleading, holding Gray tight, rubbing his back, offering comfort, companionship, love. Tempting Gray beyond bearing, making him hysterical with rage and the terror that he'd lose his chance, that he'd be trapped on the *Dee-Jay* with Scullyjon fucking him forever.

Gray hardened, pushing Shad away more brutally each day. Because surely Shad was the worst of him, the darkness in his heart. All the small, nasty thoughts, the jealousies, the rages, the dark desires—they were Shad. Bloody Shad. *Bloody, fucking* shadow. Abomination. The fissure in his soul began slowly, widening rapidly to become a fracture, a chasm.

You want the pain, the filth, the fury? he'd snarled. *Fine, fucking take it, because it's what thou art—abomination.*

And he'd thrust it all at Shad, every hideous, agonizing, shameful piece of it. Once it was done, his soul sundered, he'd find small stretches of peace, places where he could go away in his own mind, float in an echoing silence, while Scullyjon sweated and grunted over a body in a bunk. With practice, he was able to join the white spaces together, and if the first mate noticed his catamite was glassy-eyed and placid, he didn't seem to care, as long as the boy performed as instructed.

But Gray found to his horror that whenever Shad touched him, held him, the fragile peace shattered, the piercing brightness of the mental agony slashing his soul to bloody ribbons. He couldn't let Shad in without losing his mind, so he kept him at bay with furious determination.

Gray was young and healthy, after all, and he healed quickly. Delighted, Scullyjon taught him other things, shameful things. He even grew to be dully grateful that the first mate refused to share him, always ready to protect his property with his fists or a blade. Once or twice, when Scullyjon was minded to be gentle, there was pleasure that caught him unawares, made him gasp, but Gray didn't feel it. Only Shad.

He wasn't Shad. Shad wasn't him. Shad was all that was *wrong*.

Abomination.

Gray rested his chin against the top of the fire witch's skull, gazing out into the blackness. By the time he'd jumped ship, he thought he'd been as crazy as a fourteen-year-old could be. He'd sacrificed his sanity and his honor, but Judger God, he'd survived! As a mercenary, he'd fought with a reckless disregard for his own life, daring the Judger to take what he offered. A pity divinities were so fucking perverse. The Judger had obviously given up on him, so he'd curled his lip and returned the compliment.

And he'd discovered that the face and form Scullyjon had desired also attracted women. Happily, he had an innate gift for pleasuring them, thereby pleasuring himself. His instinctive desire to cherish, to protect, was a hangover from his home world he couldn't seem to shake, but when it combined with a driving compulsion to prove his manhood, he found he had more willing female flesh than he could handle. His lips curved. Ah, yes. Women and music, they'd pulled him back from the abyss.

And Shad.

In those first few years, Shad had stopped him a half dozen times, the knowing bastard, his equal in strength and guile—Gray with his hand on the *DeeJay*'s airlock or testing the point of a dagger against his throat, once at the top of the highest tower on Concordia.

Slowly, it sank in—he could never go back, never see them again. Lost, lost, forever. Alone, save for the one who'd betrayed him. Working grimly through the pain, he'd put a life of sorts together, a facsimile of a real existence.

He raised his free hand to his cheek. But he'd cried all his tears so long ago, there were none left in him.

Now all that remained was to make himself whole, to rid his soul of his personal abomination. Forever.

He looked down at the means he'd chosen, the woman in his arms, though he couldn't see her in the dark room, only feel her light, even breath against his collarbone, her trusting weight on his shoulder. The fire witch was one piece of a bigger puzzle, Deiter had said, and he couldn't solve it without her. Gods, the old scoundrel drove a hard bargain! But then no wizard or witch reached the rank of Purist without developing a ruthless streak. Still, better crafty old Deiter than the Fixer and his fucking dog. Or the Technomages in their white coats of office, sharp, shiny instruments gripped in their gloved hands.

Gooseflesh broke out over his shoulders and upper arms, tightening the skin over his nape, and he rolled his body more firmly into Cenda's, throwing an arm across her waist, inhaling the scent of her skin. Gods, she was warm! So alive.

He should be feeling steadier, surely? The first step was accomplished, the woman seduced, under his control. He'd convince her she'd be safest on Concordia. With him. But instead, everything was worse, all the conflicting emotions sharpened to razor points, a forest of evil spikes lurking in a pit. If he let himself fall . . .

Resolutely, Gray squeezed his eyes shut. He was so very tired, so weary of the whole fucking mess masquerading as his life. Counting his breaths, he drew deep, reaching for a singer's discipline. As exhaustion pulled him under, he reached up beneath the shirt to cradle the swell of Cenda's breast, feeling the steady thump of her heart against the heel of his hand.

She often dreamed of Elke, the weight of the sturdy little body on her hip, sloppy kisses on her cheek, her mouth. Every time, it was worth the pain of waking, even as it was now, the useless tears trickling over her nose and behind her ear to pool—

Cenda reared up, her heart thundering.

Luminous gray eyes gazed up at her from beneath those absurd lashes. "It's only a chest," said Gray. "I'll dry out. Weep if you want."

Chinks of light squeezed between the boards on the windows, dust motes dancing as if spotlit on the stage at The Treasure. In the fireplace, the salamander expanded, writhing happily in its fireball. If the old ballroom had looked shabby the night before, now it appeared positively derelict, the bed where they lay an island at one end of an ocean of scarred parquet flooring. Cenda scrubbed at her cheeks, her eyes growing wide. "It must have been so beautiful once," she whispered. "Before the Technomages came."

"And the tourists." Gray ran his hand up her spine, kneaded her shoulder. "You all right?"

"Yes." And she almost was. Because before Elke, the dream had been a sense-memory, so vivid she'd experienced the joy of it all over again, his lips, his hands, the hardness pumping deep inside. She'd woken in the dark, a cry trembling on her lips, her hungry sex pressed against his thigh as he slept, gone from her, fathoms deep.

And hours later, she was still pressed up against him. Sighing, she asked, "What time is it?"

"Not long after dawn." Gray tugged her down for a leisurely kiss. And another. "Mmm." Sinking his fingers into her hair, he licked a trail up her neck to the back of her ear, and she heard herself giggle. Lady, a *giggle*! Was she going insane?

His lips curved against her pulse and he murmured, "Come with me to Concordia."

Cenda stiffened with shock. Gray's lean body went very still beneath her. Lady, perhaps he hadn't meant to say it!

Slowly, she braced her hands against his chest and sat up, almost frightened of what she was going to see. But his eyes gleamed the silver color that meant he was deeply pleased about something.

"Don't you see?" he said. "It's perfect. It solves all our problems."

It took her two tries before she could speak. "Gray, I can't."

"Judger, why not? The Pures here aren't strong enough to protect you, but on Concordia, they are. Sybaris is not a good place for you to be." He tucked himself right up against her back, slipping an arm about her waist, long fingers unerringly finding her breast. As he rose, so did his shadow, until it was sitting, dark and dense, right in front of her.

Great Lady, she'd forgotten—Shad! She froze in Gray's embrace and heard the rasp of his indrawn breath.

"Shit, it's him, isn't it?" His voice hissed in her ear, low and hate-filled. "Well, I'm sorry, little witch, but I warned you. I can't get rid of him, not until—"

As the warmth of Gray's arm fell away, Shad folded his long body, leaning, down and down, until his forehead rested on her knee.

"Oh, Shad." Cenda lifted a shaking hand and stroked

the dark head, feeling the cool softness of thick hair sliding over her knuckles. She turned to meet Gray's glare full on.

"Shad won't hurt me," she said with sudden and utter certainty. Sucking in a breath, she risked a glance from under her lashes. "But you might."

Some strong feeling flickered across Gray's features, so quickly she almost missed it. His face settled into a bleak mask. "Cenda, don't say—"

"I think you will." She lifted her chin. "But the pleasure might be worth the pain."

Shad sat up, peering intently into Gray's face, and the man's stony look became more pronounced. "Then I'll apologize in advance," he said stiffly. But when he picked up her hand to press his open mouth to her palm, Gray's breath puffed warm and rapid against her skin. "Cenda, love," he said, no more than a husky murmur, "believe this, if nothing else—I'm sorrier than you'll ever know." Drawing her back against his shoulder, he rubbed his cheek against her hair. "But I'm still asking. Come with me?"

"No." Her heart was a pile of dead ash in her breast, and she was almost glad of it. A cold fire felt no pain. Wetting her lips, she forced out the words. "Don't you see? I can't leave her. Not yet."

"You mean Elke?" His arms tightened. "Ah, sweetheart." Crooning under his breath, he rocked them both. Shad patted her calf.

"She would have liked it, you know," she whispered. "That lullaby."

A pause, as if he gathered himself, and then he began, very softly.

Storm clouds gather, love,
In your eyes, in your pretty eyes.

His voice cracked, then steadied.

Cenda closed her eyes, leaning back against his shoulder. A heart of ashes. She'd taken the bright little box to the Rainbow Lakes, to the most beautiful spot she knew. It had cost all her meager savings—the dogcart, the pass for Remnant Two, the accommodation along the way. But Krysanthe had helped, Lady bless her. Still, when she'd stood on a point overlooking the still water, the box so light in her hands, it had been worth every cred. She'd waited for dawn, the multicolored light of the Dancers fading into a rainbow-shot rosiness, while the water swirled with the mysterious phosphorescent currents for which the lakes were famous.

Such a small action, a mere turn of the wrist, and Elke was gone forever, drifting away on a broad swirl of aqua shading to blue shading to indigo.

It was stupid, she knew, but how could she leave, knowing her baby was here, woven into the very fabric of Sybaris, part of its turning seasons?

Lifting Gray's hand from its resting place at her waist, she moved it to her breast, thrusting the hardening nipple into his palm. "Make me forget," she said into the sudden silence. "There's time, isn't there?"

"Cenda . . ." A pause, then, "I'll try, but—are you sure?"

Twisting in his arms, she plastered her lips against his. "Yes," she muttered savagely. "Gods, yes!" Before he could reply, she tore her mouth away and launched herself at his body, running her mouth over his shoulders and down his arms, nipping at his throat, along his collarbones. He was speaking, but the noise went over her head in a meaningless jumble. So beautiful, so hard, so *male*. Cenda licked all around a tight, dark nipple, tasting the salt of his sweat, the heat of his desire, and earned a hissing intake of breath, his fingers bunching in her hair. Obliterating the pain, erotic triumph flared within her. *Mine, all mine.*

If only for this moment.

She fumbled a hand down, brushing the head of his cock, skating her palm over the thickening length, right down over the soft, tense sac of his testicles. Gray grunted and his thighs fell open, giving her room.

With her lips, she traced the line of silky hair down his

body, all the way to his navel, licking a trail, then blowing on it to watch the gooseflesh rise, the muscles contracting beneath the skin. Slithering down between his legs, she nuzzled the inside of his thigh, inhaling male musk and running her thumb over the silky-smooth head of his cock, smearing him with his own moisture.

"Stop." The strong fingers in her hair tugged firmly. "Cenda, stop for a minute."

Five-it, what was she doing wrong? Didn't he like it? Panting, Cenda stared at what she held in her hand. Her lips curved, even as her eyes widened. Oh, yes, he liked it all right. His shaft throbbed against her palm, the blood beating hard beneath skin. The heart-shaped head was ruddy with lust, the little slit weeping, drawing her fascinated attention. What if—? She licked her lips, thinking. Barton had never managed to persuade her to do this, though he'd all but begged.

Gray froze, not even breathing.

When she glanced up, he was staring at her mouth, not blinking, his eyes the smoky dark color that she loved.

Very, very slowly, never shifting her gaze from his, she whisked her tongue over the head. Salty, a little bitter, the flesh like hot velvet, so gorgeously smooth.

Gray's mouth opened and closed, and his fingers flexed against her scalp.

"Do you like that?" she whispered, angling her head to ensure her breath puffed against the slick, wet flesh. Her hair whispered a silken caress over his hip, his thigh.

"Yes." He braced his back against the wall and spread his legs farther, making himself vulnerable, giving her his trust.

And she remembered.

Five-it! Damn it all to the seven circles of hell. No wonder he'd been trying to get her to stop. "Sorry." She whipped her hands away and put them behind her back. "I . . . forgot." Hot tears prickled behind her eyes and she willed them away. "Sorry."

"No." Gray leaned forward and seized her arm. His hips

arching up, he clamped her fingers around his girth and held them there in a hard grip. "I'll tell you when I can't take the heat anymore. Just do it, woman," he growled, "before I fucking die."

Cenda stared, her brain spinning, feeling the beat of his blood against her palm. "But you said to stop," she said shakily.

"What? Oh, yes." He grinned, fierce and wild. "The shirt. Get it off."

Her blood bubbling with a new, dark power, Cenda returned the grin in full measure. She dug the fingers of her free hand into the taut, tempting curve of his buttock. "Can't," she murmured. "My hands are full."

Immediately, dark hands slid up over her thighs and her hips, skimming her belly. Cenda gasped. Gray's brows drew down and he flicked an irritated glance over her shoulder. Long, shadowy fingers slipped the lowest button and went on to the next, knuckles brushing her skin. Great Lady, that felt . . . it felt . . .

"Don't make a fucking meal of it, Shad," Gray said through gritted teeth. But the next instant, a glint of humor lightened his eyes.

"He said something, didn't he? What did he say?"

Shad drew the shirt away and Gray's lips twitched. He considered her for a moment, his gaze dropping insolently to her mouth. "He said, 'One meal for another's only fair.' "

The blush was so fiery, Cenda felt it slide in a scorching wave from her breasts, up over her throat. Her cheeks burned. "Oh!"

Gray laughed.

Cenda muttered an invocation under her breath. Then she swooped, feeding his cock into her mouth, closing her lips over the luscious solidity of the head. Gray's laugh became a strangled gasp, and his hand fell away from hers, a clenched fist on the bed at his side.

The smooth, dense flesh quivering helplessly against her palate, the girth stretching her lips, the musky male smell of him, even the rigidity of his thighs beneath her forearms—everything told her it was pleasure she gave. Lord's balls, this was power; this was Magick! Discovering a deliciously sweet spot under the glans, Cenda rubbed the flat of her tongue over it, relishing Gray's every groan and twitch.

Lost in a kind of delirium, she gripped the root with one fist so she wouldn't choke, and licked and suckled and pulled and nibbled. Loved.

"Sweetheart, enough." Long, wonderful minutes later, he tugged gently at her hair. "Stop now, before . . . Are you listening? Cenda, stop!"

Regretfully, she levered one eye open. Every corner of the room was bright as noonday, the fireball roaring in the hearth, the salamander dancing like a mad thing. Gods, he'd left it to the absolute last minute! The tipping point between pleasure and pain must be seconds away.

Abruptly, she reared back, but a cool, dark hand pushed her calmly down again, and shadowy fingers replaced hers at the base of Gray's cock, tilting it, offering it at the perfect angle.

"No," croaked Gray, his voice barely recognizable. "Shad, don't—"

"Yes," whispered Cenda. Shad's presence was a cool veil between her and the fire, a fluid screen of twilight that gave her back control, made all things possible. Her heart gave a great, soaring leap of joy and triumph. "Great Lady, *yes*!"

Luxuriously, she slid her mouth back over Gray's shaft, savoring every throb, every hard, fat inch.

The breath whistled out from between his teeth, and his hips thrust up, helpless against the pleasure. "*Aargh!* Oh, gods, oh, fuck!"

From the corner of her eye, Cenda watched his knuckles whiten. What was it like to experience the double sensation? Shad's cool touch and the wet furnace of a fire witch's mouth? She redoubled her efforts, dismissing the ache beginning to manifest in her jaw.

Without warning, Gray leaned forward, hooked both hands under her upper arms, and hauled her off him. Ignoring her startled cry, he shifted his grip to her hips and braced her above him. "Fuck me," he growled. "Hard!"

Oh. Oh, yes. Panting, Cenda groped beneath her, but Shad's cool fingers brushed hers aside, guiding Gray's cock to the grasping, greedy little mouth of her sex. She heard Gray groan a protest. Ignored it. Her eyes slid shut as she concentrated on sinking down, impaling herself slowly, drawing out the sensation inch by excruciating inch. Vaguely, she was aware of Shad slipping a muscled arm around her ribs, a welcome support. His slick palm cradled her breast, the thumb rasping her nipple in time with the pulse thundering in her loins, where Gray's blood beat hot against hers.

Cenda whimpered. She flexed her thighs and rose, experimenting, shuddering with the delicious, fiery friction. When she dropped, Gray arched up to meet her, and she moaned as he hilted.

"More," he snarled. "Come on, little witch, give me more." A pause. "I've got her, Shad. Back off."

Gods. She found the rhythm, feeling the fire build with every luscious plunge and rise. Her fingers dug into the muscle of Gray's forearms, but all she could sense, all she could hear, was the roar of the approaching flames, a great, rolling conflagration, racing toward her like a force of nature. It bubbled beneath her skin, unstoppable. Deadly.

Cenda struggled, drowning in the firestorm, swept away like a leaf in a torrent, twisting, dizzy, helpless . . .

17

Abruptly, a lean, muscled torso pressed into Cenda's back, all along her spine. Firm, cool lips kissed her neck, her shoulder. The caresses raised gooseflesh inside as well as out, like a draft of water from the deep cistern beneath the Enclave, drunk too quickly on a summer's day. Gods, she *knew* that touch. The blaze died down, enough that she could think again.

Her eyes flew open and she turned her head, finding she was nose to nose with Shad's featureless face. She lifted a hand, seeking, needing the physical connection, and immediately, he pressed his cheek into her palm, so that she could feel the strong line of his jaw, the side of his nose.

It was the simplest thing in the world, the most inevitable, to part her lips for his seeking tongue. Her head fell back, limp as a rain-soaked flower, and Shad's hand slipped around to cradle the back of her skull. He kissed like Gray—*exactly* like Gray, the same erotic, dominating plunge and retreat. All the hair on her nape rose and she shivered, her nipples stinging as though he'd pinched them between his shadowy fingers.

As if from very far away, she heard Gray shout, "Cenda, no!" Then, "Ah, fuck!" Suddenly, he was jerking her down, hard fingers digging into her hips, hammering into her so violently Shad tightened his grip, swaying with the rhythm.

"Look at me, Cenda!"

She couldn't have done it by herself, couldn't have dragged her mouth away from Shad's dark kiss, but he cupped her face in his cool hands and eased away, with a final flickering nibble that made her whimper.

Panting, she stared down at Gray's determined, agonized face. "Come." His eyes blazed with lust and fury. He placed the pad of one finger over her aching clit. "For me!"

Shad nipped her neck. She could have imagined she felt the huff of a laughing breath against her throat, but she knew she hadn't. With both arms, he reached around her body, his fingers spreading wide over her belly, slipping down luxuriously, cool and slick over her hip bones, furrowing gently through her pubic hair until he found the lips of her sex. Ignoring Gray's warning growl, he spread them gently with his thumbs, exposing the small jut of her clit, flushed and succulent as a ripe berry, quivering beneath Gray's finger.

Cenda glanced down, and the sheer eroticism of it, the sight of their hands, so bold together on her most intimate flesh, was like a flash fire incinerating the last shred of her control. Gray pressed with his fingertip, simultaneously thrusting so deep inside her, he nudged her womb. Cenda screamed without sound, writhing. The unbearable tension shattered, Gray shouted something, and her world exploded, all hot, vicious sparks of sensation. The flames consumed her.

Cenda swayed, her eyes going wide and blank, then she collapsed over his chest, her gusty breaths hot and moist on his neck. "Oh, oh—"

"Sshh." Shakily, Gray stroked her hair, feeling the hard contraction and expansion of her ribs. His bones seemed to have turned to jelly. The aftermath of the most brutal orgasm he'd ever experienced was bad enough, but shudders ran through him soul-deep, the potential for complete dissolution utterly terrifying. Gods, what had he—what had *they*—done? He gestured at Shad, quick and curt. *Go stand by the wall.*

The shadow took his time, an insolent saunter, but he did as he was bid. Satisfaction streamed off him, so thick Gray could taste it, smooth and bittersweet as the spiced chocolat liqueur they served in high-class Concordian taverns. But Shad said nothing.

"Are you all right?" Gray asked.

Cenda moaned, and his heart stood still.

Then she raised her head, chuckling. "I pulled something in my back. I'm sure of it."

Judger be praised. "Mmm." Gray let out the breath he'd been holding. "Here?" He slid a hand down to curve over one taut, silken buttock.

"No." Cenda peeped up from beneath a forest of dark lashes, the glance an endearing combination of reproof and mischief. Reaching behind her to grab his hand, she slapped it down firmly, but higher up, above the swell of that glorious ass.

Gray heaved a theatrical sigh and let her snuggle. The knots inside him began to unravel, bit by bit. He let his eyes fall shut, walling off the uncertainties with an effort of will, allowing the postfuck lassitude full reign. After a few moments of quiet, the fire witch's hand rose to roam over his shoulder, now circling, now pressing, as if his body were a spell she must learn by heart.

Eventually, she murmured, "What do we do now?" But before he could gather his thoughts, she said, "I have to get back to the Enclave."

Well, he'd tried. Gray set his jaw. He'd try again. "Yes, I know." Cenda transferred her attention to his collarbones, tracing their complex architecture with a shy, curious touch. Gray stifled the urge to purr. "You take a nap and I'll scout a route." A pity there was no way he could leave Shad behind to keep an eye on her.

True, agreed his shadow.

Gray stroked his knuckles over the satin-soft skin at the side of her little belly and felt nerves flutter beneath the skin. "What do you fancy for breakfast, hungry one? Noodle cakes this time?"

"Uh-huh." The fire witch buried her nose in the soft pit at the base of his throat. She sighed.

Life hadn't provided him with many definitions of peace, but he thought this might be one—Cenda's limp, firm body pressed warm and boneless all along his, the sweat cooling on their skin, sealing them together, her hair a silky shawl over his chest. Shad mercifully quiet, just the quietest hum of satisfaction. Gods, it was something to savor, but time was a luxury he didn't have. The minutes passed while he floated. Just a little longer . . .

With an inward curse, Gray gently set her aside and sat up. Immediately, his skin mourned the loss of her warmth, and he shivered. Surely he remembered a similar sensation? Frowning, he sorted through the foggy landscape of sleep. Emotion and exhaustion had closed over his head like a soft sea, but hadn't she—? Yes, there'd been a moment in the dark when he'd reached out and the space beside him had been cold and empty. But then there'd been a rustle, his searching fingers had closed over her hip, and he'd pulled her back into his body.

Gray rasped a hand over his chin. "Didn't you get up?" he asked. "Sometime in the early hours?"

Cenda murmured an affirmative without opening her eyes. "I had to go."

A trickle of unease unfurled in the pit of his stomach. "To the privy?" He rose, reaching for his trews. "Did anyone see you?"

The fire witch rolled over, stifling a yawn. Sleepy golden eyes blinked at him and he got tangled up for a minute in the sweep of long, slim thighs and the sweet, dark curls springing between them. Cenda blushed and her nipples perked up. "Only a child."

Gray froze, hands on his laces. "Shit!"

She levered herself up on her elbows, the dark cloud of her hair a great inky tangle brushing the bed behind her. "A baby, Gray. No more than a mite." She swallowed hard. "So thin and hungry."

Gray's urgency drew him forward, until he was looming over her. One hand shot out and gripped her arm. "Did you speak to her? Did she see your face?"

Cenda jerked herself away. With an odd sort of dignity, she said, "I gave her the last fern-fruit cake and an oct-cred." Her jaw set. "I'm only sorry I didn't have more. Five-it, Gray, we exchanged four words, if that. I don't see—" She broke off, staring at his face.

Fuck, fuck, fuck! For a horrible instant, Shad's voice filled his head with a litany of panic. *Gods, oh, gods. Run—now, now!*

Sshh. Let me think.

Gray whirled, pouncing on his pack. He reefed out the shabby gown she'd worn last night, now woefully creased, and flung it at her. "Quick! Put this on." Disciplining himself not to fumble, he buckled the dagger harnesses around each forearm and reached for the stagehand's rough plaid shirt. But when he glanced at Cenda, she was motionless, the gown still bundled in her lap.

"But Gray, I don't under—"

"Quiet," he hissed, his ears straining. Nothing, just the faint creaks of the palazzo sagging into its old bones. Breathing a little more easily, he bent to check for the small blade in his boot. His mind leaped ahead, creating and discarding plans, sifting through possibilities. Cenda's magnificent mane was a dead giveaway. He wondered if she'd let him—

A deep, baying howl rose and lingered on the air. Then it cut off abruptly. Feet pattered past the door and away, the sound fading rapidly. An outer door banged and a man's voice spoke sharply.

Judger, they were fucked!

"The dog!" All the blood drained from Cenda's face, until even her lips went white. A moment's frozen terror, and she was scrambling into the gown, groping for her boots.

"C'mon!" Gray grabbed his instrument case with one hand and Cenda with the other, dragging the fire witch the length of the ballroom at a stumbling run.

The baying drew nearer, but now it was accompanied by an eerie, booming echo. Shit, the Fixer's men were in the building!

A splintering crash and the door burst open, the dog surging through, towing the bald thug in its wake. Another three men followed more cautiously, fanning out in a wary semicircle. Two of them bore armfuls of what looked like heavy sacking. Gray glanced at the steady drips spotting floor at their feet. *Wet* sacking. The Fixer wasn't stupid.

As if the thought had conjured him, the Fixer strolled through the door. He spread his legs, folded his hands behind his back, and cocked his head. Cenda's hand clutched the back of Gray's shirt in a trembling grip.

"Thinkin' t' cheat me, were ye, laddie?"

"No." Gray took a step backward, pulling Cenda with him, until their backs were pressed to the last of the boarded-up windows. He reached behind him, feeling for the edge of the boards he'd loosened when he'd hired the room. There was something to be said for a career as an itinerant musician. Gray and Erik had the art of getting out of town down to a precise science.

The dog lunged against the chain, its eyes pale and mad. It didn't bark. Instead, a low, continuous growl rumbled in its throat, its muzzle peeling back to show the gleam of wet teeth right up to the gums.

Calmly, Gray met the Fixer's flat brown gaze, praying the man was arrogant enough to dismiss the trembling fire witch as a negligible threat. "I never intended to give her to you."

The Fixer shrugged. He didn't look particularly surprised.

"Have it yer own way." He gestured to the men with the sacking, the novarine in his ring flashing a solid black. "T' witch is yours, lads." Nodding at the dog, he said, "Let 'im loose."

Baldy grinned, bent, and slipped the chain.

The animal launched itself across the parquet floor, its powerful hindquarters bunching, nails clacking loudly. The sack carriers darted forward, poised to throw.

Gray seized Cenda by the waist and shoved her away from him with all his strength, toward the opposite side of the room. The two men cursed and swerved to intercept her. One flung a sack, catching her shoulder, tangling one arm.

"Gray!" Her shriek piercing his skull, he spun around just as the dog barreled past his leg, ripping his trews at the thigh. He felt its hot breath on his flesh, the slime of warm spittle soaking the fabric.

Judger!

The forearm blade fell into his hand, and he flipped it neatly into the dog's hulking shoulder, deep into the flexing muscle. The animal yelped, but this was Sybaris, where dogs were bred for the ring. Pain would only madden it. Lowering its head, it stalked him, warier now, the milky eyes still glowing. The dagger dropped from the wound with a tinny clatter, startlingly loud. Bright blood dripped, beading on dirty white fur.

Somewhere on his left, Cenda screamed and a man grunted something vile, but Gray didn't dare take his eye from the dog. At the far end of the room, the Fixer's placid smile broadened, Baldy looming at his shoulder. "Good lads," he murmured, and Gray's heart sank. They must have her, then, wrapped up tight in those filthy, sodden sacks.

The Fixer put his hands on his hips. "This'll be good." He raised his voice. "Kill 'im, Tiny!"

"No, gods, no!" Cenda's voice was thin and tight. "I'll come with you, I promise. I—"

The bald man threw his head back and laughed aloud.

"Lady, oh, Great Lady." At first no more than a sobbing thread, it grew louder with each repetition.

A man swore, something uneasy in his tone.

Gray shifted around, trying to work his way back to the blade on the floor, the dog flanking him, keeping pace. Strange, the room was growing brighter, as bright as noonday. His head was full of crackling, roaring.

Cenda. *Fuck!*

Grabbing the knife, he glanced up in time to see the sacks shrouding her burst into flame, the pattern of the coarse weft brightly illuminated for an instant before it crisped and blackened. The two men holding her leaped back, shouting, and the dog launched itself into space, straight at Gray's throat.

Everything blurred. He got the blade up, barely in time, bracing himself for the impact. Judger, he'd tear the bastard's fucking throat out with his teeth if he had to!

Cenda screamed, not shrill with fear, but solidly from the gut, with a desperate, burning rage. A streak of fire sailed through the air between Gray and the dog. He thought he glimpsed a salamander leaning forward, riding the flame, its fiery mouth agape. When it hit the center of the dog's chest, the animal reared back, howling, twisting in midair. An endless second later, it thudded to the floor. There, it writhed and snapped, contorting itself into impossible positions, chasing the rills of flame scudding through its fur.

Gray looked up, and the breath caught in his throat with awe and terror.

Holy Judger God, she was like something from the seventh circle of hell, the goddess of wrath incarnate, deadly in her fiery beauty. She was advancing steadily, her golden eyes burning like embers in a face gray as ash. Her hair streamed around her as if in an unseen wind, crackling with energy. Her right hand was extended, the arm wreathed in flame to the shoulder.

Behind her, one man rolled over and over, tearing at his flaming clothes, uttering shrill, rasping shrieks. But the second staggered to his feet, pulling a short wooden bludgeon from his belt. His other arm hung useless by his side, a scorched ruin. Lips pulling back from his teeth, he lifted the weapon and brought it down in a blurring arc, toward Cenda's unprotected head.

Gray's dagger flickered past the fire witch's shoulder, a wicked slice of lightning. It caught the man under the ear with a meaty *thunk*, and he gave a gurgling cry, his eyes going wide and dark. He dropped, the bludgeon falling from his limp fingers, and a dark shadow swooped over him, steely fingers sinking into his throat.

Gray continued his forward momentum, diving to the floor and rolling aside as an armored fist struck the point of his left shoulder. The blow numbed his entire arm. Judger, it hurt! Clearly no stranger to street brawling, the Fixer stood over him, brass knuckles swinging. He was no longer smiling. Shit, that had been intended to crush his temple. Gray's eyes narrowed, even as he gripped his shoulder. How long had it been since the Fixer had done his own dirty work?

And fuck, where was Baldy, the dog handler?

"Bitch!" The thug glared at Cenda across the dog's twitching, whimpering body. Whole sections of fur had fallen away, the skin burned and black beneath it. Tears stood in the man's eyes. Slowly, he rose, a short sword with a curving blade in his big fist. "Fookin' bitch."

Cenda simply stared, her shoulders sagging, all the bright fire dead, waiting for the bastard to kill her. Gray could see every grief, every pain and failure graven on her face, her pretty eyes gone all dull and dark.

The Fixer threw himself at Gray, fists flailing, but Gray hurled himself toward Cenda in a desperate gamble. He reached her a fraction ahead of Baldy and thrust her behind him. Baldy glanced at the useless arm Gray was cradling across his stomach and grinned. "Ye first, then." He hefted his blade in a businesslike manner and lunged.

Gray didn't bother with the courtesies. When he'd been a mercenary, his first sergeant-at-arms had insisted every recruit learn to fight with two blades. Not for the first time, he blessed the vicious old bastard. Being left-handed gave a man an advantage, but being ambidextrous made that advantage unfair. Smoothly, Gray drew his remaining dagger and stepped inside the man's lunge.

The risk didn't entirely come off. Baldy scored a long slice across his ribs, the sharp edge burning like ice, but Gray shoved his point up under the man's sternum, twisting and gouging with everything he had. Baldy gave a choking grunt. He swayed. Gray stepped aside and let him fall.

"Don't move, son." Almost lovingly, the Fixer pressed Cenda into his body. He stood behind her, one arm across her throat, the other fist rammed into her neck, a short spike protruding from the knuckledusters, just beneath her ear. A trickle of blood ran down her neck, shockingly bright against the skin. "Ye listenin'?"

His guts heaving, Gray grunted assent. When he touched his side, his fingers came away bloody. Cenda whimpered.

In his head, Shad moaned, *Hurt, oh, hurt.*

No, I'm all right. Sshh, now. Concentrate. Help me.

Yes. Her. Save her.

"Reach inta me right-hand pocket, lass." The Fixer jerked her closer and she choked, coming up on her tiptoes. "Nice 'n' easy-like. Fetch me whistle out."

Wincing, Gray straightened. "A whistle? What for?" he asked, although he had a sinking feeling he could guess. The Fixer was a careful man; there'd be reinforcements waiting outside, guarding the perimeters.

"I'm thinkin' t' Technomage'll be mighty pleased wit' a pair."

"Why?" whispered Cenda, and she laid her fingers lightly over the knuckleduster. Her eyes glinted gold.

"A bonus, like. So she can kill him herself." The Fixer chuckled. "Wit' Science. They say it takes 'n endless time." He gave Cenda a shake. "Git on wit' it, lass."

"Kill him?" Slowly, she tightened her fingers over the Fixer's. Her right hand fumbled and patted, as she searched for the pocket.

Shad quivered. He lifted a dusky arm, stretching, reaching . . .

No!

Shad paused.

Wait, wait for her.

Slowly, Shad let the arm fall, but he took a step closer.

The Fixer shifted his feet, frowning. "Yah. Though I'm fair tempted meself." He shot a dark glance across the room at the bodies of his men. Only the dog still moved, and that feebly, to a constant high-pitched whine. For the first time, Gray registered the smell of burned flesh and fur and fabric. His guts heaved. He swallowed.

"No," said the fire witch. Then more strongly, "Five-it, no, I won't let you!"

Abruptly, her fingers clenched over the metal knuckles and the Fixer grunted. Then his face contorted, his mouth stretching wide in a full-blooded scream. Gaping, Gray watched the metal heat 'til it ran, flowing and dripping. It seared into the man's skin, boiling flesh and settling into bone. Gods, it must be excruciating! The Fixer shoved Cenda away to flail about the room, stumbling into the bed, careering off the walls, shrieking, shaking his hand. A small blaze broke out in the mattress, spread to the dusty hangings.

The novarine ring flew across the room in a flashing arc, rattling to a rocking halt at Gray's feet. Automatically, he bent and picked it up, hurting his wounded side and singeing his fingers. Judger! "Here." He tossed it to Cenda and she caught it awkwardly, but with no evidence of discomfort. "C'mon." Grabbing her arm, he dragged her back to the last window, Shad running ahead of them along the wall.

"But—" She turned to survey the carnage. Flames devoured the box-table, licked a hungry path toward the ceiling. Smoke billowed, obscuring the stumbling figure of the Fixer, reeling in crazed circles. "We can't—" The words were almost drowned by a series of sharp, echoing reports. Something solid fell with a shattering crash.

"Yes, we can." One-handed, Gray tugged at the loosened boards, feeling the blood trickling over his ribs, all the nerves in his shoulder shrieking a protest. "The place is a tinderbox." The last board came away. Gray seized his instrument case, still mercifully untouched, and shoved it at Cenda. "Hold the Duchess."

"But Gray—"

A wave of supercharged heat rolled toward them. The hair at Gray's nape crisped, and the fire roared like a hot breath straight from hell. He didn't give her a chance to speak again. Slipping his good arm around her waist, he hurled her out the window.

18

The world was full of dust and sparks, and screaming. Cenda landed on a sagging canvas awning, her arms flying over her head. A split second later, Gray arrived beside her in a cursing flurry. The fabric split under their combined weight, tumbling them into a pile of fusty rugs. A woman's voice shrieked in her ear, "Geroff me goods, ye daft buggers!" Wiry fingers tugged urgently at her arm.

So they weren't dead, after all. Cenda scrambled to her feet, scooping up Gray's harp from the corner of what was apparently a rug seller's stall. "Sorry," she muttered automatically, brushing at her skirts. "We—"

"No time." Gray's fingers locked around her wrist. "The palazzo's going up," he snapped at the rug seller. "Run!"

The next moment, Cenda found herself pelting down the alley, towed helplessly in Gray's wake. At the corner of the block, he stopped and caught her by the shoulders, spinning her around. "Look, fire witch," he panted. "Look what you did."

The voice of the fire was obscenely loud, a great, leering

roar punctuated by booms and bangs. She'd had no idea it would sound like that, like a huge choir singing a crackling song she could almost understand. Tongues of flame burst from the windows and snaked their way to the roof, reaching for the sky as if they could lick it to death, too. Lady save her, if she looked closely, she could see salamanders dancing, some of them twenty feet from nose to tail. Smoke and cinders rose in writhing columns, burning flakes of ash falling on the people in the street. They ran in all directions, some toward the conflagration, some away from it, their mouths gaping with insect cries, arms flapping.

Great Lady, what had she done? Her mind reeling, she whispered, "They were going to kill you."

The flinty look in Gray's eyes softened. "Yes, I know. You were wonderful, Cenda. Amazing." Wincing, he pressed a palm over the blood on his side. He peered into her face. "Are you all right? Answer me!"

The stench of roasted flesh lingered in her nose. Suffocating, hideous. She'd killed, *killed* . . . Oh, gods, her daughter's life had been the price she'd paid for the gift of death. Black spots swarmed before Cenda's eyes and her stomach heaved itself into her throat. Bending over the gutter, she was violently ill.

Vaguely, she was aware of Gray patting her back, making awkward, soothing noises. When she was able to focus again, she rubbed her remaining sleeve over her mouth. Leaning heavily on his good arm, she struggled to her feet. She hadn't even realized she'd slipped to her knees. "Take me home," she said huskily. "Please." Her head swam.

"Fookin' 'ell."

The boy stood a few feet away, well out of arm's reach. "Mistress—" He took a half step forward, then checked, shooting Gray a wary glance from under his matted fringe.

Gray raised a brow. "You want to help?" he asked, his voice curt.

Slop shifted from one bare, dirty foot to the other. Backing away, he shook his head.

"He's dead." Cenda leaned back into Gray's shoulder. "I—" Her throat hurt as if it were coated with something vile. Ashes? "I killed him." She stared over the boy's head at the tower of flame, very nearly as high as the Technomage Towers. "In there."

Slop's dark eyes went very round. "Nah," he said. "Not t' Fixer."

Cenda reached into the pocket of her skirt and withdrew the novarine ring.

The boy uttered a small, yelping cry, like a startled puppy.

Frowning, she rubbed it with her thumb. The gold setting had fused into a solid lump, but nothing could tarnish its smooth yellow glitter. Sullen and beautiful, the novarine gleamed, its dark-star heart unaffected by the inferno, impervious to human pain.

"Not here." Gray's hand enveloped hers, curling her fingers into a fist. The light winked out. He glanced at the boy. "Stay with her while I get a dogcart." He slid around the corner and disappeared.

Cenda slipped the ring back into her pocket and held out her hand. "Come on," she said, sinking wearily to a low wall. Gods, she wanted to curl into a ball and die, but she couldn't leave the child to stand by himself in the street, that strange expression on his face. Reaching up, she caught Slop's hand and drew him down beside her.

The boy flinched, pulling away, and she saw she'd grabbed at the hand with the stiff finger.

"Sorry. Did I hurt you?"

"Nah." Slop settled beside her, leaving a good foot of soot-speckled wall between them, his back ramrod straight.

"Someone broke it, didn't they?"

Slop said nothing. He stared at his grimy toes.

"Was it the Fixer?"

"Nah."

"Oh." They sat in silence, watching people rush to and fro, a few more energetic souls forming a ragged bucket brigade while others stood openmouthed, entranced by the excitement of disaster on such an enormous scale.

Cenda seized a hank of her hair and began to braid, concentrating fiercely on the familiar rhythm. She wasn't even singed, though her right sleeve was burned completely away.

"Me mam."

"What?" Five-it, why had she bothered? She didn't have anything to tie it with.

Slop lifted a dirty hand, the smallest finger askew, and let it drop.

"Your mother?"

"Yah. But she didn't mean it."

"Gods." Would this day never end? Cenda trembled, fighting the impulse to reach out and gather the child into her arms. He wouldn't welcome it, she knew. Blinking hard, she asked, "What's your name?"

He shot her a suspicious glance. "Ye know it. Slop."

She shook her head. "Your real name."

The boy stiffened. "How do ye know it isn't Slop?"

Cenda pushed her hair out of her face. "I'm a witch, even though I'm not . . . a very good one. True Names are important."

"Ye'll laugh."

"Try me."

He inched closer, until he was practically sitting on her skirt. Lord's balls, he stank. The cynical, streetwise gaze studied her face, cataloging every feature. He must have her total worth summed up to the last oct-cred.

Finally, he ducked his head. "Florien," he muttered into his ragged shirt.

"Ah." Cenda clasped her hands around her knees. "Florien, my dear," she said. "I'm going home to the Enclave and I'm never coming out again as long as I live. Would you like to come with me?"

"What fer? I ain't no witch."

"You could"—she hitched—"I don't know. Eat? Stay for a little. There'd be work for you."

"Do I hev to wash?"

"Yes," she said, and watched him think about it.

"Fookin' 'ell."

But when Gray arrived with a shabby dogcart and a villainous-looking driver, he hopped on board with surprising alacrity.

Gray got the dogcart to drop them three blocks from the Enclave, mistrusting the glint in the man's dark eyes. Cenda wove an unsteady, purposeful way through the last of the back alleys, the boy a watchful presence at her side. Gray frowned. They'd obviously come to some sort of accommodation, and he wasn't sure he liked it. The fire witch's face was as white as paper, her eyes surrounded by shadows as dark as bruises. She didn't have the energy to spare for beggar boys.

" 'Tis warded, Mistress." The boy stared at the dense, prickly wall of green in front of them. Twenty feet high, the hedge of Lady's lace stretched the length of the street and all around the Wizards' Enclave, screening it from the gaze of the Sybarite unwashed. The perfumed bellflowers tinkled very faintly, an ethereal harmony almost below the threshold of hearing. But flanking each exquisite, blush pink flower was a pair of two-inch thorns, hard, curved, and wickedly barbed. Like the Lady Herself, thought Gray, beauty sharp enough to pierce a man to the heart.

"Yes, dear, I know." Cenda sent the lad a shaky, sidelong smile. Her hand brushed his shoulder, then fell away. "But there's a place"—she stepped forward, her nose inches from the waiting thorns—"a seam in the spell. The young ones use it to sneak in after curfew." She tilted her head to one side, frowning.

Gray frowned, too. There was nothing to see and Cenda was out on her feet. "The boy can go around to the gate with a message," he said. "Who should he ask for?"

"No!" It came out a near shout. Swallowing, Cenda moderated her tone. "Don't you see?" she said. "I couldn't stand . . . the fuss. Purist Olga's the gatekeeper, and once she sees us, I'll have to explain. She'll demand every detail. This way brings us out near the infirmary. And Krysanthe." She flicked a worried gaze at the blood on his shirt. "You need a healer."

Ah, well, he'd had worse, though the slice stung like a bitch and his shoulder was still half-numb. He flexed it, wincing. Krysanthe? Gray searched his memory. Ah, yes, the woman who'd accompanied Cenda to The Treasure that first night. A lifetime ago.

"It's right here. I can see the place," she muttered. "But if I try, I'll just burn a huge hole." The fire witch rubbed fretfully at her brow. "Five-it, a first-year can do this rolling drunk. Why can't I?"

"Send t' beastie," suggested the boy. He gestured at Cenda's dark hair, where the salamander nestled, as bright as a new coin, seemingly none the worse for its adventures.

"No." Gray grasped her wrist, feeling her tremble. Gods, she was balanced on such a precarious edge, she'd likely incinerate the hedge all the way around the Enclave.

Tears coming now, murmured Shad from where he crouched at Gray's feet, squat and blocky in the morning sun.

[illegible]

We could . . . help . . .

No, said Gray automatically, but even as he formed the mental response, he was moving. Casually, he shifted position so that Shad's dark shape fell across the skirts of the witch's gown, mingling with her own shadow on the cracked pavement.

"Try now," he said.

Cenda glanced down, then lifted a startled gold brown gaze to his.

"Go on," he murmured, his heart beating uncomfortably fast.

The fire witch inhaled, squeezed her eyes shut, and reached out with one hand. A thin line of fire formed under her fingertip, crisping and blackening the vegetation. With it, she drew a narrow oval. The space inside had an odd shimmer, as if the air there were superheated. Halfway through, Gray moved discreetly aside, taking Shad with him.

Immediately, Cenda frowned ferociously and opened her eyes.

Gray brushed a curl from off her cheek. "Keep going."

Cenda pressed her lips together and lifted a shaking hand. The line of fire reappeared. It was a trifle wobbly, but she completed the oval.

She looked from Gray to Shad and back again. "Oh," she said. "Thank you." Stepping forward, she curled her fingers into each side of the oval, avoiding the thorns, and pulled the quivering space open to reveal the back wall of a stone building. Slipping though the narrow aperture, she reached a hand back for Slop. "Come on." After Gray followed, she smoothed the edges back, whispering something under her breath. The hedge rustled violently, but the gap closed over as if it had never been, save for a few charred leaves on the ground.

They stood on a flagged path that ran along the back of an elegant stone building. To one side stood a neat structure that looked like a garden shed. The walkway was flanked by narrow beds of tall, silvery reeds that sighed in the light breeze. Gray could hear the rhythmic murmur of voices, though there was no one to be seen. It sounded like a chant, half-spoken, half-sung.

"This way." Cenda opened a small door in the back wall of the building and stuck her head around it. "In here." She disappeared inside.

The room they entered was completely circular, the walls lined with shelves crowded with bottles and jars and pots and boxes, all labeled in the same neat hand. A bench ran all the way around, and on it were mortars and pestles and chopping boards and tubs full of strange plants and knobby roots and tubers. Out of the corner of his eye, Gray watched Slop's nimble fingers close surreptitiously over the handle of a small peeling knife, but he said nothing. The blade vanished as if by Magick.

"This is the still room," whispered the fire witch. "Krys should be in her study."

But of course she wasn't. Gray took Cenda's hand, but she was shaking so hard, he put his arm around her shoulders and hugged her into his good side. What she needed was a good square meal, two or three of them, a bath, and twelve hours horizontal. And so did he. Taking in the study with one comprehensive glance, he decided the daybed under the window looked mighty tempting, but its worn crimson brocade was nearly obscured by unsteady towers of books and papers.

If the still room had been organized chaos, the healer's study was chaos, plain and simple. Krysanthe must be a formidable researcher. Gods, she read enough! Dust motes danced in the sunbeams that streamed in through the open shutters, spotlighting the wizardly tomes heaped on the desk, gleaming on a rectangle of something slick and pale. Familiar. Frowning, Gray ran a finger over it. Technomagery. Why—?

"Cenda!"

A small, plump woman stood in the doorway. The cloth she must have been using to dry her hands fluttered to the floor as she enveloped the fire witch in a hug, thick salt-and-pepper plaits bouncing on her shoulders. "Oh, my dear." She grasped both Cenda's hands and held her at arm's length for a rapid inspection. "I've been so worried. Where have you been? Great Lady, look at you!" She fingered the charred remains of Cenda's right sleeve, shot a sharp glance at the salamander in her hair. "What in the world—?" She frowned at Gray's bloodstained shirt and turned back to Cenda, gripping her shoulders. "Five-it, you're not hurt?"

Gently, Cenda removed the healer's hands. "I'm fine, though Gray needs your skill. It's a long story." Her mouth twisted. "But I've been doing what you wanted." She flapped a hand in Gray's direction, flushing. "With him."

"The Duke of Ombra." The woman favored him with a cool, measuring glance, not without an element of frank appreciation. "I am Purist Krysanthe."

"We've met." Gray gave her the sketchiest of bows. "And believe me, I didn't do anything she didn't want."

Cenda went scarlet and Krysanthe grinned, her dark eyes sparkling. "I can hardly wait to hear." Her gaze fell on the boy's skinny person and her lips tightened. "And this one?"

Cenda drew a reluctant Slop forward and laid her hands on his shoulders. "This is Florien," she said. "He helped."

"That's as may be." Wrinkling her nose, Krysanthe regarded the boy with disfavor. "But you don't have time for beggar boys now."

The healer's words echoed Gray's earlier thoughts so uncannily that he blinked. And Florien? Who was Florien?

The lad stiffened and his mouth moved, though no sound emerged. "Fook you," he'd said. Gray suppressed a smile.

Cenda's fingers tightened on the boy's shoulders. "I'll make time. It's not like you to be uncharitable, Krys."

To her credit, the woman flushed. "Sorry. I—" The healer rummaged in the chatelaine around her ample waist and came up with a key. When she tossed it to Gray, he caught it one-handed. "Hmm," said the healer, her dark eyes intent. "You're moving all right. Not light-headed?"

"No."

"Show me the wound."

Gingerly, Gray lifted the shirt, hissing as the fabric pulled at the dried blood. The slash was several inches long; Baldy's blade had skidded off his ribs.

"I'll stitch it for you after you've bathed," said the healer briskly. "What about that shoulder? Can you feel your fingers?"

Gray wiggled them. "It's improving."

"Good." Krysanthe put an arm around Cenda's waist, and the fire witch sagged into her hold with a sigh. Over her shoulder, the healer said, "If you go to the end of the passage and turn right, you'll find a bathing chamber. Take the boy with you, and for the Lady's sake, get the stink off him."

She shepherded Cenda toward the door. "Come on, dear. Let me check you over, and then you can bathe and change. Matthaeus will want to see you." The fire witch didn't look back. Thick with curiosity, Krysanthe's voice floated down the hall as the two women walked away. "You used your Magick, didn't you?" It dropped a tone. "Oh, Cenda, was it good?"

Shad stirred against the wall, murky and indistinct inside the diffusely lit room. *Don't like her.* His voice was faint, but clear.

Gray snorted. *You're just jealous.*

He glanced up in time to see Slop's bony rump halfway out a window. "Hey!" Gray pounced, latching on to a thin ankle and hauling him back. "Where do you think you're going?" He gave the boy a gentle shake.

"Don' like her," muttered Slop. Interesting, that made it pretty well unanimous. "Not gunna fookin' wash."

Gray grabbed him by the collar and marched him to the door. "Yes, *Florien*, you fookin' are."

19

In the women's bathing chamber, Cenda let her soot-stained gown puddle at her feet. Lady, she was so overloaded with sensation, she'd gone beyond feeling—except for an all-pervasive sense of disaster hovering at her shoulder, a tangible presence poised to strike.

"Great Lady, you're covered in bruises," said Krysanthe, her voice sharp. "And what's that on your neck?"

"I'm all right," said Cenda dully. But when she took the first step down into the sunken bath, she wobbled. Immediately, Krysanthe's strong arm was there, and she clutched it gratefully.

"He hurt you, the smooth bastard. Lord's balls, he didn't—?" Her friend's plump little body stiffened, her dark eyes snapping. "I'll kill him, I swear."

"No." Cenda flushed, feeling the healer's searching gaze travel over the beard burn on her breasts, the purple marks where Gray's fingers had gripped her hips in his passion. Hastily, she took the final few steps and sank into the steaming water, flinching as every cut and scrape on her body sprang to stinging life. The salamander in her hair hissed in outrage and scuttled up to the very crown of her head. "It wasn't like that."

"Oh, yes?" The other woman raised a brow. Peering at Cenda's huddled body in the water, she smirked. "So what *was* it like? C'mon, indulge me."

"Krys, you don't understand."

"Try me. Was he good?"

"No, no!" cried Cenda. The words stuck in her throat, barbed with guilt and pain. "I killed a man. With Magick."

The healer froze in the act of bending to take a small vial from a cupboard. Straightening, she spun around. "You what?"

"With the Lady's gift." Burning tears rolled down Cenda's cheeks and plopped into the water. "The gift I didn't want, the Magick that cost me the most precious life in the world." She choked. "I used it for death."

Krysanthe's dark eyes opened very wide, then narrowed, intent. "You're that strong?"

"What does it matter? They were going to—going to"—she gulped—"kill him. And I—I—" Squeezing her eyes shut, she remembered how she'd channeled all her rage and terror into that fireball and *flung* it, using nothing but her will, the dog screaming, the Fixer shouting, the molten metal searing, skin crisping. The disgusting smell. Oh, gods. Though there was nothing left in her stomach, it revolted, and she doubled over, retching.

Strong hands grasped her shoulders, gave her a brisk shake. "You can go to pieces later, sweetheart. Who were these people? And tell me what you did—*exactly*. It's important."

Cenda gripped the healer's wrists, dragging in huge breaths of the warm, moist air. Opening her eyes and looking into Krysanthe's tense face took a tremendous effort. The other woman knelt on the damp floor, heedless of the water soaking her skirts. "It was a man called the Fixer. He said he had a"—the word clogged in her throat—"a *buyer* for me. As if I was . . . was a . . ." She flapped a hand, helpless with the horror of it.

"A commodity," supplied the healer, her voice tight and hard. "A tool, a weapon. Lady save us, Matthaeus said this would happen." She thought for a moment. "And the Duke of Ombra? They wanted to kill him?"

"Yes," whispered Cenda, remembering a genial voice. *Thinkin' t' cheat me, were ye, laddie?* But she said nothing. He'd sworn he wouldn't give her to the Fixer, and his word had been good. He'd very nearly died to make it so.

"No witnesses," said Krys grimly. "So what about the boy?"

"He came later. He just"—Cenda shrugged—"got attached."

The healer tipped a blue liquid from the vial onto a folded cloth. "Hmm. Well, don't you get attached to him. Turn your head." She pressed the pad against the wound on Cenda's neck.

Cenda jerked. "That hurts!" Oh, gods, the spike on the knuckleduster. The stupid tears welled again.

"I know. Hold still. It's deep enough to get infected if I don't cleanse it."

"Cenda!" The door banged back to reveal Gray, barechested and barefoot, a slim blade gleaming like frost-fire in his hand. The slash over his ribs dripped pink with blood and water.

Krysanthe sprang to her feet, shielding Cenda with her body. She put a hand to her chatelaine.

"No!" Heedless of her nudity, Cenda rose and grabbed her friend's elbow. "Krys, don't! Gray, I'm all right, truly."

He didn't lower the knife. "You cried out." The winter fury in his gaze was focused on the healer. "In pain. I heard you."

"Allow me to know my own business," said the healer in arctic accents. "The cleansing potion stings, but it's necessary." She cast a scathing glance at the cloth floating in the water and rummaged in the cupboard again. "The Lady knows what filth was on their weapons. Here."

Cenda took another pad, sank back into the water, and pressed it to her neck, willing herself not to flinch.

Krysanthe tilted her head to one side, studying Gray. Her lips curved, very slightly. "And one for you, Duke." She held out the cloth.

The damp air sizzled with challenge. Gods, the only two people on Sybaris whom Cenda cared anything about, and they didn't like each other. "Just take it," she said wearily.

Slowly, he sheathed the knife and reached for the cloth. With his hair wet and slicked back, the stark beauty of his features was startlingly apparent, though he looked older, and brutally tired. When he applied the pad to his side, his lips tightened, but all he said was, "You'd do better to get her something to eat."

"Hmm." The healer pulled one plait forward over her shoulder and played with the end. "I'll send Tai Yang. He knows how to keep his mouth shut. Where's that boy?"

Slop—no, *Florien*, she must remember—eeled out from behind Gray's legs. Cenda slipped farther into the water and crossed her arms over her breasts. Lady, why not sell tickets? Knowing if she started, she wouldn't stop, she fought back a wave of giggles.

The child looked lost in the stagehand's cheerful plaid shirt, the sleeves rolled up many times, the hem brushing his skinny calves. His hair stood up in tufts all over his head, as though ruthless fingers had tugged at it. Even well scrubbed, he wasn't prepossessing, with his pointed little chin and broad forehead. Though his face was clean enough, it was dark with offense.

Krysanthe snorted. "Great Lady!" She grinned.

"Not fookin' funny."

"Watch your mouth, young man." The healer bustled to the door, snagging Florien's ear between two fingers on the way. "You can come with me." She hauled him out the door.

They heard the boy's shrill protests fade away down the passage. Another door banged.

Gray leaned against the wall in the four-bed infirmary. The Pures were obviously a healthy lot. There'd been no patients, though all the beds were neatly made up, the covers pulled so tight and square they practically saluted. His mother used to make the beds like that and, strangely enough, so did his old sergeant-at-arms.

Now, though, Cenda sat on the side of one bed, the healer right next to her with an arm firmly around her waist. The old crone from the gate perched on another, her black eyes snapping with excitement. Squarely on the pillow beside her, a big tabby cat sat bolt upright, regarding the proceedings with a regal air. Purist Olga and Titfer.

Purist Matthaeus paced slowly up and down the central aisle, hands folded together in the sleeves of his plain black robe. Unlike any wizard Gray had ever met, he was clean shaven, his spare body fit and wiry, though the hair on his head was snowy white and thinning.

The air crackled with tension, though Gray suspected there was a fair dose of Magick in it as well. He had no doubt this was a council of war, the strangest one he'd ever witnessed. Judger be praised, they hadn't excluded him, though he thought they might try later, after his usefulness as a witness was over. He set his jaw. They could try.

He glanced at Shad, barely there, spilling onto the flagged floor at his feet. *One wrong move from you, and we're dead. Got it?*

Up yours.

Gray let out a careful breath. *Fine.*

Purist Matthaeus came to a halt. He fixed a chilly blue gaze on the healer. "Purist Krysanthe," he said formally, "do you vouch for Tai Yang?"

Krysanthe turned her head to smile at the handsome young man standing near the shuttered window. The light reflected off his spectacles as he shifted, concealing the intensity of his dark almond eyes. "Oh, yes," she said. "His loyalty is absolute."

It had been Tai Yang who'd arrived at the bathing chamber with a basket of food. Fortunately, Gray had finished helping Cenda wash the smoke smell out of her hair, though she'd had to coax the offended salamander onto a soap dish so he could do it. When Krysanthe's apprentice had seen the fire witch, dressed once more in the tattered, filthy gown, her hair drying in a cloud of steam, he'd gaped. Then he'd shut his mouth with a snap and said only, "I'll find something else for you to wear." His gaze skimmed over Gray, clad only in his trews. "Both of you."

And he'd been as good as his word. Now Cenda was dressed in the same tunic and leggings she'd worn to The Treasure, and Gray had a blue shirt and a pair of well-worn trews. He suspected they were Tai Yang's own. They were much of a size.

"Very well." Matthaeus turned to Cenda. "From the beginning," he said. "Every detail."

Gray only half heard the fire witch's soft, halting voice, the Purist's probing questions. Gods, she looked tired, gone beyond exhaustion and out the other side, rubbed so thin there was little left of her save stubborn courage.

Needs spoiling, murmured Shad, painting a picture of Cenda lying relaxed in a huge bed, Gray curled around her, feeding her chocolat, brushing her hair. Naked, of course.

Mmm.

His eye fell on Krysanthe's arm around the fire witch's waist and his lip curled. If the healer truly cared, she'd spare Cenda the interrogation 'til she'd had another meal, then let her sleep for a week. That was what she needed, poor little love. Irritated, Gray stiffened, and the stitches in his side pulled. Still, he had to admit, the healer had done a neat job, and the green translucent salve she'd smeared on the wound reduced the pain considerably.

Cenda had fallen silent at last, drooping against her friend's shoulder. The three Purists were talking, arguing.

"I agree with Olga," said Matthaeus. "It's not safe here, not for the only fire witch in the known worlds."

"But Matthaeus, surely we're capable—" said Krysanthe.

The old man overrode her. "Unbeknownst to the rest of the Enclave, I have purchased a number of properties in East Sector with our funds."

Purist Olga's dark eyes shone bright amid the wrinkles. "Matthaeus, you sly dog!" She clapped her hands. "We can use them as safe houses."

"Exactly. We keep Cenda hidden, and not only do we save her life, but for the first time, the Enclave meets the Technomage Primus on an equal footing." He paused, smiling with grim relish. "I look forward to the negotiations."

Gray straightened, pushing away from the wall. He projected his voice into the airy room as if it were a theater. "So you use her as a weapon, a bargaining chip. Which makes you no better than the Fixer or the Technomage." *Or me.* Bleakly, he stared at the fire witch. "Is that what you want, Cenda?"

Wordlessly, she shook her head.

"Neither of you knows anything about it," said Matthaeus, his tone dismissive.

Godsdammit, he wouldn't be so arrogant if he'd seen her advancing the length of that dilapidated ballroom, death blazing in her hands. Gray met the wizard's pale eyes. "I know enough to understand what you're doing. And why."

Olga ran gnarled fingers through the cat's fur, and it arched and purred. "We're protecting her, boy. Don't you see that?"

"And if the Technomage offers something sufficiently attractive in return for Cenda? Like the Enclave's continued survival, for instance? That would be for the greater good, wouldn't it? What will you—"

Abruptly, he took two steps to the door and jerked it open. The small figure on the threshold whirled to run, but Gray caught the back of his collar and hauled him into the room. "Is this an example of your security?" He gave Slop a shake and received a glare in return.

"Please." Cenda's voice rasped, barely audible. She rubbed her forehead. "Don't hurt him. Can we—" She swallowed. "Can we decide tomorrow?"

Krysanthe stroked her knuckles down Cenda's cheek. "Sweetie," she said, very gently. "The decision's already made."

Shad growled inside Gray's head, and he felt his own lips pull back in a snarl. Under his hand, the boy's heart beat like a frightened kitten's. He shrank back, pressing into Gray's side.

Cenda set Krysanthe aside and straightened up. She shoved the hair out of her eyes and said, very softly, "I will not use the Lady's gift to kill again."

"But Cenda, what if—"

The fire witch continued as if the other woman hadn't spoken. Her eyes were fixed on Matthaeus. "This I swear," she said, "on my Elke's life."

The old man stood, frowning. Finally, he inclined his head. "Understandable," he said. "Very well."

The healer rose, shaking out her skirts with a brisk rustle. "I absolutely forbid moving Cenda until tomorrow. If she doesn't eat and sleep, there won't be any fire Magick in the foreseeable future. I guarantee it."

"Wait." Cenda grasped her friend's hand. "Swear," she said. "Swear you'll look after the boy."

Krysanthe disengaged herself and patted the fire witch on the shoulder. "Don't be silly. You can do that yourself."

"Swear, Krys," Cenda insisted, her voice rising. "Swear by the Lady."

Gray frowned. That sounded too much like hysteria for his peace of mind. He took a step closer, but Purist Olga forestalled him. Hopping off the bed nimbly enough, she hobbled over to the boy. She wasn't much taller than he was. "We'll take him, Titfer and I."

"Perrowt!" The cat wound himself so firmly through Slop's legs that the lad staggered.

"Oh." Wonderingly, he bent and drew his fingers through the thick, soft fur. "Don' know nuthin' 'bout cats."

"You will, Florien, you will." The old witch laid a hand on his shoulder. "He likes you, and I respect his opinion." She cocked her head to one side, her eyes bright. "Is that a mistake?"

The boy ducked his head. "Dunno."

Bent fingers grasped his chin and forced his head up. "Answer me, lad. Am I right to believe Titfer?"

Two pairs of dark eyes met. "Yah," said Florien firmly. "But enough wit' t' fookin' washin'."

Purist Olga gave a rusty chuckle. "We'll see," she said. "Come, then." She glanced back at the fire witch. "All right, Cenda?"

Cenda smiled, the quiver of her lips making something tighten in Gray's chest. "Yes," she whispered.

With a final twinkle, the old witch shepherded the boy out of the room. They were followed by Tai Yang, neat and unobtrusive as ever.

"Excellent," said the healer briskly. "That's settled. Cenda, you stay here 'til nightfall. Sleep." She grinned. "Consider that a prescription." The smile faded as she turned to Gray. "You'll be wanting to get back to The Treasure, Duke," she said pointedly.

"Not at all." Gray crossed to the bed in a couple of swift strides.

"Not yet," said Cenda, clutching his sleeve.

The two Purists exchanged an unreadable glance. In the end, Matthaeus said, "It might be for the best." When the healer nodded, he shifted his attention to Gray. "We'll lock you in, for your own safety. And ours."

"Sleep, sweetie." Krysanthe bustled out the door. Matthaeus followed more slowly, with a final chilly glance for Gray. The door snicked and a key turned in the lock.

"Gods." Cenda released Gray's hand and fell back onto the pillow, her eyes closed. "That was awful." The muscles in her throat worked as she swallowed. "All I wanted was to get home, where I'm safe. Loved." Her lashes rose, revealing golden brown eyes sheened with tears. "But I'm not, am I?"

"No." Gray grasped her calves and shifted her legs aside so he could sit on the bed beside her. "It's not the sanctuary you expected." He didn't doubt he could pick the lock, get them out some way, but she was stupefied with exhaustion, and he wasn't much better. Her lips were so pale they looked almost white.

"You're not surprised."

"No, but I'm a professional cynic."

She grabbed his forearm. "You saved my life."

Gray patted her hand. "And you saved mine. We're even." He tried a smile, but judging by her expression, he wasn't especially convincing.

With a long sigh, her eyelids slid shut and her head rolled on the pillow.

"Wait." The general uneasiness in his gut coalesced into something specific. He leaned over her. "Cenda, why does Krysanthe have Technomage books?"

No answer.

He stroked her cheek, tugged gently on her earlobe, suddenly overtaken by a sense of urgency. "Cenda!"

20

"Nngh." The fire witch cranked one eyelid open. "What?"

"Technomage books. On the healer's desk. I saw them."

Cenda struggled. Rubbing her eyes, she said, "She told me . . ." A cracking yawn. "Research on fire Magick. She tried everything, looked . . . everywhere. For me."

"But how did she get them?"

"Mmm. Tai Yang knows . . . knows someone in the Technomages' Library. Would have cost"—she gave the ghost of a shrug—"Lady knows."

"But where would a Pure like Tai Yang find that much money?"

Cenda tucked one hand under her cheek and settled into the pillow. "The Enclave has more money than you think." Her lashes fluttered down.

It must have. Matthaeus had purchased properties, whole houses. Tai Yang was obviously more senior than Gray had first supposed. Brooding, he ran a hand through his hair, gazing down at Cenda's limp body. The sooner he got her away from the Pures, the better. But right now . . .

The beds were so narrow he wouldn't be able to fit himself next to her with any degree of comfort. Blowing out a breath, he chose the one nearest and stretched out. Deliberately, he didn't remove his boots. Best to be prepared.

He was incredibly tired, weary right to the bones. Not surprisingly, his shoulder still ached a bit, but the knife wound should be hurting like a bitch and it wasn't. Odd. Pulling up his shirt, he stared at the slash over his ribs in disbelief. The edges had begun to knit. Judger God, what was in the healer's salve?

Still puzzling over it, he turned his head to watch his fire witch sleep, her mouth slightly open like a child's. He punched the pillow in irritation, wanting to lie beside her, touch her, feel her pulse beat under his hand, reassuringly regular. Silence stole into the room, the faint rush of her breath the only noise.

Ah, shit.

Gray rolled off the bed and knelt on the floor at Cenda's side. Resting his folded arms on the mattress, he stroked a dark curl with one finger, watching her lashes flutter as she dreamed. That was better. His breath steadied and slowed. Just a few minutes more. He yawned.

The pain in his knees woke him sometime later. An hour or so, he judged. Cursing under his breath, Gray lurched to his feet, his knees and his back shrieking a protest.

Cenda hadn't moved. He was tempted to bend and lay his lips against her cheek, the way he used to say good night to Mother. But he had no right to do that.

Gray threw himself on the other bed. He was still thinking of evenings on the farm when sleep rolled over him in a dark wave.

The noise that woke him was faint, a sort of cautious rattle. Opening his eyes the merest slit, Gray peered through his lashes. Cenda stood at the entrance of the infirmary, tugging at the door handle. Two of the lamps dangling from the ceiling had been lit. No guesses as to who was responsible for that. Night blanketed the windows, the Enclave lying quiet and still under the light of the Dancers. They'd slept the afternoon away and half the evening.

Now the fire witch bent to apply her eye to the keyhole. She traced it with a fingertip, frowning. Yawning, Gray braced himself on one elbow, enjoying the pert curve of her bottom under the tunic, the long line of her thigh. What, in Judger's name, was she doing? If she was trying to pick the lock, he could do that easily. All he needed was the thin blade he kept in his boot, or even a hairpin. No, she drew back, muttering what sounded like curses under her breath.

He should get up, kiss her one last time. Enough pressure on a certain point in her neck and she'd slump unconscious in his arms. All he had to do was get them out of the Enclave and away before she came around.

Me, murmured Shad's insidious voice. *Use me.*

Gray's stomach turned over. The greasy feel of the shadow veil, the choking sensation of otherness. *I haven't done that since we were fourteen. I'm not doing it now.*

Lying beside him, half on the bed, half on the floor, Shad shrugged. *Have it your own way.*

Cenda reached up into her hair and coaxed the salamander onto her finger. Her face fierce with concentration, she crooned to it. The woman was rubbing noses with a fire elemental! Gray shook his head. Unbelievable.

The salamander stepped daintily from the fire witch's finger and disappeared into the keyhole with a jaunty flick of its golden tail. Cenda grinned, her face shining with delight. Involuntarily, Gray smiled.

With a sort of tired hiss, the lock flowed and melted, the metal of it trickling down the door in a slow stream that charred the sturdy wood.

"Yes!" Cenda executed a quick hop and a skip. "Gray, Gray, wake up." She spun around, only to meet his fascinated gaze. "Oh!" The salamander appeared over her shoulder and the fabric of her tunic began to smolder.

Gray fought the grin. "You're . . . ah . . . burning again."

"Five-it!" Irritably, she grabbed the fire lizard and shoved it back into her hair, where it hunkered down, glaring at Gray with its heart-of-flame blue eyes.

It knows, whispered the voice of doom in his head.

Yeah, so? Gray stood and stretched, feeling his bones creak. Aloud, he said, "I could have done that for you. More neatly, too."

Cenda flushed, and Shad said dryly, *Well-done, stupid.*

Gray gritted his teeth. "Sorry," he said. "I still can't get over it, what you can do."

"Never mind." With a half smile, she pressed a hand to her belly. "It's way past dinner hour and I'm so hungry I could eat a dog whole, paws and all." Abruptly, her face changed, as if a great hand had taken a sponge and wiped all expression from it.

Shit!

Gray reached her in three hasty strides. Grasping her arm, he held her steady—only to find her face already turned away from him. Shad stood on her other side, stroking her cheek with his long, dark fingers, crooning.

"Oh, Shad." She put her hand over the shadow's. Without taking her gaze from Shad's featureless face, she said, "What's he saying, Gray?"

"Nothing." He could barely force the word out.

At that, she did look around. Tears stood in her eyes.

Go on, she wants to know.

"He's . . . singing."

"Singing? Singing what?"

"The"—Gray stalled, had to drag in another breath—"the lullaby. Remember it?"

She blinked hard. "How could I forget? Oh, thank you, Shad." Leaning forward, she brushed her lips across his smooth, dark cheek.

Sweet, said Shad. *So sweet.*

If it wasn't for you . . .

What?

I could keep her . . . a little longer.

Shad didn't reply, the internal silence filled only with

the rushing beat of the blood in Gray's ears. Fiercely, he concentrated on the wine red strands of hair at Cenda's temples. There was more of the vivid color than there had been a day ago.

The merest thread of a thought, Shad murmured, *Keep us both.*

Gray had to squeeze his eyes shut for a moment. When he opened them, the fire witch was staring at him, the strangest smile trembling on her lips. "This is good-bye," she whispered. "Isn't it?"

"In a way."

She gripped her fingers together. "What do you mean?"

Gray forced a smile in response. "I'll walk you wherever you're going." He ran his palm lightly up her spine, around to her throat. Just there, where the pulse beat.

"I have to get out of here and go home before Krys comes back and starts fussing. I want to sleep in my own bed." Her cheekbones pinkened. "And I'm starving. I'm going via the kitchen."

He'd never get through the hedge, not without Magickal assistance, but the gate . . . the gate was a different matter, requiring no more than a small diversion. And her cottage was such a short distance from it.

"Good idea," he said. "But we visit the healer's study first."

Cenda's brows rose. "What for?"

"My harp. I'm not leaving the Duchess to an enclave of tone-deaf Pures."

"Great Lady, that's better." Cenda licked the last crumbs from her fingers. She was very thorough.

The cavernous kitchen had been dark and deserted save for a pair of black-and-white cats, long and lean. The Rat Patrol, she'd called them. Gray had to give them their due—not a single rodent, not even a scuttleroach. He'd stood watch while the fire witch had carved a huge slab from a wheel of cheese and another from a cooked joint.

Then she'd appropriated an entire loaf and a big jug of manda juice. Enough for three hardworking ditchdiggers.

And she'd eaten twice what he had. Amazing.

Because the rickety dresser in her little cottage was the only available horizontal surface, they'd set the meal out like a bizarre picnic, sitting on the rug before the fireplace, the curtains drawn tight. Cenda's salamander had scampered down her arm and practically leaped into the blaze to join its brethren, making the fire witch snort with amusement. "Poor little love," she said. "It's had a rough time."

When she returned from clearing the plates, Gray rose and grabbed her hand. They fell together into the depths of the shabby armchair.

You going to do it? Shad sprawled up the wall, flickering in the firelight, looking vaguely menacing.

Soon. He must have pulled another muscle somehow. Gods, his chest ached. Gray breathed in the warm scent of her hair.

A brisk tattoo on the door. "Cenda? Cenda, let me in!"

Krysanthe. And she sounded pissed.

"I know you're there!"

Cenda raised her head from his shoulder. "Not now, Krys. Tomorrow."

"Nonsense. I need to talk to you now. The Duke's disappeared."

Before he could stop her, Cenda said, "No, he hasn't."

A short pause. "That's a very bad idea, sweetie." Jingling noises as if the healer was fiddling with her chatelaine. "I'm coming in." The doorknob began to turn.

Cenda shot to her feet. "No!" she shouted. "I warded it! Don't—"

Flames flickered all around the edges of the door. A shrill scream sounded from the other side, followed by a stream of curses. Gray's brows rose. Fancy a Purist knowing words like that.

As one, the flames subsided and Cenda called, "Krys! You all right?"

"Just a bit scorched." It sounded as though the healer spoke though clenched teeth.

"You should try the green salve," said Gray blandly. "Works wonders." Heaving himself out of the chair, he pulled up his shirt to show Cenda the line across his ribs, now completely healed. Her eyes went wide. Then she shook her head and put her palm over his mouth. When he kissed it, she frowned at him in mock reproof.

"Come back tomorrow, Krys," she said, her gaze locked on his.

A much longer silence this time. Finally, Krysanthe said, "First thing, Cenda. I'll be here first thing. You be careful, you hear?" After a few seconds, her light footsteps receded, but slowly, as if she were deep in thought.

The fire witch stared at him, studying his face feature by feature, as if she'd never seen it before. Gray couldn't imagine what sort of expression he was wearing, but he felt as if he were transparent. Surely she must see the guilt, the evil in his soul?

Slowly, a tide of red worked its way up over her throat, to her cheeks. "I'll never see you again." One hand crept up to grasp his biceps. "*Never.* I don't care if I . . ."

Gray lowered his voice to a crooning murmur, the way Concordian trainers did when they spoke to high-strung horses. "If you what?"

"Look like a fool." Rising to tiptoe, she placed her mouth against his, flicked her tongue over his bottom lip. "One last time," she breathed. Artlessly, she pressed her body against him, wriggling her hips. "I don't want to think about anything anymore. I don't want to think at all."

"Sweetheart—" he began. There, the vulnerable spot was right there, under his fingers. But his other hand moved of its own volition, spreading greedy fingers over her buttock, sealing them together. He felt her gasp when blood spilled into his cock and it kicked against her. Then her moan.

Something shifted behind him, and Shad's strong, cool fingers moved in his hair. *Another hour or two,* murmured the voice of temptation. *Won't make any difference.* Gray's blood surged. What he had to do would be easier in the early hours, when the Enclave was deep in sleep. Of course it would.

"Oh. *Oh!*" Cenda's eyes deepened to a glowing amber. She shot him a sultry glance from under her lashes and scraped a fingernail lightly over the stubble on his cheek. "You look positively villainous." Lowering her voice to a throbbing murmur, she mouthed his earlobe. "Also delicious. Edible. Ah . . . um . . . Damn." She waved a vague hand. "Run out of adjectives, but you know what I mean." She drew back, frowning, but her lips curved with mischief.

Gray didn't know whether to laugh or cry. Or throw her to the floor and fuck her 'til she fainted. He cleared his throat. "Is this a seduction?"

"Oh, yes." Cenda shot him a twinkling glance. "How am I doing?"

Fucking brilliant.

"Not bad."

"What did he say?" She was looking past him, over his shoulder.

"What?"

"You get this strange look when he's talking to you. Sort of distant . . ." The light faded from her face. "Angry."

See what you've done. Shad stepped forward, right into their embrace. He slid a shadowy arm around Cenda's waist and nuzzled her throat. Gray felt the fleeting, silky brush of hair as Shad bent his head, then the firm press of his shadow's other hand against his spine, just above his ass.

He let out a hissing breath. *Stop that.*

No.

"Gray?" Cenda was staring at him, frowning.

He ran a hand through his hair. "Sorry. He . . . distracts me."

Cenda smiled. "I can imagine."

"No." He grabbed her by the upper arms, disregarding Shad's warning snarl. "You can't imagine; you couldn't possibly. Cenda, I can't"—he swallowed, feeling as though he were poised over a long drop, stripped naked, and dizzy with terror—"always control what . . ."

"Sshh." She placed warm fingers over his lips, even as she snuggled further into Shad's embrace. "He won't harm me." She flushed. "It's you who takes the greatest risk." Her lips twisted. "I'm the one with no control."

A fine pair. Shad sounded smug.

Cenda looked down at Shad's arm, a strong black silhouette curved around her waist. "I need him," she whispered, "so I can't burn you, cause you pain trying to give you pleasure. I might wish it wasn't so, but"—she lifted her chin, her eyes flashing—"I don't. He's amazing." Her breath hitched. "Wonderful."

Darling, crooned Shad, pulling her even closer. *Darling, darling girl.*

Dark anticipation and fear had pulled Gray's balls up so tight, it felt as if they were reaching for Shad's hand, still splayed firmly over the upper curves of his buttocks. A long finger insinuated itself under the waistband of his trews, teasing the cleft of his ass. He flinched, cursing under his breath.

The fire witch shrugged out of Shad's grip and stepped back. Pulling in a deep breath, she crossed her arms, grabbed the tunic by the hem, and hauled it off over her head. Her breasts bobbed, so tender and soft, so vulnerable, the dusky nipples furled and stiff.

Shad's growl emerged from Gray's mouth, long and low and hungry. Gray stepped forward, ready to pounce, but strong, dark arms circled around him from behind, pinning his arms. "Fuck, Shad. Let me go!"

Cenda's golden eyes went wide and the flames leaped in the fireplace. "No," she said in a rasping whisper. "Hold him, Shad. Hold him for me."

Gray heaved and struggled, gasping obscenities, but Shad was his exact match. As he'd always been.

The fire witch paused, slender fingers on the top button of his shirt, realization dawning in her face. "He knows, doesn't he?" she said slowly. "What you like. He has to know." When she slipped the button, her hands shook.

Shad chuckled, low and wicked. *So I do.* The tide of

his shadow's lust, all blood heat, bloodred, flooded Gray's mind, swamping rational thought in a wave of intense physical sensation. And because he knew, Shad turned his dark head, nipping the junction between Gray's neck and shoulder. Simultaneously, he spread a hand over Gray's genitals, palming his cock, the pressure firm—perfect.

Cenda froze, watching. *"Lady save me."* She flushed, a fiery red.

Gray writhed and shook. "She'd better." He forced his eyes open, pinning her with his gaze, willing her to understand, to gift him with her warmth, her foolish trust. "Because I can't."

"Gods, who cares?" Cenda gripped the fabric of his shirt in both hands and ripped it open. Buttons pinged on the floor. But when she drew another breath and reached for the laces of his trews, Shad was there before her.

Hot and cold chills chased up and down Gray's spine as cool, dark fingers cradled his cock, lifting and displaying the flushed length of it, pressing under the head with a stroke so deft and knowing that he cried out.

"Oh, yes," breathed the fire witch, dropping to her knees. The warmth of her grip around his shaft was such an excruciating contrast that he bucked, his vision fading around the edges, his last sight that of pale fingers entwined with dark ones. Shad was a solid presence behind him, his cock an iron bar nestled into the crack of Gray's ass.

Not yet. Shad squeezed the root of his cock so hard, Gray saw stars of pleasure and pain.

"Stop," he croaked, but she didn't lift her head, her tongue whisking across his slit like a flickering brand. Leaning back, he let Shad bear his weight while he gave her hair a firm tug. *"Cenda."*

She administered a searing kitten lick that nearly blew the top of his head off. "Mmm?"

"One last time." He bared his teeth. "To remember forever. Bed. Now."

21

For the first time, he noticed Cenda had worked her remaining hand free. She'd reached around behind both of them to fondle one cheek of Shad's ass, pressing him firmly forward, rocking him into Gray's body.

Words completely beyond him, Gray bent and hauled her up, feeling Shad flow away across the room. Ignoring her startled yelp, he flung the fire witch across the bed and bent to rip off his boots and trews. By the time he caught up, Shad had managed to peel her leggings down far enough to get them tangled with her boots, and Cenda was laughing so hard, her breasts bobbled.

"You're no help," Gray growled at her, his head clearing a little.

Cenda shot him a luminous glance and held out her arms. "Doesn't matter."

"No, it doesn't." He came down over her in a rush, settling into the cradle of her thighs. With a soft thump, one of her boots hit the floor. Followed by the other. Shad.

"Gods, yes." The fire witch tilted her pelvis and wrapped

her long legs around his waist. Instinct had him surging forward with a grunt, furrowing through hot, slick folds, sinking in that first tight, delirious inch.

A firm, cool touch skated all the way from the nape of his neck to his tailbone, setting off a wave of prickling sensation. He could feel Shad attempting to form words, but his head, his body, and his soul were overwhelmed by the primal urge to rut. He drew his hips back, poised to plunge so deep, there'd be no more of him to give her, and his shadow's hand skimmed over his ass and gripped his balls. *Want,* hissed the dark voice.

Shad wasn't hurting him—of course he wasn't—the grip merely cradled, his shadow's thumb moving in an insistent, gentle rhythm that made rational thought impossible. *Want,* said Shad again. *Mine.* A pause, and Gray could feel the shudders in the arm pressed against the back of his thigh. *Ours.*

Without warning, his shadow shoved a vision of the three of them into Gray's head, intimately entangled, complete in every excruciating, erotic detail. All the breath punched out of his lungs, his hips drawing back automatically, thrusting deep, burying him full length in the hot, humid clasp of paradise. Bending his head, he took her mouth, fucking into her with his tongue.

Hands were all over him, warm fingers in his hair, gripping his shoulders, cool palms massaging his flanks, his ass. Flesh surrounded him, satin smooth and searing hot against his belly, around his cock, muscled and hard and cool all along his back. His head spun and Shad leaned right down beside him and licked his throat, raising a delicious ripple of gooseflesh.

Do it, let's do it.

Gray groaned into Cenda's mouth, fighting for sense, for coherence, for any damned particle of himself that wasn't consumed by the beast. He freed his lips, just enough to rasp, "Trust me? One last time?"

Panting, the fire witch stroked his jaw with her knuckles. "What . . . what do you want?" Her eyes blazed and the sleek walls of her sheath tensed around him.

"Turn over . . . hands and knees."

The flames roared like Concordian tygres on the hunt, the shabby little room suddenly as bright as day, Shad's body dense and perfectly defined.

Gritting his teeth, Gray pulled out, Cenda's convulsive shiver some small consolation. Immediately, Shad took her hand, steadying her as she flipped over, displaying that glorious ass. Pink, flushed folds pouted from between her thighs, musky dew making them glossy, moisture shining on the pale flesh of her inner thighs.

Gray grabbed his cock and squeezed hard enough to bring tears to his eyes. Then he leaned over to the dresser and snagged the small, square pot that sat next to her hairbrush. "What's this?" he croaked. Judger, let it be what it looked like!

Cenda glanced over her shoulder and froze. "Hand cream. Krys makes it for me. Why do you . . ." She paled, her tongue coming out to moisten her lips. "Gods, Gray, I don't think I—"

"Sshh." He nibbled a line along the luscious curve where buttock met thigh and she whimpered, throwing her head back, her hair slipping off her shoulder in a lustrous, tangled shawl. "Nothing you won't want, I promise."

She gave a breathless chuckle. "That's no comfort."

He felt a truly demonic grin stretch his lips. Taking a better grasp of her hips, he inhaled deeply and speared every luxurious inch into her sheath, until his thighs were flush against the backs of hers.

"Gray!" The fire witch jerked and trembled.

"Hold on to Shad."

The shadow surged up onto the bed, tossing pillows aside left and right, some kind of furry toy flying away with them. Lying on his side, he pulled the fire witch into a firm embrace, her fingers gripping his biceps, her head nestled into the curve between neck and shoulder. *Better?*

"Lady, that's better," she whispered, as if she'd heard him. Then she arched her back, pushing back into the impalement with a lascivious wriggle. "Gray, love, please. *Move*, dammit!"

Such trust. Poor, foolish little witch. But he could make it good for her, this one last time.

What a sacrifice, hmm?

Shut up and hold her tight.

He wanted to build her up a little at a time, send her flying in the most erotic experience of her life, but the weight of Shad's desire combined with his own pushed him forward, again and again, in a brutal rhythm that brought him perilously close to the brink, his fingers flexing in the resilient, sumptuous flesh of her ass. Reaching for the fleeing fragments of his self-discipline, Gray changed angles, hitting her high and hard, knowing he had to be striking her clit full on, no mercy. The bed creaked and rattled.

Cenda began crying out, soft little gasps that blossomed into whimpers and then short breathy screams. "Gods," she keened. "Gods, oh, gods, oh, gods." The slick tissues around him had grown searingly hot. Raising her head, the fire witch swooped on Shad's mouth, kissing him ferociously, her hand drifting down the dark length of his body. The heat moderated.

Shad arched, his bass growl of pleasure filling Gray's head. "No," gasped Gray aloud. "Shad, no."

Yes. Fuck, yes. Here, feel it.

Shad shoved it all at him in one fell thrust, the beautiful, desperate heat of her mouth, the warm fingers skating over his belly, curling around a proud dark cock. She was pumping his shadow with exactly the same rhythm Gray was using to fuck her.

The multiple layers of sensation made his head reel. Choking, he reached for the pot of hand cream, ripped the lid off, and dug his fingers in.

Go on, hissed Shad. *Don't stop now.* He could have meant either of them. Or both.

"Cenda." No response. He dropped the pot, took one

pale, glowing cheek in each hand, and squeezed them together. *"Cenda!"*

"Mmm?" She sounded half-drunk. Reluctantly, she raised her head.

"Take a breath."

"What? Why? *Nngh!*"

She bucked so hard, he had to hold her down with one hand while he circled his slicked up thumb over the cute little pucker of her anus.

Shad slid his fingers into her hair and pressed her cheek into his chest.

"Lord's balls, what do you think—*Argh!*"

Concentrating fiercely, Gray pressed past the ring of muscle, rotating his thumb. Keeping the motion light enough to tantalize rather than alarm wasn't easy. He rocked his hips, fighting the urge to plunge, to hammer into her and relieve the aching pressure in his balls.

"Breathe, sweetheart, breathe. Shall I stop?"

"Yes. Oh, gods, no! It feels so strange, I—I don't know!" But her hips lifted into the caress while she burrowed into Shad's strong body, clutching him tight.

Gray glanced up the length of her slim back, to the curve of her cheek, so pale pressed against Shad's complete absence of light. Her mouth was open, her eyes squeezed shut. Something warm and huge unfurled in his chest. It felt suspiciously like tenderness, the last thing he could afford.

Gruffly, he asked, "More?"

Hard, fuck her hard, insisted Shad.

"Harder," she panted, and the hair rose on the back of Gray's neck.

What are you doing to her? he demanded.

Nothing. Ah, shit!

What?

Licking, she's . . .

Cenda twisted, peering over her shoulder, her eyes brighter than any flame. "What I do to Shad—can you feel it?"

If you want.

"Yes," said Gray hoarsely. "If I want to."

Cenda shot him a burning look, her expression brimful of what he could only describe as glee. Then she launched herself at Shad's body, lower this time.

Fuck! Shad's hips arched so high he left the mattress. Simultaneously, he opened himself to Gray, so that he felt the warm, wet heaven of Cenda's mouth wrapped around a thick, aching girth even as her burning sheath clamped down on him in a greedy vise and her hips moved under his hand. The overload was almost too much, the surge of blood to his cock so violent, that for a moment, Gray thought he might pass out.

Fuck her, moaned Shad. *Judger God, just fuck her.*

Completely beyond coherent thought, let alone speech, Gray thrust, increasing the pace so rapidly that he was thundering into the fire witch within a few strokes, still circling a relentless thumb in her ass. Cenda moved easily with the rhythm, her head bobbing over Shad's dark shaft, one hand fisting the base. She was moaning quietly, the muffled sound nearly lost under Shad's continuous bass growl, a litany of *Yes, fuck, yes! Shit, don't stop!*

The doubled sensation thickened, ramping Gray's arousal up to unbearable levels. He was going to die right here in this nondescript little room, explode in a fountain of hot, wet seed, but oh, gods, it would be worth it, worth an eternity in the grave. Hardly able to see straight, he fumbled a hand over her belly, furrowing down to where her clit stood proud and slick. Shaking with the effort to keep the touch light, he rubbed back and forth with the pad of his forefinger.

Cenda gave a choking scream and went rigid. All her muscles clamped down—the hot, succulent walls gloving his cock, the fiery velvet tunnel around his thumb. And fuck it, her mouth and tongue drew on Shad so hard, Gray *felt* the surge of ecstasy boil the length of his shadow's cock, Shad's orgasm paralleling his, the fabulous double rush of release so acute the breath stopped in his throat and his heart ceased beating. While it lasted, he couldn't make a sound, not a groan, not a shout, his entire being suspended in a universe of soft, dark fire. His and his shadow's, one again and yet not.

And then the world returned and he could move again, speak. The breath whistled out between his teeth, and he leaned over the fire witch's back. She was coughing and spluttering, Shad stroking her shoulder even as the dark outline of his stomach rose and fell with his heaving breaths.

As gently as he could, Gray pulled away. Then he collapsed next to Shad and drew her into his arms. "Cenda, are you all right?"

The fire witch wiped her mouth with the back of her hand and nodded. "I didn't expect . . . I wasn't ready . . . Sorry."

Gray shot his shadow a filthy look. *You could have spared her that.*

Shad chuckled. *She swallowed, though, the little darling.*

Gods, yes, he'd felt the movement of her throat. Curiosity got the better of him. "What does he taste like?"

Cenda frowned, running her tongue over her teeth. Finally, she said, "It's hard to describe, like a dark cloud, like mist with salt in it. Here." Without warning, she lifted her chin and swept her tongue inside his mouth.

The flavor burst on his palate, smoky, spicy, and somehow familiar. Utterly, delightfully wicked. Despite the fact he was completely drained, his cock gave a hard, hungry twitch. Shad sniggered and Gray growled a furious response, cradling her cheeks in his hands and easing his lips away.

Body still humming, Gray got them arranged on the bed, though it was a tight fit, Cenda in the middle, her head settled on his shoulder. He ensured her hair spread across his chest like a silken shroud. Fuck, it had been amazing, beyond anything he'd thought possible, being double-fucked, double-sucked. He shivered with the lingering remnants of pleasure.

Fuck it, Shad, why? Why now?

A pause, then Shad said slowly, *You didn't want it before.*

Cenda turned her head and pressed a shy kiss to Gray's shoulder. He was grateful for the distraction. "Can you stay a little longer?" she murmured.

"A little."

She sighed and reached out behind her with one hand. Immediately, shadowy fingers grasped hers, Shad's lean length curling over her back. The fire crackled happily in the grate, the room the perfect temperature for lying naked with a woman in your arms.

Gods, he was too wrung out to protest. Let her hold on to Shad if that's what she wanted. Let his sweet witch enjoy her last few moments of peace. His thoughts still muffled and slow, he sorted through his memories, one by one, picking the best, polishing them like jewels. Soon, they'd be all he had of her. Cenda's wide eyes, staring into his over the rim of a wine cup, gone golden with shocked arousal; her endearing irritation with the way the salamanders scorched her clothes; the startled pleasure as she pulled on the leather gauntlet he'd given her. Odd, he would have thought his recollections would be overwhelmingly carnal, given what they'd done to each other—his thoughts hitched—and to Shad.

The shadow reached across Cenda and laid a hand on Gray's shoulder, but he didn't speak. Gray ignored the comfort of the touch.

He was even proud of her, strange and stupid as that was. Because she'd done it all by herself, come to her powers. "What can you do?" he'd asked that night in The Treasure.

"Not much," she'd said, showing him the flicker on her palm. But now . . .

Her integrity and innocence were what made her vulnerable, because she had no concept of treachery such as his . . . Gray winced. At least she was no longer completely defenseless. Gods, was there anything stronger, more enduring, more stubborn, than a woman of honor?

The furrybear toy lay on the tiles before the fireplace and though it was decidedly cross-eyed, it looked as relaxed as he was. His eyelids drooping, Gray watched the firelight flicker over the grubby, tattered fur, the flames creeping closer and closer. A salamander skittered across the tiles and pounced, worrying at a well-chewed ear. It was joined by a second and then a third. Strange, he would never have thought such small creatures hunted in packs. The furrybear's expression didn't change, not even when the smoldering ear burst into flame.

"Cenda." Gray nudged her leg with his knee.

Her eyes drifted open and she smiled, a smile so sleepy and full of innocent warmth that she stole his breath. "What?"

"Look." He indicated with his chin.

Yawning, she turned her head.

The next moment, she'd hurtled out of bed and landed on her knees before the fireplace. "No!" She snatched up the burning toy, the salamanders scattering like fireflakes before a hot wind. But the furrybear was well alight, blazing like an odd little effigy, even though Cenda pressed it to her bare breasts, rocking back and forth, keening. "Ah no, no. Booboo."

It made Gray's guts turn over, watching the flames snake over those sweet nipples, the pale, tender skin of her breasts and belly. He leaped to his feet and grabbed the water jug from the dresser. "Hold it out," he ordered, poised to pour.

The heartbreaking sounds ceased and her head rose slowly, her eyes very wide and glowing gold. "No," she said at last. "They're right." She glanced at the fire lizards perched in a row on the grate, their eyes shining like melted sapphires. "It's fitting. And this is the right time. Tomorrow, my life changes forever. I'll leave here and I may never return. I'll never be the same—I know that." She cupped the furrybear in both hands as though offering an invocation, and kissed it as if the fire didn't exist, right on its burning nose.

The flames reached out to lick her lips, and Gray had to close his eyes.

When he opened them, the fire witch was sitting on her heels, ramrod straight, watching the furrybear burn, crumbling down to ash in her hands. On her face was a madonna's smile, terrible in its grief and power. The tracks of dried tears marked her cheeks.

Gray leaned against the armchair and watched her, vaguely conscious of Shad pressed against his side, shivering. He didn't dare speak or move, or disturb her in any way.

Tell her about Deiter, said Shad suddenly. *You have to.*

Something gave way inside him with a long sigh, a knot of tension slipping loose. *Yes.*

The toy was no more than a scant palmful of ash. Cenda stirred the little pile with a forefinger. "He was all I had of her," she said. "That she'd touched. She couldn't't"—her lips twisted—"couldn't sleep without him. Booboo."

She touched you, though, whispered Shad.

"She touched you." Gray said it aloud. "You touched her."

Cenda didn't speak, but she leaned over the fireplace and spread her fingers. Booboo drifted down in a gray spill until he was indistinguishable from the ashes in the grate.

"Bone of my bone, flesh of my flesh." She washed her hands clean in the flames. "I carried her under my heart." Coming to her feet, she spread a palm over her ribs, directly below her breasts. "I would have killed a full-grown tygre with my bare hands to protect her."

Shad grunted his agreement and, unbidden, Gray saw her as she'd been in the palazzo, advancing down the ballroom toward those who would do him harm, death streaming from her fingertips.

"I'm sorry," he said awkwardly, feeling helpless.

Shad brushed past him to wrap Cenda up in his dark arms. She leaned into his shoulder, though her bleak golden gaze didn't leave Gray's. "But I couldn't fight the gods. I saw them, you know. The Lady and Her Lord."

She'd what? Gray frowned, nonplussed.

Her pretty mouth went flat and tight. "And this"—when she flung out an arm, indicating the fireplace, flames danced in her palm—"*this* is the price I paid."

She thought the gods had bought her off with fire Magick?

Perhaps they did, whispered Shad.

Tentatively, Gray reached out and stroked her cheek. "It's possible, I suppose," he said. "Though I think it's more of a gift myself. What will you do with it?"

"Go on living." Cenda dragged in a shaky breath. "Make the price worth Elke's life. Use it for the general good." She shrugged. "Though I don't know how."

"Your control is better. Your power . . . last night . . ."

A spasm of pain crossed her face. *Idiot,* hissed Shad. *Don't remind her.*

"Last night, I used my Magick to burn two men to death, maybe more," she said, her spine stiff. "And I destroyed a refuge used by the poorest of the poor. They're homeless now, because of me."

Gray cupped the point of her shoulder in his hand and rocked her gently. "The Fixer would have made you a slave, your Magick a weapon sold to the highest bidder. You did right."

"I am a witch. Sworn to do no harm." Cenda's face set like winter iron. "What I did was *wrong*, Gray. It cheapens Elke's memory, soils my soul. I will not do it again."

"But Cenda—"

She didn't raise her voice. "I will not do it again, I swear on the life of my baby."

How long did she have before they caught her? The Technomage or Deiter or the Fixer. It was only a matter of degree. They'd force her one way or the other, break her down bone by bone, bleed all this shining resolve out of her drop by drop. What did an innocent witch know of the calculated infliction of pain, of screams without end? He wanted to vomit.

Tell her.

No need now. I can't do it. Her agony in return for his soul. Judger, what a fool! He should have known he wouldn't be able to follow through.

Gray turned away to hide the shocking rush of tears, the threadbare curtains blurring before him. *Fuck, Shad, I can't take her to Deiter. Not even for*—Blindly, he fumbled for the borrowed trews and shirt, pulling them on, giving her his back. The loss of hope was a strong black fist that sank vicious fingers into his guts and twisted.

Ah, said Shad on a note of discovery. Then, *Took you long enough to see it.*

That was all? His soul was damned, the dream of peace fled as if it had never been, and that was all Shad could say? He might as well reach deep inside his chest and rip his heart out by the roots. Well, fuck it. He seized on the familiar bright surge of anger. *Abomination. Fucking abomination.*

Yes, your *abomination.* A dark wave of comfort washed over him, and he shrugged it off.

Cenda touched his arm. "Gray?"

He couldn't bear to look at her. "What?" Grabbing his boots, he busied himself pulling them on. The sooner he got out of here, the better. Let the Enclave look after her. She'd have some sort of chance with them, anyway. A better life.

A pause, and she said, "When you sang the lullaby, who was it for?"

He glanced up to see her standing nude and unselfconscious before the fire, a salamander perched on each shoulder, another in her hair. "What do you mean?" He reached for his knife harness, buckled it on.

How was it she could look so inexpressibly beautiful and so endearingly plain, all at the same time, the firelight painting her creamy skin with flickering warmth?

"At The Treasure. You sang it for someone specific. I know you did."

Gray's throat had turned to dust. "My mother." Where was the Duchess? Ah, there. Spotting the instrument case, he slung it over one shoulder and straightened, bracing himself. "Cenda, I have to go."

But the fire witch was staring past his shoulder, her brow creased. "That's strange," she said.

Gray turned. Soft light glowed all around the window frame. Shit! His heart slamming in his chest, he leaped for Cenda, bearing her down to the floor, his body blanketing hers, her face buried in his shoulder.

With a sort of sighing *whoosh!* the wall evaporated.

22

Coughing, Cenda peered over Gray's shoulder. Her mouth fell open. Five outlandish figures loomed out of the settling dust, clad all in white—baggy coveralls, boots, and gloves, their heads completely covered by rough cloth helmets. The goggles concealing their eyes gave them a bug-eyed air, but there was nothing humorous about the weapons they held. She'd never seen anything like them before: sleek, silver metal, with bulbous noses and a handle that fit snugly in the palm.

Gray leaped to his feet and shoved her behind him, a knife shining wickedly in each hand.

"Don't." Almost casually, the tall one in the lead, a man by his voice, pointed his weapon. A beam shot out of it and scored a long furrow in the floor near Gray's foot. The other three fanned out, leaving the fifth to linger by the ruined wall.

The air smelt strange, like acrid lightning.

Gray froze, but he didn't lower the blades.

Technomages. But how had they got past the gate?

Cenda's stomach roiled. Gods, Purist Olga! "Did you hurt her?" she rasped. "The old woman at the gate?" Flames sparkled angrily on her palms, writhed up her forearms.

After a short silence, the leader's head moved clumsily from side to side, as if he were blind. The light gleamed off the opaque surface of his goggles. "We don't believe in unnecessary violence. Get dressed, fire witch. You're coming with us, both of you." There were numbers embroidered on his coveralls; she could just make them out. Forty-two. Each of the subordinates had three digits; the fifth, shorter figure, none at all.

Cenda looked down at her nakedness and flushed. Then she set her jaw, her mind racing. She wasn't going anywhere, and neither was Gray. There had to be a way. Crouching behind Gray's body, she scrambled into her leggings and tunic.

"Someone helped you, didn't they?" said Gray, his voice colder than she'd ever heard it. "You bought one of the Pures."

No one moved or spoke.

Cenda stamped into her boots, shaking with sick fury. "Yes." With a single swift step, she planted herself in front of Gray. "Because you came through the hedge, not the gate. You must have."

Five-it. Fighting a nightmare sense of unreality, she focused on the fifth Technomage, the short one without a number. "It was you."

The white, featureless head jerked up and something jingled, very faintly.

"Great Lady, why?" Heat blossomed deep in Cenda's solar plexus. She welcomed the burn, her teeth bared. *"What could they offer you?"* The words emerged as a scream of rage that morphed into the deep-throated roar of a forest fire on the rampage.

Taking a step forward and spreading her arms, Cenda let it take her. Flames burst from every pore of her skin until she stood in a column of fire that reached the ceiling, Gray safely behind her.

"Shit!" she heard him gasp as he jumped back. *"Cenda!"*

"Your choice," she said, her voice a crackle that boomed off the remaining walls, salamanders dancing in her hair. "Touch me and die. Or leave."

"Fuck." She wasn't sure which of them had spoken, but the Technomages flinched, raising their weapons.

"Last warning." Cenda pointed, and a stream of bright fire slashed from her finger. *Whoomp!* The cushions in the armchair burst into flame.

Suddenly, the tall one laughed. "Very impressive," he said. "But then so is Science." He holstered his evil-looking weapon and drew something else from his belt, a red tube about six inches long, calibrated at regular intervals. "This fabric is flameproof," he said conversationally. He walked forward. "You didn't know that, did you, fire witch?"

No. Please no. She'd been so certain, so—

The Technomage peered down at her, his head tilted. He was grinning behind the mask, the bastard—she could swear it. "Watch." With one gloved hand, he reached right through the blaze and grasped her shoulder, his fingers digging in cruelly when she tried to jerk free. Desperately, Cenda directed the fire at his arm, but the flames skittered hungrily over the coveralls, unable to gain a purchase. From the corner of her eye, she saw his other hand move, faster than a striking salamander.

Something freezing hissed against her neck. It spread from the point of contact, a spectral tide of ice surging through her veins, congealing her blood. A salamander winked out, shattering with a high-pitched squeal of agony. Then another and another.

Cenda swayed. As if down a long dark tunnel, she heard a flurry of movement, Gray shouting curses, abruptly cut off. Someone short and plump inserted herself under one arm, propping her up. "I've got you," said a familiar voice. A firm arm slid around her waist and a chatelaine jingled.

"Krys." Her lips were numb. "Why?" But nothing came

out. The ice tide reached her skull, her eyes. Lady, it hurt. Her vision dimmed.

She'd been blessed with a wonderful pregnancy; she'd never felt sick, but there'd been times she'd wept with the weariness, so drained by the demands of everyday life she wanted to huddle in someone's arms and be held. Just held.

Cenda threw an arm across her eyes. No one to hold her, no one to help. *Gray,* something small and sad wailed inside her. *Oh, Gray.* Resolutely, she pressed her lips together. As for Krys . . . She swallowed hard. Surely, she'd dreamed it, her friend's betrayal? It couldn't be true. *It couldn't be.*

She suspected the Technomage drug lingered in her system, the effort required to lever her eyes open almost beyond her. It had taken her half an hour to struggle to even this level of coherence. Muzzily, she wondered how much time had passed. Two hours, maybe three?

Already, her stomach was cramping, both with hunger and with dread. A place in the crook of her left arm stung. Wherever she was, it smelled utterly alien, pungent with a hard, metallic odor like a powerful cleanser. The surface beneath her was firm and smooth, the covering over her naked body light and well tucked in. *Naked.*

Five-it, she *really* didn't want to think about that. Experimentally, she opened one eye the merest crack, then closed it, wincing. The chamber was full of light reflecting off pristine white walls. There was nothing in it, save the mattress on which she lay.

Something hissed, a low, continuous note. Clutching the sheet, Cenda came up on her elbows. A rectangular space was opening in one wall to reveal a sheet of the finest clear glass she'd ever seen. The window gave onto another room, very similar but containing two well-padded chairs with high backs and a desk lined with banks of buttons and switches. Set into the wall above was a set of gleaming gray squares at eye level, six in all. In four of them, multicolored lines and squiggles danced and spun; the other two were blank, like great vacant eyes. It was very confusing.

A tall, rawboned woman spun around in one of the chairs. Whatever Cenda had expected, it wasn't this. She wore a flowered smock patterned with blossoms of Lady's lace, depicted in an improbable shade of hot pink and minus the thorns. "Ye're awake then," she said, in an unmistakable Sybarite accent. Her deep voice came out of a grille high up on the ceiling. It echoed a little. "Are ye hungry?"

Cenda nodded.

"She said ye would be," the woman said cryptically. Fingering her lower lip, she scanned the desk with care, selected a button, and pressed it. "An' here's t' privy."

On the wall opposite, a rectangle formed and opened with a swish, revealing a low white stool and a small basin. Cenda stared.

"Don' ye wan' t' go?"

"Yes." Ripping the sheet free, she tucked it around her chest under the armpits and lurched across the floor, her toes curling against its rubbery resilience. The privy door slid shut behind her, nearly snagging the trailing end of her makeshift garment.

So Technomages had the same bodily functions as everyone else. Darkly amused, Cenda used the facilities, noticing as she did so the perfectly circular bruise adorning the inside of one thigh. If she let herself think about it, or the smaller mark on her arm, she'd start screaming and never stop. Biting her lip, she touched the door and it opened immediately. She emerged in time to hear the Sybarite woman speak to one of the gray screens. "Yah, at once. Of course, Primus."

Cenda sank cross-legged to the mattress. "Five-it, who are you? What is this place?" Surreptitiously, she called a tiny spark to one fingertip. "Where's Gray?" She touched her finger to the bed covering. Nothing. Shit.

The woman was bustling about on the other side of the window, tapping buttons, frowning up at the squares on the wall. "Stop thet," she said absently. "I'm Sharanita. I ain't allowed t' say no more."

"Stop what?"

"Your metabolic rate spikes when you use your powers." A woman in a white coat had entered the adjoining room through a door on the far wall, a discreet number one adorning her collar. No more than medium height, she wore tailored white trews and sensible low-heeled shoes to match. "We're monitoring you." Cool blue eyes scanned Cenda from head to heels in a single comprehensive sweep. She flashed a smile as if they were at a dinner party, practiced and charming. "This is our remote research facility at Remnant Two. And I'm the Technomage Primus." She paused, waiting.

"So what?" said Cenda sourly. "Where's Gray?"

The Technomage's smile disappeared. "Everything in that room is flame-resistant. I had it made especially for you. At great expense, I might add."

Cenda rubbed her forehead. Lady, her head hurt! "Is he dead?"

The Primus seated herself in one of the chairs and crossed her legs. "Ah, love," she murmured. "So messy." Her pretty brown hair sat perfectly, waving back from her forehead, streaks of gray at her temples.

"Don't patronize me!" Cenda glared, feeling angry heat bubble in her veins. *"Is he dead?"*

The other woman glanced at the screens. "Not yet." After a beat, she said, "Interesting reaction. Do you feel dizzy?"

"A little."

"You're not functioning very well. Sharanita?" The Primus nodded to the tall woman, who pushed a button. A section of wall under the window slid up to reveal a tray. On it sat four cubes, each about the size of Cenda's fist, one pink and smooth, one green and nubby, two others mud colored. With them was a glass tumbler full of a clear fluid that looked like water. "Eat something."

Cenda drained half the water in one gulp before her brain caught up with her thirst. Shit! What if it was drugged?

"Why would I bother?" The other woman smiled kindly,

as if she'd heard the thought. "I already have you under my control." Even through the glass, the Technomage's eyes gleamed with satisfaction, tiny crow's-feet crinkling at the corners.

Gods, thought Cenda dismally, why was her face so easy to read? "What do you mean, I'm not functioning well?"

"I bought a powerful fire witch. You couldn't light a candle in your present condition. You're dehydrated and you need protein."

Bought? *Bought?* Gritting her teeth, Cenda said, "The machines tell you that?" Then she picked up the pink cube and sniffed it doubtfully.

"Clever girl." An approving nod, as if she were a dog who'd performed a clever trick. "Yes, the machines tell me that."

Cenda nibbled at a corner of the cube and pulled a face. It tasted like nut porridge and sawdust, unsalted and unflavored. "Krys says I need fuel to feed the fire." *Krys.* "I want to see her."

"Purist Krysanthe?" A raised brow. "Why?"

So it was true; she hadn't dreamed it. She bowed her head, not wanting the other woman to see the tears, but when she looked up again, the Primus was staring at her wall screens, rapt. "I want to see her face, hear her voice, know why . . ." She had to stop to catch her breath.

"No," said the Primus. "I don't think so." She turned her head. "We need to talk, Cenda, about what you're going to do for me."

"For you?" Cenda clenched her fists to hide the flames, but they escaped, licking up over her forearms. "Why would I do anything for you?"

"Fascinating," murmured the Technomage, leaning forward in her chair, mouth open, eyes bright. Then she sat back and folded her hands together in her lap, at ease once more. "Let me explain."

"No." Cenda tossed the food cube on the floor. It bounced. "Let *me* explain. I don't feel like eating, or *functioning.* Not until I see Gray and Krys."

"I can have you force-fed."

"I'm sure you could. But that'll be messy, won't it?" She couldn't prevent the curl of her lip. "Like love."

The Technomage gave a bark of laughter. "I think I like you, Cenda the fire witch."

"Gray and Krys?"

"All right." Still chuckling, the Primus waved a hand at Sharanita. The tall woman got busy punching buttons, muttering into a black disk pinned to her lapel. "I need to establish a set of benchmarks in any case. The observations should prove extremely interesting."

Doggedly, Cenda applied herself to the green food cube, washing it down with sips of water. When Sharanita rose to usher the familiar, bustling figure into the other room, her throat closed so hard, she couldn't breathe for a moment. She set the cube aside. "Krys."

"Hullo, Cenda." The healer bent her head, fiddling with something on her chatelaine.

"Krys, look at me."

Slowly, Krys met her gaze through the glass, the clever dark eyes defiant, and a little scared.

"How did she buy you?" Cenda took the few steps to the window and pressed her palm against it. "What did she offer?"

The healer's jaw tightened. "Knowledge. Understanding." Her eyes began to sparkle. "Centuries of recorded research." She braced her hands on the desk, leaning forward. "Cenda, it's a different way to think about healing. When I put Science together with Magick, there'll be no limits to what I can heal, what miracles—"

"You'll bring me back from the dead, then?"

Krys scowled. "You're misunderstanding on purpose."

Flames frisked up her arms, danced around Cenda's shoulders. "Well, it's my life. I think I'm entitled. All for the good of humanity, is that it?"

"Remember the green salve? How it healed the Duke?" Krysanthe bounced on the spot, grinning. "Complete tissue repair in a matter of hours. I worked with the Septimus to develop it. She's the senior Technomage healer. The top person."

"So the end justifies the means?" Cenda straightened, dropping her hand. "And I'm the means."

"Sweetie, I'm sorry." Her friend's face twisted with distress. "If there was any other way . . ." Tears stood in her eyes. "But they would have taken you, anyway. That's why I was there. I insisted, you know. To make sure they treated you right, didn't hurt you."

"Didn't hurt—!" The blood roared in Cenda's ears and the room spun, seen through a veil of orange blue flame. She slammed into the window, blazing like a torch soaked in pitch. "Gray?" she screamed, over the crackle of flames. "What about Gray?"

"Gods!" Both Sharanita and Krysanthe stumbled back, paling, but the Primus was made of sterner stuff. Her fingers flew over dials, levers, and buttons while she glanced repeatedly at her banks of screens, face shining with concentration. And greed.

Cenda let herself slip down the cool glass until she huddled on the floor and the flames died to a flickering shawl around her shoulders. Tilting her head back, she stared deep into her friend's eyes, wanting to inflict pain, *needing* to do it, to shatter the smug armor of Krysanthe's conviction. "And Tai Yang?" she asked, forming each word softly and precisely. "What does he say?"

The healer's chin wobbled and tears trembled on her lashes. She turned her head away.

Cenda smiled, not pleasantly. "I see."

"The Purist's apprentice?" said the Primus coolly. "A regrettable casualty. He was a most intelligent young man. Very promising."

Cenda ignored her. "Krys? Look at me."

Blinking furiously, the other woman set her jaw. "He couldn't see it, even though I explained, over and over. *Begged.* His face . . ." She turned her back, breathing heavily.

Poor Tai Yang, so earnest, so serious. She'd grieve for him later.

"So you did love him." Cenda felt her lip curl with cruel satisfaction at Krysanthe's wince. "But not as much as your ambition."

"This is the future." The healer stiffened, running trembling fingers over the console set into the desk. "If you don't keep up, you get left behind. Tai Yang made his decision. I'm sorry, Cenda, more sorry than I can say—"

Cenda snorted, but Krys persevered.

"—that you choose to be so willfully blind, so wrongheaded. Sweetie, please." Her whole body inclined toward the window. "Please, if my friendship means anything. Just think about it, all right?"

"Matthaeus and Olga and the rest of the Enclave? Are they dead, too?"

"No. No!" Krysanthe looked appalled. "How could you think such a thing?"

The Technomage waved a hand, the nails neat, well-shaped ovals. "The incident was well contained. You were extracted with the minimum of fuss." She drew a flat, shiny case toward her and took a half dozen translucent sheets from it. "Ah," she said, scanning the page in a single comprehensive glance. "Good work, Nita. You did well to get the samples through the lab so quickly. Is everything in place for the stress tests?"

"What tests?" asked Krysanthe, craning her neck, an anxious furrow between her brows.

"You still here?" The Primus glanced up. Then she shot a measuring glance at Cenda. "Finished with her?"

A ball of ice seemed to have taken up residence in Cenda's stomach. "Yes," she said dully, turning her back. "Good-bye, Krys."

"But, Cenda—"

The Technomage's voice was brisk. "Off you go now, dear. You've had your chance. Now it's mine."

"But what are you going to do?" asked the healer.

Cenda spun around, glaring at her friend. "Surely you can guess?"

The Technomage's laugh was attractive, low and musical. "I doubt it," she said. "Nita?"

The tall woman strode to the door and held it open in a very pointed kind of way. "Off wit' ye." Looking down at Krysanthe, she jerked her head in dismissal.

A last troubled look over her shoulder and the healer was gone.

"I want to see Gray."

"All in good time." The Primus remained unperturbed. "Aren't you wondering what I'm going to offer for your cooperation?"

23

Cenda stared, the pulse pounding in her ears. "Offer?" she repeated. "I thought you'd just take."

The Technomage Primus inclined her head. "I have the power to do that—I wouldn't want you to think otherwise—but I also believe in the value of investment. I'm giving you the opportunity to defray what I've spent on you. I'm sure you're perceptive enough to realize you're worth more to me if you're willing?"

Cenda gave a bark of laughter, the sound deadened by the rubbery substance of the floor and walls. "You're joking!"

"Not at all." The Primus turned to the woman in the flowered smock and held out a hand, smiling.

Sharanita bent to retrieve a shiny silver box about a foot square from beneath the desk. Biting her lip with concentration, she removed the lid and set it aside, her big-knuckled hands surprisingly deft. Reaching in, she extracted wads of some cottony material, obviously packing of some sort. Finally, she used both hands to lift something free with the greatest of care, setting it gently on the desk. Another cube, this one a matte gray like the wall screens, a little smaller than what had passed for food.

The Primus beamed.

Cenda frowned, her heart thudding. "What is it?"

"Something you'll like. But first I have to activate it." The Technomage took the stylus Sharanita handed her and poked it into the underside of the cube, her brow knitted. "They're so fragile 'til the sequence is locked in. Ah, there!" Even through the ceiling grille, Cenda heard the tiny, decisive *click* quite clearly. "Now you couldn't scratch it with a fission cannon."

A what? But the other woman was bending to place the new object in an aperture low on the wall.

The tray slid in and then reappeared, bearing the cube.

Cenda stretched out a hand, snatched it back.

"It's safe," said the Primus encouragingly. Over the top of her head, Sharanita grinned and nodded.

Slowly, Cenda reached forward and closed her fingers around the cube. At the moment of contact, it gave off a clear, sweet tone like a silver bell. One side shimmered and rippled, the image of a young woman swimming out of the gray. After a few seconds, the outline firmed up, and Cenda stared at it, puzzled.

"Who's this?" She passed a fingertip over the pretty, smiling face. The woman was probably in her early twenties, with a cloud of dark hair rather like Cenda's own. Her face was round and cheerful, given definition by a stubborn chin and level brows. Cenda frowned, irritated by a nagging sense of familiarity.

The Technomage placed her palms flat on the desk and leaned forward, her face intent. A brow arched. "Can't you guess?"

When Cenda shook her head, the other woman said softly, "Turn it around."

There was Elke, just as she remembered her, chubby baby cheeks dimpled with giggles, soft curls waving around her little head. The lips of the image moved, showing the small, white baby teeth. "Mama," gurgled Elke, though no sound emerged from the thing. "Mama."

Cenda grunted as if she'd been gut-punched. The cube dropped from her nerveless fingers to bounce off the flexible surface of the floor. A heartbeat later, her brain creaked back into gear. Elke! Desperately, she flung herself after it, scrabbling on her knees.

"Ah, perfect," said the Primus, her face wreathed with satisfaction. "I knew it would be."

Sharanita sniffed and wiped away a tear with the hem of her smock.

Cenda touched Elke's face with wondering fingers. "She moves. It's exactly—How did you—"

The Primus folded her arms. "Science," she said briskly. "Look a little harder, fire witch."

Dashing away the tears with the back of her hand, Cenda turned the cube, holding it steady with difficulty. A girl of about twelve with the familiar dark curls. And on the next side, the same child at six or seven, wearing a blithe, gap-toothed grin, a smudge of dirt on her cheek.

Cenda's heart began a slow, slamming beat, like a death knell. She twisted the box, her hands shaking so hard she had to fight not to drop it. Six sides, and they were all Elke, all her darling, caught at every stage between infancy and adulthood. Her head swam with longing and terror. "What evil is this?" she croaked. "Her soul, my baby's soul . . ." She couldn't complete the sentence.

The Technomage clucked her tongue with impatience. "Superstitious nonsense," she snapped. "It's just a picture series, a holo, no more. Quite an advanced one, though." Her bosom expanded beneath the spotless white jacket. "Age projections are particularly difficult, but I flatter myself I got them pretty well flawless."

A *hollow*? That was a good name for it. She was scraped raw inside, her soul an empty, blood-splattered space echoing with pain and fear. Cenda passed gentle fingers over the face of Elke the woman, noting the calm good humor in the blue eyes. Elke had had her father's eyes.

This was what the gods had stolen from her—a whole life—not just the brief, precious months of a baby's existence, but all the potential, the bright promise of a normal span. She would never see Elke blossom into womanhood, never be her friend as well as her mother. All those possibilities were displayed before her, made manifest in a way so cruel, it robbed her of breath. Grief and rage rose up on a slashing wave, so keen, so razor sharp, that Cenda doubled over, slain by the intensity of it.

Moaning, she clutched the cube and rocked herself, the edges digging into her palms.

Dimly, she was aware of the Technomage rising to stand right up against the window glass, saying the same sentence over and over, with a kind of grim patience. "You can have her, Cenda. You can have her back."

Cenda wiped her nose with the sheet. "She's dead. Gone forever. My baby."

"For Science's sake, you stupid woman, will you listen?" snapped the Primus. "That's the whole point. I can give her back to you. Pretty much exactly as she was, if we use the same male." Her eyes blazed. "It will be as if she never died. What do you think of that, fire witch?"

Cenda gaped. "What?" she said weakly. "No, that's not possible, that's . . . How?"

"Science."

"But . . . she's dead."

The Technomage sighed. "Look, you'd never understand. The concepts are too complex for someone without a Technomage education. But believe me when I say"—she pressed a small, square hand against the glass, the pads of her fingers whitening with the pressure—"I can re-create your daughter. Elke, wasn't that what you called her? Funny little name, but never mind. Cenda, I will plant her in your womb again." She nodded at the *hollow*, her voice dropping to a murmur. "All those faces, you will see them in the flesh."

Her hair was stuck to her cheeks with sweat and tears. Cenda shoved it back one-handed because she couldn't let go of the cube. The sterile room swooped and swung around her. Panting, she struggled for sense. "Try me," she said huskily. "Explain."

The Technomage's lips went tight. "It's a gross oversimplification, but think of it as a combination of the codes imprinted in your flesh and that of the father. Krysanthe brought me a few strands of the child's hair, so I know what sequences I'm aiming for." Her spine stiffened. "I am the Technomage Primus because I achieve my objectives. *Always*. Do not presume to question me again."

"She said she wanted some of Elke's hair to put in a locket. Weeks ago. So I took some from the one I had. Fool that I am, I didn't even think."

Walking on her knees, Cenda made her way to the mattress and sank down. Her heart thudded behind her ribs, a heavy, choking beat, a chant of *My baby, gods, my baby.* Oh, to hold her again, to hug that precious little body to her breast, to touch her plump cheek . . . Little arms in a stranglehold around her neck, sloppy, openmouthed kisses pressed to her eyebrow. Real, not just a dream of longing and empty arms. Ah, the return of hope was a painful thing! She tried to think through the fog. "And the price?"

"Mm, yes." The other woman relaxed. "Batteries of tests, I'm afraid. A couple of . . . procedures." She waved a hand. "The usual."

"What sort of procedures?"

The Technomage smiled that practiced smile. "Nothing very dreadful."

Behind her, Sharanita shifted abruptly. Then she dropped her head, biting her lip.

Cenda brushed her fingers over the raw patch on the inside of her arm. She didn't think the Technomage was practiced at lying in person, face-to-face. "What is it you want from me?"

The other woman studied her. "I want to know how it works, how you do it. If it's reproducible." Calmly, she seated herself. "Everything about it, really."

"Reproducible?" Cenda stared. "Why?"

"For Science's sake, why do you think?" The Technomage's knuckles whitened on the arm of the chair. "Just imagine, all that energy . . . an almost infinite power source. Think of the possibilities for us all . . ."

"And the damage," murmured Cenda, remembering the Fixer's agonized face, the flames rising hundreds of feet into the air above the palazzo. Charred corpses on a battlefield. Gods . . . She squeezed her eyes shut.

"Of course, it will have to be harnessed, controlled. That's why I need you."

Cenda ran her thumb over the face of the twelve-year-old Elke. That was a willful chin. Would they have fought? Argued? Would Elke have been a door slammer? She looked up, keeping Sharanita's face in her peripheral vision. "Will it hurt?"

"A little, perhaps. But I'm sure it'll be worth it."

The tall woman's face went completely blank. She blinked rapidly.

Cenda shuddered, cold sweat breaking out on the palms of her hands, over her ribs. Death she thought she could face—Elke was waiting at the end of that bright tunnel—but not pain, pain without end. Even if she discounted half of the rumors about what went on in the Technomage's labs, she was helpless, destined for a world of hurt, measured and dispassionate, inflicted in the name of progress. For Science and the ambition of the Technomage Primus.

"You seem a sensible woman." Coolly, the Technomage rose, tugging her jacket straight. "But I'll give you an hour or so to think."

"Wait." Resolutely, Cenda put the images out of her mind. White-gloved hands grasping slim, shining blades, honed to a wicked edge. High, narrow beds with white, tight sheets and long, dark straps and buckles. Bright blood welling scarlet against cool linen. Forceps, little saws—*Great Lady!*

She cleared her throat. "I want to see Gray."

"The Duke?" The Technomage's lip curled. "Are you sure?"

"Yes. I can't decide until I see him."

"Mm." The Primus shot her a glinting glance. Her smile grew, though it was grim. "Very well," she said. "You should know the truth." She nodded at Sharanita. "Bring him."

Gray was leaning up against the wall, dozing, when the godsbedamned thing started *humming*. The vibration traveled through his shoulders, centering on the sore spot on his jaw, making his teeth ache. For the fiftieth time since he'd come round, he ran his tongue over his molars. All there, thank Judger. No thanks to Number Forty-fucking-two and his fucking boots.

He opened his eyes a slit. He'd been in enough jails to recognize the feel of one right away, though there were no bars here, and no door or windows, either. Like a rat in a box.

Shad stirred beside him, not much more than a gray, amorphous shape in the diffused light that came from the ceiling fittings. *A rat with a shadow.*

Yeah. It was a kind of comfort not to be completely alone. It wasn't his imagination, he was sure; the place smelled of despair, as if the sweat of terror had soaked into the thin mattress on the floor.

From beneath his lashes, he watched a rectangular opening form on the far wall of the bare, dusty room, a tall figure advance.

"Well, well. My friend Forty-two." Gray tilted his head to one side and opened his eyes very wide. "You looked better in the helmet."

"You should use the proper form of address. I am the Quadraginta Secundus." The man scowled, knitting sandy brows.

"Nice," said Gray. "What do you want, Quad?"

"Childish taunts don't bother me," said the Technomage. He gave a prim smile. "You're to go before the Primus, *Duke*." He gestured with the weapon he held. "Up."

A lasegun. Gray had seen them before, on the black market, though for some reason, they stopped working once they were out of Technomage hands for longer than a few weeks.

The gods be thanked, action at last. She wasn't dead, his fire witch—he knew that much already. Shit, what had they done with her? He'd woken on a flitter, jaw throbbing, guts heaving, strapped down so tightly all he'd been able to move was his head. Squinting across the craft, he'd managed to make out her still body, that glorious hair spilling over the side of the gurney, and a small woman, bending over her, white trews straining over substantial hips.

The flitter side-slipped and the woman braced herself. "We're coming in," she snapped to the tall, sandy-haired man beside her. Quad. "Secure the woman."

"Yes, Primus."

And then Quad had turned and seen Gray watching. He frowned. "Damn. He's not supposed to wake for another two hours."

The Primus straightened, her blue eyes calm and cool. "Dose him again."

But Quad had frowned. "Uh, Primus, it says here on the tube"—he pulled a red cylinder from a pack on his belt—"not to exceed, ah, thirty units."

The flitter banked, and Gray's body pressed against the straps. Surreptitiously, he strained his fingers, feeling for his forearm knife.

"Science!" hissed the Primus. "I developed that drug myself. He can take his chances." The craft began to vibrate, a deep buzzing coming from under the floor. "Don't argue. Knock him out!"

His lips compressed, Quad had jammed the evil thing against Gray's neck, and the flitter and everything in it had faded away, submerged under an icy tide of black.

All of which indicated quite clearly that he was expendable. Ah, well, nothing new.

He stood and rolled his shoulders as far as the manacles on his wrists would permit. They weren't at all heavy, being made of what looked like the same slick substance as Technomage paper, but Judger, they were strong! The thin blade he kept in his boot might as well have been on one of the Dancers for all the use it was. His mouth still felt as though he'd swallowed a dog hide with the fur left on, but he'd drunk as much water as he could hold and used the noisome little privy concealed behind a sliding section of the wall.

He was about as good as he was going to get. Which didn't fill him with cheer.

Me, you have me.

For once, his heart lightened when Shad spoke. *True. And they don't know.*

Like the old days. Us and them.

Waving the lasegun, Quad ushered him into a passage with featureless beige walls, pierced at regular intervals by beige doors with beige knobs.

The tall, angular woman waiting there stood out against the neutral tones like an exploded bouquet of tropical flowers. Gray blinked. "You're not a Technomage."

"Nah." She turned and strode away, Quad bringing up the rear, the lasegun caressing Gray's spine.

"This is the Prime Assistant," said Quad, in a voice completely devoid of inflection.

As they turned a corner into another corridor, Gray raised a brow. "Oh, no, trouble in paradise?"

"Nah." The woman placed her palm against a plate on a door no different from the rest. The smile made her plain face almost pretty. "T' Primus depends on me, ye see."

She stood aside, Quad shoved with the lasegun, and Gray stepped into a light so bright it made him screw up his eyes. The door clicked shut behind him.

"Gray!"

A flying figure launched itself across the room and into his arms. "Oh, Gray. I thought—Are you—?" Cenda clung, babbling, patting his cheek, his shoulders, rubbing her hands up and down his arms. Then she pulled away, so she could peer into his face.

"I've been better." Awkward because of the cuffs, he cupped her cheek. "You?"

Her lips trembled. "Me, too."

She looked terrible, the harsh light emphasizing the bony shape of her skull, her cheekbones thrown into sharp relief by the hollows under her eyes. The sources of illumination were in the ceiling, so bright and all-encompassing that casting a shadow wasn't possible.

Over her shoulder, he could see straight through a window so large it was virtually a wall of glass. The room beyond was full of Technomage machinery, not unlike the deck of a starship. His guts crawled.

"Duke." The Technomage Primus nodded, her face alight with what looked like grim relish. It didn't bode well. A door behind her opened, and the tall Sybarite woman walked in to loom quietly at her shoulder.

Gray ignored them both. Taking Cenda's hand in both of his, he tugged her close. She landed against him with a sweet little sigh. "You got the superior accommodations," he said. "But why are you wearing a sheet?"

In the other room, the Technomage seated herself at the console and began to adjust knobs and dials, her intent blue gaze flitting from the wall screens to Gray and Cenda, and back again.

"Doesn't matter." The fire witch cast a dark glance at the preoccupied Technomage. Bracing herself on Gray's shoulders, she whispered in his ear. "I feel like a scuttleroach in a jar."

"Speak as softly as you like. I can still hear you." The Technomage chuckled. "There's only one scuttleroach in that room, my dear, and it's not you."

How long did he have before the bitch exposed his treachery? Only minutes. This close, looking into Cenda's face, he'd hear the crack as her heart broke. The Technomage was delaying, savoring the anticipation, but she didn't strike him as a woman who denied herself her pleasures.

No use trying to stave off the inevitable; he wouldn't give her the satisfaction of watching him squirm. Anger moved in him, deep and bright. And cold purpose. He didn't bother to look at the other woman again. Cenda was going to hate him. There was nothing he could do about that, or about the hurt, but it didn't matter, not really, not when he knew what he was going to have to do.

He had nothing left now, only the last shards of what had once been his honor. The fire witch stood before him, shaking with nerves, stripped of everything save a sheet. And yet she was cloaked in the dignity of her innocence, the goodness of her soul. Judger God, he owed her recompense! He didn't doubt she would have ended up here eventually, and at least he'd managed to keep her in one piece. But nonetheless, it was his fault, his and Shad's. He'd swaggered into her life, selfish and stupid and desperate, and turned it upside down. That made Cenda his responsibility, and by all the gods, he'd honor that obligation! Because if he didn't, he might as well bare his throat for the blade right now.

Cenda didn't have anyone but him. He was going to get her out of here, and if it killed him, as it probably would, what did it matter to the fucking universe, anyhow? No one would know, no one would mourn, but his life would have been worth *something*. His lips twisted. Shad would approve; he was sure of it.

As for the Technomage Primus . . . He growled under his breath. Presumably, her blood was the same color as everyone else's. He intended to prove the truth of the hypothesis in a suitably violent and Scientific manner.

"Gray . . ." Cenda stumbled to a halt, her eyes enormous, full of some emotion almost too great to be borne. She tugged him around, so that their backs were to the interested gaze of the Technomage. Wordlessly, she opened her fingers, so he could see the small gray box that sat on her palm.

Frowning, he touched it gingerly with a fingertip. "What is it?"

"The price." Cenda's mouth worked. "Elke." Her golden eyes swam with tears.

Gray took the thing from her with both hands and examined it. All six sides. Judger God. His mouth went dry. Twisting, he glanced over his shoulder at the Technomage. She gazed placidly back through the glass, her head tilted.

"What do you mean?" he asked the fire witch, dreading the answer.

"She says"—Cenda swallowed—"she can give me back my baby, exactly as she was. I'll give birth to her, hold her, watch her grow . . ." She trailed off, her breath coming in shallow pants.

"Not possible," said Gray flatly.

"I believe her," whispered Cenda. She caressed the cube with a fingertip. "Look how she moves, my darling." Her smile was misty. "She grew up so pretty, much prettier than her mother."

"Here." He shoved the filthy thing back at her. "Cenda, love . . ." Desperately, he grasped her arm with his bound hands. "You can't trust her; you know you can't."

An amused voice issued from the ceiling grille. It said with immense satisfaction, "You're a fine one to talk of trust, Duke."

Oh, shit, here it came. Automatically, Gray reached for Shad, but there was nothing there in the bright room. Only his aching, angry self.

The fire witch stared up at him, the tears spilling over. She didn't cry well. Her nose was red, her skin blotchy. "It was Krys," she said in a ragged whisper. "She betrayed us." She flicked a look at the woman behind the window and flames leaped in her gaze. "The Technomage bought her."

The Technomage's smile broadened. A final twist of a dial, and she leaned back in the big chair. *Fuck.* Instinctively, Gray released Cenda and stepped away.

"The same way I bought you, Duke," said the Primus, savoring each word.

24

Cenda tossed her head and glared at the window. "No, you didn't."

"You think?" The Technomage Primus raised her brows. "Look at his face."

He'd had no concept of how bad it would be, watching the light die in her eyes. The seconds ticked by and her face stiffened, until it could have been a pallid mask plastered over the bones of her skull. This was how she might look on her deathbed.

Words tumbled out of his mouth, stupid, pleading words. "I didn't give you to the Fixer."

"No," said the Technomage, "but you took my money and then reneged on our bargain. I take a dim view of a man without honor. Don't you, Cenda?"

Slowly, the fire witch reached out and clamped her fingers around his forearm. Flames danced in her eyes. "So it was all a lie?"

"*No!* Not all of it, I swear." He could smell the fabric

of the ragged shirt beginning to scorch, his flesh heating beneath her touch.

Her grip tightened. "You set out to seduce me, didn't you?"

"Only at the start." A bracelet of bright agony seared across his skin. "Shit, Cenda!" He ripped himself free.

"I must have been so easy." The fire witch tossed the gray cube to the mattress and lifted her hands. When she flexed her fingers, flames shot toward him. "So *pathetic*!"

As Gray backed away, she stalked him, magnificent in her fury, hair crackling with rage, her cheeks flushed. Judger, with his hands bound, a shoulder charge was his best chance. He should be able to take her down without doing more than jar the breath out of her. But after that . . . Shit, shit, *shit*!

"Gods, whoring yourself out like that." Her lip curled. The sheet had slipped to her waist, exposing her breasts. She looked like a warrior goddess thundering across a temple frieze. Terrifying. "You must *really* need money."

A ribbon of flame flicked out to caress his calf, and he jumped aside, cursing. "I had my reasons," he growled. "And it wasn't the money."

"But you took it just the same," said the smug voice from behind the window. "Cenda, your output is off my charts. Don't stop."

Without releasing Gray from her gaze, the fire witch paused, haloed by a flickering nimbus. "What?"

The Technomage tweaked a dial, adjusted a lever. She stared at a wall screen, frowning. "We don't need him anymore," she said absently. "Go ahead and save us the trouble." Her blue eyes snapped with excitement. "It's amazing. Your metabolic adjustment is extraordinarily efficient."

The high color drained from Cenda's face. She squeezed her eyes shut. "Great Lady, save me. I almost—" She spun around, showing Gray the flat, angular planes of shoulder blades shifting under creamy skin as she hunched into herself, hitching the sheet up under her arms. "I swore an oath to do no harm." Her chin went up. "I will honor it."

"For Science's sake, woman!" The Technomage's lips compressed into an irritated line. "I've got all the instruments calibrated and running. Time is money; you know that. We've got the perfect setup, ready to go."

Gray found his voice. "Setup for what? Murder?"

Cenda shot him a single agonized glance before turning her face to the wall.

The Technomage Primus gave no sign of having heard. He might as well have been invisible. Or already dead.

"Cenda," the Scientist said urgently, "complete the test."

But the fire witch only shook her head, her breathing rapid and shallow.

The other woman sighed. "Very well," she said. "I'll let it go this time." She made a mark on one of the translucent sheets with a stylus. "Nita," she murmured, "tell the Quadraginta Secundus to stop by with a cleanup crew, would you?"

Gray's heart somersaulted into his throat and tried to choke him. *Shad.* Oh, Judger God, Shad. Would he have the chance to say good-bye?

"Yah, Primus." The Sybarite woman moved to the door.

The stylus paused. "Oh, and Nita?"

"Yah, Primus?"

"Tell him to use the healer woman. It's time she earned her keep." The Technomage signed the bottom of the page with a neat flourish.

Gray walked up behind the fire witch, his footfalls soundless on the cushiony floor. Gently, he touched her shoulder, feeling the tremors that ran through her, over and over. "I swear it was never about money, sweetheart," he murmured. "And it was you who seduced me, though you weren't supposed to." He stroked her hair, aching. "I'm sorry. For everything. Kiss me good-bye?"

Cenda flinched, but slowly, she turned, her eyes great

golden pools in her pale face. Wordlessly, she lifted her chin and wrapped her hands over his, her fingers brushing the strange, lightweight manacles.

Gray shot a glance at the window. The Primus was frowning, absorbed in her sheets of information.

Their lips met and clung in a lingering, closed-mouth kiss. Her fingers moved against his, gripping the cuffs. Gods, what he'd give to be able to wrap her up in his arms, his sweet, hot witch. But he couldn't, and that was that. It was better this way. Behind him, the door whooshed open and he drew away, blinking hard.

"Tell Shad—" She broke off.

"Yes, I will."

"Come on," said Quad from the doorway, the lasegun much in evidence.

Gray touched her cheek with the fingertips of both hands. "Don't trust her," he whispered fiercely, knowing it was a lost cause. "Just don't."

Then he turned away, brushing rudely past Quad and out into the beige corridor.

Heartbreak was a strange thing. Considering it was born in your thoughts, intangible, incorporeal, it had the most amazing effects on the body. She should have been used to it, able to cope with the boulder of pain and grief and rage crushing her chest, but it seemed she'd forgotten how. Cenda pressed the heels of her hands into her eyes and, just for a moment, let herself fall into the glowing dark. *Great Lady, You took my joy from me, my Elke. In return, You gave me the Magick of Your fire. Now grant me Your strength to do what I must do.*

She opened her eyes as the Technomage gathered the translucent pages together and slid them into her shiny case. The other woman rose, smoothing her hair.

"Wait."

The Primus paused and set the case down again. "I said I'd give you time to think."

"Don't need it." Cenda's voice was so creaky, she barely recognized it herself. She coughed. "I've decided."

"Ah." Smiling, the Technomage leaned over the tall back of the chair. "I knew it."

Cenda wet her lips with her tongue. "Don't kill him."

The Technomage's brows flew up. "You want *him*? The Duke?"

Cenda nodded.

"After what he did?"

She nodded again.

"But why—?" The other woman broke off and shook her head, apparently baffled. "Your logic escapes me."

"Doesn't matter. Let him go. Unharmed."

"I was right," said the Technomage sternly. "Love *is* messy. Cenda, my generosity is not without its limits. I will not give you two lives. Think carefully. Which do you want?" She glanced up at the wall screen on the left. "And think quick."

She couldn't afford to be clumsy, not now. Concentrating fiercely, picking her words with care, Cenda said, "I want to see him walk free of this place. No tricks. Then I'll do whatever you wish."

"Are you sure, my dear? What about your baby?"

Cenda met the cool blue eyes though the glass. "Elke is dead because she's meant to be dead. There's a reason. I can't imagine what it is, but the gods know. Nothing and no one can replace her. What you want to do is an abomination. *Wrong*."

"Very well." The Technomage straightened, tucking her case under one arm. Her face was stiff. "At least this option has the virtue of bringing the project in well under budget. Refreshing." Briskly, she moved to the door. "I'll let you know." It closed behind her, and the section of wall slid across to cover the window with a definitive hiss.

Cenda crumpled to the mattress. Gathering up Elke's cube, she curled into a fetal ball, clasping it to her breast. Biting her lip, she willed herself to hold back the rising tide, to wait until she could be sure the other woman was out of earshot. But the sobs began, anyway, deep in her chest, and as they tore free, they hurt, as if they were barbed. Her mouth distorted into a helpless, ugly gape and she pressed her face into the cool surface of the mattress, trying to muffle the sounds. In a small, bleak corner of her mind, she wondered if the Technomage's machines were still ticking, estimating the depth of her despair to the last sixteenth of an inch, measuring the exact volume of her tears.

After what felt like an eon, she rolled over, throwing an arm over her eyes. Her throat burned. Blotting her face with the sheet, she thought bitterly that the Primus had the right of it. Love was messy. Love screwed you over, ruined your life, made you see yourself for what you were—skinny, awkward, *old*. Five-it, she was pathetic! Desperately, hopelessly in love with a beautiful bastard, shadow and all.

Even now, the fear for him had long shudders running through her limbs, over and over. She couldn't seem to keep her hands steady, even though they were clenched around the *hollow*. Her thoughts swung like an off-kilter pendulum. Gray, Elke. Gray, Elke.

Gods, to bring Elke back from the dead, like some living, breathing ghost! Once again, she saw her baby, her precious darling, cradled close in the arms of the Lady, where she was meant to be, loved and laughing. *Laughing.* For one incandescent instant, she'd been tempted almost beyond bearing. But then the totality of it had come crashing down, the thought of something so unnatural making her skin crawl with horror.

As for Gray, he wouldn't thank her for saving his pretty hide, even if the Technomage kept her promise, which was by no means certain. Any man with such a finely honed instinct for self-preservation would seize his chance and run far and fast. He might think of her now and then, with vague regret. He wasn't all bad; he'd be sorry to hear of her death. He'd liked her well enough, she thought now, enough to lie patiently after they'd fucked, stroking her hair with absentminded affection. She couldn't call it making love; it had been *fucking*, nothing more. Ah, but Great Lady, it had been amazing, wonderful. With Shad—

Cenda sat up and hugged her knees. A sad smile curved her lips. With Shad, she'd been making love. Poor sweet shadow, so much Gray and so much not. She wondered if he'd cry dusky tears for her.

She peered at the far wall though puffy eyelids. If she could just splash her face with cool water . . . Carefully, she set the *hollow* aside and approached the wall. The seam had started about *there.* When she pressed her palms against the area, something buzzed, and the familiar rectangular opening appeared. Cenda blew out a shaky breath. Thank the Lady for small mercies.

When they reached Gray's cell, the healer was waiting inside, together with a lumpish Technomage with 379 on the collar of his shirt. He was solid enough through the shoulders, but he had the small paunch of a man unaccustomed to physical exercise, and he stood flat-footed. The lasegun was lost in his beefy paw.

Shad sprang into existence, a smoky, wavering shape on the wall. Immediately, Gray reached for him. *Shad?*

Here.

Quad shoved Gray in the small of the back so that he stumbled forward onto the mattress. "Kneel," he said brusquely. The door hissed shut.

As he fell to his knees, Gray shot Krysanthe a hard glance. Her plump, pretty face looked doughy with tension. Between her fingers, she twisted one of the Technomage tubes, a white one. Around and around and around.

Gray bared his teeth, his heart beating right into his throat. "Killing someone in cold blood isn't easy," he said. "I think it's the eyes. What do you think, Quad?"

"I don't think at all." Quad pressed his palm against a shiny plate to the left of the door.

Gray's snort of laughter was lost in a loud hiss as an opening about three feet square appeared in the floor just beyond the end of the mattress. Judger God! A gentle, rhythmic humming floated up from far, far below, like a giant sleeping in the bowels of a mountain. His guts cramped. Machinery. Fucking Technomage machinery.

Get ready. The lumpy one's yours. He flexed his wrists in the manacles.

Yes. Determination, focus. Not hot with rage, but cold and steely.

"Efficient, aren't you?" His voice was remarkably steady, all things considered. "No fuss, no mess."

"Yes," said Quad. "Humane, too. You won't feel a thing." He turned to the healer. "Against the neck." He pressed his fingers to a spot behind his ear. "Here."

Krysanthe shook her head, the chatelaine jingling softly at her waist. "I—I *can't*."

Gray stared into her panicked eyes. "Is this how they killed Tai Yang?" he asked quietly. "Or did you do it yourself?"

"No!" The healer lurched forward a step. "I'm sworn to do no harm. No, he—I couldn't—Not in time." She swallowed hard and her mouth worked.

"Go on," said Quad, not unkindly. "It's unpleasant, but it's over quick. Just take a breath and do it."

Tears streamed down Krysanthe's cheeks. Her skirts billowing around her, she slumped to her knees at Gray's side. "Forgive me," she whispered, lifting the white tube. "Please, say you forgive me."

Gray held her eye. "You've got to be joking."

A sharp, two-toned chime echoed in the confined space. Quad dug a small black disk out of his belt pack and clapped it to his ear. "Yes," he said, frowning. "Yes, but—All right, yes, I've got it." Brow still furrowed, he returned the disk to his pack.

Flexing his shoulders, Gray poured every particle of strength he possessed into pulling his hands apart. The muscles in his forearms writhed. A half second of unbearable tension and the substance of cuffs stretched along the line Cenda had weakened for him with the touch of her fiery fingers.

"Wha—?" gasped Krysanthe.

Gray drove his shoulder into the healer's soft belly, pushing her hard into Quad's legs, simultaneously ripping the manacles apart with a desperate surge of strength. Technomage 379 came off the wall as if he'd been goosed, lasegun waving wildly, but long, smoky arms wrapped around his meaty thighs from behind, tackling him in a powerful charge that sent him headlong across the mattress and into the dark opening in the floor. He disappeared with a startled, choking cry, the soles of his boots thrashing in a final instant of terror and panic.

That left Quad.

Gray had to give the man marks for brains. Still tangled in the healer's skirts, sprawled full length on the floor, he was lifting the black disk to his mouth with one hand, the lasegun clutched in the other. Gray launched himself across the room, all his attention on the disk. A sizzling bolt scored the top of his shoulder and he bit back a scream. Fuck, it hurt! Fuck, fuck, fuck!

Furious with pain, he raised his elbow and slammed it into Quad's Adam's apple. The man gave a horrible choking gargle and fell back, both hands rising to claw at his throat, his face congesting with blood, the eyes protruding from his head.

Krysanthe scrambled to her knees, her eyes stretched wide with terror, mouth open to scream. A dark shape rose out of the floor directly in front of her and a shadowy fist clipped her neatly on the chin. With a startled grunt, she collapsed, barely missing the opening in the floor, one arm dangling over the depths.

Gray pushed to his feet, breathing hard. Quad was still rolling around on the floor, fighting a ghastly battle for breath. He was beginning to bubble, bright blood trickling from the corners of his mouth.

Over there, said Shad, still crouched over the healer.

Gray retrieved the white tube from near the door. He knelt, grasping Quad's shoulder to hold him steady. "Here," he said, jamming the thing into the Technomage's neck, behind his ear. "It's better than drowning in your own blood."

Quad froze, his eyes going so wide the whites were visible all around. Then they glazed over and the hideous rasping stopped.

The silence seemed very loud, save for the hum of machinery, miles deep.

Strong, dark arms slid around Gray's waist, lifted him to his feet. Beyond words, he turned into the embrace and rested his forehead on Shad's shoulder. Gods, he couldn't remember the last time he'd done that. A long, rolling shudder shook him from head to heels. "Did you hear?" he said aloud.

Poor bastard. Was quick, though.

One more second of comfort. He dug his fingers into his shadow's biceps, hanging on. *Once he hit the bottom.*

For such a big man, Technomage 379 had had a surprisingly high-pitched scream. Carrying, too. It had taken agonizing minutes to fade as he fell, cutting off in a sort of soft, wet thud. The faint crunching that followed was something Gray preferred not to think about. When he stepped back, Shad's arms fell away.

Cenda, said his shadow.

Yes. Let's get our fire witch.

25

The pacing helped. She should have been praying, but her head was full of a particular gentle rhythm, a husky tenor.

Storm clouds gather, love,
In your eyes, in your pretty eyes.

When the door to the observation room crashed open, bouncing against the wall, Cenda stumbled. "Gray!"

He had Krysanthe's limp body slung over one shoulder, and what she could see of his shirt was dark with seeping blood. The separated manacles dangled from his wrists. His face was as pale as paper, the slashing brows very marked. In his free hand, he held a pair of white Technomage boots and a wad of rolled-up cloth. The hilt of a lasegun gleamed balefully from his waistband.

Without ceremony, he straightened, dumping Krys on the floor. She moaned, rolling over so that Cenda could see she'd been gagged and her wrists lashed together with a belt. Gray hauled her to a sitting position by the front of her dress and ripped the gag away. “How do I lower the fucking lights?” he growled. He shot a glance at the array of buttons and dials on the desk. “Which one?”

Krys shook her head and coughed. A dark bruise decorated her jaw, blood on her mouth.

Gray’s lips tightened. In a single smooth motion, he drew the lasegun and aimed it at one of the light panels in the ceiling. A sizzling beam, a high-pitched buzz, and a rain of shards tinkled down to the floor. The lights dimmed and shadows pooled in the corners of the room, Shad springing up at Gray’s heels.

Cenda felt a wild grin stretch her lips.

Gray hadn’t looked at her once, not since that first blazing glance as he came in the door. He glared at Krys. “Open Cenda’s door.”

The healer shook her head. “They’ll kill me,” she whispered.

Shad moved in front of Gray, directly into Krysanthe’s line of vision. Her mouth fell open. When the shadow held out his hand, Gray placed the butt of the lasegun in his palm and stepped aside. His smile made Cenda’s blood run cold. “Ah, but so will he.”

“Lady, a demon!” Krys scooted backward, heels scrabbling against the floor. She tried to make the sign of the Five, but her bound hands brought her up short.

Shad spread his legs and took aim two-handed.

The healer whimpered, her face shiny with tears, her nose running. “The plate on the wall,” she croaked. “I have to . . . touch it.”

Gray hoisted her to her feet one-handed and propelled her in the right direction. “You,” he barked at Cenda, “stay there.” The door to her prison whooshed open.

An instant later, Krys stumbled in, Gray right behind her. Immediately, he used the lasegun to shoot out two light panels. Shad flowed past to wrap Cenda in his long arms, his cool, dark cheek pressed against hers.

“For the gods’ sake, Shad, there’s no time for that.” Gray flung the bundle of cloth at her, then the boots. “Here, put these on." He turned on Krysanthe. "Strip, healer. Quick, I want the gown!"

Krys shrank back, fumbling for her laces with bound hands, shaking. Gray's patience evaporated. "Help me, Shad." They pounced.

The healer's eyes rolled up in her head and she fainted. "Good," grunted Gray, busy unbuckling the chatelaine, wincing as the fabric of his shirt pulled across his injured shoulder.

The bundle of cloth turned out to be a pair of Technomage trousers, six inches too long in the leg, gaping around the waist, but snug over the rear. Shad untied the healer's hands and tossed Cenda the belt. By the time she'd struggled into the strange boots and tucked the trews into them, Gray had hauled the gown over Krysanthe's head, leaving her well-upholstered form clad only in a light shift.

The boots felt as if they were made of the same flexible substance as the floor. Cenda wriggled her toes. They were pretty well the right length, but too wide for her long, narrow feet. She gasped as the boots tightened, conforming themselves to the shape of her foot. Fighting the desire to laugh like a crazy woman, she took her friend's dress from Gray and pulled it on over the trews.

He crouched over Krys, ripping her shift into long strips, exposing white, dimpled thighs.

"Gray—"

Efficiently, he stuffed the gag back into the healer's slack mouth and tied it tight. "I know you want to stay. And why." He shifted his attention to the other woman's wrists. "But I'm not giving you a choice." Binding Krysanthe's ankles, he dragged her into the privy and dumped her.

Cenda scooped up the discarded chatelaine and the *hollow*, shoving them both into the deep pocket of the borrowed trews. As an afterthought, she grabbed the strange food cubes, too.

"C'mon." Gray darted past her, his hand closing over her wrist and yanking her out into a featureless corridor painted a uniform beige, Shad running along beside them against the wall.

From their right came the sound of brisk footsteps, the murmur of voices. "Shit!" hissed Gray. They broke into a trot, skidding around a corner into yet another passageway.

"Here!" gasped Cenda. The door was as featureless as all the others, except it had the words CLEANING TECH stenciled across it. There was no lock.

Wrenching the door open, she had time for only a glimpse of shelves stocked with bottles and boxes, a bucket and mop in one corner, before Gray crowded in behind her, knocking her forward. The point of her hip struck something hard, but Gray's hand clamped over her mouth, stifling her yelp of pain. They stood rigid, pressed together chest to chest in the dark, listening.

Gray's heart thumped against hers. Even over the sharp, acrid odors in the closet, she could smell him, blood and sweat and scorched cloth, and under it all, that essential Gray smell, hot and piercingly masculine. Her stupid eyes filled with tears. Great Lady, how could she feel so many different things for one human being? He was only a man, and a bastard to boot.

Turning her jaw, she curled her fingers over his and pulled his hand away from her lips. For a moment, he resisted, then he released her. His fingers dug into her shoulders as the conversation drew closer. Three voices, two male, one female.

"I bet she was furious," said the woman. "About the spaceport budget, I mean."

"I'll say." One of the men chuckled. "Heard she ripped the Quartus a new asshole."

They must be right outside the door. Cenda gripped Gray's wrist, staring into darkness so complete, she couldn't even see the gleam of his eyes.

"Science, but power struggles are a waste of time." The second man sounded older, exasperated. "I've got work to do. Bah!" The door vibrated as a fist struck it.

The female voice said, "Look, even if the Quartus goes over to the Secundus and they bring her down, your funding's all signed off. You're safe." The doorknob rattled. Cenda's heart stopped. Gray tensed against her. "What do you want in there?"

"Some cleanwipes, the superstrong kind."

"Got some yesterday," said the other man. "The green ones?"

"Oh. Yeah, good. It'll be all right, I guess," added the older man morosely, his footsteps receding. "It's safer to be a nobody, thank Science." He sighed. "Let's get back. Is the tissue analysis finished?"

"Slave driver." The woman chuckled. "Of course." The voices dwindled to a murmur and the humming silence returned.

"That was close," whispered Cenda.

Gray tightened his hold. "Sshh."

Finally, he set his lips to her ear, his breath hot and rapid. "We have to get out of this place, *now*." His long fingers moved to grip her jaw. "If you so much as squeak, if you hold back for a second, I'll knock you out and carry you, I swear it."

Cenda stiffened, reaching for him. A rill of flame flickered across her fingers, and Gray wrenched his hand away with a hiss. "Idiot!" she snarled. "Why do you th—"

"Save it." Gray eased the door open a crack. "C'mon." He yanked her out. A shadowy hand patted her shoulder as Shad rose off the wall outside to join them.

Endless corridors, door after door after door. Gray frowned. "Where are they all?" He glanced around "Why don't they have guards?"

"The Primus said"—they came to a T-junction—"this is a research facility. I guess they're working. Great Lady, it all looks the same. Which way?"

Gray gave a bark of laughter. "Look."

A neatly lettered sign on the wall pointed to the left. It read LABORATORIES 40–53. An arrow indicated the opposite direction. EXIT. Typical Technomage efficiency.

Without a word, they turned in to the corridor, following the EXIT signs through another three turns, Shad slipping ahead to peer around corners. Once, he came rushing back and Gray pulled Cenda flat against the wall as a dozen Technomages trooped through an intersection thirty feet away, two of them pushing a trolley piled high with cages. Cenda wrinkled her nose and all the fine hair on her body stood up. Rats, dozens of them.

But after that, the trip was surprisingly uneventful, the passage increasing in width, until it gave out on what she supposed must be a loading bay for flitters. There was certainly one of them there, squatting like a sleek-winged bird, stacks of boxes lined up behind it. A blast of sunlight poured in like glory through wide doors twenty feet high, casting dense, sharp-edged shadows. The area was deserted, baking in the heat. A breeze whispered in from the outdoors, bringing with it the green scent of vegetation. Remnant Two, the Primus had said.

No wonder there were no guards. Who did the Technomages have to fear on Sybaris? On Concordia, the Enclave was powerful enough to enforce an uneasy peace, but not here. And out in Remnant Two, an area so restricted the only visitors permitted were the escorted tourist parties who came in by flitter, they could do as they pleased.

The air filled with a crackling noise that hurt the ears. A short pause, and a well-modulated baritone said calmly, "Emergency situation. Repeat, this is an emergency situation. Stand by for further information."

Cenda craned her neck, staring at the roof. It seemed to come from everywhere.

Another crackle, the clipped voice of a woman this time. "This is the Technomage Primus. There are unauthorized personnel at large in the facility. One male, one female. Do not approach. Repeat, do NOT approach. Activate all comm devices immediately and report to supervisors."

Gray grinned, grim and fierce, pulling Cenda behind a large crate marked FRAGILE, THIS WAY UP. "Judger, she's pissed."

"Staff are not to panic. The situation is well in hand. This message is for information only. Primus out."

"Science, you're them!"

They whirled. A burly man had emerged from the other side of the flitter, a good fifteen feet away, a greasy rag in his hands. Immediately, he dropped it, reaching for the black disk pinned to his shirt.

Five-it! Too far for Gray to reach him. Or even Shad. Acting purely on instinct, Cenda flung a thin ribbon of flame across the intervening space. It licked over the back of the man's knuckles and the disk fell at his feet, a small, melted lump.

"Shit, shit!" He was still bent over, cradling his hand, when Gray barreled into him. They hit the floor with a resounding *thud*. Gray dug his fingers hard into the man's thick neck and he went still, his limbs flopping. Breathing hard, Gray rolled aside and sat up. Shrugging off Shad's solicitous hand, he stared at Cenda across the loading bay. "I'd say you just burned your bridges, fire witch. So to speak." He smiled without humor. "You have to come with me now."

Cenda glared as she trotted over to the huge doors. "I never intended to stay." Cautiously, she peered out, squinting as the light hit her eyes. The building stood foursquare in the center of an expanse of white gravel, windowless. Twenty yards away, a wire fence about twice her height separated the Technomage compound from the shifting, sighing mass of the blue feather forest.

Remnant Two. So near. So impossible.

From this angle, she could see only one gate. Next to it was a small, square building, a Technomage sitting comfortably on a stool in the shade, leaning against the wall.

"If they're all checking in, they'll miss this one any minute," said Gray in her ear, and she jumped. Shad slid a comforting arm around her waist.

At the gate, the Technomage sat up, bent his head, and spoke into his disk. Lady, they'd be exposed like bugs on a griddle out there. The Primus wasn't stupid. The Technomages would already be watching the perimeter, for sure.

"How long before dark, do you think? A couple of hours?" Gods, where could they hide? She glanced into the loading bay. The flitter, perhaps?

Gray grunted an affirmative, but he was staring past her at Shad, all the color draining from his face.

Cenda grabbed Gray's arm. "What's he saying?"

Gray's mouth worked. "I—I—*can't*—"

"He's got an idea, hasn't he?"

Shad's dark head dipped.

Gray wet his lips. "I used to—We used to—"

"*What?*" She danced with impatience. "Gray!"

"Hide in the shadows. Behind the veil." His eyes blazed. "I hate it; it's foul, *wrong*. I haven't done it since—since we were children."

He'd been going to say something else—she was sure of it.

"*In* the shadows? Really? Is that what you mean?" she asked Shad, ignoring Gray.

A nod.

"And you can take me, too?" Shad picked up her hand and pressed a cool kiss to her palm.

Boots coming closer, many boots. Converging on the loading bay. Voices shouting.

Shad muscled between them, sliding an arm around each waist. "Now!" croaked Gray. "Run!"

Shad launched them headlong out of the building into the blinding sunlight, but only for a few stumbling paces. Gray groaned, "Fuck!" and then a cool, translucent substance was streaming over her head and neck, her chest, her legs. She blinked. Great Lady, the shadow of the Technomage building! Lying across the graveled perimeter, dense and rectangular in the strong afternoon sun.

On reflex, she reached up to claw the film from her eyes, but Shad's gentle hand squeezed hers. *No.* He shook his head, then put a finger to his lips. *Quiet.*

All right. Cenda nodded, blowing out a careful breath, shivers running up and down her spine. It was strange, certainly, more than a little weird, but Magick was never an easy thing, or without cost. She gave a wry smile. As she well knew.

Shad led her over to the wall of the building and pressed her down until she was settled against it, more or less comfortably. In the strange twilight world of shadow, she could almost make out his features, a dusky copy of Gray's, but somehow younger looking, not as bleak. For the first time, she wondered if Shad was some particular part of Gray, splintered, split. She rubbed her forehead, glancing at Gray's set face from beneath her lashes. No, she'd never had the sense that Gray was less than whole, as complex and as complicated as any worthwhile human being.

Her thoughts came to a shuddering halt. *Worthwhile?* He'd betrayed her for money, seduced an awkward, ugly fire witch because he had to. She gripped her fists together to keep the angry blaze hidden, but sharp blades of hurt twisted viciously inside her, scooping her out, leaving her hollow. A plain-faced, unwanted nothing. Bastard. *Bastard.* And what he thought he was doing now, she had no idea. Why hadn't he run the moment he was free?

A small, stupid voice whispered, *He came back. He risked his life to come back for you.*

He'd have reasons of his own, no doubt. Probably another buyer with more creds than the gods. Enough money, and he'd do fucking anything, the whore. Cenda closed her eyes, her treacherous memory painting a picture of Gray rubbing her feet, his beautiful eyes luminous with tenderness.

Or a reasonable facsimile thereof.

Gravel crunched as a half dozen Technomages marched out of the loading bay in a tight phalanx, laseguns waving. Cenda almost smiled. They were Scientists, not soldiers—that much was blindingly obvious. Nonetheless, it hardly mattered who was on the other end of a lasegun when it blew a hole in your chest. She held her breath. Gods, that stout woman was looking right at her!

Gray's hand closed around her throat in silent warning, his eyes gleaming very pale in the swimming half-light.

The stout woman's gaze skimmed right over her as if she weren't there. Cenda breathed again. She met Gray's narrowed eyes and laid her fingers lightly against the back of his wrist, next to the remains of the manacle. She raised her brows. *Care to try?*

Slowly, Gray released her and drew back. She thought she heard the click as his teeth snapped together. She smiled. How delightful. *Bastard.*

The Technomages separated into two groups of three and trotted around the building in opposite directions. Five minutes later, they reappeared, puffing, and conferred with much shaking of heads. More muttering into the black disks and two were left outside on sentry duty, one to wait, the other to patrol the perimeter.

Five-it.

Shad nudged her shoulder and pointed at the sharp leading edge of the shadow.

Huh? She pantomimed an exaggerated shrug.

He moved his hand sideways, toward the gate. Then again.

Oh. Of course. It was late afternoon, the shadow of the building stretching closer and closer to the gate. All they had to do was wait.

Shad moved away to hunker down next to Gray, his whole posture indicative of anxiety. Cenda glanced sideways at Gray, slumped against the wall next to her. His eyes were closed, those absurdly luxuriant lashes lying like tiny fans against his cheek. Every muscle in his body was tense, his hands clenched into fists, the tendons in his neck standing out clearly. His lips were folded tightly together. Every now and then, a shudder ran through him, from head to heels.

When Shad slid down next to him, shoulder to shoulder, he didn't stir. Instead, one hand flashed out to clamp over Shad's wrist, the first time she'd seen him touch his shadow voluntarily. Beneath the bloodied rags of Tai Yang's shirt, his chest rose and fell with his rapid breaths.

Great Lady, his wound. He was in shock!

26

Cautiously, Cenda reached out to touch his cheek. Cold and clammy.

His eyes flew open. Even in the twilight, she could see that his pupils were enormous.

What? she mouthed. *Are you all right?*

Curling his hand under her hair, he drew her down and placed his lips against her ear. "Hate this," he breathed. "*Hate* it."

"The shadow?" she whispered back.

He nodded, his jaw bunching as he gritted his teeth.

Cenda pointed to where the far edge of the dark was nearly nudging the fence. Only a couple of feet of sun-bright gravel separated them. "Let's go."

"No." His grip tightened. "See the red wires?"

She squinted. Three thin lines of red were threaded parallel through the mesh at regular intervals, all the way around.

"Seen it before," breathed Gray. "Touch it and fry." His eyes fell closed again.

Cenda leaned back against the gritty wall and thought. She thought about fire Magick and about Elke and the price she'd paid and the oath she'd sworn. Glancing across the perimeter, she estimated angles and distances. It would be about another hour before the shadow extended as far as the gate. She flexed her fingers, checking her inner resources. Whatever had been in the pink food cube, it was nourishing enough that she felt strong. Ready.

How much more could Gray take? She couldn't tell what the problem actually was, but coping with it was draining him. He'd played his part—whatever it was—now she must play hers.

A strange little spark of excitement glowed within her, even as her belly cramped with apprehension.

Slowly, she climbed to her feet and walked slowly to the outer limit of the shadow. She motioned to Shad. *Get him up.*

Shad inserted himself under Gray's arm and heaved. A gasp and a flurry, and Gray was standing at her shoulder, pulling her around to face him, his face dark with fury. "You'll get us killed, you fool," he said in a harsh whisper.

Rudely, Cenda elbowed him in the guts. Ignoring his strong fingers digging into her flesh, she raised her arms. *Great Lady, help me.* As she let out her breath, the heat rolled through her, billowing across the few yards to the fence in a great ball of roaring flame.

The result was all she could have hoped for and more. Her jaw dropping, Cenda watched the red wires whip back, writhing, sparks arcing back and forth, crackling all the way along the fence and around the corner. The section of wire mesh in front of her buckled and sagged, but not quite enough. Her blood singing with power, she sent another blast. The fence peeled back, the ends of the melted wires dripping, leaving an opening about three feet wide.

Shouts and screams burst out behind them. The Technomage at the gate catapulted out of his seat and stumbled into the feather forest, arms wrapped around his head.

Hard hands grabbed her biceps, one on each side, and

shoved her bodily out of the protection of shadow and through the gap in the fence. "Run!" panted Gray. "Gods, *run*!" Shad flowed along smoothly at her other side, hauling her along, keeping her steady.

As they pelted toward the bluish line of forest, a man's voice yelled, "Don't touch—" Someone gave a choking cry, abruptly cut off, and a lasegun bolt cut directly in front of them, kicking up a long line in the dirt. Another passed right through Shad's thigh, but his stride didn't falter. Gray whipped the lasegun from his belt and squeezed off a shot over his shoulder. The gatekeeper collapsed, grabbing at his leg and howling.

The forest closed about them, feathery fronds whispering across their faces, caressing their arms. "Keep going," grunted Gray, towing Cenda along at a breakneck pace. Without warning, he tugged her off the narrow trail and struck off down a gentle slope. "Where the hell are we?" He detoured around a fern tree log.

"Remnant . . . Two," puffed Cenda. "The Primus said." She batted at a vine with scarlet flowers and it squeaked a protest. "Sorry," she muttered automatically. "Please, can we slow down?"

But it wasn't until after another fifteen minutes of strenuous jog-trotting that Gray drew her to a halt under a huge fern tree. "Can you hear anything?"

The sounds of the forest reasserted themselves, the sighing of the breeze through the feather leaves a soft, continuous susurrus. Somewhere farther down the slope, water tinkled. The contrast felt surreal, as if she'd strayed into a stranger's dream of peace. A flock of a half dozen hummers whirred past, tiny, living chips of cobalt, magenta, aquamarine, and heliotrope. Cenda planted her hands on her knees and bent over, sucking in air. With Shad beside him, Gray stood at her elbow, blinking, his gaze traveling from the hummers to the silky, iridescent feather leaves of the fern trees. Undergrowth was almost nonexistent, except for a tall, gray blue grass that swayed in a silver dance with the breeze.

"How come," she gasped, "you can still breathe . . . and I can't?"

"Fight scenes with Erik," Gray said cryptically, but he grimaced, flexing his shoulder. "Is there anything here that can hurt us?"

Cenda snorted. "Only humans."

"Are you sure? Where are the predators?"

"Sybaris is not like other worlds," she said curtly. "It's truly benign. The hunters here are so tiny, they're no threat to people. They kill sonically, anyway."

Gray sank to a log and plucked gingerly at his bloody shirt. "Sonically?"

"The hummers emit a noise so high-pitched humans can't hear it, but it makes the bubble dancers burst. Then they feed." She straightened. "We'll need to soak that to get it off. What happened?"

"Quad hit me with a lasegun. So I guess it's cauterized." He squinted down, wincing, and Shad crouched at his feet. Absently, Gray rested his hand on the shadow's shoulder.

Little chills raced up and down her spine. "Not if you're still bleeding." The thought of his pain made her dizzy, breathless.

And caring made her a godsbedamned fool.

"It'll be dark soon," she said. "What do we do now?"

"Find a safe place for the night." He pushed to his feet. "I've never seen anything like this. It's beautiful."

"Wait 'til you see the Rainbow Lakes." Cenda fell into step beside him. "Most of Sybaris was exactly like this. Until the Technomages came eight hundred years ago."

"And then?" Gray cocked a brow.

"They opened the planet up for development and for tourism, but they didn't set any limits. Too greedy, I suppose." Tilting her head back, she gazed up into the rustling canopy. "This is all that's left, about eighty square miles of it." She shrugged. "And Remnant One, which is even smaller."

From somewhere behind them came the deep thrumming buzz of a flitter. With a curse, Gray dragged her under the huge, rounded leaves of a featherbrella bush. "Shit, a search party."

"Could be." Cenda watched the shadow of the craft skim the forest floor. "Could be a day trip."

"A *what*?"

"They bring the tour parties in by the flitterload. In high season, you can hardly move in Remnant Two for off-world tourists. Except for the mountains beyond the lakes. There's nowhere to land there."

Gray shook his head. "We need to be undercover before dark. Somewhere near water." He strode off downhill, Shad flickering at his side. But after a few steps, the shadow turned. Two paces farther on, Gray stopped and looked back. "Coming?"

Judger, it was amazing. Gray stood in the dense forest on the edge of Orange Lake and stared. The body of water was almost perfectly circular. In the long rays of the afternoon sun, orange was a barely adequate description. It glowed like a gigantic copper coin baking in a furnace. It wasn't much of a stretch to visualize Cenda rising out of it naked, pale, and glowing, liquid flame flowing over that flawless skin. Without turning his head, he said, "Can you swim?"

"Yes."

Somewhere around an hour ago, she'd stopped speaking except in monosyllables. Now she stood, vibrating with tension, an angry set to her mouth. She hated him.

Well, of course. He hated him, too.

Shad's fingers brushed his arm. *I don't.*

Shit, Shad had touched him more in the last twelve hours than in the previous twenty years. And he'd permitted it. In fact, he'd wanted to burrow into the comfort of that dark embrace like a child. Gray breathed carefully through his nose, staring unseeing at the far shore of the lake. A flitter rose out of the setting sun and skimmed away to his right, back to "civilization," so low he could even make out the pale blobs of the faces pressed against the windows. That made six since the first one. He was certain at least two had been the Technomages, looking. Fuck them.

He clenched his fists at his sides. The remains of the manacles were driving him crazy, and the lasegun burn on his shoulder made his breath hitch every time he moved. Fuck, he was one big ache, but that wasn't the worst. No, the worst part was a tight, empty place deep inside, where he couldn't touch, couldn't soothe.

Not that it mattered. He'd done what he'd done and it was over. His priority was to get them out of here in one piece. After that? He shrugged. Concordia for him. Cenda could please herself, choose her own way to hide and die. A warm touch, a hug, soft lips against his . . . Longing for them like a lovelorn youth wouldn't make any difference.

Wearily, he sank down on a flat rock, pried his boots off, and unlaced his trews.

"What are you doing?" Her voice came out a little shrill.

There was a spot there where a stand of featherbrellas hung over the water. Should be safe enough from spying eyes. "I need to soak this shirt off. And I feel filthy."

The subsequent silence felt very loud.

Wearing just the shirt, he worked his way down to the water, Shad running ahead. He smiled sourly, wondering if she'd averted her eyes.

Nuh-uh, she's staring at your ass, said Shad with satisfaction.

The silvery mud-sand squished under his toes, the water retaining the heat of the day for the first few feet. Hauling in a breath, he launched out into the deeper water at the outer limit of the featherbrellas, where it was cold and dark. Shit, that hurt, like an icy flame searing his skin. Gritting his teeth, he braced his knees against a rock and plucked at the shirt.

Shad knocked his hand aside, the dark head bent. *Let me.* Shadowy fingers eased the fabric away, every time stopping the split second before he was about to flinch.

Gray exhaled and tried to relax.

An eddy of warmer water swirled around his hips just as Shad pushed the shirt off his shoulders. Cenda stroked past, lithe and confident. He caught a glimpse of the rounded curve of a buttock as she slipped by, the fiery water parting softly before her. His cock jerked, hard and hungry despite it all.

He snorted. Because of it all, more like. He'd been fighting the insistent buzz in his balls since their last stop. He knew what it was: the primitive urge to reaffirm life in the most direct way possible, to plant his seed. Instinct was amazingly resilient, but it wasn't going to happen. She hated him.

Gray caught Shad's wrist as the long fingers slid over his thigh. *No, don't.* His cock could wait, but the practicalities couldn't. He had to get his fire witch fed, and quickly. If he was hungry, she must be ravenous. What had the healer said? She needed fuel to feed the fire.

"Show me." Cenda stood waist-deep in the water in front of him, her breasts high and tight with cold, the sweet chocolat nipples puckered even though rivers of liquid fire streamed over her shoulders and down her torso.

Gray narrowed his eyes. Judger God, she was *steaming*, tendrils of mist curling up from the heavy curtain of her wet hair, the dark red more evident than ever.

"The burn," she snapped. "Let me see it."

He stiffened. "It's fine." Turning, he waded back to shore. "I'm fine."

An instant's pause, then splashing from behind. The fire witch stalked past him to the shore, that gorgeous ass flexing with the angry vigor of her long-legged stride. Snatching up something from a rock, she whirled, shoving it under his nose. It jingled. Krysanthe's chatelaine.

Gray gave a surprised bark of laughter. "Well-done."

"Don't patronize me, *Duke*." With a sneer, she slapped the spiky thing into his chest.

Growling under his breath, Gray examined it more closely. Gods, how had the healer remained upright with so much hardware slung around her middle? Frowning, he sorted through the strange objects. Between a pair of scissors and a huge bunch of keys was a small pot that looked familiar. Judger be praised, when he ripped the lid off, there was the green salve, the stuff of miracles. Suddenly suspicious, he sniffed, but the smell was as he remembered—fresh and minty, with an odd metallic undertone. Huffing with relief, he smeared it over the lasegun burn on his chest. Someone lifted the pot out of his hands to daub the stuff on the awkward place on his back.

Thanks, he said grudgingly.

A dark chuckle. *Not me.*

Gray's head whipped around. Cenda stood at his shoulder, so close he could have kissed her. Their eyes met.

He had the oddest fancy that he actually heard the hungry roar of flames, sucking all the air out of his lungs and every thought from his head. His cock hardened so fast, he felt dizzy. A single step and he had the fire witch backed up against the silky trunk of a fern tree, devouring her mouth with desperate urgency, one hand gripping her thigh and lifting it high over his hip. The pot slipped from her fingers and rolled against a rock with a decisive *clink.*

And oh, gods, she was kissing him back, purring deep in her throat, giving him the blessed, wet heat of her mouth, his cock already prodding at the slick entrance to her body, her hips tilting up at the perfect angle. Ah, fuck, yes, *yes*!

Gray's buttocks flexed and Cenda stiffened. Her fingers speared into his hair and yanked, so hard his eyes watered. Her eyes glittered gold with rage and passion, her lips swollen. "Wait," she gritted. "I don't"—she swallowed—"want this."

"Liar." Keeping her pinned against the tree, Gray swiveled his hips, a mind-numbing slide of hot, wet pleasure against the sensitive head of his cock.

Cenda lifted her chin and glared. "Not with you, Duke." She placed a fingertip against the pulse thundering just under his jaw. "Let me go."

As a threat, he knew it was real enough, but the touch burned all the way down to his groin, as if she'd petted him instead. A cool, dark hand closed over his good shoulder. *Let her go,* whispered Shad.

Slowly, Gray stepped back, his chest heaving, battling the beast within. His balls aching, he reached down to cradle himself. All right. Fine. He could do this. The cold water of the lake was right there. But he couldn't bear to look at her, posed against that godsbedamned tree like something from an adolescent wet dream, her sexy little belly quivering with her breaths, the moisture of arousal shining on her thighs. Wanton and there for the taking.

As he turned toward the lake, he heard her whisper, *"Shad."* A shuddering sigh. *"Please."*

The hair rose all the way down his spine. He spun around.

Shad had taken his place, Cenda's arms milk pale around his dark neck, one long leg wrapped around his hips. The bottom dropped out of Gray's stomach.

Cenda's eyes opened. Taking her time, she freed her mouth from Shad's and he bent his head, nibbling the side of her neck. Those molten eyes lifted, fixing on Gray's. "Your shadow's a—*Five-it!*"—she jerked as Shad surged forward and her head fell back against the tree—"better man than you are, Duke." Her lashes fluttered down and she moaned, writhing with pleasure.

27

A small, detached part of Gray wondered if this was what hell was like, this dark, echoing maelstrom of the soul. In the void, he seemed to hear the rush of leathery wings, demons jeering, pointing, gibbering. Everything lurched, the sensation of falling so vivid, he dropped to his knees, his fingers scrabbling in the sand. Nothing, he was nothing, a mote, a cipher— Drifting, lost, lost forever.

For you, for you. He became aware of a voice, calling, desperate, urgent. *Feel it, damn you! Come on, feel it!*

Shad? He rubbed his eyes and abruptly, sensation surged inside him, flooding his cock again, tightening his balls, making his head spin. A hot, gloving pressure, sliding against his length, glorious rubbing. More and more and more. Gods, so good.

Shad's mental voice was breathless, punctuated by little grunts of effort. *Fool . . . love you . . . would never . . . For you . . . touch. Quick!*

Gray stumbled forward, coming up hard against Shad's spine. Cenda's eyes flew open, glazed with passion, her cheeks flushed. "No," she gasped. She must be very close; she was incredibly tight and bearing down deliciously hard.

Gray felt his lips draw back in a feral snarl. *Slow down. Don't let her come.* "Oh, yes," he mocked. "Fuck him and you fuck me." He shoved his knee inside his shadow's. *Open.*

Obligingly, Shad widened his stance, a warm wave of anticipation washing out of him. *Do it.*

It was a little awkward, because they were exactly the same height. Gray had to dip his knees, but he managed, sliding his cock between Shad's strong, dark thighs, hissing as his shadow shifted, closing on him hard.

"Lady, what are you *doing*?"

Gray didn't answer. He dropped his forehead to Shad's shoulder, relishing that weird doubling of sensation, the flesh of Shad's thighs muscular and cool and slick, compressing him with hard masculine strength, Cenda's sheath tight and searing and giving. Judger, it was amazing! *Fuck us,* he demanded. *Make us come.*

Shit, yeah! Shad laughed, the sound ringing in Gray's head, loud and frankly joyous. *Just be careful with that thing. It's hard.*

Gray chuckled, sinking his fingers into his shadow's hip. With the other hand, he grabbed the fire witch around the upper thigh. *Go.*

The glory didn't last long. He hadn't thought it would, given how primed he was—they all were. A half dozen strokes and he was right on the edge, the seed boiling at the root of his cock—or was it Shad's? He couldn't tell anymore. Cenda was crying out, those high, formless noises women make in extremis. So sweet.

Shad swooped, ravishing her mouth, taking her whimpers down his throat, wrapping her up, giving her back to Gray. Acute, pinpoint pleasure streamed out of him, more than doubled by Shad's. Gray groaned as if the Judger had reached down and torn out his still-beating heart. Somewhere a long way off, Cenda screamed, the sound muffled by Shad's busy tongue. Everything clamped down, wringing the last of his orgasm out of him.

Slowly, consciousness returned. He was plastered up against Shad's back, his mouth open and slack against his shadow's dusky shoulder blade, fingers buried in his hair. The whole thing had taken only a few minutes.

Good?

Gray blew out a shaky breath. *Good.*

Carefully, he straightened and stepped back, his gaze meeting Cenda's over his shadow's shoulder. Gods, she looked lovely, flushed with that just-fucked glow only women seemed to get. As he watched, she turned her head to the side and pressed her lips against Shad's cheek. "Thank you," she whispered. "That was good."

And as if she'd repeated the words aloud, he felt it again, that rapier thrust to the heart. *Your shadow's a better man than you are.*

Shad nuzzled her hair, gently lowering her leg to the ground, holding her steady.

"Why—?" Gray's voice came out a rasp. He cleared his throat and tried again. "Why did you do that? Do you hate me so much?"

The fire witch stared at him in a measuring sort of way, all the pretty color fading from her face. "I'm not generally cruel," she said, "so I suppose I must. Surely you're not surprised?"

Wordlessly, he shook his head.

Cenda stroked a dark shoulder. "I'm sorry, Shad. I used you. That was wrong."

Shad pressed a quick kiss to her knuckles. *Anytime, sweetheart. Was fucking fine.*

"What did he say?" But before Gray could answer, she squeezed her eyes shut. "No, you smiled. I don't want to know." Pushing away, she strode back to the lake and waded out waist-deep.

Gray swallowed. The ropey smears on her slim thighs had been shiny, smoke and cream mixed.

By the time she returned, he'd dressed in trews and boots and secured their hiding place for the night. Resisting the urge to apologize, he disregarded the scarlet-flowered vine's squeaky protests, binding it around the bent branches of a featherbrella to form a rough bower. There'd barely be room for the two of them, but they'd be concealed from anyone more than ten feet away.

The fire witch didn't speak, pulling on Quad's trews with jerky movements, the healer's gown going over the top.

"You must be hungry," he said. "What's edible around here?"

Cenda looked across the lake to where the sun was setting, the water blazing with the force of its farewell. She shrugged. "Fern fruits. But it's almost dark." She dug in her pocket. "Here." She tossed him a yellowish cube.

"Technomage food," she said, correctly interpreting his expression, fishing out another for herself.

Would she never cease to surprise him?

Taking the knife from his boot, Gray carved off a corner and chewed gingerly. For cardboard, it was extraordinarily filling.

The sun trembled on the horizon, the crescent of Arabesque, the first of the Dancers, showing as a mere sliver to the north.

Going, going now. Shad sounded wistful.

All right. Gray glanced up. *Thanks.* Night advanced across the lake in a swooping rush, swallowing Shad whole, before Gray realized what he'd said.

His back turned, Gray slept beside her as neatly as a cat, his breath coming soft and regular. What would it be like to lie next to him like this every night of her life? Cenda stared into the dark, sensing the swaying movement of the featherbrella leaves above their heads, trying to imagine it. Her lips curved in a wry smile. Loving him had turned out to be disastrously easy; not incinerating him would be the hard part.

Well, it hardly mattered, because she'd never find out. Slowly, Cenda lifted a hand and laid her knuckles against his shoulder blade. *Good-bye,* she thought. *Good-bye, you beautiful dream.* Because that's all he'd ever been. A foolish dream.

Aching, she turned her head, breathing him in. Blinking away the tears, she closed her eyes and kept them closed.

Cenda woke with a start in the cool of predawn, her heart thudding. A hard hand clamped over her mouth. Gray. He was sealed against her spine from neck to knee, rigid with tension. Quite distinctly, a man's voice said, "I've got a reading. Bearing 27 by 193. Closing in."

Gray slithered out of the bower in complete silence. Cenda strained her ears, but all she could hear were the night sounds of native Sybaris, the barely perceptible buzz of the hummers, the gentle lapping of the lake waters, a booming hoot from some creature she couldn't identify.

She peered out between the featherbrella leaves. Two dark shapes flowed together. One grunted, and then the other stepped back, letting the first one tumble to the ground.

Gray said, on a thread of sound, "Light."

Only a single moon remained in the sky. Pirouette, its face a dusky blue. Cenda crawled out of their night bower. Trembling, she created a tiny fireball, no brighter than a small candle, dancing like a sprite at the end of her finger. "Did you kill him?" she whispered, staring down at the Technomage sprawled at their feet.

[illegible] in the man's neck. "Shit. Yes." He wiped his narrow blade on the man's sleeve, and she caught a flash of metal as he returned it to his boot.

Shivering, Cenda made the sign of the Five. "Lady keep his soul."

Gray unclipped a small box from the Technomage's belt. "We're screwed. This is some sort of tracking device." He hurled it into the lake. "C'mon, the others won't be far behind." Grabbing her hand, he towed her onto the lakeside path.

Cenda frowned. This looked familiar. A few hundred yards farther on, the track opened up into a grassy area. The sun peeped over the horizon, illuminating the picnic tables, the bins for waste, the marked landing square for the flitters. Yes! She'd been this way before, when she brought Elke's ashes. The breath left her in a whistling hiss.

Concentrate, concentrate.

"Green Lake is just beyond those trees." She pointed. "It's very popular with the day trippers. Do you think if we—" She broke off, uncertain.

"Mingled with them?"

Now Shad stood at Gray's shoulder. He blew her a kiss of greeting, all cavalier, dusky charm. Her loins clenched as though a great fist had cupped her and squeezed. Great Lady, he'd been incredible, moving inside her, so broad and cool and smooth, furrowing deliciously through sensitive tissues, filling, stretching . . . Such a contrast with the human heat of Gray, his hand burning on her thigh. His eyes had been so deeply shadowed with lust, it seemed as though Shad lived within him as well as without.

She jerked her gaze away, frowning so ferociously at an innocent gourd-gourd bush it withered a little under her regard. "We might confuse those tracking things. The Technomages don't seem to have much woodcraft without them."

"Maybe." Gray strode over to a shelter shed. Picking up a rock, he broke the transparent plas-shield on one wall and reached inside.

"What's that?"

His lips curved with satisfaction. "A map." His head jerked up. "Shit, here they come! Run!"

They'd barely reached the sanctuary of the fern trees when a flitter darkened the sky above the clearing. With a high-pitched whine, it settled, wings rocking, and the doors hissed open.

"Wait." Gray hauled Cenda back before she could hit her stride. "Look. What the hell—?"

The half dozen men who climbed out of the craft wore the rough garb of Sybarite slum dwellers. Two of them had laseguns.

Cenda's stomach turned over. "Lady, it's the Fixer!"

"No." Gray narrowed his eyes. "Not the Fixer. His successor, chasing the original investment." He shot her a glance. "You. Cenda, they don't know we're here. You could—"

Her head shook of its own volition, even as her stomach turned a somersault. The Fixer, reeling about the ballroom, screaming, out of his mind with agony. "I swore. Never again."

Gray sighed. "Come on, then."

Quietly, they faded into the forest as another flitter flew over, heading for Indigo Lake. A tourist party.

Tourists, Technomages, the Fixer's thugs. *Great Lady.* Cenda's head ached. Drifting along beside her, Shad rubbed the back of her neck.

"Rest." Gray pushed her down behind a boulder, well off the trail. He squatted beside her, the map rustling as he unfolded it. "Dammit all to hell."

"What now?" She leaned forward to look. Five-it, his shirt was still damp. Automatically, she spread her palm over his shoulder blade and let the heat flow, drying the fabric on his body.

"Mmm." He rolled his shoulders, turning to gaze at her, his beautiful eyes silvery with surprise. "Thank you."

Cenda pressed her lips together, castigating herself for a weak-willed fool. "You'll get sick."

"No, I won't. And the salve worked again." He pushed the shirt aside, revealing a long red weal marring the smooth skin.

Gods, it must have hurt! Ruthlessly, Cenda suppressed the wince.

His lip curled. "Thanks for asking, witch."

The manacles had raised weals on his wrists. If she were a better person, she'd offer to burn the cuffs off. After a moment's tingling silence, he went on. "There are landing squares for flitters all over the Remnant. Except here." He flicked the map with a fingernail. "The Smoking Range. You been there?"

"No one goes there." She snorted without amusement. "The mountains really do smoke. Too dangerous for flitters, for the precious tourists. Two hundred years ago one actually exploded."

"Really? What's on the other side?"

She shrugged. “The outskirts of North Sector. People, slums.”

Gray’s eyes shone. “If we cut past Indigo Lake—through here”—he indicated the route with his forefinger—“we can walk out of the Remnant via the Range.”

Cenda opened her mouth to tell him he was insane, that the mountains would kill them, that she couldn’t bear even to glance at Indigo Lake, to be reminded of her darling. Then she closed it. Shad held out his hand, and she let him pull her to her feet.

Judger, it was a fucking nightmare. Two steps forward and one back. For a remote native forest, Remnant Two was busier than a Sybarite bazaar on sale day. Beyond belief. It took them hours to work their way past Indigo Lake. First, there were the tourist parties straggling along the path, three of them, one after another, each led by a smiling guide carrying a brightly colored pennant on a pole. “And here we have the famous Indigo Lake, formed in the dead heart of a volcano. Note the amazing phosphorescence of the water. Souvenir bottles, two creds. Why, thank *you*, sir.” Blah, blah.

And Cenda had as near as dammit got them killed, standing to stare out across the deep blue water, a bleak expression tugging down the corners of her mouth. When three Technomages stepped unexpectedly out of the forest to confer over their godsbedamned black boxes, he’d had no choice but to roll them both deep into the shadow veil. He’d turned to look at her, his heart hammering as the greasy caress of it slid over his skin. Tears had been streaming down her cheeks, and automatically he lifted a hand to brush them away. Would the tears of a fire witch scald his skin? But she’d slapped at his fingers and shot him a glare fiery enough to raise blisters.

One consolation was that he seemed to be growing more accustomed to the shadow veil. Shad at his side, he’d walked carefully through the swimming twilight, across a clearing, and right up to a tourist flitter. The feeling of exposure had been the worst part, his instincts screaming, his spine prickling, even though the entire party was down at the shore, pointing and exclaiming. Working quickly, he and Shad had appropriated a bag from the seat nearest the door. A child's backpack, in a virulent shade of pink. As he tossed aside a battered doll and a little fleecy jacket, Gray felt guilty, but only for a moment. The fire witch was beginning to look gaunt. Fern fruits were all around them, but she needed something decent, something solid. He stuffed the pack full to bursting with the food laid out ready for the offworlders' lunch. The remains of the tasteless Technomage cubes would be best kept as a reserve.

By midmorning, the Technomages had got themselves organized into a sort of sweep, each Scientist armed with a tracking box, a black disk, and a lasegun. Spaced at intervals of a couple of hundred yards, they came forward in a line. Inexorably, crashing through the bushes like the clumsy milkbeasts of Gray's childhood. It must be his imagination, but it seemed to him that the feather forest recoiled, as if in disgust.

The day became a test of endurance, of ducking and weaving, in and out of the shadow veil, so many times Gray lost count. He almost ceased to care. Once, when he climbed a tree to fix their position, he thought he glimpsed the Fixer's men skulking in the rear, but it was hard to be sure beneath the shifting bluish mass of the feather fronds.

Past Indigo Lake, Cenda seemed to pull herself together, but by early afternoon, when they left Violet Lake behind and the terrain began to rise, she was stumbling, her mouth set in a stubborn line. Gray stepped into the pool of dense shade cast by a small bluff, drawing her with him. The thick twilight closed over their heads.

He gripped her shoulders, feeling the internal tremors running through her. "It's not much farther to the mountains proper," he said, "but it's all uphill. Are you all right?"

She tried to shrug him off. "I'm fine."

"No, you're not. Where are your salamanders?"

28

Cenda's lips twitched with genuine amusement. "Wherever I want them." She uncurled her fingers to reveal one of the tiny creatures, sitting bolt upright and regal in the center of her palm, glowing brighter than any lantern. It favored Gray with the customary sapphire glower.

Gray frowned. "I thought—" He broke off.

"You thought wrong. They're a focus, but I don't seem to need them anymore."

Yes. Gray thought of the ferocity of the fireball that had reduced a wire fence to sludge, the delicate ribbon of flame licking precisely across the knuckles of the Technomage in the loading bay. Gods, she'd dried the shirt against his body without giving him a moment's discomfort.

A full-fledged fire witch, mistress of one of the primary elements. Come to her powers alone.

Just a woman, holding herself together with stubborn courage, footsore and frightened. His guilt, his responsibility.

You've lost her, the only one. A voice of doom in his head, acid and accusatory. *Fool.*

What the fuck are you—? Gray pinched the bridge of his nose. No time, no time.

"Cenda," he said urgently. "Can you lay us down a line of fire?"

"I won't—"

"Kill. Yes, I know. But can you put a wall of flame and smoke between us and them? Say, along the line of that gully there?" He indicated the area in question below them, then turned to stare up into the foothills, feeling grim. Clad in a sparse skirt of scrubby bushes and stunted tress, the mountains marched away, clear-cut against the soft afternoon blue of the sky. A single plume of smoke drifted up to mate with a passing cloud. "It's so rocky, there's hardly any cover farther up. They'll just pick us off. Target practice."

Her smile was ghastly. "That's you." Her throat moved as she swallowed. "I think the Primus wants me alive. You're lucky she doesn't know about . . . about Shad."

Gods! For a moment, he couldn't breathe. "You didn't—?"

Shad stepped between them to brush a wisp of bloodred hair off her sweaty cheek, tucking it gently behind her ear. *Stupid question.*

Cenda shot Gray a killing glare from under her lashes. "You forget, Duke. I don't betray those I—" She broke off, pressing her lips together.

Then she stepped forward, raising her arms. A single measured exhalation, and fire crackled from her fingers, igniting a stand of featherbrellas with a joyous whoosh, writhing to the top of the fern trees, leaping from branch to branch, racing along the gully. The sky shimmered with the heat haze, fireflakes and billows of smoke dancing in an upward spiral. Perfect, pinpoint control. Purist Matthaeus would be so pleased.

Someone bellowed an order. A second, thinner voice shouted a long stream of unintelligible words brimming with panic. Gray smiled.

Whirling, he grabbed Cenda's elbow, heading for the narrow path that wound upward, over the shoulder of the hill.

Her calves were packed with bright, burning daggers of pain. Cenda staggered around the brow of yet another slope, the soles of her Technomage boots sliding on the gravel. Shad hauled her up the last couple of feet, all smoky, sinewy strength. The flash fire had bought them about half an hour.

Behind her, Gray cast a look over his shoulder. "Bastards are about half a mile back. A half dozen or so. I don't suppose—?"

Nausea roiled in her belly. "No."

Abruptly, Gray hauled her against him, his lips coming down hard on hers in a desperate, closed-mouth kiss. His mouth tasted coppery, like blood. "I'll draw them off, then. Promise me you'll at least defend yourself."

Her head swam with terror, but she sank her fingers into his biceps, fighting to keep her nerve. "I won't let them take me."

"Cenda, I—" His head jerked up and he spun around. "Where?" he snapped. "Show me!"

From behind a scrubby fern tree, a dark arm beckoned.

"A cave! Quick!"

The entrance was so narrow, she had to turn sideways, but Gray set his hands to her hip and muscled her inside. With her last particle of sense, Cenda locked her fingers around his wrist in a death grip and hauled. Then rocks clattered on the slopes and Gray squeezed in beside her, swearing as he lost layers of skin against the unyielding stone.

Cautiously, Cenda straightened, raising a fireball in the palm of her hand. Shad sprang back into being, a charcoal silhouette. Shielding the light with her cupped fingers, she took in their refuge with a single comprehensive glance. About ten feet across, bare and dusty, smelling of earth.

But at the far end was a dark opening no more than four feet high. Gray reached it one step ahead of her, the pink pack still slung over his shoulder. "Light me," he grunted, crouching to enter.

Five-it, there could be anything hidden down that close tunnel, an endless shaft, a boulder poised to drop and crush. "Wait, wait."

Hurriedly, she bent and released a salamander, a little one, no more than six inches long. It scampered past Gray and into the passage. There it stopped, haloed by a gentle nimbus, head tilted to one side.

Gray huffed out a laugh. "Judger, woman, you're incredible." He reached a hand behind him and she gripped it gratefully. Bent double, they stepped into the tunnel.

After about twenty feet, it opened up. And up and up. Cenda tossed a fireball straight high above their heads. The flash of it illuminated a vast chamber, sparkling off jutting buttresses of rock, some pinkish, others tending to orange. The left-hand side flowed like a waterfall caught in a flash freeze, all sculpted, parallel lines. Shad stood beside Gray, a black mirror of his posture, their heads tilted back to look at the ceiling.

"Which one?" Cenda waved at three tunnels. The air smelled of ancient stone and unimaginable weight.

"No idea." Gray slid an arm around her waist. "But they'll figure out where we went eventually. We can't stay here."

The salamander skittled over to the center passage and paused, every fiery inch of it conveying impatience.

Without further speech, they followed.

By the time Gray called the first halt, Cenda was almost certain about the salamander. She slid down the wall to sit on the floor. "I think it knows where it's going," she said, working her way through the provisions in the pink pack. Noodle cakes, but sweet enough to make her gag. Three manda fruit, only slightly squashed. A bottle of some sort of cordial, as sugary as the noodle cakes. The sort of food Elke had enjoyed. She'd been completely indifferent to stickiness, the little rogue. Cenda smiled, leaning against Gray's firm shoulder, watching Shad drift around farther down the tunnel, running his fingers over the walls.

Gray turned his head to look at her, his eyes narrowed. "The salamander?"

"It stopped hesitating about half an hour ago; didn't you notice? And it's bigger now."

"Yes." Gray considered the fire lizard, perched on the apex of a rock needle. "You're right." He shrugged. "Well, I'm sure it won't let any harm come to you." His lips twisted in a wry smile. "But it doesn't much care for me. Finished?" Coming to his feet, he pulled her up, right into his arms. Their eyes met and the muscles in his jaw bunched. "Cenda, I—"

Gods, she couldn't bear it! Cursing herself for a fool, she smoothed her thumbs over those flyaway brows, feeling the rasp of stubble under her palms. He'd risked his life for her today, many times over, when she knew beyond doubt he'd be able to travel farther, faster, without her. And she had no idea why.

"Just this once," she whispered. "Kiss me like you mean it."

He frowned. "Cenda—"

She put her hand over his mouth. "No excuses, no reasons. I don't want to hear them." Rising on tiptoe, she pressed her lips to his and let the bittersweet joy of it wash through her.

Gray held her so gently, as if she were precious, his palm open against her, warm on the small of her back, the fingers of his other hand stroking her nape. Ah, gods, it was like the very first time, a lifetime ago, leisurely and deft and excruciatingly thorough. Cenda relaxed into his strength and let him take the lead, hot chills chasing deliciously up and down her spine. Shad nuzzled her throat, his lips cool and smooth, tingling against her skin. Oh, they were so very good at this! Somehow, they made it so tender, she felt as if she'd come home to a refuge where she was loved and valued. She breathed into Gray's mouth, welcoming the hot, muscled velvet of his tongue against hers, loving the feel of his hard body. She let her soul drift away to float on an ocean of quiet delight.

Her head fell back, the salamander dimmed to an ember, the fireball winked out, and Shad disappeared. Gray was all there was, giving her the world in his kiss.

But it couldn't last forever. Gently, he pulled back to place light-as-air nibbles over her jaw, her ear, an eyebrow. It was too dark to make out his expression, but his whisper was fierce against her cheek. *"I do mean it."*

Blinking back the tears, Cenda sighed and stepped back, away from the comfort. "Right now?" she said quietly. "Yes, I think you do." The fireball spluttered back to life and Shad stood before her, reaching out to run his hands up her arms. She glanced at the shadow and her smile came out lopsided. "And so do you, Shad. I know."

Gray said, very low, "Forgive me?"

When she turned to look, he was standing in his usual graceful way, one hand braced against the rock wall, but his chest rose and fell as if he'd been running.

Cenda shrugged. "Forgiveness isn't so hard, Gray. It's forgetting that's difficult." The salamander sizzled, dancing with impatience. "We should go." Steeling herself, she walked away from him, following the fire lizard.

The passage sloped downward, growing hotter.

A half dozen turns later, Gray snagged her elbow, drawing them both to a halt. "We're going deeper," he said. "And I smell smoke."

Cenda opened her mouth, then clamped it shut again. She killed the fireball. The dark fell like a smothering blanket, the glow of the salamander the only remaining illumination. "Listen!"

A long way away in the dark, a rock tumbled into an abyss, the noise hard-edged, endless. No sooner had it finally died away than it happened again, what sounded like a small avalanche this time, a gravelly rush. A man's voice cried out and then cut off abruptly, echoes lingering in the hollow places under the mountain. One less pursuer—perhaps.

Gray spat out a curse, pulling her into a rapid lope. The salamander, now almost as big as a small dog, flowed along in front, crackling with excitement.

"What?" Cenda gasped to it. "Where are you taking us?"

The fire lizard sprouted small wings and rose off the floor, flying down the tunnel, sparks rising with the speed of its passage. It disappeared around a sharp, right-angled corner, Gray and Cenda on its tail.

"Fuck!"

Gray's iron grip hauled her back from the brink. He went to one knee and Cenda staggered, squinting into the blaze of light, her eyes watering.

"Judger, that was close!" Gray slammed them against the rock wall at their backs, Shad hovering protectively a yard in front of them, floating above a lake of seething fire. The salamander perched on the ledge, teetering over the drop. She could hear it crooning, a crackling, burning song of love.

The chamber was vast, the ceiling finally lost in shadow hundreds of feet above their heads. Dwarfed by the scale of it, they stood like insects on a ledge about ten feet wide, the heat of the fire lake beating against their cheeks, drying the sweat on their skin.

Gray shielded his head with his arms. "I thought you said the mountains were dormant."

Cenda nearly laughed. "They're supposed to be." She drew a shaky breath and took a cautious step forward. "Great Lady, I'm so glad I've lived this long. So beautiful." She spread her arms, luxuriating in the heat.

"Cenda, this can't be safe. I'm starting to crisp here."

The fiery surface of the lake heaved, a long, smooth roll. "No, it isn't," agreed Cenda, absently. The salamander took to the air, circling, emitting a trail of sparks. The fire swirled, a pool of blue forming. Then another.

The pools blinked. Slowly.

"Lady!"

Gray swore. Shad jerked and trembled.

The great head lifted, staring, the air around it shimmering with a heat haze. Dipping and swooping, caroling at the top of its voice, the little fire lizard sang a sizzling greeting to its kin.

Lady, save her. A salamander, a monstrous salamander.

With ponderous grace, the huge creature climbed to its feet, and now Cenda could see it had been curled up on a bed of molten rock. Gods, how big was it? The eyes of molten sapphire were about a foot in diameter, the sinuous body, made of flickering, interlaced flame, forty feet long, perhaps more.

Oh, no—*Gray!* Cenda interposed her body between them, staring up into huge orbs the same blue as the heart of flame. "Move back," she hissed at him, still holding that burning gaze. "This is for me to do. Get into the tunnel."

Boots scraped on rock. Gray's voice said, "All right, I'm behind a boulder, to your left. Gods, Cenda, be careful!"

When she held out her hands, palm up, two more salamanders sprang to life, skittering up her arms to sit on her shoulders, their little throats swelling as they joined the fire chorus. Five-it, as usual the fabric of her dress began to smolder.

The giant salamander extended its neck, the huge head drawing closer, level with the ledge, the eyes fixed on her. Flame dripped off the long jaw.

Cenda's heart hammered. She couldn't look away. Every particle of Magick within her yearned toward the creature and its perilous beauty. Gods, how long had it been here? Centuries? Poor thing. Before she knew it, she'd stretched out a commiserating hand.

Ribbons of fire wreathed up her arm as the creature nudged her gently with its nose. Then again. "Oh!" she exclaimed, and flexed her fingers, scratching. It was the oddest sensation, hot and cool at once, the shape of scales ghostly beneath her fingertips, silky and hard. The entire sleeve of Krysanthe's dress turned black and fell away in flakes, but she couldn't think of that now.

The rocky floor beneath her feet vibrated with a bass

reverberation so deep, it filled her head to bursting, made her ears buzz. Cenda laughed aloud. The salamander was purring its pleasure. When she sank down cross-legged on the ledge, the creature tried to lay its head in her lap, but it was too big. Instead, she threw her arms around its nose and hugged with all her might.

"Gods, Cenda," said Gray, his voice tight. "What the fuck do you think you're doing?"

"Making friends." She patted and soothed. "Isn't it beautiful? And so lonely, poor darling."

"Hmm. The Technomages should be thrilled. You realize they're only minutes behind?"

Cenda barely heard him. "Ah, sweetheart," she crooned, "you need a friend, don't you?" She looked up at her fire lizards, now perched in a row on a rocky shelf, their eyes whirling blue with fascination. "Three of them." When she scratched behind an eye ridge, the long lids fluttered down, each fiery eyelash nearly the length of her forearm. The salamander's gusty sigh incinerated the left leg of her trews. It tickled.

"Cenda!"

"What?"

"I can hear them." His fingers brushed her shoulder. *"Get up."*

29

Judger God, if he lived through this, he'd have a tale to tell his grandchildren.

Not likely, said Shad dryly, and Gray didn't dare ask him to elucidate—on either count.

The fire witch had looked . . . exalted, her hair streaming behind her like a river of melted garnet, her golden eyes as fiery as the monstrous creature attempting to crawl into her lap. Shit.

His brain quivered like jelly with the effort of believing his eyes. Gods, forty feet of muscle composed of equal parts flame and Magick. Suddenly, he grinned. With any luck, the skulls of the Technomages would cave in as their assumptions were punctured, one by one.

"Hmm," he said, as calmly as possible. "The Technomages should be thrilled. You realize they're only minutes behind?"

But Cenda was murmuring under her breath, glancing back and forth between her trio of fire lizards and the giant salamander. She looked as if she were performing introductions at some high-toned garden party.

They're coming! Shad rushed back from the entrance of the tunnel. *Lights. Voices.*

"Cenda!" Gray made a grab for her shoulder. There was nowhere else to go but forward, along the ledge, to the tunnel opening twenty feet farther on.

"I can hear them. *Get up.*" Throwing an arm over his eyes, he pulled her to her feet.

She came reluctantly, bestowing a kiss on the end of the fiery nose that made his eyes water. " 'Bye," she whispered. "Be happy."

With a grumbling, flaming snort, the salamander settled back onto its lava bed and they took off at a stumbling run, Shad flowing easily beside them, Cenda bouncing a fireball ahead. The tunnel began to rise and they leaned into the gradient, their breath rasping. Surely it was growing lighter? Gray could make out shapes, just barely, even without the fireball.

They raced around a corner into a shaft of light. His heart soared. Then it sank.

The passage debouched into a spacious, roughly circular chamber, the roof pierced by a shaft like a primitive chimney. He tilted his head back. The ceiling was a little lower there. If the fire witch could stand on his shoulders, she'd be able to scramble into the narrow pipe. Judging by the softness of the small patch of light, it was late afternoon up there. In the real world, the one he would never see again.

A man's startled shout echoed out of the fire chamber. But no screams. Pity. Boots clattered and slipped on rock.

Well, there must be worse places to make a stand. Gray drew the small blade from his boot and braced himself against a rock shaped like an irregular table. "Get over here. Hurry."

Stand next to the doorway, he ordered Shad. *Get ready.*

He got the sensation of a fierce grin in return. *Together,* said his shadow, with tremendous satisfaction.

And three figures erupted into the chamber, laseguns waving.

Gray dived for cover behind the rock table, pulling Cenda down with him.

"Finally!" said a male voice, sounding massively pissed. "Thank Science."

Gray hitched a cautious eye around the rock, studying the three men as they fanned out. Well, well. He grinned. "You look a little the worse for wear. Real life's not a precise science, is it?"

"Fuck you," said a short, chunky Technomage with close-cropped gray hair. A bruise along his jaw oozed blood, the once pristine white coveralls filthy, ripped in several places. Though the number on his collar was partially obscured, Gray thought he could make out two digits. His brows rose. The Primus must be pretty desperate if he and Cenda rated more than mere rank-and-file. The other two looked even worse, if that was possible. Only one appeared to be uninjured, though his face was drawn with exhaustion. A skinny individual wearing spectacles cradled his wrist with his gun hand, his lips white with pain.

Shad chuckled. *They're hurting.*

"Give us the woman," said Chunky, "or I'll blast you out of there."

Crouched beside Gray, Cenda growled in her throat. "I'm not his to give," she called.

Lost her, sniped Shad. *Told you, lost her.*

Not now. Shut up.

Chunky frowned. "You've cost me three good people already." He shrugged. "Be damned to you. Have it your own way." As he raised the lasegun, Shad surged out of the wall and knocked his arm up. The bolt arced across the chamber and struck a protrusion high on the wall. The vicious crack of it echoed across the room, again and again, as the blast ricocheted off stone buttresses at odd angles, slicing through the air, forcing the Technomages to duck and roll. Rock chips sprayed in a deadly shower. A man screamed, a high, animal sound of shock.

Endless minutes later, Gray raised his head, Cenda still pinned beneath him, protected by his body. *Shad?*

Chunky's dead. Skinny's passed out. Other one doesn't look too good.

Slowly, Gray rose from behind the rock. The gray-haired man lay in a gradually widening pool of blood, Skinny moaning beside him, his spectacles askew. The last Technomage slumped against the wall, breathing hard, the lasegun dangling from limp fingers.

"Put it away," said Gray wearily. "It's no use in here."

"Yah." A tall, bulky figure stepped out of the tunnel. "Hard steel's better by far."

Fuck. "Who the hell are you?" Though he knew. Four men filed in behind the first. Workingmen's trews, rough shirts.

"Chief." A missing tooth showed in the man's tight smile. "Pleased ta meetcha."

Cenda's fingers crept up to clutch Gray's arm. "Is the Fixer dead?"

Chief's flat black eyes brightened with what looked like satisfaction. "Near 'nuff. Thanks t' ye, witch." He waved a hand. "Banty. Wace." A short, square thug and a taller, wiry one advanced on the two remaining Technomages. A brief struggle, a couple of grunts, and the Scientists were weaponless.

"But how did you find us?" asked Cenda.

The big man chuckled. "Follered along, sweet as ye please." He nodded at the wide-eyed Technomages. "Stupid bastards never knew we was there." Casually, he reached down, grabbed Skinny by the front of his coveralls, and hauled him roughly to his feet.

Skinny choked on a scream, clutching his wrist.

Chief thrust his face into the other man's. "An' ye're goin' take us oot agin, aren' ye? Wit' yer little machine."

The Technomage nodded frantically, then sagged in Chief's grip, moaning.

"But didn't you see the creature? Out there?" Cenda pointed.

Chief let Skinny drop. "I saw a fookin' great fire lake. Yah. So what?"

"Magma, you peasant," muttered the third Technomage under his breath.

The man standing beside him drew back a tattooed fist and punched him over the kidney. "Watch yer lip," he growled.

"Thanks, Wace, lad." Chief nodded his approval as the Technomage reeled back, gasping. "Bah. No more talkin'." Drawing a long knife from a sheath at his waist, the big man sauntered a few steps closer to the rock table. "Ye sure ye're t' fire witch, lass? Don' look like much t' me."

Gray thrust Cenda behind him, his brain spinning, sorting and discarding possibilities. They were fucked, no doubt of it, but if he and Shad could create a divers—

A small thunderclap reverberated in the chamber. Purist Matthaeus stepped out of a puff of smoke in the doorway, not a single snowy hair out of place, a long, knobby cane gripped in one hand.

Gray blinked, ears still ringing. Then he sniffed and his eyes narrowed, remembering. A smoke bomb—Erik used them onstage. Excellent for conjuring demons out of thin air.

"Purist!" gasped Cenda. "What are—"

"Git 'im," snapped Chief.

But the old wizard skipped nimbly aside. A quick thrust of the cane and Banty and another man went sprawling in a thrashing, cursing tangle. Puffing a little, Purist Matthaeus stepped behind the stone table. He patted Cenda's arm. "I made an error," he said stiffly. "I am here to correct it."

Judger! Was there anyone left behind in East Sector, anyone at all?

Cenda stared. "Yes, but . . . Where . . . How—?"

The Purist's lips twitched. "Olga's great-grandnephew."

"Oh." Cenda nodded. Suddenly, she thrust out a hand, flames shooting from her fingertips. "Stop right there," she hissed, and Chief froze, caught in midstride.

"Fook!" whispered Banty. "Lookit thet!"

"Well-done, my dear," murmured Matthaeus.

Doesn't know the half of it, said Shad.

You got that right.

I'm always right. Lounging against the wall, Shad gave him the finger.

Gray bit his lip.

Matthaeus raised a chilly brow. "I think retreat would be the best course, don't you?" he said to Chief.

The big man ignored him. "So it's fookin' true, what t' Fixer said." He fixed a glittering gaze on Cenda. "He was lettin' ye go cheap, the fool."

"What do you mean?" said the old wizard sharply. "Letting her go? To whom?"

This time, Chief flicked him a glance. "T' Technomage," he said. Suddenly he grinned, but it wasn't a pleasant expression. "But now I'm thinkin' I might use ye meself. What else can ye do, lass?" He poised the knife in an expert thrower's grip. "But do it careful like."

"She has powers you cannot imagine." Matthaeus stepped forward. "Stand aside, young man."

Without taking his gaze from Cenda, Chief lifted a meaty hand and backhanded the old wizard across the face. Everything happened at once.

Cenda screamed in fury and burst into flame. Gray flung himself at Chief, bearing his knife hand down, taking him to the dusty floor, where they grappled, rolling over and over.

Another voice shouted, "Witch!" Gray looked up to see a blade flash through the air like a hideous shard of light, straight for Cenda's heart. Wace. The one with the tattooed fingers.

Time seemed to slow to a trickle as he lifted away from Chief, stretching out a futile hand, knowing he was too late, too fucking late.

Gathering the skirt of his robes in one fist, Purist Matthaeus lurched forward. The move was hardly graceful, but it was extraordinarily effective. The old wizard's body arched in front of the fire witch, the dagger blooming suddenly in his breast like an evil flower. He made a strange noise, a high-pitched grunt, swaying on his feet. A momentary hesitation, and he toppled, hitting the floor with a muffled thud.

"No!" Immediately, Cenda's fire died and she dropped to her knees to cradle his head in her lap. "Purist . . . ah, Great Lady, no!"

Gray shoved Chief aside, and they rolled to their feet.

Matthaeus blinked once, slowly. "I knew . . . had a dream . . . vision . . ." He coughed, and a trickle of blood ran out of the corner of his mouth.

"Don't talk," said Cenda. "Save your strength."

"No use. Listen."

Cenda bent her head. Gray had to strain to hear the old man's labored whisper. "Saw it, the Pentacle. P-pattern. Was why"—the pale blue eyes warmed, even as they clouded—"came." He fumbled a hand up to touch hers. "You, you're part. The fire . . ." His breath bubbled, and for a moment Gray thought they'd lost him. But the old wizard was tougher than that. "Live, Cenda. You have to . . ." His cold fingers closed hard over Cenda's. "Good girl."

A racking cough, a river of blood spilling over his chin, and the Purist's head fell back against the fire witch's arm.

In the silence, a thready voice moaned, "Oh, shit. Science save us." Skinny.

"Take care o' that, Wace," ordered Chief.

Wace grunted his assent, drew a second blade, and bent over the Technomage, gripping him by the hair to pull his head back. Before the man could struggle, he cut his throat as precisely as a surgeon, the sweet, coppery reek of fresh blood now so intense it masked the odors of earth and stone.

Gray dragged Cenda to her feet and put their backs to the wall. He gripped his blade.

Shad's growl echoed in his head, a long, low rumble of fury. Or was that him? No matter.

We won't die alone, Gray promised, getting another visceral snarl in response.

Chief gestured at the remaining Technomage, and two thugs went to prop him up, one on either side. "I only need one o' ye bastards t' work t' machine, geddit?" The Scientist nodded vigorously, his head bobbing.

"Git oop, lass," the big man said impatiently. "We're

goin'. An' as for ye . . ." His flat gaze swung around to Gray. "How d' ye wan' it?"

"Enough." The fire witch straightened, brushing off her tattered garments. Her voice had the oddest undertone, as though she controlled something huge with her will alone.

Gray watched the tears on her cheeks evaporate, her long tresses begin to lift away from her shoulders, floating out behind her, and the short hairs rose all along his spine. Fuck. Oh, fuck.

Cenda raised her molten gaze to Chief's. "I am a witch," she said, still in that gentle, muted roar. "I swore an oath to do no harm."

Chief smiled. "I like an easy woman," he said. "Let's go, lass."

"You are an evil man." Her gaze swept across the cave. "All of you. But the Lady gives every soul a choice."

Chief's face darkened. "Gods, woman, stop t' fookin' yammerin'. We have t' go."

"Yes." The small breasts trembled beneath the ruin of Krysanthe's dress. Cenda passed a shaky hand over her eyes, but when she looked up, Gray caught his breath.

Something ancient and immeasurable blazed out of her molten stare, distant and all-encompassing. The scrutiny of a Judge, balancing honor against will on the Great Scales. Gray braced his knees so he wouldn't slide down the wall.

Without further warning, flames licked up from her feet, as if she stood bound at the stake on a pyre. "I have called your death," she said in that crackling, otherworldly voice. "It is coming. Down that tunnel." She pointed, and ribbons of fire danced up and down her arm. "The choice is yours. The only way out is up the shaft over there. Leave us, help each other, and live. Otherwise . . ." She shrugged, her face set behind the veil of fire. "You will burn. I guarantee it."

"Don' be daft," Chief snorted, his hands clenching into fists. "Nothin' burns forever. We'll wait ye out, and then I promise . . ."

The floor shuddered beneath their feet. "Chief . . ." muttered Banty uneasily. A wave of heat rolled out of the passage. Sweat prickled under Gray's arms, popped on his forehead.

"I need to be higher." Bathed in her inferno from head to heels, the fire witch beckoned. "Shad, help me up." Krysanthe's dress began to curl and blacken on her pale body.

Shad's featureless face turned to Gray. *Love you.* An infinitesimal pause. *Love her.*

Gracefully, looking neither right nor left, his shadow walked across the chamber and gripped Cenda's flaming hand in his dark one.

"What t' fook is that?"

Light poured out of the tunnel, accompanied by a monstrous, rushing roar, as if a thousand searing desert winds whirled together within its confining walls.

Gray took a breath, the hot dustiness of baked minerals sharp on his tongue. "Mine," he said. "He's mine." The words felt strange in his mouth. His heart twisted in his breast, full of pain and regrets and might-have-beens.

Shad reached right into Cenda's column of fire, set his hands at her waist, and lifted her easily to the top of a large boulder. She stood there pale and naked, as if she bathed in a firefall, the clothes burned off her body.

"Who t' fook cares?" Wace rushed across the chamber and scrambled onto the stone table. "Forget 'er. I'm off." He stretched up, the opening in the roof just beyond the reach of his seeking fingers. "Shit."

The cave reverberated to a regular, thundering cadence, the steps of something monstrously heavy. A huge voice spoke from inside the tunnel. Gray imagined an exploding sun might cry out like that, a great crackling howl, incandescent with loss and grief and fury.

Three small winged salamanders shot out of the doorway and circled around the ceiling, trailing sparks, diving at the six men standing frozen, their mouths open.

"Choose," said the fire witch, her voice deeper than Gray's.

30

Chief came to life. "Move it, fookers!"

The men made a concerted rush for the stone table, but Wace fended them off with boots and fists. "Chief," he panted, "ye're tallest."

Chief leaped up. "On me shoulders. Then ye help pull. Got it?"

"Yah." Wace swarmed up Chief's broad back and launched himself into the shaft, bracing his shoulders and the soles of his boots against the narrow walls, puffing and swearing. He'd barely got situated before the other three thugs collided in their rush to get to the big man, cursing, punching, and kicking. When a swooping salamander set fire to one man's hair, Chief simply snapped out a big fist. The man flew off the table and hit the wall headfirst. He slid to the floor and didn't move again.

"Go, go!" Chief lifted Banty's compact body, the muscles beneath the coarse shirt bunching. Wace braced himself and reached down, but a salamander dived with a shrill, crackling cry, striking at him.

"Shit!" Wace winced, pulling back, shaking his hand. Searing light spilled out of the tunnel, so bright it made the eyes tear. "Fook this!" Using the muscle in his shoulders and thighs, he began to work himself up the shaft, a foot at a time.

Without hesitation, Banty pulled the lasgeun from his belt and squeezed off a shot. Wace's head vaporized in a cloud of blood and bone and brains, the bolt bouncing around inside the stone chimney until it was spent. The remaining Technomage screamed, "No, you fool, no!" and Wace's body dropped out of the shaft, driving Chief and Banty to their knees. The Technomage and the last thug vaulted to the table and over the top of the heaving bodies, reaching for the opening above their heads.

A gout of flame belched out of the tunnel, followed by a huge, reptilian head formed of a hundred infernos knitted together, the eyes twin furnaces of burning blue. The hair on Gray's arms curled, crisping.

"Gray." Cenda's voice. He hadn't realized he'd fallen to his knees. *"Hurry."*

What?

In his head, Shad bellowed, *Run! To us, run!*

Standing on her boulder, Cenda faced the giant salamander, smiling a terrible smile, an effigy all aflame, but somehow not consumed. Behind her, a solid patch of shadow extended across the floor, dense and hard-edged in the bright, unrelenting light of the creature's fire.

Gods! Gray pushed off the floor like a runner from the blocks, his body hurtling parallel to the floor in a long, shallow dive. In a single movement, he hit the shadow and rolled into the twilight of the veil. Shad's arms wrapped around him and held him in an iron grip, chest to chest, belly to belly, shielding and protecting.

The salamander's fiery body flowed inexorably into the chamber, taking up its entire width. When the huge maw opened in a roar of rage, the air exploded, fire roiling right up to the roof. Even through the shadow veil, Gray blinked, blinded, stars bursting behind his eyelids. Cenda screamed, a high, thin note, and he thought he heard echoes, sustained instants of unendurable agony, hanging in the air.

Silence crept back slowly, punctuated by a muffled, desperate keening and the soft crackle of flame.

Gods, *Cenda!*

Gray struggled to his feet, swaying, gripping Shad's strong arm.

You cut that close, said his shadow.

Yeah.

Gray set Shad aside and stepped up to the small, huddled form of the fire witch. Before her lay the salamander, its long nose resting on its paws, glowing like an enormous banked fire. It stirred, the sapphire eyes tracking his progress. When it growled, Cenda raised her head. "Not him," she said huskily. The creature subsided with a grumbling crackle.

Gray stroked her hair. Then he shrugged out of his ruined shirt and wrapped it around her bare shoulders. "Let's go," he said gently.

"I felt them . . . die." Cenda looked around the empty cave, her eyes blind with pain. "There's nothing left," she said. "Six—no, nine lives—and there's nothing to show they even existed." She bowed her head. "Only ash."

Shad took her other arm and they lifted her to her feet. "They made their own choices, Cenda. Even Matthaeus. Come on, sweetheart."

"Especially Matthaeus." Sighing, she leaned heavily against him. "Lady, I couldn't light a candle."

Shad scrabbled behind a rock and produced the backpack, so battered and singed the bright shade of pink was but a memory. *Eat?* He extracted a Technomage food cube, squashed almost flat.

Cenda pulled a face. "Later."

Warily, Gray eyed the monstrous salamander. "What about him? It? Whatever?"

"Yes." The fire witch knelt before the creature and stroked its jaw. "Thank you," she said. "I will never forget you, I swear." She glanced up at the three fire lizards, perched in a row on the stone table, their eyes swirling cobalt with interest. "And they will stay and keep you company. You won't be lonely anymore."

A final pat and she rose, wincing. One of the fire lizards whirred into the air above their heads, darting toward the tunnel. "Oh!" said Cenda. She smiled, her lips trembling. "Thank you."

"What for?"

"It knows a quicker way."

The shorter route was almost entirely uphill, and if it hadn't been for Gray and Shad, Cenda knew she would have given in to the temptation to lie down in a dark corner under the mountain and die. When they emerged from the narrow opening and she glimpsed the Dancers, high in the night sky, the flood of relief was so intense it made her lightheaded.

So when Gray jerked her suddenly behind a scrubby stand of fern trees, she was already off balance. She tripped and fell, choking back a curse. Lady, she knew it was ridiculous after all they'd been through, but she couldn't help tugging the shirt down, uneasily aware of her ass, gleaming round and pale like Arabesque and likely as big.

Gray bent, placed his lips next to her ear, and whispered, "A flitter. Look."

Below them was a dark winged shape, squatting directly across the path. Cenda suppressed the urge to burst into tears. She couldn't take any more; she *couldn't*!

Wait a minute! Her tired brain spun, creaking with effort. Matthaeus had said—

Suddenly, Gray was no longer beside her. A scuffle erupted a few feet away. "Who the hell are you?" hissed Gray.

Abruptly, a lantern flared and a young male voice said, "There's a lasegun trained on your spine, friend. Back off slow and easy. Did he hurt you, Auntie?"

Cenda's jaw sagged.

Purist Olga shrugged herself free of Gray with an irritated shake strongly reminiscent of Titfer the cat in a huff. "No." She glared.

Cenda shut her mouth. "I gather this is your great-grandnephew, Purist?"

The young man smiled, but he didn't lower the gun. He had a freckled, open face, a head of unruly brown curls, and a shielded lantern in his left hand. "Thoby," he said cheerfully, "the one who went to the bad." His interested gaze dropped to Cenda's legs. "Auntie Olga's the only Pure who still speaks to me."

"Hah! You're more useful than the lot of 'em. More interesting, too. Nothing like a handsome space pilot." Chuckling, Purist Olga nudged Thoby's gun arm. "You can put that nasty thing away, dear."

Thoby complied, but slowly.

"How'd you know we'd be here?" asked Gray.

"I'm a gatekeeper, lad. I know all about entrances and exits." She glanced shrewdly from one face to the other, and her expression grew bleak. "Matthaeus is dead, isn't he?"

Cenda nodded, unable to speak.

"Did he make it right? That's why we came, once we knew about Krysanthe."

Cenda bowed her head.

Gray said, "He sacrificed his life for Cenda's."

"Stubborn old fool." After a short silence, Purist Olga sighed. "Come on then, let's get you back to the Enclave." She hobbled off toward the waiting craft. "We've got a blanket in the flitter."

Cenda thought she heard Thoby mutter, "Pity."

In her comfortable private office at the Remnant Two facility, the Technomage Primus flexed her shoulders, reaching up to massage the tightness at the back of her neck. Science, stress had amazing effects on the body! When she'd first been informed of the fire witch's escape, she'd actually felt her heart leap into her throat with fury and fear. Though, of course, that wasn't physically possible. Even now, her respiration was slightly elevated despite the fact that she'd always prided herself on her self-discipline.

Not to worry, it would all be over soon enough. Glancing at the deskvid display, she permitted herself a small smile. She'd regrouped, initiated the appropriate emergency response, and set out to retrieve her investment. Superimposed on a contour map, a cluster of green dots was converging on two red dots.

Fire Magick. If it hadn't been for the readouts, she wouldn't have credited the evidence of her senses. Science save her, the woman had literally burst into flame! And then— Chewing the end of her stylus, the Primus activated the perimeter security vid and ran it back, calculating distances and angles. Hmm. It didn't look as if Cenda had expended any particular effort.

With a tailored diet and the right training, the fire witch could wipe out advancing armies, devastate cities. She scanned the list of potential clients Sharanita had compiled. A warlord on Palimpsest, a space pirate from the Horsehead sector, the oligarchs of Green IV, a mystery figure calling itself the Necromancer. And this was only the beginning.

Of course, there'd have to be demonstrations, a sliding scale of fees established. The Primus consulted her budget summary sheet and jotted a few figures in the margins of Nita's list. She blinked.

The most powerful Primus ever known. A legend. So far beyond—

The thin, disapproving face of the Secundus appeared in her mind's eye, and she smiled. Ah, what pleasures in store! And the Quartus, that oily bitch. She'd have to think of something special for them.

She rolled her shoulders. So much sustained, intelligent effort, but oh, so worth it. She'd always been famous for a ferocious work ethic.

The Primus leaned back in her chair. A neck-and-shoulders massage—that's what she needed. Nita was probably still awake. Reaching for her comm disk, the Primus caught sight of the deskvid.

She froze.

All the dots on the screen were now clumped together, but why was there only one green dot? As she watched, it winked out.

The stylus snapped between her fingers.

The flitter was small and battered, but Thoby flew it like the rich man's toy it had once been, low and very fast. Gray sat sideways across two seats, braced against the window, the unconscious fire witch half slumped over his lap, wrapped in the blanket. His brain felt soupy with exhaustion, his thoughts ponderous and muffled. His fingers moved in Cenda's hair as she slept, separating the wine red swathes over her temples from the dark mass of the rest. They were well-defined now, unmistakable.

Fire witch. Gods!

Purist Olga sat across the aisle, mouth open and eyes closed, emitting a regular ladylike snuffle.

Shad stirred restlessly, kneeling on the floor. *You listening?*

Gray yawned. *I'm asleep. Later.*

No. Now. Steely fingers gripped his knee. *You lost her.*

Not quite. Absently, Gray kept playing with the red silk beneath his fingertips, twisting it into a narrow braid, letting it uncoil and spring back against her temples. *She's here, isn't she?*

Thoby glanced over the high back of the pilot's chair, his eyes bright with male speculation. "She all right?"

Shad growled and Gray's lips drew back from his teeth. "She's fine. I've got her." His hands stilled, cradling the precious, stubborn shape of her skull.

Thoby raised a brow, grinned, and returned to his instruments.

The only one. Lost.

Will you stop *that!* Gray pinched the bridge of his nose, feeling the empty place open up inside him like a wound that would never heal. *Moan all you like, it doesn't change anything. Yes, we lost her, but we never really had her, did we?*

He was too tired to fight, to prevent the slow slide of Shad's grief from filling him like a rushing tide. His shadow dropped a dark head to Gray's knees and shook with the sobs Gray wouldn't release. He shifted a hand to Shad's nape, the silky hair brushing cool across his knuckles, and the breath rattled out of him in a shaky sigh. *Let me sleep, Shad, please. I can't—*

Can't bear it? Shad clambered up to press into Gray's other shoulder, his body a perfect fit. As it always was. *The only one who could love us both. Lost, lost, oh, lost . . .*

Both? The word dropped like a pebble into a pool, ripples spreading.

Lost, oh, lost . . .

Shut up. Both? The world began to tilt sideways and Gray groped after it, his vision going blurry at the edges.

Shad sniffed. He huffed out a rasping laugh. *Idiot. She loved you.*

You said—Gray swallowed, trying to force his heart down out of his throat—*both*. Because that would mean—it would mean . . . He and Shad . . .

Yeah, stupid. A soul. Together.

Shit, it was too much, a seething mass of emotion, of frantic, leaping hope and pain and the dislocation of everything he'd believed about himself and Shad and the world for years. He'd thought he'd come to some accommodation with himself, as much as any man with a shadow could do, but now he could see that the fissures had been widening, pretty well from the moment he'd seen Cenda across the footlights. Because now his soul was beginning to crack and bleed, fragmenting, flying into a hundred little pieces, shards of his essential self, like a mirror fractured and gone mad. And Shad—bloody Shad—who always knew exactly where and how to push, was nudging him off his perch. He'd shatter, spill, die . . .

In desperation, Gray snagged a single thought out of the morass and clung to it, something marginally safer for his sanity. *What about you? You think she . . . loved you, too?*

Shad's cool chest rubbed against Gray's as he shrugged. *Love you, love me. Same thing.*

And just like that, Gray was drowning again, going under.

Wait, wait. Yes, there were things he had to say to Shad. In the name of honor, he could do no less. The rest of it—in a panic, he shoved it all aside—he'd deal with later, when he was rested and ready. Thinking straight.

Carefully, he counted to ten, conscious of Shad's ironic attention. *You saved my life. I thank you.*

His shadow gave a vulgar snort. *Yeah, I do that a lot. You never thanked me before.*

Gray felt his cheeks warm. Shit, this was ridiculous. Shamed by his own shadow. Stiffly, he said, *Well, then, it's overdue.*

Hard fingers gripped his chin and forced his head around. Fathomless eyes glared into his. *Why do you think I bother?* Each word was clipped out, precise and angry.

Gray gave a harsh bark of laughter. *You have to.*

Because?

Without me, you're nothing.

Uh-huh. And without me, you are what, precisely?

The world stopped. Just fucking stopped. Gray gaped, blinking.

Shad released him. *Nothing. That's what you are. Or worse than nothing, half a man. Ah, shit!* He turned his face away.

Gray flailed. *I thought—I thought if I could . . . if you . . .*

I kept trying to tell you there was no way, but you wouldn't listen. You stupid, stubborn shit, you'd die without me. Judger knows why I love you so much.

Gods! Now he was totally out of his depth. He choked.

Shad leaned into him, nose to nose. *This is the third fucking time I've said it. What fucking part of I—Love—You don't you understand?*

Gray squeezed his eyes shut. *I'm not having this conversation. W-why?*

A dark brow rose. *Why do I love you? How can I not?* Shad's cool, sweet breath puffed over his lips. *Someone has to. And it might as well be your shadow, don't you think? Because you love me, too.*

"I—?" It was too much. His head spinning, Gray struck out blindly, banging his knuckles hard against the cabin wall. "Fuck!"

An irritated voice said, "Lord's balls, lad." Purist Olga levered herself out of her seat and hobbled over. "You're keeping me awake." A gnarled finger tapped him lightly between the eyes. "Go to sleep."

Gray opened his mouth to protest, but the finger, the flitter, and the world receded into a dark, cottony fog.

It seemed like a few minutes later that Cenda exclaimed, right in his ear, "Not my vegetable patch!"

How strange. Gray forced his eyes open. The flitter's hum had changed to a deeper whine. They were settling, coming down slowly, lights off. Below them was a large patch of darkness, lit only by sporadic soft glows. The Enclave.

Thoby gave a preoccupied grunt. "I generally do this with the lights on, sweetie. Pray I only roast the taters and not the dining hall."

Sweetie? Gray sat up. The fire witch was leaning across his body, very close, staring out of the window. The blanket slipped, baring one shoulder, the bones showing strong and angular beneath creamy skin. He smiled.

And it all came crashing back. The smile slid away as his gaze sought his shadow. Shad made a rude gesture.

No, no, he couldn't have— Shad hadn't— Gray threw his arms around Cenda and hugged her tight. She squeaked a breathless protest, but he hung on.

A shudder, a scrape, and a rocking thump. Thoby blew out a breath and leaned back. "Am I good or what?" he asked no one in particular.

"Yes, yes," muttered the Purist. She dropped a hasty

kiss on his freckled cheek. “Don’t wait,” she ordered. “Lift off the moment we’re out.”

Thoby hit a lever and the night air rushed in, perfumed with Lady’s lace.

“Come on, you two.” Grabbing her stick, the old witch scuttled down the ramp.

“Give us a kiss, darlin’.” Thoby held out his arms to Cenda and waggled his brows. “For luck.”

Gray snarled. He grabbed the backpack with one hand and a chuckling Cenda with the other, hustling her out of the flitter. “Thanks,” he threw over his shoulder. Then he thought better of it. He turned on the threshold. “You’re bloody good,” he said. “What did you say you did?”

Thoby’s teeth gleamed in the glow of the instrument panel. “I didn’t.” He flicked something on the console.

The ramp retracted under Gray’s feet and he jumped off, swearing.

“I’m a smuggler.” Thoby’s cheerful voice floated back to him. “Good luck, friend. Don’t get your balls burned.” He laughed, the door hissed shut, and the flitter lifted, hovering like an improbable bird. Then it accelerated, shooting away in the general direction of Tap and Tango, still hanging low on the horizon.

Purist Olga cast a worried glance at the night sky. “You’ve got five minutes in your cottage to pack,” she said. “Then you go to a safe house. I hired a dogcart.”

31

"Slop!" Cenda stared at the diminutive figure holding the reins of the four-dog team. She tossed her bundle in the back. "I mean—Florien!"

"Mistress." The boy nodded awkwardly, but he grinned. He shot Gray a cautious glance from under his lashes.

Olga ruffled the lad's hair. "There's only the two of us will know where you are. Use the boy to run messages."

"Purist"—Cenda turned to look down into the old woman's face—"tell me truly. Do you think I'll ever be safe on Sybaris?"

"No." Gray and Purist Olga spoke together.

The old witch leaned on her stick. "No, dear," she said quietly. "You're dangerous now, in so many ways, to so many people. The Technomages must be looking for you already. Lie low, and we'll move you to another house tomorrow and another the day after that. But then"—she sighed—"I don't know. Do you have any money?"

Cenda drooped. "Only the few creds I had in my rainy-day box. Not even enough to get me out of the Sector."

Purist Olga patted her arm. "Go now," she said. "Cook put together something for you." She handed over a small sack. "We'll talk again tomorrow. Duke." She nodded at Gray.

Gray climbed into the cart and pulled Cenda up beside him. Florien snapped the reins, gave the dogs a muttered command, and they were off, racing through the crooked alleys and mean streets, past the taverns and inns. Gray braced an arm behind her as they bumped along, completely impersonal. His features were pale and set, showing no trace of his thoughts. She could have dreamed it, that expression of startled joy and relief when he'd found his harp, lying half under the bed in her ruined cottage. She hadn't seen him smile quite that way before, sheer happiness lighting his handsome face like a bright dawn, his eyes gone silver with it.

The safe house turned out to be a shabby, two-room apartment above a block of shops, not far from a bazaar. Florien turned the cart into the yard at the back and the dogs hunkered down, panting, their eyes avid. Hastily, he pacified them with bloody scraps taken from a noisome bag, and led Cenda and Gray up a narrow staircase at the side of the building.

The light of a battered lantern revealed a sitting room of sorts with a door leading to a poky bedroom. The boy turned to face them, bracing himself against the side of a half-sprung couch upholstered in faded, stained chintz. His dark eyes burned huge in his wizened face. "Take me wit' ye."

"With us?" echoed Cenda, staring.

"Where do you think we're going?" said Gray, his voice hard.

"Offworld. Ye have t' be goin' offworld." A small hand clutched a fold of Cenda's skirt. "Take me." A pause. "Please."

Cenda knelt down to peer into the boy's face. "But Florien, I thought you liked Purist Olga? And Titfer."

"Yah. Do." He drew a clenched fist out of his pocket. "But I wan' go wit' ye." His cheeks pinkened. "I like ye better. An' I can pay." Hands shaking, he unwrapped a dirty rag from around a small object.

The light sparked dull gleams from the novarine lying like a black star in his small palm, the gold setting lumpy and distorted. With a gasp, Cenda recoiled.

"Judger!" Gray gave a short laugh. "The Fixer's ring. I'm definitely losing my mind. I'd forgotten all about it." He took it from the boy and turned it over in his long fingers. "You little thief. Technically, Cenda, it's yours."

Great Lady, she didn't care if she never saw the evil thing again! "Gods, no, you keep it." She rubbed her forehead, trying to think, achingly conscious of Gray at her elbow. She hardly knew how to speak to him, what to feel, how to act. Every time she looked at him, the world sideslipped toward confusion.

Every move Gray made was deliberate, rigid with tension, as if he were holding himself together with sheer willpower. Exhaustion must be making her stupid, because she was beginning to think she'd have more luck trying to read Shad, lounging against the wall. His head turned toward her as if he'd caught the thought. Wistfully, Cenda wondered if he'd smiled.

She rose and moved to the sofa, clasping her hands in her lap. "I thought," she said slowly, feeling her way, "I thought we might leave with the Unearthly Opera? We can go our separate ways once we reach Concordia."

The silence seemed to last forever. Gray's face showed nothing. "You've never been to a spaceport, have you?"

Cenda's heart sank. "No. Why?"

"The Technomages make most of their money out of space travel. They invented slingshot sails, after all. Every passenger, every ship, has to have papers. They keep records and they check." He looked her in the eye, one dark brow quirked. "If you were the Primus and you discovered your prize fire witch had got clean away, what would you do?"

"Five-it." Cenda sagged into the squashy embrace of the sofa.

Gray laid a hand on Florien's shoulder and drew him closer to the light. "Chief is dead. So are Wace and Banty. Still want to come?"

The boy's jaw sagged. "Fook, ye killed 'em?"

Gray shot a glance at Cenda. He shrugged. "Near enough." He squatted to stare into Florien's face, both hands gripping the skinny shoulders. "If you want our trust, you have to earn it. Do you understand, Slop? Sorry—Florien."

Cynical black eyes met hard gray ones. "Yah. An' ye'll kill me if'n I let ye down."

"Very likely." Gray studied the boy's face. "The ring's worth more than the whole bloody Sector. All we need is some cash, papers for a family of three, and passage to Concordia."

The lad flushed brick red. "A family?"

"Yes. They won't be looking for a couple with a child. A son."

Florien's mouth opened and shut. Eventually, he whispered, "Concordia? Is thet where t' choc stuff comes frum?"

Through a haze of tears, Cenda saw Gray's lips twitch. "That's right," he said gravely.

Florien's skinny chest expanded with his intake of breath. He thrust out a small grubby hand. "Yah. All right, then."

Gray shook it firmly. "Agreed."

"What about me?" Their heads whipped around so fast, Cenda almost laughed. She offered her hand. "I'm in this, too."

The boy took one step, then two. He arrived at the sofa in such a stumbling rush, she opened her arms, ready for a hug, but at the last minute, Florien skidded to a halt. His little body stiff with tension, he grasped Cenda's hand and squeezed it gingerly. Her heart ached.

"Do you know where to find Thoby?" asked Gray.

Florien turned. "Yah."

"Come, then." Gray stowed the ring in an inside pocket.

"You're leaving?" Cenda surged to her feet. "Wait for me."

"You'd be a liability where we're going." The cool gray gaze didn't waver. "Get some sleep. Eat something."

"Here." Cenda grabbed her cloak and flung it at him. "Wear it, Duke," she gritted. "It's too short for a man, but it's got a hood." Krysanthe's cloak. Her friend would be dead now. Or wishing she was.

"We won't be gone more than a couple of hours. I'll lock the door behind me." Warm fingers feathered her cheek, a cool, dark touch smoothed her hair. The door snicked shut and their footsteps padded softly down the stair. Out in the yard, the dogs whined; Florien gave a shrill command, and they were gone.

Cenda took the lantern to the bedroom. Seated cross-legged on the narrow bed, she opened the food sack. Gods, she was starving! Abruptly, she teared up again. Cook had packed all her favorites, bless his gruff old heart.

Five-it, if she was going to cry, she might as well do it properly. Hardly daring to breathe, she unwrapped her own meager bundle. When she reached for the gray cube, her hands were shaking so hard she could barely grasp it. All this way, shoved deep into the pink backpack. She still wasn't sure if the *hollow* was good or evil, or if it just *was*. Nonetheless . . . She bowed her head. *Thank you, Great Lady. Thank you for these scraps of my darling. For letting me see what might have been.*

And then she allowed herself to look, *really* look, to trace the beloved features with wondering fingertips.

An hour later, she slid over the edge of exhaustion and grief into sleep, a place of the oddest fragments. The day after Elke had been born, Krysanthe had brought her an ingenious toy made of chips of colored glass in a tube. Every time you shook it, a new pattern was produced, breathtakingly bright and lovely. And somehow, every design had a *rightness* about it, each color clicking into its appointed place, and you couldn't conceive that it had ever been otherwise. Cenda had put it away carefully, for later, when Elke was old enough.

That day would never come, but now the gods held the toy and shook it for her, the scenes forming in rapid succession—Elke's first bath, Cenda's hands trembling, her heart thudding with delight as the tiny limbs uncurled in the warm water. Titfer maintaining his dignity by the merest whisker as Elke crooned baby nonsense into his ear. And then, strangely, a young voice saying decisively, "Mother, you can't wear that!" Followed by a hand thrusting a dramatic length of jewel-toned velvet into her arms. "Try this one."

Cenda smiled in her sleep. "Bossy child."

The visions flowed, flashing behind her eyes, faster and faster. A life—two lives, intertwined. Two strong wills clashing, the joys, the moments of quiet communion, a mother's pride. Ah, so Elke would have been a healer, but not in the ordinary way. Her gift was with animals. No wonder Titfer had loved her.

A Great Hand rattled the toy. "Look, dearest one," said a beautiful Voice. "See how it works."

And there was the Pattern, laid out beneath her. She frowned, following the path of sparkling lines that broke and met in a dance whose significance she could almost grasp. Yes, there was the fire Magick, emerging from the node that was Elke's death. Or was it her life? Other Magicks glowed, twisting to form a familiar five-pointed shape. A Pentacle. A laughing breeze lifted the hair from her forehead and she held up her palm to feel its passage. Air Magick, like a breath distilled from pure joy.

Fire coursed around the Pentacle, crackling with excitement, but it missed one side entirely. How odd. A four-sided Pentacle. Cenda peered and her head swam.

"Later," sang the Voice. "Sleep now, little witch."

Yawning, Cenda turned her whole body, snuggling into the comfort of loving arms. She slept, deeply and without dreams.

Sometime later, she fought her way to the surface, a smile still on her lips. The building was quiet, the room swimming in the cool light of dawn. Gods, she felt crumpled. And sticky.

Apprehension jabbed her stomach. Gray! Where—?

The next thing she knew, she was in the sitting room, staring at the limp figure stretched full-length on the couch. The breath whistled out of her. *Thank the Lady.* Of the boy, there was no sign. He must be at the Enclave, gathering his things, such as they were.

His head resting on one arm, Gray looked younger, his hair mussed and his mouth relaxed, all that fierce intelligence soothed away. But there was a crease between the slanted brows, his eyes flickering beneath the lids. What was the substance of his dreams? She'd never know, because he'd never tell her.

Shad rose from the sofa and drifted across the room. Cenda leaned gratefully into his shoulder. As they stood together, watching Gray sleep, time slipped loose, running through her fingers. It had been so long since she'd felt any kind of peace that wasn't the numbness of despair. But now? These bittersweet moments were very, very good. Absently, she stroked Shad's knuckles with her fingertips, and his grip on her waist tightened.

No parent recovered from the death of a child—that was a given. She would never "get over it," but she didn't want to. Until the day she died, grief would be her close companion, woven through the fabric of her soul. But the fury, the slashing edges of the pain? Gingerly, she explored her memories. The little husk that had once been her darling, the ashes drifting away across the surface of Indigo Lake.

Sad, so sad. But steady. As whole as she would ever be.

A shadowy finger stroked her eyebrow and she looked up into Shad's featureless face. He pointed at the jug and basin set on the corner table.

Cenda's lips twitched. *All right, I can take a hint.*

Quietly, she disengaged herself and poured a basinful of water. In the bedroom, she ripped a threadbare pillowcase in half, with a wry smile for her own daring. Five-it, by the time her wickedness was discovered, she'd be offworld. Or dead.

She was standing naked in the basin, shivering, before it dawned on her to heat the water. Shaking her head at her own stupidity, she glanced up to see Shad lounging in the doorway, his dark gaze intent.

Her first instinct was to cover herself with her hands, her second to drop them. She squared her shoulders, turned to face the shadow. "You like?" she whispered.

A nod.

Slowly, Cenda passed her makeshift washcloth over her breasts. Her nipples had furled up into hard, aching crests. Shad didn't move.

"But you can't come in, can you? Not if Gray's out there."

Nod. *That's right.*

Cenda shifted her thighs. She was warm, throbbing. "You want to watch?"

Nod. Shad cocked his head to one side and she was almost certain he was smiling.

If she propped her foot on the bed and reached between her thighs, her flesh would be hot and slick. Gods, she could imagine it so vividly. When she inserted a finger into her sex, her internal muscles would grab at it. Hard. "I have a price."

The dark figure froze.

"Make him dream of me, of this. Can you do that?"

Nod.

"Yes, but will you?"

Shad turned sideways, staring into the other room, at Gray asleep on the couch, out of her line of sight. The shadow's dusky silhouette was perfectly framed in the doorway. One hand slid down his body to palm his genitals, cupping them firmly. His back arched with pleasure and his head turned, his gaze fixed on Cenda.

He didn't need to speak. *Keep going.*

Her heart thundering, Cenda shuffled around until her back was to the door. *Lady, help me.* Meticulously, she washed her neck and shoulders, twisting around to reach her lower back.

She'd never be voluptuous, but if she moved carefully enough, she should be able to keep the show more or less graceful. She stole a peek over her shoulder and smiled, a warm curl of triumph blending with the desire. Her audience of one was still cradling his cock. She had his absolute attention.

Cenda leaned forward, sliding the washcloth down over her knee, her calf, her ankle. Behind her, Shad moved sharply. From the other room, Gray muttered restlessly. Heat bubbled in her blood, evaporating the water from her skin faster than she could apply it.

Gods, she had to see! Abandoning the other leg, Cenda turned.

Oh, yes.

Shad was completely motionless, save for the hand caressing his shaft, sliding up and down with casual competence. His chest rose and fell with the hard breaths she couldn't hear.

Raising one hand above her head, Cenda stroked in a single long sweep, all the way down her arm from her wrist to her breast. Then she circled the cloth around and under, before dropping it with a wet splat. Five-it, she couldn't stand it! Panting, she rasped her thumbs over her nipples until they tingled, widening her stance as far as the basin would permit.

Gray moaned and the sofa creaked.

Cenda froze. "I don't want to wake him. Shall I stop?"

The dark head shook decisively. Shad jerked his chin at the bed.

Her eyes must be stretched so wide. Cenda swallowed. "You mean . . . ?"

A nod. *Yes.*

Her gaze flicked down to the intriguing shape of his erection, to the black weight and girth of it, clasped in his fist. "I . . . can't."

The words hadn't actually come out, but Shad seemed to have no difficulty lip-reading. He pointed sternly at the bed. But then he blew her a kiss. *Please?*

Her heart had migrated to a new home between her legs, the pulse of it shaking her whole body. Trembling and still damp, Cenda lay back against the pillows.

Shad gestured with his free hand. *Open.*

How hard could it be, after all the other things she'd done? Images tumbled through her head, each more lascivious than the last. Shad, restraining Gray so she could take him in her mouth; the cool length of a thick shadow cock, buried to the balls inside her; Gray's head thrown back in mingled pleasure and pain as Shad nipped his neck.

How dirty.

Gods, how *wonderful*!

As her knees fell open, Gray's groan bounced off the walls of the small apartment, but Cenda was gone, flying, the fingers of one hand strumming her wet flesh, the other tugging a nipple, so hard it was a sweet pain. She could smell the arousal slicking her thighs, hot and musky, the primitive odor of it ratcheting her desire up another excruciating notch. Panting, she watched Shad through her lashes. He was standing spraddle-legged, squeezing and tugging on his cock, his head thrown back. The tendons stood out clearly on the side of his neck.

All because of her. Yes, yes. Gods, yes! She knew a more sexually accomplished woman would drag it out, make it last, but she was too close, too desperate.

Cenda thrust a finger deep into her body, feeling the muscular walls clamp onto it. The sensation was so luscious, so welcome, it had her curling up off the bed, adding a second finger. Peripherally, she was aware of Gray's rattling breath, his hoarse gasps, but she had no attention to spare. Ruthlessly, she pressed with her thumb, right on her quivering clitoris, rasping the hot spot that was driving her mad.

When the orgasm finally rolled over her, the relief was so blessed she screamed aloud, but she was so short of breath, all that emerged was a strangled wheeze.

Gray groaned, one of those deep, guttural sounds only a man could make. That was followed by a thud so loud the walls of the apartment trembled. "*Aargh!* Shit!"

Cenda opened her eyes.

32

Shad had sagged against the door frame, his belly still heaving with the final spasms. A pause for an impenetrable stare, and he dipped his knees, reaching out a long arm to snag the abandoned washcloth. Then he straightened, bowed extravagantly from the waist, and sauntered out of view.

"What the fuck—?" said Gray crossly. A grunt, as if he'd levered himself off the floor. "Here, give me that."

Cenda had to bite her lip to hold back the chuckle. She strained her ears. The water jug clinked, and Gray swore under his breath. Boots hit the floor; clothing rustled. She clapped her hand over her mouth. *Oh, Shad, you're wicked.* The approaching pad of bare feet had her diving under the threadbare cover and burying her face in the pillow.

"Cenda?" Gray's quiet voice. A hand ghosted over her bare shoulder. "You awake?"

"Wha—?" she mumbled, keeping her eyes shut tight, praying the blush wasn't visible.

As Gray drew the cover up to her neck, cooler fingers

stroked her cheek, tugged her earlobe. Cenda took her lower lip firmly between her teeth. The silence seemed to last for a long time, and she had the sense of a tense conversation going on over her head. Finally, Gray padded away, which meant Shad had gone, too. With a long sigh, she relaxed, burrowing farther into the pillow. Sleep washed over her.

"The dossiers?" said the Technomage Primus, settling into the comfortable seat in her customized flitter.

Damage control. She'd always been good at it, at keeping her nerve. The right lever, a steady, ruthless hand to apply it, and all would be well.

Sharanita handed the documents over without a word, her brow furrowed.

"Did the spaceports acknowledge?"

"Yah, Primus. An' I sent t' pictures."

"Good. And the search?"

"Started. But Primus . . ."

"Mmm. What?"

"This come." Nita proffered a sheet of transplas. Her hand trembled. "Frum t' Secundus. He's callin' a Conclave of t' Ten."

"Is he indeed?" The Primus pressed her lips together. "Then it's just as well we compiled the dossiers, isn't it? No one has a blameless past, Nita." She smiled grimly. "Especially a member of the Ten."

Science, she couldn't afford to have her Prime Assistant go to pieces. She *depended* on Nita. Well, for the moment.

The Primus patted a big-knuckled hand. "Relax, dear," she murmured. "The fire witch problem is just a matter of time. You can trust me to put things right with the Ten. You know that, don't you?"

"Yah, Primus." The worried look lifted a little.

"Good. Leave me now." The Primus allowed herself to gaze out the window at a sleeping Sybaris. Dawn kept pace with the flitter, the tide of light racing them back to the Sector. Her responsibility, this world, and no one would take it from her. Resolutely, she opened a folder at random. Ah, the Quartus. Scanning the sheets, her lips curved.

At the end of an hour, she had the beginnings of a plan and a massive headache. Just tension, that's all. Not at all dissatisfied, she leaned back and composed herself for a well-earned catnap.

The flitter hummed.

Someone gave the back of her hand a vicious pinch. "Ow!" Her eyes flew open.

Seated opposite was a tall figure in a dark cloak, the hood so deep she could see no details whatsoever, not even the shape of a nose.

The Primus shot upright. "Guards!" she barked. "To me!"

"Useless." The sexless, whispery voice had an odd distortion, as if it came from underground, or somewhere far away. "Observe." One side of the cloak lifted in a floating gesture.

The Primus shut her sagging jaw with a snap. She was no longer on the flitter. How—? She and her sinister companion sat in the familiar seats in an island of diffused light. Beyond, she thought she could discern the hulking shape of an ornate wardrobe, a swagged and brocaded curtain.

"You are dreaming."

"Nonsense." It must be a trick. Science, it had to be! The Primus rose, but before she could take a step, an empty sleeve brushed over her knee. Pain flashed up to her groin, as if merciless fingers had seized a major nerve and tweaked it. The leg collapsed beneath her. With a strangled grunt, she fell back into the seat.

"You made inquiries about me. I am the Necromancer."

Her head spun. Slowly, she sank her fingers into the seat rest and hung on. Real. Solid.

"You were careless, Primus, losing the fire witch."

"I'll get her back."

"Perhaps." A sinuous shrug. "Perhaps not. In any case, your position is under threat."

Her mouth went dry. "I have taken precautions."

"Admirable. But not sufficient, I fear. The Secundus has secured the support of the Tertius."

"What?" The Tertius was wasted by an incurable muscle disease, confined to a motorized chair. He devoted his brilliant mind and his frail reserves of strength to an abstruse field of space research. Because he publicly abhorred Technomage politics, the Primus had left him out of her reckoning entirely. The Tertius was sacrosanct. There wasn't a Technomage on Sybaris who didn't accord the old man awed respect.

Science, his opposition spelled disaster!

"Don't be ridiculous," she snapped. "You know nothing about it. If this is a dream, then I'm waking up. Right now."

"Not so fast, my dear." A hidden hand rose threateningly.

The Primus subsided, her leg aching, the pulse in her ears pounding like surf. "Science save me," she gasped. "What *are* you?"

"It's not like you to be so slow, Primus. You know what Necromancy is, surely?"

"Death Magick." She was too rattled to pick her words. "Filthy. Evil."

"Powerful." The cowled shape leaned forward.

"Superstition. Preying on the ignorant."

The toneless voice could have been amused. "I perceive a demonstration is required."

The Primus recoiled, huddling back into her seat. "What do you want with me?"

"Cooperation. An alliance, if all goes well."

"Then show yourself."

"The skepticism of the Scientific mind. How delightful." Now the Necromancer was definitely amused. "I am bored, my dear Primus, and I find Science . . . ah, how shall I put this? . . . somewhat intriguing. I am ever curious, and I have thought for some time that Technomage skills and abilities would be a useful . . . adjunct . . . to my activities. The Dark Arts in harness with Science. So to speak."

"Do not patronize me." A pause for a steadying breath. "I am the Technomage Primus of Sybaris."

"Not for much longer, I imagine." The dark shape drifted toward the ceiling, expanding. "I will take a life you value. A demonstration and a price." The voice dropped to a hiss. "And a punishment. I do not care to be insulted."

The cloak became a black cloud, obscuring her vision, making her blink.

"Uh, Primus?" A gentle touch on her shoulder. Nita's face hovered above her. "Wake up. We're landin'."

Five-it, how did he stop himself from scratching? Surreptitiously, Cenda stole a glance at Gray, the heels of his tall leather boots clicking on the polished plasfloor as they strolled through the concourse of West spaceport. They both wore the white, powdered wigs of minor nobility from Green IV, but while Gray's only enhanced his severe good looks, Cenda's itched as though it were infested with bitemes. She longed to scour her scalp clean with a rill of flame, but she dared not risk turning her head into a bonfire.

Gray looked down and patted the hand resting on his black velvet sleeve. "Glad to be going home, my love?" he asked with absentminded affection, using the clipped Greenish accent, but his gaze was bright with tension. He'd darkened the color of his eyes with drops until they were as black as Florien's. In fact, he looked like his own brother, the shape of his nose and jaw subtly different, a thin mustache giving him a dapper air.

"Yes, dearest," said Cenda dutifully, forcing a smile. She ruffled Florien's hair. "You, too, beloved?"

Looking grossly uncomfortable, the boy nodded, his mouth clamped shut. Gray had drilled it into him. No speaking, not even if his life depended on it. Privileged little boys from Green IV didn't talk like Sybarite guttersnipes.

The impact of the novarine ring had been amazing.

Thoby had arrived not long after she'd finally woken, loaded down with mysterious bundles and cases. Gray had specified an identity that allowed Cenda to cover the distinctive red streaks in her hair; hence the Greenish costume. The boning in the gown cinched her waist and thrust her breasts up under her chin, enforcing a rigid posture. She didn't think she'd ever felt so *tall.* The emerald green brocade looked expensive on first glance, but the cuffs were shabby, the seams worn. Even the rings she wore on her fingers were glass.

A perfect little family, Florien a smaller copy of his "father." Except for the over-the-knee boots. Those boots had the strangest effect. Every time Cenda looked at them, at the way they emphasized the power of Gray's muscular thighs in the cream breeches, her thoughts stumbled and hitched.

They passed another two Technomages leaning against the wall, four-digit men. Cenda concentrated on breathing, trying to think like a Greenish noblewoman. She was a diplomat's wife. She and her dearest husband traveled frequently.

Lady save her, Scientists were everywhere, checking papers, directing people into queues. Her hand clenched on Gray's arm and he murmured, "Steady."

Calmly, he attached them to the end of the shortest queue. As they shuffled toward the checkpoint, the banging of Cenda's heart became so loud in her ears that when the Concordian man in front of them turned to speak with Gray, she half expected him to inquire about the noise. But no, he only wanted to complain about the delay. Did the Greenish Scion know what the problem was?

"Escaping criminals." A plump, middle-aged Technomage looked up from scrutinizing the Concordian's papers. Number 692. He made a mark with his stylus and passed them back. "Guilty of murder and sabotage. A male and a female."

Cenda knew she went pale. Gray's grip tightened. "Indeed." He raised an aristocratic brow. "Then I trust you will apprehend them swiftly."

Technomage 692 smiled politely. "Your papers, Scion? And I need to check the tickets."

The tickets were genuine; the papers were not. Florien's hand clutched a fold of Cenda's skirt.

The man's face softened. "Going back to school, son?"

The boy froze.

"Shy," blurted Cenda. She moderated her tone, trying to imitate Gray's cut-glass consonants. "He's very shy."

The Technomage shook his head, grinning. "Looks bold enough to me."

"You have no idea," said Gray with faint hauteur. "Have you finished?"

"What? Oh, yes." Technomage 692 handed back the papers, marked the tickets, and waved them through. "Good trip to you."

Relief turned Cenda's knees to water.

"Almost there, my love," said Gray solicitously, his grip the only thing keeping her upright.

Ahead was a young woman with some sort of wand with a broad tip. A wire led from it to a black box clipped to her belt. Technomage 977.

Recklessly, Cenda smiled. Over the woman's shoulder, she could see the passage leading to the boarding dock.

Something beeped loudly. Technomage 977 said, "I'll have to ask you to come with me."

Cenda's stomach disappeared, leaving a cold, queasy space behind. "What?" she stammered. "Why?"

Gray's arm circled her waist, warm and comforting. "What is the meaning of this?" he said icily. "I have diplomatic immunity."

"I'm sorry, Scion." The woman didn't look sorry. Her thin, dark face was alight with purpose. "It is forbidden to take Scientific devices offworld."

The mist cleared. Everything went still and quiet as if time itself had slowed. Cenda slipped a hand into her pocket and gripped the gray cube, the *hollow*. A voice that must be hers said cheerfully, "Oh, no, my dear. I'm sure you're mistaken. Try again."

"I insist," said Gray, his tone colder than frozen granite. He dropped a hand to the hilt of the short sword at his waist.

Cenda withdrew her clenched fist and spread out her arms. Frowning, Technomage 977 ran the wand over her three times, recalibrating the box each time. Eventually, she stood back. "You're free to go," she said grudgingly. "It must have been a false reading."

"Of course." Cenda seized Florien's icy little paw, smiling brilliantly. "Thank you." She swept down the passage, skirts swishing.

She waited until they were seated in a dark corner of the passenger lounge of the *CF8919* before she dusted the ash from her fingers.

"Any sign?"

Sharanita paused the scrolling display on her deskvid. "Nah, Primus." She glanced at the half dozen Technomages similarly employed in the adjoining office. "Don' worry, dear," she said soothingly. "We'll find 'em."

The Primus gritted her teeth. The Conclave had been entered in her calendar, first thing tomorrow. The rest of the Ten had already signified their attendance, even the Tertius. "Make it soon."

Nita peered at her screen. She rewound and replayed. "Primus . . ."

The Primus leaned over her shoulder. "Enhance," she snapped, her heart thundering. "Where was this?"

"West spaceport. Log just come in. False reading for contraband."

The woman's features sharpened, leaping toward them.

"*Yes!*" hissed the Primus. Nita flinched under the fierce grip of the fingers on her shoulder. "We've got them! Who's supervisor there? Never mind. Just comm the office."

The Prime Assistant rose slowly, towering over her employer. She pressed a hand to her flowered smock. "Sorry, Primus. I feel . . . funny."

"All right, I'll do it. Get out of the way."

But when the Primus shouldered her aside, Sharanita staggered, dropping to her knees. "Gods, can't . . . breathe." She clawed at her throat, her face a strange shade of bluish gray. The long body jerked. "Pri—" Her eyes bulged, fixed on the Primus, then they rolled up until only the whites were visible. When she sprawled across the floor as if her bones had liquefied, the Primus had to skip out of the way.

Nita's head thrashed back and forth. A final, choking rattle accompanied by a violent convulsion, and she went still.

Shit! Who'd have thought it? Nita had passed all the physicals with flying colors. She was as strong as a dray dog; slum survivors generally were. Grimly, the Primus knelt to feel for a pulse. Dammit, nothing. She glanced up at the circle of horrified faces and stood, brushing the knees of her trews. "Get her out of here," she barked. "You!" She beckoned a Technomage at random. A young man with thick spectacles. "Attend me."

She wrinkled her nose. In her extremis, Nita had soiled herself. "Move it!"

They moved it.

"Excuse me, Primus."

Now what?

The Technomage at the door stood aside to allow the others to remove Nita's body. She held out a shallow box. "This arrived for you, marked PERSONAL. We've screened it. It's safe to open."

"Oh, for Science's sake, not—"

Suddenly, she couldn't breathe.

"I've got West spaceport on the comm," said her new assistant.

But the Primus was ripping the box open, her fingers shaking.

A feather? She frowned. A single feather, dusty black.

Gingerly, she reached into the box and picked it up, revealing a knot of small, brown bitemes clustered in the bottom of the box. Another stream of them skittered out of the feather and across her fingers, nipping as they went.

"Aargh!" The Primus dropped the feather and brushed them away, shuddering. Red welts rose on her flesh and bile bubbled in her throat. She gulped, fighting for control.

A demonstration and a price, murmured a toneless voice. *And a punishment.*

"The subject embarked on the *CF8919*," said the bespectacled Technomage. "Hours ago. Heading for Green IV."

The Primus leaned against the wall, panting. Gone, gone, gone, out of her grasp, the slingshot sails deployed, the starship running before the space winds, down a Discontinuity Tunnel and away. Shit and Science! Her brain scrambled to catch up. She hadn't exactly endeared herself to the Technomage Primus of Green IV, but perhaps a judicious bribe, even a part-share in the fire witch . . .

She pointed to the feather. "Take that to the lab and test it. For everything, you hear me?"

"Yes, Primus." Her new assistant crouched to scoop it up with a sheet of transplas.

"I'll be in the Tower of Residence." Packing. "Keep me updated."

33

The floor beneath Gray's feet shuddered as the Technomage engineers engaged the sail winch. He glanced at the vid in their modest suite. Transit 55A spun beneath them, a [illegible] [illegible] spindle of shiny metal rotating to create its own gravity. A deep female voice crackled out of the grille under the screen. "Attention, passengers. This is Technomage Captain Number 212. *CF8919* will be docking briefly with Transit 55A to refuel and reprovision for your comfort. This is not a disembarking point. Only crew will leave the ship. We depart for Green IV in approximately two hours."

"Ready?"

Florien grinned. "Yah." He patted his nondescript shirt and trews. "Hated that fookin' suit."

"Well, you get to leave it behind." Their bags sat on the floor, fully packed. "Along with everything else." Except the Duchess, of course. "Cenda?"

The fire witch turned and smiled. "I'm fine."

Liar, mumured Shad.

She'd spoken barely a dozen words in the two days they'd

been aboard the starship. They'd retreated to the suite straight after launch. Cenda had spent most of her time with the boy, watching the stars blur in the vid screen as they skimmed through the Discontinuity Tunnels. She'd slept fully dressed next to Gray on the big bed, not touching, while Florien took the foldout bunk on the wall.

In fact, she'd spoken to him directly only once. He'd been hunched over the Duchess, picking out desultory chords because it helped him to think. And the Judger knew he had so much to think about, his head was about to explode. Cenda had touched his arm and said simply, "I'm glad you found it."

And he'd known then, what he'd only guessed. It had been the Technomage cube she'd had in her pocket at the spaceport. He couldn't be sorry it was gone, the evil thing, but his heart ached for her. Judger be praised, he'd never know a grief like it.

But Mother had. And Father.

Carefully, he inhaled, steadying himself. When all this was over, perhaps he could go home. Little Gracie would be a grown woman now, with children of her own.

Because of us, murmured Shad.

Yes. His eyes stung. *I'd like to see them.*

Now the fire witch wore the familiar, practical tunic and leggings, her cloak slung over one shoulder.

Shit, look at her hair, said Shad. *I could cry.*

Gray sighed his agreement. They'd loved her in the Greenish costume. The line of the gown had brought out a queenly grace, the wig defining the clear-cut features and emphasizing the glory of golden eyes under strongly marked brows. But when she'd removed it, running her fingers through her butchered curls . . .

Catching his expression, she'd shrugged. "It was easier."

And she was undoubtedly right. Now she looked like an adolescent boy, slim and long-limbed and completely beguiling. But the vulnerable nape of her neck was what undid him. Gods, he'd had such dreams of her—standing nude, cloaked in her hair, then pleasuring herself with ruthless abandon, her thighs splayed, fingers plunging deep into the folds of her sex, vividly pink and glistening with—

It'll grow. Shad sounded as though something had amused him.

Gray hauled in a breath. *Yeah.* He released it. *And we'll be there to brush it for her, I swear.*

He suspected he might be more than a little mad at the moment, acutely conscious of Shad's every move. He'd been avoiding his shadow's touch with scrupulous care. Gods, he tried not to speak with him or think about him at all, but he kept forgetting, the habits of a lifetime so deeply ingrained they were second nature.

Shit, he was doing it *again*!

"What are we waiting for?" he snapped. "Let's go."

Jumping ship wasn't particularly difficult, not when he'd followed Thoby's recommendation as to the right palm to grease. Smugglers were everywhere, after all, and the mention of Thoby's name, together with the code word he'd supplied, brought a raised brow and grudging acceptance. The bag of creds helped. Taciturn and snaggletoothed, the man led them into the bowels of the ship by a circuitous route that involved a great many ladders, and therefore numerous opportunities for the bastard to leer up at Cenda's perfect ass. In the hold, the man boosted the fire witch up onto a wheeled platform between two huge crates, leaving Gray and Florien to follow as best they could.

When he turned away and immediately tripped over a shadow, Gray grinned. *Well-done.*

Shad rumbled his disgust. *Why didn't she scorch his filthy fingers?*

Ten minutes later, they were striding through the crowds in the docking bay of Transit 55A. Gray clamped a hand around Cenda's arm and drew her close. "Grab my belt," he ordered the boy. Like all Transit stations, 55A was grimy and rough, purely industrial, a frontier town inhabited almost entirely by men. And whores of both sexes.

Slab-sided, prefabricated buildings stretched away in a

narrow strip that curved up and back in a decidedly unnerving manner. Both his companions looked a little queasy. Gray dropped a steadying hand to Florien's shoulder and tightened his grip on the fire witch. Transit 55A hadn't changed much in the decade since he'd last passed through. Even The Spacer's Spot, the bar where Thoby had contacts, looked as dingy as ever. By way of introduction, a three-man brawl tumbled out the swinging doors and landed almost at their feet, all flying elbows and thrashing boots. The boy swore and jumped neatly aside, but Cenda clung to Gray's arm, trembling. "Hey," he said, "don't forget, you could toast their asses."

Her startled look made him smile, but his good humor evaporated very shortly thereafter. "What do you mean, it's not enough?" he demanded.

The fat man looked like he'd been born on a heavy gravity planet and allowed himself to run to seed on the transit station. His flesh jiggled when he shrugged, but his small eyes were shrewd in their pouches of fat. The local equivalent of the Fixer. "Price's gone up," he said blandly.

All they had were the clothes they stood up in and the last of the creds Thoby had provided. Shit! It wouldn't take long for the Technomage Primus to discover where they were. But a starship left Transit 55A every few minutes. Once on board the first flight to Concordia, they'd be safe enough.

"Ye could make up t' difference." With a sausagelike finger, the fat man drew a pattern in the spilled beer on the table top.

Gray clenched his fists. "How?"

"There's always a market fer new meat here. Give me t' use of t' woman for a night. Or t' boy."

Beside him, Cenda choked. A small hand clutched Gray's knee, bruisingly hard.

When Shad growled, a red mist descended in front of Gray's eyes. It took him precious seconds to realize he'd risen to lean over the table, a blade naked in his fist.

The fat man didn't move. Neither of his hands was visible. "Or you, mebbe," he said. "Ye be a likely lad."

The table burst into flame.

The fat man pushed his chair back so swiftly, he toppled over and the lasegun clattered to the floor. Cursing, he lurched up on one knee, pillows of flesh wobbling. "Wha—?"

"Who knows?" Gray shrugged. He didn't dare look at Cenda. "The place is a fire trap." He gritted his teeth. "Show me a pawnbroker."

"Third on t' left." The fat man gestured at the door as the bartender threw a bucket of dirty water in the general direction of the smoldering table.

Cenda seethed beside him all the way to the *KT5177.* The *KayTee* was more a tramp ship than anything else, down at heel and decidedly shabby. Their accommodations were far from luxurious, consisting of two single cabins on a lower deck, but then they were no longer playing happy Greenish families, were they?

"Out," she snapped at Florien and then bit her lip, obviously regretting being so brusque.

The lad glanced from one set face to the other. "Can I go to t' galley?"

"The galley?" Cenda frowned. "Are you hungry again? Already?"

"Well, yah." Florien grinned. "But they'm playin' cards. I seen 'em."

"All right." Sternly, she held the boy's eye. "But not for money, understand?"

"Yah, sure." Florien gave her a wide-eyed look and disappeared, his light footsteps pattering down the passage.

The moment he was gone, Cenda shut the door and leaned against it, her eyes burning gold with agitation.

Signs of life at last. And he thought he knew why. Or he hoped he did.

It was Shad who'd pointed it out. *Using her powers is good for her,* he'd said, striding along at Gray's heels in the artificial light of the spindle.

I know. The Technomage crewman at the *KayTee*'s boarding gate didn't bother with more than a cursory glance at their tickets and travel documents.

She saves the real firepower for you, though.

Me? Gray halted so abruptly in the narrow passage of Deck G that Cenda's nose collided with his spine. She huffed with irritation.

Shad's tone grew creamy with satisfaction. *Anytime you're threatened. Whoosh!*

Gray's heart leaped, thinking of the table in The Spacer's Spot, the Fixer's men in the old ballroom. *Gods, you're right.* A chance, they had a chance!

And she purely loves to fuck us. Ghostly fingers had trailed up the inside of his thigh and his cock reared like a happy puppy. *Remember?*

Stop that!

Shad chuckled, the sound so wickedly infectious, Gray's lips had twitched despite himself.

Now Cenda tossed her cloak onto the bed. "How could you do it?"

"Do what?"

"Pawn the Duchess."

Gray raised a sardonic brow. "You preferred the alternative?" He winced every time he thought of his beautiful Duchess in that tawdry shop, but the sacrifice was worth it. No question.

"Of course not! But we could have done something!"

Gray folded his arms, relishing the sparks. Gods, he'd missed this part of her! Standing beside him, Shad followed suit. "Like what?"

"I don't know!" She flapped a hand. "I should have burned the place to the ground!"

"A great help."

"But that harp's your life!"

"Not anymore." He let the silence run on and on, growing

in significance, until her flush rose and faded away. Then he shrugged. “I’ll get it back.” And he would, too. He’d threatened to dismember the pawnbroker if she sold it.

Go on. Ask, urged Shad.

“What about you, little witch?” He reached out to touch her hand.

Cenda stared, the pulse fluttering in her smooth throat. “What do you mean?” He couldn’t decide if the cap of soft curls made her look older or younger, but he was getting used to it.

Shad sauntered over, all dusky grace, and bent to nuzzle her cheek with his nose.

Gray said, “You gave up something precious, too, didn’t you? I’d say we’re even.”

She tried to speak but failed. In the end, she buried her fingers in the silk of Shad’s hair and produced a shaky nod.

“Ah, sweetheart.” He couldn’t bear it, that lost look. Gray stepped forward and took her in his arms. He pressed his cheek against her hair. “I’m so sorry. If I could fix it, I would.”

A trembling hand clutched his waist. “The Primus offered. I said no.”

“She’d what?” Gray pulled back. “You refused? But I thought— Your baby . . .”

“It was wrong.” She shuddered. “Abomination.”

There you go, said Shad with a trace of the old bitterness. *Just like me.*

No, nothing like you at all. Now be quiet and let me concentrate.

Cenda hesitated, the golden gaze studying his face, feature by feature.

The floor beneath their feet began to tremble and a high-pitched klaxon sounded.

“Shit, that’s liftoff. Come on, over here.” Scooping the fire witch off her feet, he lay down on the narrow bed, pressed her slim length against him, and fastened the safety webbing over them both.

"Florien," protested Cenda, wriggling.

"The crew won't allow a passenger to come to harm. Don't worry. They'll strap him in. Sshh, now."

He'd always enjoyed the rush, the acceleration pressing into his spine, a pale reflection of sex. By the time the winches rumbled, deploying slingshot sails in mile-wide clouds of gossamer silver, he was hard. And judging by the delicate shade of pink on Cenda's cheekbones, she'd noticed.

Purpose settled inside him. Losing her again wasn't acceptable. He couldn't conceive of it.

The only one . . . Shad's shaky whisper.

Gray unbuckled the webbed harness and settled the fire witch more comfortably against his shoulder. Whatever it took. Even the truth.

"You're bubbling with questions. Ask."

Cenda propped herself up on one elbow, her face troubled. "But will you tell me?"

He compromised. "If I can. I don't . . . I'm not used to sharing."

"All right." She inhaled. "Why did you come back for me? Do you have another buyer?"

Judger! He blinked and his erection shrank to a nub.

Don't fuck up, warned Shad, but his strong fingers wrapped around Gray's wrist, holding firmly, anchoring him.

"Gray?"

"I owe you a debt of honor," he said, sparing himself nothing. "I accepted a commission from the Technomage Primus, just as she said. And I reneged on it, just as she said. I did mean to seduce you, at least at the start, and I did intend to hand you over, but not to the Fixer."

"Oh." She thought it over, fiddling with the top button of his shirt. "For money?"

"As a means to an end." His guts clenched. "For the Magick to rid myself of Shad. You were the price."

"You hate him that much?"

Shad lowered his head and nipped the side of Gray's

neck, hard enough to break the skin. Gray hissed and batted him away. "I did. I did hate him."

"And now?"

And now?

They said it together, his shadow and his fire witch, with exactly the same inflection. The only living creatures he cared anything about.

Gray's mouth worked while thoughts scrabbled around in his head like scuttleroaches in a panic. "Uh . . . I don't know." The strength of Shad's grip was crushing the bones in his wrist. "I'm confused."

The corners of Cenda's mouth tipped up. "Confusion's progress, I suppose." She leaned down and licked the spot Shad had bitten, a warm, gentle swipe of the tongue.

Immediately, his cock stiffened again, while his guts churned. An unsettling combination.

"Why did you change your mind about me?" she asked.

Gray wet his lips. Gods, this was difficult.

Go on, you can do this. Just say what you have to say so we can keep her.

He turned his hand under Shad's until they were palm to palm, their fingers interlaced. "Because you're you."

Idiot. Not good enough.

Cenda had folded her lips together, and he hurried on. "You saw Shad, really *saw* him. And me. No one's ever"—he shook his head, fumbling for words—"touched us both like that, accepted . . ." He smiled painfully. "And with so little fuss."

The golden gaze flew to his, skittered over to Shad and then back again.

Shad raised his head so that his lips were pressed against Cenda's cheek. *You're the only one,* he said, very slowly and clearly. *The only one for us.*

"Oh!" She quivered, her eyes going wide.

"The only one, Cenda," said Gray, the words pulled out of him. "I don't think we can live without you."

All the color drained from her face and she swayed.

Gray's heart stuttered and stopped. "Cenda, are you all

right?" In a panic, he rolled her beneath him, peppering her face with anxious kisses.

Her eyes were enormous golden pools gazing up at him. Her lips formed a single word: "Why?"

Gray stared back. "Why what?"

"Why can't you—?" Her voice trailed away.

Because we love her, you fool! roared Shad, knocking him out of the way to peer into her face.

"Because I love you," Gray said. "Ow, shit! And so does he," he added when Shad elbowed him in the ribs.

"It's not"—they watched in fascination as a small pink tongue crept out to lick her lips—"because of the fire Magick?"

"No. How does this undo?" Gray fiddled with the tabs of her tunic, feeling light-headed with relief and lust and joy. That hadn't been so bad. He'd got through it. "Though I admit, I love knowing we're the only man you'll ever fuck. Gods, that sounds weird." His blood pumping, he grinned. "But good."

She hasn't said it back, said Shad suddenly.

Shit. Gray froze.

34

Gray's eyes were as clear as the cool, sweet water of a mountain stream. For a moment there, she'd seen all the way to the depths of him. Great Lady, what a beautiful gift! But then, because he was only human, they'd darkened, as if clouds had moved over the water. Wonderingly, Cenda lifted a palm to her tingling cheek. *The only one,* Shad had said, his cool, soft lips breathing the words into her skin as Gray spoke them aloud.

And Great Lady, it was true, wasn't it? She, Cenda the Pure, who'd never been particularly good at anything, had been truly superb at one thing. At loving a sorcerer of shadows, at laying her foolish heart at his feet. To be honest, there'd never been a possibility it would be otherwise, not from the beginning.

Warmth unfurled in the pit of her belly, spread softly to the base of her spine. *Because I love you,* he'd said.

He meant it. All she had to do was glance at Shad, stroke his smoky shoulder, touch his hand, to know they meant it. She'd thought Gray beautiful from that first glimpse across the footlights in The Treasure, but it was Shad who was his true beauty, the keeper of his soul, the custodian of the open, loving heart of the boy within. He was so sweet, Shad, so rough and funny and lusty and direct. Gray without the civilized veneer.

For the first time, it occurred to her she'd seen a soul made manifest. Real and raw. How many people could say they'd seen that? Let alone made love to it?

The warmth swept up over her torso in a mind-sizzling wave. She didn't need to look down to know her breasts would be flushed, her neck and her cheeks burning. But with Shad's lean, smoky muscularity pressed against her, it didn't matter if she self-combusted with desire; she couldn't hurt the man she loved, not physically. Her heart quivered. Then it soared.

Her sex clenched and moistened with the vividness of sensory memory, trickles of flame running through her fingers. Both of them using her body, Shad's cool, satiny length in her mouth while Gray pounded his heat into her from behind until she died of the pleasure. The only man she would ever fuck.

Shad being so brave, showing himself to strangers, to their enemies, walking gracefully across that horrible cave to take her hand because she'd asked it of him. And gods, the glance he'd sent Gray as he did it!

She looked from Gray's handsome face to the dark mirror beside it. Gray's slashing brows had drawn together with concern, every muscle rigid with tension. She should put him out of his misery. When she lifted shaking fingers and drew them along his jaw, he turned his head to press a heated kiss into her palm. "Cenda?" he said. "Sweetheart?"

The way they occupied space relative to each other fascinated her. Thinking back, their body language had always been both confrontational and intimate. The change was subtle, but definite. Cenda doubted Gray realized it, but he was no longer at war with his shadow. Something in his face, some pain or tension, had eased, so that she was conscious of it only because of its absence. He seemed steadier, more grounded. Whole.

Slowly, Cenda smiled. What would it take for them to truly make peace, to be one? She placed her fingers over Gray's and slipped the tabs on her tunic.

"Cenda?" he said hoarsely. "Godsdammit, tell me what you're thinking. I'm dying here."

Shad tugged a dark red curl in a reproving sort of way, but he helped her fold the tunic back, exposing the upper swell of her breasts.

"How long do we have?" she asked. "Before we reach Concordia?"

"Three days. Shit, woman, you're supposed to say it back!" His eyes were a little wild, gone that smoky color she loved.

"Let me up."

Gray gave a huff of impatience as they moved back to give her room. A dark arm slid around her shoulders, supporting her, while Gray stuffed a pillow behind her back.

Cenda reached out a hand to cradle each jaw, one warm, the other cool. Her smile was wry. "I never had a chance," she said. "Not from the first time you kissed me."

Gray leaned hard into her palm, his jaw clenched hard. "Say it! Give me the words!"

Her eyes filled with tears. "I love you. Both."

As one, they surged forward, but she held them back. "Wait. There's a price."

"Ah, shit!" Gray ran his hands through his hair. "What the hell do you mean, a price?"

"You say I'm the only one who can love you both, right?"

"Yes." Two heads nodded.

"Great Lady, I can't love two halves of a whole. It's not possible." They froze. "I can't . . . I *won't* do that unless you love each other."

The ensuing silence was very loud. Shad and Gray faced each other across her body. Tentatively, Shad placed a hand on Gray's shoulder and Gray's face got that *listening* look.

Except now, it wasn't so much angry as thoughtful. Finally, Gray blew out a breath and turned to gaze at her, his eyes as dark as his own shadow.

Cenda's heart wobbled in her chest. "What did he say?"

His grin was fierce. "We'll let you out morning and evening to check on Florien. I'll do midday. The rest of the time . . ."

"Yes?" A rill of flame scorched all the way around the hem of her tunic. Helpfully, Shad whipped it off over her head.

Gray's gaze locked on her breasts and her nipples stiffened. "We're going to fuck you every way we can."

"A very male solution." Cenda clutched Shad's hand while the blood beat heavy between her thighs. "How is this going to help?"

Gray rose and adjusted the glowglobe until Shad's outline was clearly defined, his silhouette dark and dense. Still without speaking, he kicked off his boots and stripped off the shirt and trews. He was mouthwateringly stiff, his cock fat and full, a delicate tracery of veins throbbing visibly beneath the pale, satiny skin, the heart-shaped head dense and smooth, shiny with excitement.

As his hand dropped to cradle it, he and Shad exchanged a predatory glance. "Because," said Gray, "we're going to do it *together*."

They lunged.

Soft, cool lips surrounded her left nipple, suckling with exquisite delicacy. Gray swooped on the other side, his mouth hot and hungry and urgent. The breath whooshed out of Cenda's lungs, and her head fell back as her hips rose.

She writhed, reaching out with flailing hands for some way of anchoring herself in a world made of soft, dark fire, high, whimpering cries spilling out of her mouth. But Shad snared one wrist and then the other, holding them together over her head in an unbreakable grip. Gray pulled back, licking around her areola with lingering relish. He blew a stream of warm air over the screamingly sensitive flesh and she yelped.

He chuckled, deep and wicked. "Together, Cenda. And there's nothing you can do, except"—he bent his head and sampled the soft skin just above her navel, nipping and licking, making the nerves flutter—"take it. Until you're so hot, you're on fire." His grin became demonic. "Literally." He tugged off her boots and peeled her leggings down, mouthing her knees, her calves, her ankles, his breath hot and moist.

Cenda's head swam, her sex softening, glowing, longing to be filled, arousal coiling behind her clit like a spring already wound beyond bearing. Great Lady, Shad's gentle domination, Gray's determination, they did something to the very core of her. She'd loved him; she knew now she'd always loved him, but she'd had the innate caution to withhold her complete trust. Now, using his own body and that of his shadow as the instruments of his will, Gray was demanding she offer it up and give herself entirely to them—no reservations, no ifs or buts.

Shad's mouth descended on hers, his tongue deft and dark, a tender plundering, kissing her just like Gray, and her mind spun away, bedazzled. Gray lay between her legs, laving the delicate juncture between hip and groin and thigh, fingers drifting gently over one stiff nipple.

Two of them, two of them at once.

Being fucked by two men, both utterly focused on your pleasure, that must be a fantasy common to many women, but *this*—! Gods, this was better!

Because it wasn't *two* men; it was one man and his shadow. Four hands, two mouths—*Ah!* Her neck went loose with pleasure and she spread her thighs—two cocks. But orchestrated by one mind, one soul. In complete accord. They worked so instinctively together, pressing, licking, stroking, every sensual assault perfectly coordinated to drive her insane.

As if they were one.

"Please," she moaned into Shad's mouth. She bucked her hips and Gray held her down.

"Please what, sweetheart?" Gray shifted down an excruciating inch. "This?" Draping Cenda's leg over his shoulder, he used his thumbs to part her sopping labia and ran his tongue luxuriously up through her vulva. "Mmm." Meticulously, he twirled his tongue around the throbbing knot of her clit. Shad coiled his tongue around hers, in a delicious echo.

It was more than she could process. Conscious thought departed. Gratefully, Cenda abandoned control and let herself burn, trusting Shad to keep Gray from harm, enjoying the cool rub of his twilight flesh against hers.

Shad kissed his way down her neck, licked over her collarbones. Grasping her other leg behind the knee, he pulled it back against her chest, exposing her to Gray's attentions in the most shameless way possible.

"Don't move your hands." Gray's hair brushed silky-soft across the inside of her thigh as he licked over her perineum. He slid a finger into her sex, rotated it gently.

Cenda pressed her palms against the wall behind her head, her whole body vibrating with the intensity of her pleasure.

Gray withdrew the finger, slipped it over the pucker of her anus, and massaged, very lightly. Cenda squeaked, but he ignored her, doing it again and again. Then he took her hips in both hands and lifted so he could lick her all around, swirling and jabbing with his tongue, loosening the tight ring of muscle. Gods, it felt wicked, so *naughty*!

Before she could speak or move, Shad swooped on her mouth for a wet, incendiary kiss, long fingers plucking at her nipples.

Cenda quivered, caught between sensations, thrumming like a harp string.

After an endless time, Gray sat up, wiping his mouth. "Ready?"

For what? Her brain reeled with possibilities. "No-o," she gasped.

Shad rose and pulled her into his arms, her breasts spreading against the hard-muscled planes of his chest. Sparks fizzed up and down her spine, filled her belly, her head.

Gray took her place against the pillow, his cock rearing out of a nest of glossy black curls, testicles drawn up tight and plump between his tense thighs. He smiled, wild and fierce, and held out his arms. With a glad little cry, Cenda straddled his hips, almost overbalancing in her eagerness. Shad gripped her waist and Gray chuckled. "Hold still, love. Let Shad— Ah . . ." Those absurd lashes dropped to half-mast, his lips falling open.

Oh, gods. Shad's hair brushed the curve of her ass. Something broad and hot and velvety furrowed between her folds, all the way up and all the way back. Cool knuckles stroked in its wake. A tingling pause, and the first inch of Gray's shaft nudged inside her, Shad's clever fingers urging it all the way, petting them both. Cenda panted, trying to control her breathing, wanting a slow, luxurious impalement she could remember forever.

"Ah, fuck!" Gray's hips punched up. Two thrusts, and he'd slid deep, buried to the balls inside her, wedged all the way to her womb. He bit his lip, growling low in his chest while Cenda sat with the scream strangling in her throat, feeling the throb of blood where they were joined, so heavy, beating like a temple gong.

Gray's eyes fluttered open, so dark they looked black. He cradled her breasts in his hands. "Suck him for me, little witch. I want to feel your mouth on his cock."

When she turned her head, Shad stood beside the bed, his dark shaft an intriguing jut at eye level. Cenda's nostrils flared as she leaned forward to take a lick.

"Judger!" Inside her, Gray rippled.

Gods, how amazing. How gorgeous.

Avidly, she opened her mouth as wide as she could and sucked Shad down, wrapping a fist around his base. His fingers gripped her hair and beneath her, Gray moaned, reaching up to roll her nipples between his fingers. Even with her eyes closed, she would have known which of them she suckled. Shad tasted unique, of spice and salt and smoke, the taste of the dark, the forbidden. Oh, it was good.

Under her hand, the shadow trembled, his buttocks

flexing with the need to thrust. Gray panted, "Get him good and wet. *Hurry*." He moved inside her, tiny, controlled movements, as if he didn't dare let himself go but couldn't keep entirely still.

Humming her delight, Cenda did as she was bid, setting up a rhythm that pleased her—a long, pulling suck, a lash of her tongue under the head, a squeeze of her sheath on Gray's stone-hard bulk. Again and again and again.

"Fuck, enough, enough!" Gray pulled her off his shadow. "Kiss me. Let me taste."

Shad's hands caressed her spine, encouraging her forward. As she went down, he dotted kisses all down her back, bending to take a slow, lavish bite of the fleshiest part of her buttock. His touch skated down the soft crease, feathered over her anus. A cool tongue followed, a wet, inquisitive finger pushed. After a brief initial reluctance, it sank in to the first knuckle.

Cenda gurgled into Gray's mouth. "What are you—?" Instinctively, she jerked backward and gasped as the unwary movement forced her farther back onto that diabolical finger. *"Aargh!"*

She twisted, trying to peer over her shoulder, but Shad pushed her head back around to face Gray's devilish grin. "Together, like we promised you," he said breathlessly. He tucked a curl behind her ear with a hand that shook. "Trust me? Us?"

"It'll hurt," she protested, her stomach doing flip-flops. Shad was kneeling behind her, his dark chest pressing against her back, his fingers digging into her hips.

"Sshh, love." Gray's smoky gaze melted with tenderness. "Not if Shad does it. He's a shadow, remember? Barely there until he wants to be. Come back down here."

In a daze, she leaned down for his beautiful mouth, which canted her bottom up for whatever Shad cared to do with it. The sensation began slowly, slipping past the tight sphincter, lengthening by the merest increments. Cenda quivered, the breath leaving her body in panicky gusts. Gray licked over her lower lip, from one corner to the other, murmuring encouragement. She'd never felt such a firestorm of lust in her life, but she couldn't decide if it was wonderful, weird, or just plain embarrassing. Or all those things.

"All right?" whispered Gray, and she nodded, swallowing. "He loves it. You're so tight and hot in there."

Shad thickened gently, cramming her full of dark cock, still wet from her mouth. One palm skated over her belly in cool, soothing sweeps, keeping the hungry flames at a simmer.

Gray's eyes had closed, sweat gleaming on his forehead, his throat. He groaned, as if he were dying. "Fuck, I can feel him." Excruciatingly slowly, he pulled out, two pairs of hands holding her down so she couldn't writhe, couldn't ease the pressure. "Against me . . . oh, shit . . . so hard." He speared back in, a little faster, his cry mingling with Cenda's.

"It's good?" she panted, all her pelvic muscles clenching in arousal and terror and delight.

His eyes flew open, unfocused and glassy. "Everything's doubled. I feel what he feels. Fuck, I'm—" He spasmed inside her, a swelling ripple. "Shad," he gasped.

Shad shifted behind her, reaching between them, to where the small mouth of her sex stretched to accommodate Gray's girth. The shadow's cool fingers flexed against her thighs. "Fuck!" Gray winced. Then he steadied, blowing out a breath. "Thanks," he gritted. "Do it."

Shad dipped his head until his lips were sealed to Cenda's shoulder, then he began to flex, gliding back, stroking forward. Over and over. It didn't hurt, but it felt . . . peculiar . . . burning . . . wicked. Gray reached up and hooked a hand behind Shad's neck, pulling him down over them both, the masculine weight of the shadow's chest sealed all along her spine, Gray's muscled belly hard against her softness, her breasts squashed against his chest. And then Gray was thrusting, too, in erotic counterpoint.

Was that her voice, that keening wail? She was so full, conquered and invaded, trapped between two hard male bodies, surrounded by masculine musk and muscle and sinew and bone. So utterly and hopelessly in love.

Cenda's senses slipped the leash, spiraling away in a blaze of Magick and passion and trust, all entwined, the bright and the dark plaited together. Fireflakes dancing, higher and higher and higher . . .

The orgasm rose, a wave of dark fire that cramped her loins, the tension ratcheting up to an agonizing level. An instant poised on the brink and she fell into the flames, screaming all the way, trusting Gray and Shad to catch her.

Their arms tightened brutally around her, but it didn't matter because she'd given up breathing, anyway. She thought she heard twin roars of completion, or perhaps Gray had shouted so loudly he'd set up an echo in the small room. Their cocks ground into her, shoved high and hard, throbbing with their simultaneous ecstasy.

Her vision still a little hazed, she opened her eyes to see Gray and Shad nose to nose over her shoulder, both mouths open, gulping in air. Gray blinked and his lips quirked. Wordlessly, he turned his head to kiss the corner of her mouth. "Oh, love." Shad mirrored the action. "You all right?"

Gasping, Cenda smiled and pressed her thighs together. They were still semihard inside her. "I thought I was going to die, but yes. You?"

Gray didn't answer, because Shad had gripped his chin in one hand and turned him back. The high sexual flush faded as Gray stared his own shadow in the eye. His throat moved as he swallowed. "Shad, I—I—"

Whatever he'd been going to say was lost as Shad shifted the last half inch and sealed their mouths together.

35

"The lab says there's nothing diseased or infectious about the feather, Primus." Her new assistant's voice came out of the comm unit slightly distorted.

Grimacing, the Primus scratched at the welts on her hand. Two cases sat open on her bed, the smaller for clothes and personal necessities, the other for her files and books. A lifetime's worth of original research. "And the bitemes?"

"Same. Just small bloodsuckers, but there's an irritant in the saliva."

"Origin?"

"Uh, I don't think . . . Wait a minute—it's here somewhere." Sheets of tranplas rustled.

The Primus clenched her jaw. Science, she missed Nita. She was only just now realizing how much.

"Here we are. Says, um, 'Bio-profile consistent with Palimpsestian corpsebird and parasites.' Picture coming through on the deskvid, Primus."

Ah, so the Necromancer was on Palimpsest.

The image on the deskvid firmed up to show a hulking,

ugly bird sitting hunched over a bloody carcass. The Primus huffed in disgust. The long, featherless neck was stained with dried blood, the big, curved beak well suited for tearing dead flesh. Something stringy dangled out the side of it.

She sneered. A carrion eater—an invitation and a warning in one. Melodramatic nonsense.

The Primus sat, her fingers flying, calling up information on Palimpsest. Her brows rose. A thriving monarchy and a large Enclave, but only a single Technomage Tower and spaceport. Interesting balance of power. Plenty of scope.

The Conclave had met without her and she'd sent no apology. Her lips twisted. If she escaped with her life, she'd be lucky to be demoted to a five-digit janitor. Insupportable humiliation. Switching off the vid, she snapped the cases closed and took a nondescript cloak from the wardrobe. She was cutting it fine; they'd be coming for her any minute.

Life was certainly full of challenges, some of them truly formidable. Like the Necromancer, for instance. Her lips curved. She wouldn't underestimate the task. She'd have to begin research, start a dossier. Magick tricks and sleight of hand might impress the credulous, but they were no match for a Scientific approach—and plain hard work.

The Technomage Primus allowed herself a single long sigh. She'd built one career; she could build another. A better one. She squared her shoulders and walked out of her apartment without looking back.

A deep, tuneless crooning filled Gray's head so that he couldn't think. Shad's mouth was uncompromising on his, his tongue strong and deft, much stronger than any woman's. But he wasn't demanding; he wasn't imposing. He was . . . giving. *Here,* he was saying, over and over. *I am always here. I love you. I will never leave you. Take me, please, please take me. Take me back. Make me yours again.*

The kiss was so tender, so sweet, it was almost chaste. Gray's eyes burned with tears. Everything inside him slowed, creaking to a halt, leaving only a breathing, echoing silence. Space that was empty and aching.

C'mon, we can do this. You *can do this. With her.*

Warm, feminine fingers moved in his hair, soothed over his scalp. Cenda. They were still buried deep in her body, their shafts pressed together, beautifully sated, too comfortable to move.

Let me in, love. Let me in.

Even though Gray knew his shadow had no real need for respiration, he felt as if gusts of the essential Shad were streaming into his lungs—no, it was more than that, the essential *them*—whatever it was that made them a single viable being, a true soul. Something in his addled brain shifted and realigned. Coalesced. All those years, rejected, spurned. But he'd never truly been able to do it, had he? Shad had slipped under his guard, time and again. His humor, his insight, that cool, knowing touch, his sheer guts. Such loyalty, such unconditional love. And it had taken a fire witch to show him—them—the truth of what they were.

Indivisible.

He still had one hand gripping Shad's nape and he hadn't even realized it. *Can't keep you out.* A long pause before he took the final step, trembling. *Oh, Shad . . .*

Even though he hadn't willed it, some instinctive part of him knew. All of a piece, the barriers gave way, dissolving like night shadows fleeing before dawn. Shad surged forward, shedding dusky tears, his mind-voice a deep, inarticulate cry of love and relief and joy. Abruptly, Gray was drowning in a smothering flood of comfort and concern.

He fought his way free, choking back a laugh. *Give over. You're worse than a bloody nanny.* Blinking hard, he hung on, hauling in huge, rough breaths in an effort to control the bone-deep shudders. But it wasn't any use. Shad knew, just as he always did.

His shadow huffed in mock disgust and ripped his mouth away to give Gray an evil glare. *See if I'll help you fuck her again.*

Gratefully, Gray accepted the lead back to normalcy.

Scrambling for some sort of balance, he arched a brow. *Oh yeah?*

Still smiling, he turned to see Cenda hanging over both of them, her wide eyes shimmering amber with tears. "Great Lady," she whispered. "You've done it, haven't you? Oh, Gray."

Grayson, Duke of Ombra, that elegant, self-contained adventurer, felt himself blush like a girl.

Shad chortled and Gray punched his shoulder.

Cenda giggled. Then she winced.

"Sorry, sweetheart. Shad, get off her." Gently, the shadow disengaged himself, dropping an apologetic kiss on her shoulder blade as he did so. And then Gray was able to take a few minutes in the tiny ablutions cubicle to clean up and recover his equilibrium. He still felt as though his knees might fold at any moment, so he made a production out of tending to his fire witch, making her comfortable with a cloth wrung out in warm water.

By the time he finished, her eyelids were drooping, so he tucked her in firmly. As he dressed, he watched her give up the battle to stay awake, smiling at the way she snuggled into the pillow with a sigh, the long, slender limbs unfolding and relaxing. "Won't be long," he said, stroking his knuckles over the satin of her cheek. "I'll check on the boy and bring back something to eat. Sleep tight, little witch."

But before he left, he allowed himself a final kiss, a real one, from warm, sleepy lips that murmured loving nonsense beneath his.

She was in much the same position when he returned, a loaded tray in his hands. Chuckling, Shad removed the lid from the steaming bowl of noodle broth and wafted it about under her nose. It twitched. "Mmm." Cenda stretched and Shad helped her to sit up, thoughtfully peeling the covers down to her waist as he did so.

Blushing, she made a futile grab. Gray *tsk*ed at her, feeling as giddy as a boy. "Very nice," he said, grinning. "Leave it. We like to look." Immediately, those pretty chocolat nipples drew tight and his mouth watered.

"Florien's all right?"

Gray handed her a fork, chuckling. "The boy's a natural. He's already a fixture in the ship's galley. When I left, he was introducing the cook's crew to the Sybarite version of the shell game. We'll have to take him in hand."

Cenda's eyes grew large. "The shell game? What's that?"

By the time he'd explained, demonstrating with the two wine cups and a napkin, every scrap of food was gone and Cenda's nipples were as hard as pebbles.

Takes a power of feeding, said Shad, surveying the empty dishes.

Gray leaned forward to cup a warm breast. *But oh, so worth it.*

Yeah.

A happy little tremor made Gray's balls buzz. *Do you think—?*

Oh, yeah.

This time, it was languorous, a gently torturous buildup through successive peaks and a final explosive release. Cenda luxuriated, every muscle humming with pleasure. Kissed and licked and sucked and fucked. Gray and Shad actually made her feel voluptuous, which was astonishing in itself. And thankfully, they'd left her aching bottom alone, Gray just patting it and saying cryptically, "Later."

And Lady, that alone was enough to make her wet! What had she become?

Happy, that's what. Such a banal word for such all-encompassing joy.

The last time she'd had this soaring feeling was when Krysanthe had handed her the red-faced, squalling bundle that was Elke. Ah, Elke . . . The familiar ache returned, but muted. When she'd closed her fist over the *hollow* in her pocket and burned it down to ash, she'd felt the heart rip out of her chest. But now?

The faces flicked past, one by one, seared into her memory. Would Elke have liked him? She rather thought so, though she wasn't sure Gray would know what to do with a toddler. It would have been such fun to watch him fumble and learn.

But it would never happen, not with Elke or any other child of her womb. Krys had made that very clear. Too hot for a man's seed to survive.

But the healer hadn't known about Shad, had she? The breath clogged in Cenda's throat. About the way his cool touch moderated her heat, making it possible for her to love Gray without harm. Gods. She gulped, squeezing her eyes shut.

Great Lady, she prayed, *I give this one to You; it's too much for me. Let it be as You will.*

Like a divine gift, she remembered Patterns forming, the glass chips falling in perfect order each time, every time. Her pulse steadied. *Whatever You will.*

She glanced down. Shad sprawled half off and half on the bed, his head pillowed on Cenda's thigh. He didn't appear to be uncomfortable.

"What did he do that was so bad?" she asked dreamily, drifting her fingers through the smattering of hair on Gray's chest, following the silky trail down to his navel. The muscles under the fine skin fluttered.

After a long silence, Gray cleared his throat. "You mean Shad?" The shadow turned his head, suddenly intent.

"You said I could ask questions."

"He— Shit, Cenda, I can't—" He dried up. Casually, Shad laid his hand on Gray's calf, but the skin under his fingers dimpled white with the pressure of his grip.

Cenda became painfully conscious of every individual beat of her heart. "You've never spoken of it? To anyone?"

"No."

Everyone mourned the death of a child. At least she'd had companions in her grief. Cenda stroked the hair off the shadow's forehead. "Shad, darling, I'd ask you, but you can't tell me, can you?"

Shad tilted his head back, gazing at her. Then he shot to his feet, urging Gray forward so he could settle behind him on the bed. With ruthless dispatch, he arranged the man in his arms, ignoring Gray's bemused protests. They finished up with Gray cradled securely against Shad's chest, the long, shapely legs spread to accommodate him. The shadow slid his arms around Gray's waist and turned his head to nuzzle his neck, holding on tight.

Five-it, that bad? Cenda's heart sank. Slowly, she leaned forward, until her head rested on Gray's chest, his heart pounding beneath her cheek. "Let's start with something easy. You're from Concordia, aren't you?"

"No." He rubbed his cheek against her hair and some of the tension left his body. He sighed. "Judger's Gift. Heard of it?"

"No, tell me."

Hesitant at first, Gray described his home world, Cenda prompting in soft murmurs when he stalled. In fits and starts, she heard about Hope and little Gracie and Mother and Father. The life of a child greatly loved—secure in the moral order of a good society. But when he got to the terrible day itself, his voice cracked and he dried up completely.

Patiently, Cenda waited him out, petting his chest, cuddling close.

The words emerged, a few at a time, with long, dreadful pauses between.

Cenda's heart cracked and broke. Poor little boy, poor darling. "So you stowed away?" she whispered. "Good for you. Did they make you work for your passage?"

His skin felt clammy, cold, his breath a harsh rasp in her ear. Cenda looked up in sudden alarm. His face could have been hewn from granite, only those beautiful eyes alive with pain. Shad had curled right into him, rocking, face buried in the curve between neck and shoulder.

"No," she said in dawning horror. "Please, no."

His lips barely moved. "Yes."

Hot, salty tears dripped off her chin, dampening Gray's chest. She buried her face there, unable to bear the expression on his face. Shad's body heaved with sobs she couldn't hear, shaking the bed.

Lady, Great Lady, give me Your strength. Let me be enough to love him, love them both.

Wiping her eyes, she sat up in time to see Gray raise Shad's chin with a gentle hand. When he stroked his shadow's cheek, his fingers came away dark with smoky tears.

Cenda wrapped her arms around both of them as best she could. "It's all right," she said foolishly, the way she used to comfort Elke. "I'm here now."

Pale and grim, Gray smiled with difficulty. "Yes, you are."

And then his head dropped to her shoulder and she held him as the tears welled, slow and hard.

There were beautiful creatures called *horses* in Nakarion City on Concordia. Fascinated, Cenda watched the tall, glossy rump bobbing in the shafts of the carriage, the hooves making a crisp noise on the wide, paved road. *Clip-clop.*

They'd been here three days and she still couldn't get over it. A city with green spaces in it for the gods' sake, parks and trees and fountains. Buildings of pinkish stone with carved balustrades. So *clean*, all of it. Great Lady, even the modest boardinghouse where they'd found the Unearthly Opera Company was scrupulously maintained.

It had given her such pleasure to hang back and watch their faces light up with relief and welcome. Grinning, big Erik had wrung Gray's hand 'til he winced. She was even inclined to forgive Sydarise the dancer the smacking kiss she'd planted on Gray's elegant mouth. Almost.

Besides, Syd had promised to keep an eye on Florien while she and Gray were out visiting. The boy didn't seem to mind the fluttery attention of the dancers. In fact, Cenda suspected he enjoyed it, as much as his innate wariness would permit. While the lad would never be prepossessing, his face had filled out so that he no longer reminded her of a half-starved stray. Five-it, he'd allowed Cenda to peck his cheek in farewell, though he screwed up his nose. Progress.

She tucked her hand into Gray's, smiling. The tiny salamander perched in her hair purred its content. Shad sat opposite, behaving himself beautifully, save for the sly, booted foot that rubbed against her calf from time to time. "So who is this Deiter?"

Gray stared at the back of the driver's head. "A Purist. Probably the most powerful wizard on Concordia. And in all the known worlds—at least, according to Deiter." His fingers gripped hers. "He insisted on seeing you, even though I told him—" He folded his lips together. "Don't worry. I won't leave you with him, I promise."

What an odd thing to say. Cenda frowned, puzzled. "Is he dangerous?"

Gray gave a grim laugh. "Oh, yes. Drunk or sober, it makes no difference."

Drunk? A wizard? "But—"

The carriage rattled to a stop and Gray jumped down to pay the driver.

Cenda gazed around. "This can't be the Enclave." In front of a prosperous-looking mansion, a sign swung in the cool breeze. On it was a horse wearing a quizzical expression, a wizard's hat tipped over one eye. THE RUNED MARE.

"No, it's an inn." Gray took her arm and led her up a neat graveled path to the wide front door. "It's Deiter's hobby as well as his home. He's taken over the whole top floor."

All she could think was that Pures must be very different on Concordia.

A brisk serving man showed them up the stairs and into a large sitting room, furnished with big squashy sofas and thick rugs. A banked blaze glowed a cheerful welcome from the fireplace, tucked under a mantel of that pink stone, deeply carved with swags of improbable blooms, Lady's lace among them. Beneath a large, round window, a table groaned under the weight of cakes, pastries, savory pies, glazed fruits. There seemed to be no end to it. A wisp of steam rose from a silver chocolat pot with a long spout. Next to it sat a fine crystal jug full of clear water, and a squat wine jug, still corked.

"All for you, fire witch," said a creaky voice. Deiter entered from a door at the far end of the room, another wine jug dangling from one finger.

Cenda blinked.

His embroidered robe trailed over the rugs in the approved stately manner, but there was a large, dark stain all down the front, and one sleeve looked as if an animal had chewed it. Purist Deiter didn't resemble the ascetic Matthaeus at all. He had jowls and pouchy eyes, a little bloodshot. Only his grizzled beard was groomed, divided neatly into three thin plaits and tied off with gold ribbon.

Cenda shut her sagging jaw. "Uh, thank you."

The old man snorted. "If you really are her, which I doubt."

Icily, Gray said, "She is." He slid an arm around her waist.

"Oho. So that's how it is." The old man gave a lascivious chuckle. "I always said you were a devious bastard." He stroked his beard, his eyes traveling over her body in a way that made her skin crawl. "Lucky, too."

Cenda thought she could hear Gray's teeth click together. Hastily, she said, "Gray said you wanted to see me."

"Aye. And here you are. Good for you, Grayson, my friend." The old wizard plunked the wine jug on the table. He had a drinker's paunch, soft and wobbly beneath the satin robe, though he wasn't a fat man. Casually, he reached out, grasped a handful of her buttock, and squeezed.

Cenda spun round, choking. A spark leaped from her finger and burned a hole in Deiter's robe, right over his heart. The old man jumped back, surprisingly nimble. Gray grabbed his shoulder with an oath.

But when he spoke, Deiter's voice was clear and placid, carrying easily over the angry roar of the towering blaze in the hearth. "Not bad, lass," he said. "Not bad at all." Calmly, he fished a grubby handkerchief from a pocket and wiped his forehead. "Do you mind? It's stifling in here."

36

Cenda gaped, but she waved a hand and the fire settled back into its bed of coals with an irritated crackle. "You did that on purpose," she said slowly. "Lady, you're not like any Purist I ever met."

"No, I'm not." Deiter chuckled. "Brings back memories, an ass like that. My compliments." He ignored Gray's snarl, his rheumy gaze very direct on her face. "And well-done on the control." He pulled a chair out from the table and bowed with an ironic flourish. Flicking a finger at the little fire lizard in her hair, he said, "Take a seat, fire witch, and tell me, how big can you get your salamanders?"

"He just played you like a fiddler's jig," growled Gray. "C'mon, Cenda, let's go."

"Then I can't help you," said Deiter.

"Help us? What do you mean?" said Cenda.

"I don't need your fucking help, old man," snapped Gray.

Deiter shot a thoughtful glance from Gray to his obedient shadow and back again. "Hmm. Perhaps you don't at that."

Cenda stared, her head spinning. Five-it, the wizard knew about Shad!

"I was going to wait until after we'd eaten, but if you're going to be difficult . . ." Deiter shrugged and extracted a long roll of parchment from somewhere beneath his robes. He anchored the edge with a cold deep-dish pie on one corner and a plate of chocolat confections on the other.

Then he paused, as if taking the time to gather his thoughts, but Cenda suspected he was far from calm. His ink-stained fingers trembled and his mouth was tight. "The rumors out of Sybaris have been extraordinary. Literally unbelievable, even for me, and I believe something incredible every day before I drink my breakfast. I'm not sure what I expected." He shook his head. "I still don't know . . ." Scooping up the wine jug, he tilted it to his lips and took a healthy gulp, his wrinkled throat working.

"What I'm about to show you can go no further. Even if it means nothing to you." He straightened, wiping his mouth with his sleeve, his gaze flat and hard as flint. Suddenly, he seemed much taller, broader, no longer an old man who drank too much. The air buzzed with power. "Especially if it means nothing. Know that I will make this so if I must." A chill slid down Cenda's spine and she shivered.

The gnarled fingers surprisingly deft, Deiter unrolled the parchment.

"Lady!" Cenda's chair toppled over as she leaped to her feet. "That's—that's—I saw it."

"Yes? Tell me, lass. What is it?"

Cenda wet her lips. "The Pentacle. But see"—she pointed to the elaborate drawing of a five-pointed star—"yours has one side missing, too."

Gray's hand touched her arm. "Where did you see such a thing, sweetheart?"

"In a dream." She stared helplessly at the old man's intent face. "The Lady showed it to me in a dream. There were Patterns, such beautiful Patterns, but when I woke, they'd gone, faded away like morning mist. I can't remember . . ." Her eyes filled with tears. "Except for the Pentacle."

Tenderly, she reached out to brush a fingertip over the clean, symmetrical lines. A thin ribbon of flame leaped from her finger to the parchment. "Oh, no!" Desperately, she reached out to smother it, but Deiter's hand clamped onto her wrist.

"Leave it," he grated.

Openmouthed, Cenda watched the fiery little tongue lick all around the Pentacle, tracing the endless, interlocking lines, save for that one side. The drawing glowed without being consumed, as if illuminated with blazing gilt. All down one side, tiny, tiny salamanders danced and capered in an excess of joy.

"Thank the Lady." Deiter lifted his jug with both shaking hands and drained it in two long swallows. "Lord's balls, lass, it's proof. You're the first Side; you really are. I never thought—" He scratched his beard.

"Deiter, you're not making sense," said Gray. "Have you been drinking?"

The wizard shot him a withering glare. "Don't be stupid," he snarled. "I'm an alcoholic. Drinking is what I do."

Cenda groped her way to another chair. "Purist, please . . ."

Deiter sighed. "I don't know much more than you. I've had the same dream consistently for the last year." He shrugged. "Call it a vision. Whatever." With a kind of eerie calm, the cracked old voice went on. "Something terrible is coming. And we are pawns of the gods. Hell, I should be used to it, but they're driving me insane. Visions, bah!" His mouth worked as if he were about to spit. "Cryptic, arrogant bastards, the lot of 'em."

"There are rules, even for the gods," said Gray quietly. "They say the Judger plays fair. What is this evil thing?"

Deiter huffed in irritation. "If I knew, I'd bloody tell you, wouldn't I? But it's growing. I can feel it, like shit smeared across the Pattern. *Faugh!*" And he did spit, the gobbet of moisture sizzling on the grate. "Someone somewhere has found a way to reach . . . to touch . . ." His mouth contorted again.

"Hell?" offered Gray.

The wizard stared at him, his face bleak. "That's a name for it, I suppose." He shrugged. "Distilled despair. Destruction incarnate. A bottomless well of soul-poison. Dissolution."

"But why?" said Cenda. "Why would anyone want—?"

"Don't be naive." Deiter snorted. "For power of course. And the dark joy that comes with wickedness well-done. There are those who live for it. And others who are prepared to die."

"But what about the Pentacle?" asked Cenda, absently picking up a noodle cake.

"There are four Sides, one for each of the elements—fire, air, earth, and water. The Lord and the Lady showed me that much. The fifth Side . . ." Deiter warmed his gnarled fingers around the chocolat pot. "That's not for us to know. It could be intellect or love or spirit. Maybe. Different philosophies say different things. Or death on a pale horse, or any bloody thing."

"Air," said Cenda suddenly. "In my dream, Air was there." She smiled. "It touched me. So bright and happy and light, bubbling like a giddy girl."

"You saw it?" Deiter leaned across the table, his fingers fastening around her wrist like a manacle, surprisingly strong. "Air? Where? Who was it?"

"No idea." Cenda frowned, struggling to retrieve the dream-memory. She shook her head. "Most if it's gone now, but I don't think I ever really knew."

"Sod it." Deiter ran a hand through his stringy mane. "Whoever it is, they don't know, which puts them in incredible danger. All the Sides are at risk, you included, lass."

Gray put his arm around her shoulders. "What do we do about it?"

The old wizard pushed the chocolat pot across the table. "Pour, fire witch. We're going to be here awhile."

"Awhile?" said Gray sharply. "What do you mean, awhile? We have things to do."

"I can imagine. Bah! You can go make babies later."

Deiter regarded Gray with profound disfavor. "After we save the world."

Cenda's heart sank. "But I thought . . . It's all over." She clutched Gray's hand. "We got away."

Deiter cackled. "It's only just beginning, lass. Even random events have a purpose." He studied her shrewdly, his head on one side. "The Lady's hand is over you. It has been from the beginning. We have work to do, Cenda."

"You always were a cold bastard, Deiter." Gray leaned forward, his eyes as dark as slate. "If you want to use her, hurt her, you'll have to go through me first. Understand?"

The old Purist relaxed, his grin exposing teeth stained with wine. "The gods work in mysterious ways. I don't know how you did it and I don't care. I put in an order for the only known fire witch in all the worlds, and you brought her to me alive and in a working condition, as agreed. I never renege on a bargain."

The silence seemed to last forever.

As she watched the color drain from Gray's face, Cenda's vision narrowed to a blurry tunnel. She couldn't take much more, her emotions swooping from one extreme to the other in a dizzying rush. Her fingers felt icy, her palms clammy. A fire witch? What nonsense. She'd never be warm again, not as long as she lived. Oh, gods, she should have known, should have known, should have known . . . She swayed, her hands closing hard on the chocolat pot.

"Whoops," said Deiter, unperturbed. "You didn't tell her? Grayson, you're losing your touch."

Boiling chocolat bubbled out of the pot and splashed across the table in a glossy brown stream. Cenda jerked her hands away.

Gray raised haunted eyes to the old man's face. "There's no Magick to it, is there? There never was. You lied to me. Shad was there all along. Inside me, part of my soul, just waiting to be accepted, loved."

"I'm wounded." Deiter rose, chuckling. "I never lie, or if I do, no one knows. That's the whole point. Grayson, my friend, everyone has an interior monologue. Up here." He tapped his temple. "We argue, we chat, we listen. Sometimes, we even do what the little voice tells us. Yours is just, ah . . . a little more substantial than most."

"It wasn't money, was it?" Cenda rose, holding on to the back of the chair so she wouldn't fall down. She was drowning in Gray's eyes, in the anguish there. "You always said that."

Prudently, Deiter skipped back a few steps. "Mind if I watch?" he inquired. "I've never seen a fire witch in full blaze. That upholstery is expensive, by the way."

Gray's jaw bunched. "You wily old bastard." To Cenda, he said, "He promised to rid me of Shad if I brought him the fire witch, alive and unharmed."

He whirled on his shadow, stirring restlessly behind him. "You stop right there! Don't move, no matter what." Shad gave him the finger and Cenda's head began to clear.

Gray stalked toward her, his slashing brows drawn together, so formidable that she quailed a little. "I don't care what it looks like, Cenda. I don't care what you think. I decided a long time ago to fuck Deiter and his bargains. I'm keeping Shad and I'm keeping you." He loomed over her, breathing hard. "I'm not giving you up after everything we've been through. You're mine, and sweet Judger God, I'm yours!"

One hand flashed out to grab the salamander in her hair. With a strangled groan, Gray closed his fist over it, the startled creature giving a loud, crackling squeak of alarm.

"Gray!" Cenda seized the water jug from the table, gripped Gray's wrist, and shoved his hand into it. With an indignant sizzle, the salamander shot out of his grasp and fled across the floor toward the fireplace, scorching the rug with its tiny footprints.

Shad arrived in a sinuous rush to clasp Gray's forearm, shoving a strong shoulder under his arm, propping him up.

Gray's eyes were fixed on her face, wide and smoky and utterly focused. "Yours," he said. "Got it?"

Cenda dashed away the tears. "Yes. Show me." Oh, gods, what if he'd ruined his hand so he couldn't play?

"Back in a second," said Deiter. The door at the far end of the room swung shut.

Beads of sweat dotted Gray's hairline. When he withdrew his hand from the jug, Cenda sagged with relief. "It's going to blister badly, but you'll be able to play," she said. "And you'll have a scar shaped like a frightened salamander." She fought back a hysterical giggle.

"Do I still have you?"

She melted. "Oh, Gray."

Behind them, Deiter made a gagging noise. "I'll be in the bar. Here's a numbing salve." He slammed a small, square pot down next to a bowl of crystallized manda fruit. "Don't thank me. Just call when you've finished." The door clicked shut.

"Over here." Between them, Cenda and Shad guided Gray to a sofa and Cenda smeared the burn with Deiter's salve. The tight lines around Gray's mouth relaxed. Ruthlessly, Cenda sacrificed the Purist's napkins, soaking a couple in water and wrapping them loosely around the wound.

Finally, she leaned forward to brush the hair off his forehead. "Any more secrets?" she said. "Let's get them all done, shall we?"

Gray caught her chin with his good hand and kissed her slowly and thoroughly, with a lot of tongue and murmured endearments. Shad knelt on the floor between them, his arms around their hips. She'd drifted off somewhere delightful, her body buzzing pleasantly, when Gray pulled his lips from hers and whispered against her cheek, "There *is* one thing."

Cenda's spine straightened with a snap. "What? Gray, I was joking!"

"I know." Gray smiled, his handsome face alight. "But I can't ask you to marry me without telling you my real name." He frowned. "Gods, it's been so long, I can barely remember it."

Cenda gurgled.

"You recall how folk are named on Judger's Gift? The idea being that you live up to your name?"

"Yes." Modesty, Justice, Grace, Hope.

With less than his usual poise, Gray joined Shad on the floor at her feet. He laid the injured hand palm up on her knee and placed the good one over both of hers. Shad contented himself with nuzzling her thigh.

"Please don't laugh." His lips twisted. "It's pretty bloody funny."

Cenda shook her head. "Never."

Gray took a deep breath and pink stained his cheekbones. "Know that I love thee, Cenda, fire witch of Sybaris," he said in the language of his childhood, the cadence stiff and charmingly formal. Beside him, Shad's mouth moved, so that they spoke the words together. "I am . . . Honor . . ." When he swallowed, so did his shadow. "Honor of Judger's Gift. I would pledge thee my troth. Wilt thou be mine?"

Shad gave him a nudge in the ribs. "Ours. Wilt thou be ours?"

Tears stung her eyes. She bent to kiss Shad's cool, dark mouth and Gray's warm one. "Honor of Judger's Gift," she whispered. "Your True Name. They couldn't have chosen better; it's what you are, through and through. And in the end, it's what you saved. Your honor."

Gray's eyes shone, suspiciously bright. When he opened his mouth, she placed her palm over it. "Don't argue. It's true. And I will. I'll pledge whatever you like, whenever you like."

"Really?" Gray blinked. Then he laid his head in her lap and slid one arm around her waist. The breath whistled out of him on a long sigh, the soot dark lashes fluttering shut.

Cenda stroked his hair. Shad snuggled up behind him, resting his dark head on Gray's shoulder blade.

Ah, Great Lady. Peace, perfect peace. Deiter could take his time.

As if he'd read her mind, Shad rose and flowed over to the door. The bolt slid home.

The pain woke Gray a few hours after midnight, as he'd known it would. The moment they'd reached their room in the boardinghouse, Cenda had dived for Krysanthe's chatelaine and the green salve. There'd been only the tiniest dab left, but it had helped a little.

Gray stared into the dark, his hand throbbing. Shit, what a stupid thing to do! But he couldn't find it in himself to regret the impulse. He turned his head on the pillow, smiling. He could hear Cenda's regular breathing, feel the warmth radiating from her body, smell her skin. She was curled up against him, her nose pressed to his biceps, the palm of one hand resting lightly over his heart.

Life was strange. He would never have expected to have the most significant experience of his life in old Deiter's sitting room. He smiled. Whatever happened with the Pentacle, and the Judger knew, it probably would, he had *this*—this utter, shining joy. Someone to love him. Someone to love. His eyes stung. Ah, he was getting maudlin!

Slowly, he inhaled, remembering. How many times had Deiter knocked and been ignored? Was it hours or only minutes he'd clung to his fire witch, too deeply moved for speech?

But then . . . Oh, *yes*.

Despite the pain of the burn, his balls tightened with the memory. They'd taken such care of him, Cenda and Shad.

You look debauched, Shad had said.

He'd barely been able to open his eyes. *I'm being pleasured.* Between them, Cenda and Shad had got him sprawled naked across Deiter's sofa, the plushy velvet a sly caress against his shoulders, under his ass. His injured hand was supported by a pile of cushions, his head buzzing with a pleasant alcoholic haze. Cenda had poured him a huge mug of wine and Shad gripped the back of his neck, refusing to release him until he drained it to the dregs.

With a shameless little grunt, Gray had arched his hips, begging for more of the gorgeous distraction, the warm lips and tongue drifting teasingly over his genitals. *So fucking good.*

Yeah, she is. Voluptuously, Shad swiveled his hips and Cenda's whimper vibrated over the head of Gray's cock.

Her fingers dug into his thigh. Shad withdrew slowly, drawing out the wet friction to an exquisite degree. *Feel that?*

So tight, so wet. Gods, do it again. Can you feel her mouth on me?

The eroticism of it made his breath hitch. They had Cenda trapped between them on her knees, two eager cocks plunging into the welcome heat of her body. Her leggings and boots were still tangled around her ankles, restricting the spread of those slim thighs. Shad knelt behind her, smoky fingers grasping her hips, furrowing his dark cock into the tight fist of her sheath.

Cenda braced her elbows across Gray's thighs and compressed his glans carefully between a finger and thumb. Shooting him a glinting look, she inserted the point of her tongue into the weeping slit and lapped. "Mmm." With a happy sigh, she licked her lips, wiggling her ass against Shad's unyielding hips. "Gray?"

"Nngh?"

"What's a troth?"

The sweetheart. He'd laughed aloud then. Recalling the moment now, he grinned into the darkness.

He'd spoken truly. If she was his, then he was hers. Not alone. Never again.

Alone.

The smile faded. Gray considered the word, tasting the flavor of it.

Carefully, he rolled away from the fire witch, ignoring her sleepy protest. Cursing every time he knocked his injured hand, he managed to light the candle on the nightstand. Flickering shadows sprang up in the room, one larger and denser than the others.

Gray settled Cenda back on his shoulder, kissing her hair, murmuring and petting until she relaxed again.

Then he stared across the room, holding out the other arm in invitation. "Come to bed," he whispered, his voice not entirely steady. "I missed you."

Turn the page for a special preview of
the next novel in Denise Rossetti's
Four-Sided Pentacle series

THIEF OF LIGHT

On sale November 2009 from Berkley Sensation!

1

Choose.

When the Lady's dark velvet voice spoke in Erik's dream, the power of Her will vibrated deep in his bones. He struck out, jarring his arm clear up to the shoulder as his fist hit the wall next to the bed.

But he didn't wake.

Anger and dread banged about in his chest. "Choose?" he rasped. "Choose what?" Gritting his teeth, he tried to lever his eyes open, but they were sealed shut. The goddess had him cornered in his own body.

Twenty years ago, My Lord and I gave you a great gift. Or had you forgotten?

Erik stiffened.

A Voice so enchanting, so compelling, it captures the beating heart of all who hear it. And what did you do with this blessing, hmm? The Lady's tone dropped to the ear-aching pitch of thunder in the mountains. *You made of it a curse. In your vanity and your lust, you spoke a command. To an unwilling soul.*

"You don't need to remind me, Great Lady. I know what I did." Every muscle in his jaw—his neck, his shoulders—locked tight.

Do you, indeed? A huff of displeasure. *We see little evidence of this.*

Out of the corner of his eye, Erik saw the movement of a graceful, star-dappled hand, the palm so big he could have curled up in it to sleep.

Or to die.

In the waking world, men trod warily around Erik Thorensen, with his massive shoulders, his chest muscled like a warrior's. The Dark Lady could snap him in two with the flick of a thought.

Should he risk it? Hell, why not? All he had left to lose was his life.

Bracing himself, he said, "Why not see for Yourself?"

An impatient exclamation, and the Lady was rummaging around in his head, turning his soul inside out to look at the underside, inspecting all the dirty little nooks and crannies. When Erik groaned in involuntary protest, She withdrew, but without haste.

Another voice, so deep as to be almost below the threshold of human hearing, rumbled, *Well?*

The Lady turned to Her Lord. *No better and no worse than many others.* Either the goddess shrugged, or every star in the cosmos shifted in its cold bed. *His soul remembers, but his conscious mind chooses to forget.* Her voice dropped. *He doesn't think of her if he can help it. Only in his dreams.*

Nightmares, more like. Erik squinted into the sparkling nimbus that marked the presence of the Horned Lord. He caught the impression of a vast, nebulous figure, antlers spanning the stars. Without being obvious, he tried to angle himself toward that huge male presence. His heart hammered in his chest, fast heavy beats that hurt.

"I can't—" Hiding from the gods was useless. He'd learned that lesson at seventeen. "I have to live in my skin, face myself in the mirror, day after fucking day." Vaguely, he was aware his cheeks were damp. Must be sweat.

He raised his head a little, resentment burning a sullen hole in his belly. "It's the way I function, stay sane." Fuck it all to hell. Say it. "My Lord, when I was a boy and You gave me the Voice, You said You had a task for me. A broken tool can be of no use to You, surely?"

Dead silence.

The Lord's rumble of anger thundered through every cell in Erik's body. He grunted, squeezing his eyes shut, willing himself to endure.

But the Lady sounded amused. *Only you, Erik. Only you would dare. Little one, you cannot bargain with Us.* The sensation of Her smile tingled over his skin, both fond and terrible. *The day will come, my dear, when you'll encounter one you cannot charm, cannot control.*

"So?" he panted, still fighting for breath. "Doesn't matter about anyone else. I have my own rules, and they work for me." Cautiously, he sat up. "I live. Exist."

Last chance, growled the Horned Lord. *Choose.*

Erik set his stubborn jaw. "I want my life to have been worth something. I'll do it. Just tell me what You want."

You misunderstand, purred the goddess. *You've already committed yourself to Our service. The promise you made as a boy cannot be undone.*

"Then what—?" He shook his head. "Never mind. What is it I have to do?" Give me my destiny.

You will know when the time is right, said the Lord. *The Pattern is what it is. Beyond Our touch.* The weight of the god's attention was like a sun burning his skin.

"Soon? It will be soon?"

I am not in the habit of repeating Myself.

Erik resisted the impulse to roll his eyes. "It's all a trifle . . . cryptic." Nothing like going in blind.

Enough! The goddess moved abruptly, and a freezing wind ruffled Erik's hair, chilling the sweat on his chest. *You cannot know more without affecting the balance. It is a different choice We offer you tonight.*

Shit, shit, shit. Despite himself, Erik's hands shook. He laced his fingers together into one big fist, the knuckles white.

Listen well, Erik Thorensen. If it is truly your desire, you will never again compel another with your Voice. We will take it from you.

His heart leaped. Gods, yes! No more rules, no more boundaries, no need to censor every word he spoke, constantly alert lest he . . . slip. Again.

But inexorably, the Lady continued. *By your own actions, Erik, you besmirched the blessing of the Voice. You used it to steal a soul dear to Me.*

Judge and jury.

The blessing and the curse cannot be separated. So you will lose everything. No more of the music, my dear, the music that makes your soul soar.

Executioner.

He couldn't make a sound, but a full-body shudder raised all the fine hairs on his skin. Because the music was all he was—Erik Thorensen, also called Erik the Golden—that, and the easy, unruffled charm he wore like armor.

When he concentrated, the Voice flowed out of his deep chest like a stream of purest, golden air. It made people think of silk or the best chocolat liqueur from Concordia or the glorious, sliding friction of sublime and endless sex. It was a miracle, that Voice. The rest of the time, he was still a damn fine singer, if a trifle run-of-the-mill.

"No." All he could produce was a hoarse rasp. "No."

Despite the way he'd corrupted the gods' gift, music brought his soul as close to the warmth of human connection as any artifice could do. His magnificent baritone gave him passion that was real, more satisfying than any sex he'd ever had. It kept him sane, focused on the here and now. If the gods took the Voice from him, there'd be nothing left that was *Erik*. He'd be a shell that walked and talked, a big golden body women would desire for its own sake. Nothing more.

Hell, there were dark nights of the soul when he suspected he'd already reached that state.

A huge forefinger stroked the length of his naked spine from nape to buttocks, excruciatingly lightly. Erik shivered.

You're lonely, murmured the Lady. *Aren't you, little one? And yet women tumble in and out of your bed, smiling as they leave.*

"Yes," he said. "But it means nothing. *They* mean nothing."

You don't enjoy sex? asked the Horned Lord. *How is this? You control the women, the bedsport. You get the release you need, and all of it on your own terms.*

"True, my Lord, but I want . . . "

What? A growl like thunder. *More?*

Erik gritted his teeth. "I presumed."

You wield your charm like a weapon. The threatening pressure of the Dark Lady's disapproval rolled heavily down his spine, bringing with it a drifting scent of ice and ancient stone and warm woman. *What need do you have of anything more?*

Pressing his lips together, Erik shook his head.

Answer My Lady's question, rumbled the Lord. *Or would you prefer I peer into your miserable soul Myself?*

Fuck, he'd never survive it.

Erik cleared his throat, the heat rising in his cheeks. "There is no one who cares for me, who knows me. The real me." Humiliation washed over him, a warm, greasy wave. He clamped his mouth shut.

Audiences adore you. You have friends, said the Lady. *Grayson, for example.*

"I suppose so." Erik ran a hand through his hair. "Gray's a good man, but we're not close, not really."

It helps if you don't hold people at arm's length. Hell, She was *teasing* him.

"I have to," he snapped. "In case I—It's the price I pay for the Voice. For the music."

She'd have to be your match, Erik. So she can fight you every delicious step of the way.

"What? Who?"

The woman whose love you crave, the lover whose trust you desire. The very thought of her makes you hard with longing, doesn't it?

"Don't be stu—" Erik bit his tongue in the nick of time. "She doesn't exist. Anyway, she'd have to know. And once she did . . . " He dropped his head, breathing hard. Then he shrugged. "Ah, well."

The Lady's tone softened, became almost regretful. *A moment ago, you chose to keep the Voice, the power to compel any woman to your will. Why not use it?*

Insult the Dark Lady and he'd be dead before he hit the floor. But couldn't She see? Or was She testing him? "Great Lady, You know as well as I do that love compelled cannot be real. How would I know the difference between what she gave me and what I just . . . took?"

You are finely caught, are you not? The Horned Lord sounded thoughtful, and not particularly displeased. *Use the Voice to command what you so deeply desire, and by its very nature, you can never be sure you have it. Neither trust, nor love.*

Correct, said the Lady. *And yet, We offer you a choice. Think again, Erik. Shall We take the Voice from you?*

The Lord's deep tones: *Be very certain, Erik. All or nothing.*

Silence fell, so profound Erik thought he could hear the small bright tinkling that was the crystal song of the stars. Or it could have been the mental speech of the gods.

"Without the music, I am nothing, no one," he snarled. "I'll keep the Voice—the blessing and the godsbedamned curse."

2

Caracole, Queendom of the Isles, Palimpsest

On the stage of the Royal Theater, a chorus of devils and angels sang their hearts out, but Prue McGuire listened with only half an ear. She didn't particularly enjoy opera.

"A demon king?" she'd snorted to Rosarina as they settled into their seats. "The plot doesn't make sense." Frowning, she scanned the program. "Why does he carry her off when she wants to go with him anyway? It's plain silly."

Like the experienced courtesan she was, Rose gave an elegant shrug. "Who knows?" Her beautiful lips curved. "It's opera."

As the queen and her entourage swept into the Royal Box, Prue put her head next to her companion's. "I got us a discount," she murmured over the sound of the applause.

Rosarina patted her hand. "And these excellent seats in the bargain." She surveyed the dozen or so exquisite young people in their box with maternal pride. "Well done, dear."

"It was an investment," said Prue. "We'll get more clients out of this, you'll see."

"Not that we need them." Her friend and business

partner waved a graceful hand. "But never let it be said I argued with a bookkeeper about profit." Casting Prue a twinkling, sidelong glance, Rose flicked the playbill with one finger. "They say the Unearthly Opera Company's really very good, and this Erik the Golden is something quite exceptional." The twinkle became a naughty grin. "In every possible way."

"Rose!" She did her best to look scandalized.

"Don't *Rose* me, you wicked woman." A slim finger tapped the dimple quivering in Prue's cheek. "Not with a dead giveaway, right here." The orchestra struck up and the curtains swished open. "Shut up and enjoy, sweetie."

But Prue spent the first scene writing a tutorial on compound interest in her head. She'd rather die than admit it to her friend, but she'd come to find teaching the apprentice courtesans even more fulfilling than balancing the ledgers.

And every extra cred went into her strongbox. For peace of mind and her daughter's future. Despite herself, her breath caught.

Never again.

With some difficulty, she wrenched her mind away from the brutal slum the people of Caracole called the Melting Pot—the way her nerves had quivered at every shift in the shadows, the hilt of a small kitchen knife cold as death in her palm, her daughter's tiny fist clutching her sleeve.

The music was catchy. Tapping her fingers on her knee in time, Prue pulled in a deep breath, forcing herself to relax. It was over. Finished a lifetime ago. Slowly, she exhaled, stealing a glance at Rose's perfect profile.

By the Sister, she'd done better than merely survive! In Rosarina, she had a dear friend and a partner both. Prue smiled her satisfaction. Every courtesan at The Garden of Nocturnal Delights was the owner of an independent business with but a single product—themselves. How she loved it when it all came together for them, comprehension dawning on those beautiful, clever faces. Rose wouldn't tolerate stupidity, no matter how gorgeous the package it came in. Still, compound interest . . . Not the easiest of topics . . .

So when the demon king appeared in a clap of thunder and a cloud of smoke, she was completely unprepared.

As the lights came up for intermission, she was still trembling on a deep, visceral level that dismayed her more than anything had in years. Erik Thorensen had come striding out of fire and brimstone and clasped the shrinking heroine to his chest. And yes, he was a marvelous-looking man, his hair loose on his shoulders like dark-spun gold under the stage lights, the neatly trimmed goatee a shade darker. His eyes were such a vivid blue they pierced Prue all the way to her soft, silly soul. He was big too—so big only the athleticism of his tall muscular frame prevented him from looking blocky. Gods, exactly the physical type she preferred, right down to the mischievous glint in his eye.

But Prue had spent almost two decades surrounded by the most beautiful people on the world of Palimpsest. She was accustomed to perfection, even to the delightful frisson of sexual dominance Erik projected so effortlessly. He was a finc actor.

But merciful Sister, that voice!

He'd glanced directly at their box and his face had lit up with a grin that had pure devil in it. Then he'd opened his mouth. From the first effortless bar, her foolish heart had tumbled into his keeping. Every note was round, rich, deeply masculine, filling the auditorium as if supported on smooth columns of air. Utterly enthralled, Prue had found herself leaning forward, her mouth hanging open, trying to breathe him in, keep him forever, hers alone. She felt feverish, tingling, her breasts tight and her sex swollen and slippery, as if he were stroking her naked body with velvet.

Even worse, the costume, in an old-fashioned style still worn only by the oligarchs on Green IV, suited him to perfection. The over-the-knee boots emphasized the power of thighs and buttocks encased in tight cream breeches. Prue's mouth watered.

The tenor hero had pretty well disappeared in comparison. During one of his uninspiring arias, she managed to tear her eyes away and glance to her left. "Gods," gasped Rose, a flush mantling her cheeks. Her hand closed hard over Prue's forearm, the fingers digging in. "Have you ever—?"

"No." Every face in the theater was rapt. "Sshh. He's starting again."

The tenor had won the duel that ended the act, and the demon king lay wounded, his pain and heartbreak throbbing in a cascade of low, exquisite notes. Tears prickled behind Prue's eyes. Godsdammit, he was good! No, not good—superb, superlative, magnificent.

All through the thunder of the applause, the stamping of feet, the shouting, she sat frozen, putting herself back together, a piece at a time.

She could do better than this. She wasn't some silly girl to lose her head and heart to a handsome singer. She was Pruella Takimori McGuire, business manager of The Garden of Nocturnal Delights, a woman for whom numbers held no terror. Rose's friend and silent partner, Katrin's mother. That helped, the thought of Katrin, serious and steady, only nineteen, but so deeply in love with her Arkady. He was a good boy. That had her grinning ruefully, trying to relax.

Unfortunately, the second act was even worse. Or better.

When **Denise Rossetti** was very small, she had an aunt who would tell her the most wonderful fairy tales—all original. Denise grew up, as little girls do, but the magic of story still dazzles and enthralls her. On the good days, she likes to think of herself as Scheherazade's sister. On the bad days—not so much. She remains an incurable romantic who loves happy endings, heart-pounding adventure, and the eventual triumph of good over evil. All hail the guys in the white hats—unless the ones wearing black are more . . . um . . . *interesting*?

Denise lives in a comfortable, messy old house in the Australian suburbs. She's small and noisy, and tends to wave her hands around a lot, which can be unfortunate if the tale she's telling happens to have explosions in it.

You can e-mail Denise at deniserossetti@gmail.com or visit her website and blog at www.deniserossetti.com for updates, excerpts, giveaways, and idle chatter.